"*The Promise* is a dual-time novel that addresses themes of human trafficking and racial prejudice, as well as healing after depression and suffering loss. Newlywed Gracie is given a cedar chest with a false bottom, holding letters from World War I, a wedding dress, and Grandma Mary's Wedding Ring Quilt. But why would a family member object to having any of it displayed in a WWI exhibit so many decades later? A compelling mystery for Gracie to resolve."

~Joy Neal Kidney, author of
the Leora's Stories series

"In contrasting tales of young love, a century apart, a beautiful hope chest with a secret false bottom becomes a symbol for the truths of loss, of post-partum depression, of white supremacy and women's rights."

~Barbara Lounsberry, Author of:
Virginia Woolf Diaries trilogy

"*Grandmother's Treasures: Book Three, The Promise*, takes readers on a spirited road trip with newlyweds David and Gracie as they trace the path of family history, uncovering never before known details attached to yet another family quilt. If you like dual-timeline reads with twists and turns, interesting glimpses of American history, and poignant family relationships, *The Promise* will leave you satisfied and smiling. Enjoy!"

Sheri Smith Shonk, Author of
the Houses of Hope series

"Dargan connects all the dots, weaving her dual timeline featuring Grace in the present and Mary in the past during WW I. [*The Promise*] brims with rich, well-researched history, and it's easy to follow the changing eras, each with its daunting challenges. Midwesterners, in particular, will love the vibe and feel at home on the pages of *The Promise.*

~Patti Stockdale, Author of
Three Little Things and His Treasured Bride

I love the history of the honeymoon and its juxtaposition to a modern form of slavery. My grandmother was a quilter, and I've helped her, pieced a baby quilt of my own, and am starting another for my eldest daughter's only daughter who is due in June. My mother was the genealogist in our family, and I've inherited her work, which I've not had time to maintain. This was a fun read for all those reasons.

~Judith Roby, Speaker and Author

"As with Cherie's debut novel, this story [*The Legacy*] intermingles Civil War history and modern-day events, a strong combination."

~Gail Kittleson, author of:
The Winds of Change

"Cherie Dargan delivers a second charming historical cozy in *Grandmother's Treasures Book 2: The Legacy.* In this dual timeline book, a bloodstained Civil War Era family quilt stirs a search for answers rooted in mystery and history. War, injustice, danger, romance, and reconciliation—How could a reader ask for more?"

~Shelly Beach, Christy Award winning co-author of:
Love Letters from the Edge

"*The Gift* is a peek into an Iowa farm family. It pieces the present day and past into a quilt filled with details about World War 2. Through the eyes of Gracie, the main character, readers see how past trauma and life choices impact family relationships for generations to come. Those who enjoy books about family, quilting, and the 1940s will find this one to be a comfortable read."

~Jolene Philo, Author of:
Does My Child Have PTSD?

"I love this story! Cherie Dargan can sure paint a beautiful word picture! She spins a gorgeous adventure in the first installment of her *Grandmother's Treasures* series where she treats us to an up-close look at one of her personal family stories in *The Gift*. I, for one, am grateful. It's a colorful, lush and adventurous story, infused with grit, determination, and gutsy, likable characters (especially the females!). Her descriptive style had me craving corn muffins and chili as well as traveling and travailing with her on her journey of discovery. I would highly recommend this book and I can't wait for the next in the series!"

~Wanda Sanchez, Christy Award winning co-author of: *Love Letters from the Edge*

"Cherie Dargan captured my imagination with the first heartwarming book in her five-part *Grandmother's Treasures* series, *The Gift*. It was inspired by her marvelous collection of antique quilts and other heirlooms and the strong women in her family, especially her mom and aunts, who have been Dargan's lodestars."

~*Melody Parker, Author of* "Five Memorable Stories"—*Waterloo Courier*

the promise

GRANDMOTHER'S TREASURES
BOOK 3

the promise

a dual time-line novel

CHERIE DARGAN

WordCrafts Press

The Promise
Copyright © 2024
Cherie Dargan

ISBN: 978-1-962218-61-0

Cover concept and design by Mike Parker

Map & Family Tree designed by Patricia Tiffany Morris for Tiffany Inks Studio LLC

Published by WordCrafts Press
Cody, Wyoming 82414
www.wordcrafts.net

To my Marshalltown 'tribe,' who helped us through our darkest days after my divorce—my sister Cathi and brother-in-law Bill; lifelong friend Beth and Jim; cousins Charlene, Anne, Lee, Jim, and Ed; childhood friends Deb & Gerry and Deb, Darla and Ed; friends Pam, Sam, Kevin, Glen, Michelle, and Melissa.

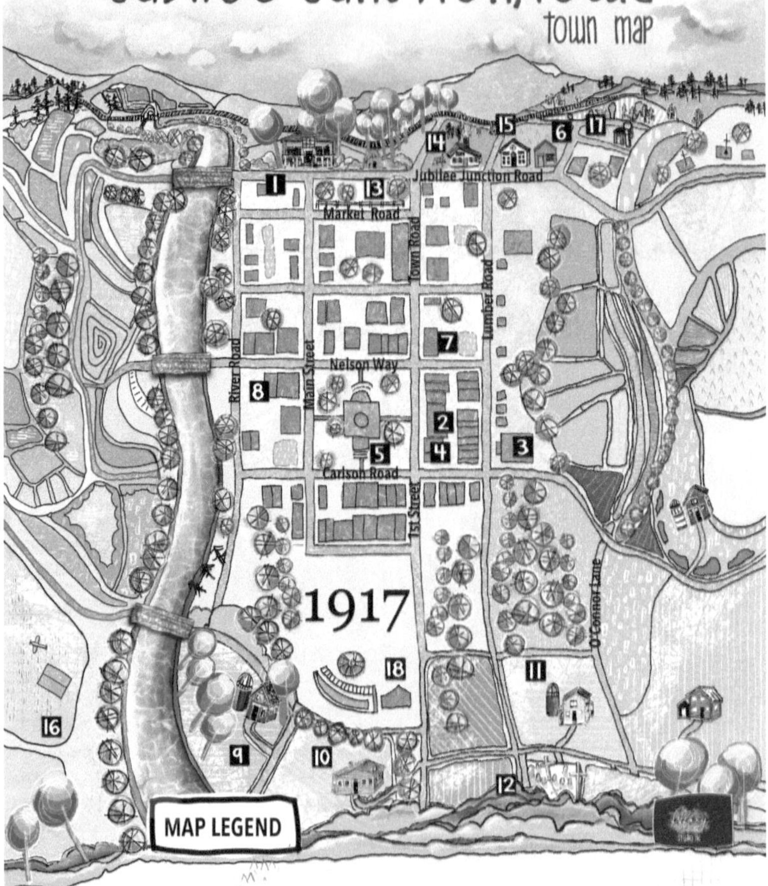

1. Jubilee Junction Depot
2. Carlson General Store
3. Teacher's School
4. Jubilee Café
5. Courthouse
6. Carlson Lumber Yard
7. Jubilee Times
8. Hotel
9. Nelson Family Farm
10. Carlson Family Farm
11. O'Connor Farm
12. Cemetery
13. Telegraph Office
14. Livery Stable
15. Blacksmith
16. Municipal Airport
17. Gas Station
18. Jubilee Memorial Park

Jubilee Junction, Iowa
town map

MAP LEGEND

1. Jubilee Junction Depot
2. Retirement Home
3. Community College
4. Jubilee Junction Café
5. Courthouse
6. Museum
7. Newspaper
8. Ruby's Restaurant
9. Vern's Farm
10. Mark & Kathy's Farm
11. Rich's Farm
12. Cemetery
13. David & Gracie's Farm
14. Library
15. Quilt Shop
16. Airport

When Gracie refers to Michael O'Connor as her 3rd great-grandfather, this is a reference to how genealogists on Ancestry.com refer to distant relatives.

"The middle west is open to the eye. There is no pretense about it."
~Ruth Suckow

*W*elcome to Jubilee Junction, Iowa, an old railroad town near the Jubilee River founded by three big families. My name is Gracie O'Connor MacNeill. My family has published the town's weekly paper, *The Jubilee Times*, since the 1850s. David and I just got married, and we're off on our honeymoon. Later this summer, we'll move to a farmhouse with our cat, Agatha.

I'm named for my grandma, Grace Nelson Walters, who died two years ago, shortly after Grandpa Richard passed. When Great-Aunt Violet, grandma's younger sister, moved to a retirement community last fall, she gave me a gift from Grandma Grace: a large wicker basket filled with a quilt, aprons, and two shoeboxes. One shoe box was full of cassette tapes with a tape recorder tucked underneath. Great-Aunt Violet and I listened to the tapes together as grandma told the story of three sisters taking the train to California to help on the home front during World War Two. Grandma Grace was the big sister, and the twins were Violet and Vera.

Grace and Vera found jobs at an aircraft factory building bombers while Violet nursed injured sailors at the base hospital in San Diego, California. Then, something happened between the twins that shattered the family. The "California quilt," hidden away for sixty years in my great-grandma Ginny's bedroom, held the answer to the dispute.

Grandma Grace revealed the secret about what Vera did to hurt her sister Violet in California and asked me to tell the rest of the family. I was nervous, but my friend David offered to be there to support me, and it helped. My family gathered, and the twin sisters reconciled. David and I grew closer, and our friendship became romantic.

Listening to the cassette tapes inspired me to add oral history to my quilt exhibits at the museum. I recruited my friend, Tiara, who taught oral communications at my college, and her students to help. They interviewed—and recorded—women in Jubilee County who talked about the quilts and shared the stories told by their mothers and grandmothers. We used snippets of those interviews with the displays. This entire story unfolds in *The Gift, Book One of Grandmother's Treasures.*

Next, David and I investigated the origins of a red and green quilt that Grandma Molly rescued from Great-Grandma Mary's house forty years earlier. What were its origins? David and I enlisted Carl, my boss at the museum, and Charlotte, our town librarian. As we looked at sources, we put the puzzle pieces together. My 3rd great-grandfather, Michael O'Connor, fought in the Civil War, with his best friend James, and their younger brothers. They were part of Iowa's 24th Regiment in the Union Army.

Using military databases, we traced the movement of the 24th Regiment. After engaging in a fierce battle near Winchester, Virginia, Michael and three other soldiers pursued a group of rebels. As they fought, the Confederate soldiers shot one of Michael's soldiers and attacked another, injuring him. So the Union soldiers sought shelter in a barn where the owner, a young widow named Sarah, found them. She took them into her home, where she and a freed slave named Rebecca attended to the wounded men, providing them with food and water.

Sarah had just brought home three freed slaves from a nearby plantation and planned to take them to freedom. She and Michael made a deal. The soldiers would escort her group to Baltimore in exchange for her looking after the two injured soldiers and taking them home to Iowa. Along the way, they rescued two more slaves. Sarah and those five freed slaves traveled to Jubilee Junction, Iowa, to start new lives. She married Michael, becoming my 3rd great-grandmother. And as we got our answers and set up the new quilt exhibit featuring Civil War quilts, David proposed.

Weeks later, we got married at the courthouse with just our families, and now we're about to drive cross-country in a Class C motorhome loaned to us by my Uncle Rich. Learning about my ancestors and the Civil War gave us a rather unusual idea for our honeymoon.

David and I are going to retrace the route taken by my Grandfather Michael's regiment and visit some Civil War battlefields. Then we'll travel to Washington, D. C. and find my uncle Patrick's name on the Vietnam memorial. We have several other stops planned for the trip home. I can't wait to have three weeks together and the chance to explore family history with David.

One

The Antique Hope Chest
Gracie

"The travel impulse is mental and physical curiosity. It's a passion. And I can't understand people who don't want to travel."
~Paul Theroux

Saturday, June 1st.

*D*avid and I sat outside the RV, holding hands and sipping our bottles of water, as we waited for Angela's arrival, and with it, our next quilt adventure. Hope chests are old-fashioned today, but in Grandma Mary's time, young women made quilts and linens and stored them in a chest. I imagined opening the chest, inhaling the aroma of sweet cedar, and discovering a set of embroidered pillowcases, quilts, or tablecloths.

Angela drove up to our campsite thirty minutes later, accompanied by her husband, Judd. I recognized her because she had her mother's beautiful grayish-blue eyes, and short, dark hair with gray streaks. I'd just graduated from high school the last time I'd seen her. She was my mother's age.

Judd's short-cut grayish brown hair suggested he might have been in the military. They introduced themselves, and when Judd asked David to help him get the hope chest out of the back of their Suburban, he spoke with a southern accent.

When Judd opened the rear hatch, I caught a whiff of something delicious coming from inside their vehicle. Angela saw my facial expression and gestured for my help. She and I grabbed two large takeout bags from the backseat and set them on our outdoor table.

Angela looked at her husband. "On second thought, let's eat first."

He grinned and closed the hatch.

David found the fourth folding chair.

Angela said, "We thought you might be hungry. Judd's brother owns a barbeque place. We called in the order as soon as I got off the phone."

David sniffed. "This food smells amazing. Thank you!"

David got out four sodas, and we dug into some fabulous barbeque beef and chicken. Other containers offered tangy coleslaw and creamy potato salad. We found crusty rolls and butter pats in one small bag and chocolate brownies for dessert in the last bag. I was thankful for the extra-large takeout napkins.

"Oh, my," I said, "This is wonderful."

Judd smiled. "They make great barbeque. My baby brother was a cook in the navy. Then he met and married Isabella, a creole woman from New Orleans, and man, oh man, can his woman cook. She's taught Jimmy a thing or two about smoking meat."

Judd and Angela were professors at the University of Missouri-St Louis. He taught computer forensics, and Angela taught English Literature. Judd was a military veteran who worked as a computer analyst based in London. They met when Angela won a fellowship and worked at the Globe Theatre for a year.

Her host family introduced them when Judd attended a play and went to the reception afterward. They began talking and hit it off. After a whirlwind romance, they married. They worked for the State Department, Judd continuing his regular job and Angela teaching on bases across Europe for a decade. As we chatted, Judd told us he shared David's enthusiasm for history, specifically Civil War history.

"My second great-grandfather was a free Black man living in Missouri, who fought on the Union side. Wounded in battle, he escaped capture. His best friend brought him home on a horse. Then his friend returned to his unit to fight. His friend survived the war and married my great-great-grandfather's little sister, Bess. She was the family story writer and genealogist."

David retrieved his notebook, and he and Judd spent a few minutes looking through our itinerary together.

Angela looked over. "Can you put up with two weeks of this Civil War mania?"

"I hope so—and we decided we needed three weeks. We got the idea for our honeymoon from investigating the rustic rose quilt that dated to 1860 that your Great-grandma Mary had stored up in a closet. It's a romantic reason to borrow an RV, right?"

Judd held up the big takeout bag. "Okay, cleanup time."

We piled plates back into the bag and saved the leftovers, which Angela left with us.

Then we discussed the hope chest.

Angela retrieved a large cardboard box from their car and explained what'd happened. David and I listened.

"My mother gave me the hope chest ten years ago when we moved here. I remembered seeing it at Grandma Emma's house. She told me it belonged to her mother, Mary. The lid had pretty carvings of roses and vines, and I liked to rub my little hands across the top. Grandma Emma told us the hope chest was in her mother's bedroom, but she didn't want to talk about it because it made her sad. Finally, an aunt told my mother we shouldn't ask about the chest anymore, so the message got carried down to our generation, too."

Judd looked at David, and David shrugged. "I was waiting for a crazy aunt to show up." Judd snorted.

Angela regarded the men. "Hey, settle down. I'm getting to the good part. So I couldn't figure out the big mystery until I used a rag and some wood cleaner. I cleaned the outside, the lid, and started on the interior—then, when I cleaned the bottom of the chest, the bottom wiggled. I yelled for Judd, and he came running and looked at me like I was crazy." She glanced at her husband.

"Yep. Certifiable. Nuts," he said.

Angela said, "I noticed a small piece of fabric sticking out. Judd used a kitchen knife to pry open the bottom, uncovering a hidden compartment almost the length of the chest. We found a beautiful red and white quilt, several aprons, some kitchen linens, and a small wooden box with a packet of letters and a little photo album."

"I called my sister Vikki because I didn't want to do the wrong thing. I didn't call my mother because I didn't want her to flip out. Vikki asked me to take pictures. I emptied it and flipped it over, saw Mary's name and a date, and took pictures. We were intrigued— there was a story here, and we'd never heard it. I emptied the contents of the false bottom into a cardboard box, and here it is."

"May I see the quilt?" I asked.

She nodded. "Of course."

I pulled a pair of cotton gloves from my backpack and put them on, then lifted the red and white wedding ring quilt out of the box, noticing its pristine condition for being almost a hundred years old. It didn't appear to have ever been used. The turkey red dye had faded but was still lovely. I admired the tiny stitches, thinking, *She made this for the bed she planned to sleep in with her husband. Instead, she hid it away in a secret compartment. What happened?*

"This would fit a full-size bed?"

Angela nodded.

I folded it back up and put it back in the box, mesmerized by the mystery of a quilt hidden away and the woman who created it.

David and Judd turned the hope chest over. On the bottom we saw the name engraved, **Mary E Carlson, 1915**. It was maybe five feet long and almost three feet wide. The lid was beautiful, with some fancy carvings of roses and vines.

David took photos of the chest, its underside, and contents, knowing that Charlotte and Carl would want to see it.

Angela said, "Gracie, I've been waiting ten years for the chance to learn the story about this chest—and the beautiful old quilt. Please find out why Grandma Mary hid the quilt, letters, and linens in the false bottom of a lovely old chest. Vikki told us you helped bring closure to some old secrets about a Civil War quilt belonging to our family."

David and I summarized what we'd learned.

She and Judd looked thoughtful.

"There are stories of light-skinned Blacks passing as white and how white slave owners treated Black women as their property. I'm a much lighter shade of reddish brown than the rest of my family, but growing up, we didn't talk about it in my Black family. What would it be like to pass for white a hundred and fifty years ago and then marry into a white family and wonder if they would welcome you or not?" Judd shook his head.

Angela patted his arm. "What an incredible story, Gracie. I hope you can find answers to this mystery as well."

David examined the chest, running his fingers over the carvings on the lid.

Judd looked at Angela. She shrugged. "Why don't you take the chest with you, if you have room, and I'll get it back later?"

David grinned. "Let's see if it fits in the exterior storage bay. Then we can take a tour."

Judd fetched several bungee cords and an old blanket from his vehicle. The men secured the chest in the storage bay, wrapping it in the blanket and using bungee cords to keep the blanket in place. I grabbed the cardboard box of linens, and Angela followed me into the motorhome.

"The RV belongs to my Uncle Rich on Mom's side. He loaned it to us for three weeks."

Angela looked around. "This is very nice, Gracie."

David sat in the driver's seat, swiveled to the interior. "It's comfortable to drive. We're hooked up, or I'd take you for a ride."

Judd sat in the passenger's chair. They debated the efficiency of gas versus diesel engines.

I placed the box of linens and quilt in the bunk over the cab. We had to guard these precious treasures during our travels. Then, once home, we'd begin our investigation into Great-Grandma Mary, her quilt, and hope chest.

Two

Grandma Mary's Note
Gracie

In glades they meet skull after skull
    Where pine-cones lay—the rusted gun,
Green shoes full of bones, the moldering coat
    And cuddled-up skeleton;
And scores of such. Some start as in dreams,
    And comrades lost bemoan:
By the edge of those wilds Stonewall had charged—
    But the Year and the Man were gone.
"The Armies of the Wilderness"
~Herman Melville

"Middlewestishness: an authentic quality, a freshness."
~Ruth Suckow

*E*arlier this year, Grandma Molly asked us to investigate the red and green Civil War quilt and discover its origins. When she did, Grandma Molly shared the note written by Great-Grandma Mary that Molly found wrapped up inside the quilt decades earlier. The note titillated our interest, but I realized that Angela and Judd knew nothing about it. I invited them to sit down while we shared what we knew.

I found the picture on my phone and handed it to her. "Your Grandma Mary wrote this note and rolled it up in the red and green Civil War quilt, but Grandma Molly was the first person to see it. Someone else—either Sarah or Beth—safety-pinned a large legal envelope to the quilt. We're sure Mary never opened it because if she had, it would have answered all her questions. We now know Great-Aunt Trina took the legal envelope forty years ago to prevent another great-aunt from burning the envelope and quilt. But I keep reading Mary's phrase, 'we should reward the kindness of strangers.'"

Angela nodded. "Yes, I see what you mean. Was a stranger kind to her? Did she suffer some tragedy? And why do you hide linens and quilts inside a hope chest after all? Isn't that its use?"

She jumped up and reached inside the box and lifted out a bundle of letters tied up with a ribbon and a small photo album.

I reached for the bundle of letters, and she hesitated for just a moment. I sensed she was entrusting me with something precious—a treasure from her grandmother. They were part of her great-grandmother's story.

"I'm confident you and David will unravel this mystery, Gracie. Give us the tour, and we'll get out of here so you folks can rest up for tomorrow. After all, this is your honeymoon." She dug in her purse for her university business card and wrote her personal email and phone number on the back, then handed it to me. Slipping it into the packet of letters, I thanked her.

We stood, and I pretended to be an RV salesperson. "Here you have the kitchen and dinette, with a microwave, small fridge, three-burner stove, a small oven, and some counter space. Cutting boards that fit on the sink give us more prep space. The TV swivels, and there's another TV in the over-the-cab bunk."

"Stepping back here, we have kitchen storage, the controls for the RV, and a bathroom divided into a shower and toilet. Here we are in the bedroom with a queen-size bed, a small closet, and a tiny end table on each side."

David took over the tour. "We have a portable gas grill in the exterior storage bay. It's the perfect size for two people, and we plan to use it."

Judd looked around. "We've talked about driving an RV across the country. This looks very comfortable."

Parting with hugs and congratulations, Angela said, "If you're ever in the area without an RV, you can stay with us."

We thanked them again for the barbeque. Once they left, we sat outside, holding hands, and enjoyed the sunset—fantastic array of colors with dark yellows, oranges, blues, and purples. *It looks like a child has spilled her crayon box onto a creamy piece of paper*, I thought.

David leaned over to kiss me. "Life is never boring around you, is it?"

I kissed him back. "Nope!"

We stood, folded our chairs, and put them and the table away, then David rolled up the awning. A family walked by, with the mom pushing a stroller and the dad hanging onto a couple of cute kids. They called "Hello," and we waved as we entered the motorhome.

David and I lay down on the bed and watched the sunset through our window. We talked about the visit with Angela and Judd and the new puzzle to solve, and our route the next day.

"Your cousins seem very nice. They have great taste in food. I'm full, but I keep thinking about those leftovers." He rolled over and kissed me, caressing my face.

"Don't you think it's strange the chest had a false bottom? I wonder what happened?"

"We'll find out. But yes, I'm hooked." David stood. "I need to brush my teeth. Don't go too far, Gracie. I'll be back."

He undressed and walked into the bathroomy wearing only his boxers.

I watched him, smiling as I got up too. I walked into the cabin and lowered the privacy curtain hiding the cab and pushed the button to shut the shades. Then I turned out the lights and locked the doors with the control panel. My attention went to the box of linens, photo album, and bundle of letters tucked away for safekeeping.

Why was Grandma Mary sad, and why did she write the note about rewarding the kindness of strangers? I wondered.

Then, I hurried back to the bedroom—and David.

Three

Sewing & Sweethearts
Mary Carlson

"Somehow it pleased him to think of how deeply rooted they were."

~Ruth Suckow's "A Rural Community"

Jubilee Junction, Iowa
Late March 1917

I sat on the horsehair sofa in the parlor, dutifully stitching a pattern of pink roses with green leaves on a cream-colored pillowcase. Mama was reading poetry by Robert Frost. It was a sunny afternoon, and I was thankful for our large windows letting in the light. I loved his poetry with the imagery of the two roads, the spider, and New England's stone fences.

My younger sister Anna fidgeted beside me, her needle stabbing into the fabric and sometimes into her thumb. She gave me a sideways glance, winced dramatically, and rolled her eyes. We'd been working for almost two hours, and she was tired of stabbing her finger instead of the pillowcase. I realized my sister was in danger of saying something to annoy our stern grandmother. I gave Anna a look to warn her.

Fortunately, Mama took a breath, having finished a poem. She looked at her mother-in-law.

Grandma acknowledged her. "Now, girls, we're done. Let's see your needlework."

Grandma Carlson inspected mine first, an embroidered

pillowcase. "Very nice work, Mary. You have how many items in your hope chest now?"

She knew better than I did, but I replied, "A dozen, Grandma. I have two pillowcases, two hand towels, four kitchen towels, two potholders, and two aprons."

Grandma then turned to Anna with her eyebrows raised. "What are you doing, young lady?" She stared at Anna's pillowcase with a frown and put it aside. "I will rip out the thread, and you can work on it tomorrow." She rummaged in her basket. "My seam ripper must be at my house. I'll be right back." She left the room.

Anna looked at our mother. "Mama, do I have to sew, too?"

Mama exhaled. "You should know the basics of sewing even if you don't make your own clothes. We're working on your sister's hope chest, and she enjoys your company."

I put on my best fake smile. "Yes, Mama, and I love it when you sew with us," I told her in a high-pitched, artificial voice. She and I both giggled, and even Mama smiled. Anna hugged me and whispered, "You aren't running off to marry Charlie, are you?"

I blushed. I was almost eighteen and experiencing my first romance. Charlie O'Connor was a classmate who started leaving sweet notes for me a few weeks ago. I hid them in a decorative wooden box in my dresser and thought we were being clever. I blushed.

"Why do you think I'd marry Charlie, silly?"

Anna looked mischievous. "Because you're filling up the hope chest, and I see how he looks at you and how you look when you read his notes." My cheeks warmed as I realized my secret wasn't such a secret after all.

Anna complained, "Mama, I hate sewing. I want to work in an office in Chicago and live with Aunt Eva. I love Grandma, but I'm no good at sewing."

My sister was an intelligent girl who loved to read, got good grades at school, and enjoyed baking with Mama and tending to our gardens. However, Anna had been sitting by me for the past four weeks, and I could only remember one day when she succeeded in the task. I think it was sewing on a button.

Mama had heard this fantasy before. "Why would Aunt Eva want you to live with her, and what company would hire a teenager who doesn't type?"

Anna sucked on a sore finger. "I could learn."

Mama said,"You can learn to sew, too."

Anna was a wonderful sister, two and a half years younger. We shared a bedroom. Anna loved to talk with me at night, and she kept my secret about Charlie. However, her hope of moving to Chicago with our Aunt Eva was just a fantasy. Eva, our father's baby sister, was a nurse, a suffragist, and had a busy life.

Mother placed her bookmark on the next page, closed the book, and cleaned up the parlor. I stood, flipped my long blonde braid over my shoulder, and put my things back into the small sewing kit Mama had given me. Anna did the same.

Anna and I stowed our sewing kits and fabric in my hope chest. It was a lovely cedar chest that Papa made for my sixteenth birthday. He carved beautiful roses and vines on top, and whenever I opened the lid, I inhaled the scent of cedar. Grandma had been working with us for months, and I had perhaps a dozen pieces inside.

We were starting work on my quilt next week. I'd already selected the colors and the fabric. I was looking forward to it, but my little sister dreaded it. We talked about it last night. I remembered seeing grandmother's quilting frame set up but had paid little attention to the work of creating a quilt. Anna had been more observant.

"It's so much work," she said. "We'll be sewing the blocks for weeks, and I'm running out of fingers to poke."

Mama headed for the kitchen. "It's a lovely day. Go take a walk."

Anna and I grabbed our sweaters and walked out into the fresh air. The sunshine welcomed us, and we linked arms as we neared the flower garden. Just like that Anna's mood lifted, and we both inhaled the wonderful scent of the flower gardens, just emerging.

We lived in a big house on a large corner lot, and Grandma and Grandpa Carlson lived next door. Between the two households, we managed a flower garden and a vegetable garden, and we enjoyed a little arbor and bench where we loved to sit and talk. The flower garden was filled with creeping phlox, azaleas, iris, daffodils, and snowdrops. They created a colorful and fragrant display. We grew tomatoes, cucumbers, peppers, kale, onions, assorted squash, and many other vegetables in the plot in our spacious backyards. Every summer, our garden was alive with butterflies, hummingbirds, grasshoppers, and bees.

Anna and I walked down the street away from our house, and I heard a whistle. It was Charlie with his best friend, Frank Wilson. They sauntered down the street across from us in the opposite direction. Charlie was a handsome fellow, with wavy reddish-blond hair, brown eyes, and a ready smile. Frank was a sturdy young man with brown hair and kind blue eyes.

Charlie waved and called, "Hello, Mary. Hello, Anna." Both boys waved. We waved back and called hello. Just seeing Charlie made me happy. The boys kept walking, and we did the same. We turned the corner and went around the block, waving at several neighbors. Then we returned to the house so we could read for half an hour before supper.

I found my book and settled on the sofa in the parlor. My bookmark was one of the sweet notes Charlie left for me last week. I was reading *O Pioneers!* by Willa Cather and enjoying it. Anna appeared with one of her books and sat across from me. Mother bustled around in the kitchen with supper. I wanted to finish the chapter before she called for us to help.

As I mused about seeing Charlie earlier, I wondered, *is there a future for us? We're both seniors in high school. I don't have any experience with boys because Papa doesn't approve of girls dating before they turn eighteen.*

Whenever I read Charlie's notes, I felt lucky to have caught his eye. *Charlie wrote that he loved me, and I perhaps I love him, too. Surely our love would triumph, wouldn't it?*

Four

On the Road to Helena
Gracie

*"Twenty years from now, you will be more disappointed by
the things you didn't do than by the ones you did do. So throw
off the bowlines. Sail away from the safe harbor. Catch the trade
winds in your sails. Explore. Dream. Discover."*

~Mark Twain

Sunday, June 2

*W*e slept in the next day, cuddling, talking, and
kissing until David got up. He said, "You sexy wench. I meant to
get up earlier. I need coffee." He grinned and walked out to make
it while I jumped in the shower and dressed.

Then it was David's turn in the shower, so I got breakfast ready.
I refilled my travel mug from the pitcher of iced tea in the fridge. I
grabbed chopped-up berries and two Greek yogurts and took them
over to the dinette with spoons and napkins. David's coffee was
ready, so I poured him a cup in his travel mug. I found the toaster
and plugged it in. I grabbed a small plate, a table knife, and the
loaf of wheat bread, and placed them on the counter.

I put the packet of letters and photo album in my messenger
bag. I wanted to read them, but this was our honeymoon, so that
was a task that could wait.

Angela's business card caught my eye. I'd tucked it in with the
letters. I took a picture so I could have her contact information handy.

David appeared, smelling like he'd just stepped out of a men's cologne commercial. His hair was still wet, as was mine. He looked handsome with his thick brown hair tousled. We smiled at each other. I felt a rush of emotion, happy to be married.

"Good morning, Mrs. MacNeill."

"Good morning, Dr. MacNeill. Would you like some breakfast?"

I embraced him, and he kissed me gently and then with more passion, pulling me closer. I would have gone back to bed if he'd kissed me any longer.

David thanked me for setting things out and made his toast. We sat at the dinette to eat breakfast. David sipped his coffee and ate some toast, fruit, and yogurt, and I sipped my tea and ate yogurt with fruit.

"Thanks, Gracie. I'll help with the cleanup." He stood and stowed his coffeemaker away in the cupboard.

David and I washed our dishes and tidied the kitchen area. I imagined myself wearing one of my grandma's fancy aprons as I wiped the dinette and put the dishes and the toaster away since we were going on the road.

After breakfast, we walked outside with Uncle Rich's checklist, unhooking our RV to the park utilities.

"We did it, Gracie. I'm glad Uncle Rich gave us the checklist."

David swiveled to face the cab and started the engine. He looked forward to driving through the Ozarks. We had a five-hour drive to Helena, Arkansas, so we settled in.

"Here we are, retracing my grandfather's regiment's route. They traveled by crowded trains, boats, and on foot. They slept in terrible little tents on the hard ground, ate awful food, and suffered from the elements while we're traveling in comfort," I said.

"You're right. Typical fare during the Civil War was very basic. Union soldiers ate salt pork or beef, along with coffee, sugar, salt, vinegar, and sometimes dried fruits and vegetables, if they were in season," David agreed. "They needed to be careful about where they got their drinking water. A lot of them got sick from the contaminated water. Two out of three deaths were from diseases like pneumonia, typhoid, mumps, measles, smallpox, and tuberculosis. Even if they wanted to practice good hygiene, they used crude latrines and didn't wash their hands."

I shuddered. "They spent their days either being bored or terrified—the life of soldiers. Mark told me that after he returned from Iraq. It's silly to compare our journey to my ancestors."

"Yes, you're so right, Gracie. Luckily for us, a hundred and fifty years later, we have better traveling options. I wouldn't ask you to go on a honeymoon, driving across the country, if we were tent camping."

I couldn't imagine a more uncomfortable experience for a honeymoon. After all, I'd been a girl scout. Shelly talked me into it and made it fun, especially the s'mores part. But I knew about sleeping on the hard ground or half-inflated air mattresses, which was much less fun.

We listened to the radio for a while and then discovered that once we got below I-70, AM was country-western, and FM was southern gospel. So I dug in my backpack and got out several CDs from Adele, Shania Twain, The Dixie Chicks, Rihanna, Katy Perry, and Nickelback.

David told me about Crowley's Ridge. "It's a land formation that created a crescent-shaped raised spot from about Cape Girardeau, Missouri, to Helena, Arkansas. The Loess Hills that formed the ridge aren't high, maybe five hundred feet above terrain. They're remarkable because they're surrounded by the northern reaches of the Mississippi Delta, which is flat as a pancake. The crescent shape on the delta meant that riverfront towns were flood-prone, therefore not very safe."

David glanced over to see if I was listening, and I asked, "Should I be taking notes? Is this on the test, Dr. MacNeill?"

"No test, but it's a great example of geography determining history. Helena was the only town on the Mississippi between Memphis and Vicksburg. The Union forces captured this strategic point to protect Grant's siege of Vicksburg. The Confederates realized the importance of Helena and tried to capture it but failed. Grant soon captured Vicksburg, and the rest is history. Helena hosted an obscure battle, but the reason for its importance is fascinating—for history geeks, anyway," he said.

We arrived in Helena around 3 pm and found Kelly's RV park,

where we had reservations. We set up camp, and it went more quickly this time. Getting the RV level and steady makes it a lot easier to pour coffee and walk around, let alone try to sleep, or canoodle.

We biked around the park dedicated to the Underground Railroad and visited the welcome center. Then we explored the Confederate cemetery, where we saw a fifteen-foot-tall memorial for Confederate General Patrick Cleburne.

The Underground Railroad memorial was inspiring and made me think about the courage of my Third Great-Grandmother Sarah. She took three slaves from a plantation in Virginia to freedom in Iowa with the help of four Union soldiers and the Underground Railroad.

David glanced over. "Thinking about Sarah, Rebecca, and the others?"

"Yes, of course," I said.

When we got tired, we stopped and found something cold to drink. Later, we picked up burgers, fries, and cokes at the Burger Shack, a famous local eatery that flavors sodas with various syrups—vanilla for David and cherry for me. We found a picnic table with a view of the Mississippi and happily ate our supper. All our senses were engaged with delicious smells and the addictive delight of devouring hot, salty French fries dipped in ketchup, between bites of a juicy burger loaded with cheese, lettuce, pickles, mayo, and onion.

"Oh my goodness, these burgers are amazing." I tried to wipe my chin. "And very juicy!"

David grinned and reached over with a napkin to dab the juices running down my chin. "Yes, maybe the best we've had."

Then we headed back to the Greyhawk. I moved my messenger bag off the couch and debated getting out the letters, but this was still our honeymoon. I wanted to focus on my new husband. We'd have plenty of time later to read the letters and solve the mystery of why Grandma Mary hid a quilt inside the hope chest.

Five

Touring Helena
Gracie

"War at the best, is terrible, and this war of ours, in its magnitude and in its duration, is one of the most terrible."
~Abraham Lincoln
16 June 1864, speech at Philadelphia

Monday, June 3

We slept in again. I was still getting used to sharing a bed and going through my morning routine around David. I'd been shy about undressing around him at first, but he made me feel safe.

David looked at me from his side of the dinette. "I'm liking this RV honeymoon adventure so far. How about you?" He wore a big cheesy grin, which I found irresistible.

"Me too. We're a good team." I grinned back.

After breakfast, we grabbed our small backpacks and headed out on the bikes to tour the new Fort Curtis. David was especially interested in seeing the huge 24-pounder guns.

Perhaps sensing the big guns didn't impress me, David asked, "Did you know they used these cannons starting in the Mexican-American war? They could fire an 18-pound shell for over thirteen-hundred yards."

I stared at the guns, imagining 18-pound frozen turkeys, not cannon balls, being fired. After all, I'd held 18-pound turkeys, but I couldn't imagine watching one fly 1,300 yards.

Next, we biked to the Helena River Park, where many of the Iowa regiments camped, including my third great-grandfather's regiment. Thousands of freed slaves gathered here when the area was under Union occupation. Many of them joined the United States Colored Troop regiments. The Battle of Helena was the last major Confederate offensive launched in Arkansas. The Confederates failed, and Major General Benjamin Prentiss was the victorious Union commander.

Runaway slaves sought shelter in one of St. Catharine's barns, and the Sisters of Mercy took care of wounded soldiers from both sides after the Battle of Helena.

"Once the battle was over, the troops moved on, leaving someone else to bury the dead and care for the wounded—and clean up the debris of war. Not a simple task," David said.

I shook my head, unable to imagine the aftermath.

By mid-afternoon, we'd seen enough. We headed back to Delta Ridge Park, strapped our bikes to the back of the RV, completed the checkout process, and looked over our maps and plans.

"Is it silly to leave today instead of tomorrow?" I asked.

"No, we saw what we came to see." David was opening my door for me when we heard a commotion nearby.

"You always ruin our trips, don't you?" An angry male voice startled me, followed by the slamming of an RV door. "I'm so sick of it!"

"Me? You're the one who screwed up our reservations," countered an angry female voice, slamming her door.

I glanced over to see a couple standing outside their RV arguing. He was waving a clipboard close to her face. She was defiant, rummaging through a large tote bag for something. They continued to bicker, and I tensed up.

David hesitated. "Are you okay, Gracie?"

I exhaled. My voice was shaky. "His angry voice made me think of my ex-boyfriend, Steve."

David nodded. "I saw you tense up," he said. "But I'm not Steve, and we aren't that couple."

I climbed into the cab.

David leaned inside and kissed me. "Shall we get going?"

I nodded. He walked around and got into the driver's seat. He checked his mirrors, and we took off.

I was quiet as we got our bearings and set off for Pleasant Hill, Louisiana, 300 miles away and a six-hour drive.

David made small talk, noting the contrast between the rolling hills of central Iowa to where we were, the flat delta farmland.

He glanced at me. "I think we should talk about what's troubling you."

I blinked back tears. "You're calm and logical, and I'm emotional and sometimes impulsive. How do we get along so well? Are we going to argue like that? Steve yelled at me when I didn't do what he wanted me to do, like take that job in Des Moines last year. Hearing that man's voice triggered me. Did you and Cynthia argue?"

David hesitated, choosing his words. "Yes, we had some doozies, but I'm not a yeller. Cynthia wasn't either, but she would say sarcastic remarks or cry if she didn't get her way. In the end, I had to break it off. She wanted us to get a condo in downtown Chicago, but I wanted to move back to Iowa and be near family—and start a family of my own."

We'd had this conversation. We both wanted children someday.

"Cynthia told me she never wanted children, and she knew I did." He looked over. "Two people who love each other can disagree on some things. We don't have to agree on everything. Say, you don't like chili cheese dogs, and I do. Does that mean I'll never have one again?" He put on a sad face.

I couldn't resist. "I like chili cheese dogs."

"Good. See? We can do this, Gracie. We're still learning about each other, but we share core values and our faith in God. We have a strong support system in our families. Don't worry, babe, because we will never be like that couple." David took my hand. "Exploring your family history has taught us important lessons, like don't keep secrets, be persistent, ask for help, and help others. All lessons we could find in the Bible."

"Thanks, David." I let go of the tension. We drove for a few miles in comfortable silence.

I read about the area's significance from David's three-ring binder. Historians agree that the Battle of Pleasant Hill was a Union victory. They caused almost double the casualties on the enemy's side compared to their own losses. I looked at David and told him what I'd just read. "So the winner of these Civil War battles was the one who inflicted the most harm?"

"Don't shoot the messenger. Many historians are nice professors like me."

We admired the scenery, and the hours passed. I checked my phone's KOA app and found some possible RV parks. "How are you holding up? We're close to an RV park near Rayville, Louisiana."

"Sounds good."

I called and got a reservation. We stopped at a Kroger grocery store and bought a few essentials. Ten minutes later, we pulled in, registered, found our space, and set up. We got out the ingredients to grill asparagus and chicken breasts. David seasoned the meat and vegetables with garlic powder, Italian seasoning, and salt and pepper. Then he drizzled them with a little olive oil, while I made a spinach and strawberry salad and a simple dressing.

I took pictures of David flipping the asparagus and chicken breasts on the portable grill on a picnic table and posted them on Facebook for our families. We sat at our little table and enjoyed the meal.

"You did an amazing job with the chicken and asparagus," I told David.

"Thanks. The salad is excellent, too." He speared a strawberry and fed it to me.

I ate it, smiling. This honeymoon was wonderful. I felt so bonded to this man. David had shown me how much he loved me in the past few months. And he'd been so tender and considerate these past few days.

Nearby, we heard some music with a strong guitar and vocals, but it wasn't anything I recognized. My feet tapped the ground, and so did David's.

"What is that music? I like it." I asked.

David grinned. "It's the blues. That's Stevie Ray Vaughan—he was a famous guitarist with a group called Double Trouble and that song is called "Pride and Joy.""

He jumped up and took my hand, so I stood too, and we did an impromptu dance.

Our neighbor playing the music looked over and waved. "Is our music too loud?"

"No, not at all!" I called back.

The man walked closer. He was wearing faded jeans, a t-shirt, and a cowboy hat.

"Hey, there. I'm Jimmy, and that's my wife Jolene over there. We're from Clarksville, Mississippi. Lots of blues down there."

"I really like the guitar. It's amazing. I'm Gracie, and this is my husband, David."

"It's the first time she's heard Stevie Ray Vaughan." David stepped forward. "Yeah, we're newlyweds, from Iowa. Nice to meet you."

The man waved at his wife, who walked over, and we introduced ourselves.

We listened to more of the blues and danced, chatted, and laughed.

After half an hour, Jimmy looked at his wife. "We better leave you two honeymooners to enjoy the rest of your evening." He winked and tipped his hat and left with his wife waving, "Nice to meet y'all!"

David said, "Yes, thanks. That was fun!"

We cleaned up together, stowed the table and chairs, and rolled up the awning.

Once inside, we ate a few more strawberries and snuggled on the couch with a soft blanket. We watched the movie *O Brother, Where Art Thou?* starring George Clooney. The story is about three escaped convicts looking for treasure in Mississippi. It's set during the Great Depression. I loved the music, and we recognized the plot's parallels to Homer's Odyssey.

David held me in his arms on the couch after the movie ended. I got sleepy and dreamed I was a young woman whose parents had given me a lovely hope chest. I opened the lid and saw a quilt, aprons, and linens folded up. Then I saw myself with a telegram in my hand, sobbing. I slammed the lid of the hope chest.

I jolted up, disturbing David, who was almost asleep himself. "What is it?"

"I think I just dreamed about Grandma Mary." My heart was beating fast. Did I dream of the answer? Did Grandma Mary's fiancé die in the war? David stood up, yawned, and went back to the bedroom. I sat down and jotted down what I remembered from the dream. Then I turned out the lights, locked up, and followed my sleepy husband to bed.

Tuesday, June 4

The following day, our blues-playing neighbors were gone. But they left us a Stevie Ray Vaughan CD, wrapped around our side mirror with a rubber band. A note included their email address and phone number.

I removed it from the mirror and handed the note to David while I examined the CD.

We were two-thirds of the way to Pleasant Hill, so we had several more hours to drive. We listened to our new CD while David told me more about Stevie Ray Vaughan's short but memorable life.

David glanced over. "Look him up on Wikipedia. I'm sure there's an article and lots of links."

I grabbed my iPhone. Stevie Ray Vaughn was part of a blues rock trio, considered one of the greatest guitarists of all time. He died in an airplane crash after a performance.

"What a gifted musician." I looked up. "And what a tragic end."

David agreed.

We drove into Pleasant Hill, parked the RV, and grabbed the bikes. David and I headed for the welcome center and walked out with a handful of brochures. We found the Soldiers Memorial monument and spent some time biking around the cemetery and battlefield.

We ate catfish wraps from a food truck vendor as we perused the brochures. David told me about the battle here, considered a Union defeat. It was part of the Red River campaign, and it had been a bloody slog, with fierce fighting and losses on both sides.

Next, we headed to Port Gibson, Mississippi. We saw signs for the Kisatchie National Forest but left it for another trip.

I complained, "Three weeks isn't enough time to see it all, is it?"

David agreed. "Yes, we could have taken a month off and not seen it all. But remember, we thought we could do it in two weeks. We're making memories and noting what we might like to see next time."

I liked that phrase—next time.

David and I are just beginning our lives together. We'll take more trips in the future and have more adventures. Our story together has only begun.

Discovering Port Gibson
Gracie O'Conner MacNeill

"That this nation, under God, shall have a new birth of freedom, and that government of the people, by the people, for the people, shall not perish from the earth."

~Abraham Lincoln

As David drove, I opened our guidebook and checked the list of things to see in Port Gibson. The first was the Windsor Ruins, the remnants of an old plantation built in the Greek Revival style. It burned down in 1890, leaving 23 chimneys still standing in a surreal display. We walked around, amazed at the size of the house and the enormous chimneys.

"This is cool. But I don't think my smartphone is going to do it justice."

David looked around, craning his neck, and taking a few pictures himself. "This is incredible, but you're right. We can always Google it."

I did just that and exhaled. "David, I found a Wikipedia article about these ruins. This plantation house was five stories tall, had twenty-three rooms, and there was an observatory on the top. The article estimates it cost on hundred and seventy-five thousand dollars for the building's construction and furnishings and points out it would cost more than four million today."

David looked at my phone, intrigued. "Send me the link."

I sent the link to the article to David and kept reading. "Confederate soldiers used the observatory to monitor the Union troops.

Later, the Union troops did the same thing, tracking enemy movements from the cupola."

We both stared up, picturing the intact building and soldiers climbing flights of stairs to the observatory to monitor enemy troops.

Next, we drove to Bethel Church. David told me that Grant's troops passed the church on April 30th, 1863, while marching towards Port Gibson on Rodney Road. It was a moonlit march, and some soldiers used the steeple for target practice. The battle the next day took place just a few miles west of the church.

David pulled over to look at Bethel Church. He picked up the travel guide, and we read it together.

The battle of Port Gibson cost Grant 131 killed, 719 wounded, and 25 missing out of 23,000 men engaged. This victory not only secured his position on Mississippi soil, but enabled him to launch his campaign deeper into the interior of the state. Union victory at Port Gibson forced the Confederate evacuation of the Grand Gulf and would result in the fall of Vicksburg.

The Confederates suffered 60 killed, 340 wounded, and 387 missing out of 8,000 men engaged. The action at Port Gibson underscored the Confederate's inability to defend the line of the Mississippi River.

I asked, "So this battle helped Grant become more important?"

"Yes, it was a crucial battle, but at a heavy price." David chose his words. "Deaths because of illness were much higher than the casualties from battles. It was a brutal war, but crowding men in camps led to diseases breaking out and doctors had few tools to use against them."

I nodded, remembering visits to rural cemeteries. Seeing tombstones where multiple members of a family died from diseases we could now easily prevent with vaccines.

We located the next RV park, checked in, and set up, feeling more confident each time we set up and broke camp.

"This isn't so hard," he leaned in and kissed me.

David was relaxed and happy, and so was I. So far, we've been getting along nicely. David put his dishes in the sink. He picked up his dirty socks and underwear and was the best roommate ever.

My silly worries about cooking on the trip had dissipated. We ate simple breakfasts and ate out during the day. David enjoyed grilling our burgers or chicken breasts outside with the portable grill, and we looked for ways to add some veggies. I hadn't cooked anything more complicated than microwave popcorn or a toasted bagel. We ate fresh fruit and yogurt every day and had a green salad or vegetables. Our moms would be proud.

Uncle Rich was right. It's fun traveling in the RV and so different from traveling by car and stopping at hotels. We have more time to relax and get to know each other on a more intimate level. What could be better?

Seven

The War in Europe
Mary

"Two armies that fight each other is like one large army that commits suicide."

~Henri Barbusse, 1916

1917

𝒫apa says America shouldn't get involved in the war in Europe, but we may not have a choice. German submarines are sinking ships with Americans on board, like the Lusitania, where over 120 Americans lost their lives two years ago.

I heard Papa talking with my grandfather and uncles again last night. One of my uncles said he would go enlist today if they would take a man his age. Papa agreed—they should send old men, not young men with their whole lives ahead of them. He worries many of the boys in Jubilee Junction would end up overseas, including his son. My grandpa said each generation had its challenges, and as long as men—and nations—were stubborn, sinful, and unwilling to negotiate, we would have wars.

I wished I could be part of these conversations, but Mama and Grandma say girls and women shouldn't discuss such things.

I sat at the kitchen table, peeling carrots on a cutting board, as Grandma and Mama worked on the stew for supper. Grandma sat across from me, cutting up peeled potatoes and onions while Mama sauteed the beef in her big cast-iron skillet.

"That's not fair! After all, it is the women who pick up the pieces during a war. Women wait at home and take care of everything. They should be more involved in deciding about war," I argued.

Mama sighed, and Grandma looked at me with a little exasperation. "You've got your Aunt Eva's spunk, Mary. But men control the world."

My family members had fought in every war for generations, according to Grandma. I'd studied the Civil War in school and read about the sacrifices made by women who had to open their homes and care for wounded soldiers. Women shouldn't read or discuss such matters? What nonsense.

I picked up *The Jubilee Times* and read the articles, but would like to discuss them. The stories about the war in Europe make me sad and angry.

Men may rule the world, but I think women could do a better job. Aunt Eva says we wouldn't have so many wars, so many weapons, and so many rules about what women can and cannot do if more women were in the government. I agree with her. She's Papa's younger sister, and she's working with a group of women called suffragists to pass laws so women can vote. Aunt Eva has marched in lots of parades. I hope the law changes because I would like to vote when I am older.

My older brother Bruce is almost twenty and going to college, and my younger brother Aidan is twelve. Mama says her babies are growing up too fast. However, I think she enjoys us more now. Mama's busy with her volunteer work at the hospital, library, and church, and with her women's club.

Papa owns the Carlson general store in town, and he and his brothers own the Jubilee lumberyard and hardware store as well. He's a hard worker and built us this beautiful house with the help of his father and brothers when I was just a little girl.

It's why our grandparents moved into town when they retired from the farm, and Papa's oldest brother took over. Our grandparents wanted to experience life in town and help Mama and Papa with us children, so they built a house next door. I remember Grandma taking care of us when we were younger, and Mama had just given birth to Aidan. When it was bedtime, Grandma would hold both of us girls on her ample lap, read us a story, and then tuck us into bed with a kiss and a prayer.

Grandpa takes care of the gardens, trees, and shrubs and helps at the Jubilee lumberyard and the store. Grandpa told me once he cared little for just sitting around because he liked to be helping his family. He's a religious man with a cheery disposition.

I'd like to talk to Aunt Eva about it all, because it's much easier than talking to Mama. Aunt Eva doesn't treat me like I'm a child.

I worry my older brother and his friends will go to war—that Charlie will go to war. I cannot imagine such a horrible thing. Our President has kept us out of war. Surely the war will end before America has to get involved. Please, dear God.

But I kept my fears to myself, remembering what Papa said. "The war in Europe has been going on since 1914, and President Wilson's 1916 re-election campaign motto was, *He kept us out of war!*"

We began work on my quilt this week, which we are doing in turkey red and white using the double wedding ring pattern. Grandma and Mama explained making the quilt, involving many steps. But Mama tells me that grandma has made over 100 quilts and not to worry.

She and Grandma laid out the fabric, applied starch and then ironed the fabric. She explained this made the fabric stiffer and easier to work with. Next, she laid the fabric on the table and used scissors and special measuring tools to cut angled pieces to create a circle.

I can't believe all this fabric will be reduced to a stack of blocks of different shapes.

"And that's when the fun begins," Anna complained to me later, "because then we'll spend weeks creating the blocks."

Last week, Charlie sat by me at the Carnegie Public Library, where we worked on a group report for our social studies class. The teacher assigned us the topic of how the war in Europe has changed America's exports. Two other students were in our group and left to return books to their shelves. I read over the notes I'd been taking, and when I looked up, he moved to sit by me.

Charlie smiled. "I'm glad they left. You look beautiful today, Mary. Have you thought about what I asked?"

I blushed. "Charlie, you need to talk to my Papa. He won't let me date until I'm eighteen."

Charlie took my hand and gently kissed it as we gazed at each other for a moment. "Very well. I shall call on your Papa. You're almost eighteen. I'm tired of secrets. I want the world to know I love you and want to marry you."

When Charlie saw the students coming back, he winked. He kept smiling but dropped my hand.

I picked up the pen again. "Our report will be just fine. I want to recopy it, of course."

"Well, thank you for your hard work."

Charlie escorted me home. He paused on our steps and took my hand. "See you tomorrow, Mary."

I watched him step off the porch, wave, and keep walking.

I went into the house, feeling wonderful. Anna was doing homework in our room when I came up the steps.

"You're in a good mood."

"Can you keep a secret?"

"Sure. What's it about?"

"Charlie walked me home. He's going to talk to Papa about us getting married."

Anna hugged me. "I knew it!"

"Please say nothing until it happens."

Anna said, "It will be our secret."

I opened my little diary and jotted down a few notes to remember this wonderful day when things came together for Charlie and me.

My eighteenth birthday is coming in just a few weeks. Charlie and I will graduate from Jubilee High School in June. Mama agreed I can have a birthday party with all my friends—boys and girls. Charlie's going to talk to Papa about us getting married. We'll have a happy future together. Surely, America can avoid the war devastating Europe. After all, there's an ocean between us.

Eight

Exploring Vicksburg
Gracie

"Without slavery the rebellion could never have existed; without slavery it could not continue."

~Abraham Lincoln

Wednesday, June 5ᵗʰ

We arrived in Vicksburg, where we found the welcome center and got brochures on the museums, cemetery, and national park. We debated where to go first.

I found the section on Vicksburg from battlefields.org in David's notebook and read it out loud. "The Siege of Vicksburg is one of the most notable battles in the Civil War. After holding the city for 47 days, Confederate Lt. General John C. Pemberton surrendered to General Ulysses S. Grant on July 4, 1863. The Battle of Vicksburg, and the Battle of Gettysburg the day before, turned the war in the Union's favor."

David agreed. "Yes, many historians agree with that statement. However, I'd pick the 1864 capture of Atlanta, Georgia."

We toured the two museums downtown, the Old Depot Museum and the Old Courthouse Museum. The Old Depot had a lot of railroad memorabilia and forty war-themed paintings by Herb Mott depicting various battlefields. He was a wonderful artist and captured the horrors of the war.

The Old Courthouse Museum's courtroom looked ready for a trial, with its arrangement of furniture. However, we found the exterior of the structure fascinating. Over one hundred and fifty years old, with its majestic columns, the courthouse housed an archive of Civil War research.

We continued our exploration by driving to Champion Hill near the small town of Edwards. We drove on to the infamous Hill of Death. I got out David's notebook and read out loud as we drove.

"Walk the sunken Old Jackson Road to 'The Hill of Death'where so many soldiers, Confederate and Union, fell in battle. In the Official Records, Union General Alvin P. Hovey, Twelfth Division, Thirteenth Army Corps, wrote, "I cannot think of this bloody hill without sadness and pride. Sadness for the great loss of my true and gallant men; pride for the heroic bravery they displayed. No prouder division ever met as vastly superior foe and fought with more unflinching firmness and stubborn valor. It was, after the conflict, literally the hill of death; men, horses, cannon, and the debris of an army lay scattered in wild confusion. Hundreds of the gallant Twelfth Division were cold in death or writhing in pain, and with large numbers of Quinby's gallant boys, lay dead, dying, or wounded, intermixed with our fallen foe. Thus ended the battle of Champion's Hill at about 3 pm, and our heroes slept upon the field with the dead and dying around them. From this site some of the burial pits can be seen."

I put the notebook down. "Oh, David. How terrible! It sounds like chaos. Where were the medics and ambulances?" I grabbed a tissue. The description was graphic.

We had pulled over and parked by now. David cupped my face with his hands and kissed me. "It's okay to cry, Gracie. I know you're tenderhearted." He grabbed a box of tissues for me. "Remember, their ambulances were horse-drawn carts. They didn't have our modern medications and took over private homes to set up hospitals. The weather was warm, and they were dealing with the rotting bodies of people and horses, and vast numbers of flies. It took a strong stomach to bury the dead and care for the living."

I almost gagged at his description, holding a tissue to my mouth. *That's horrible. How could anyone stand those smells and sights?*

David turned towards me, apologetically. "Gracie, I'm sorry. I don't know if I did an adequate job of preparing you for this trip and explaining how upsetting some of these stops might be." He reached out and touched my arm. "Are you alright?"

"I wanted to know what my ancestors experienced. I'm getting a better idea."

By late afternoon we'd seen enough, so we headed to Jackson, Mississippi, about an hour away, and checked into a RV park. We asked the manager to recommend a restaurant.

"Try Jerry's Catfish House, and I suggest the catfish and hush puppies."

Back home after a delicious meal, I told David about my dream about the cedar chest.

"Your dream presents the most obvious solution." He nodded. "We'll look at the photo album and letters on our drive to Virginia."

After supper, we moved to our recliner couch, found a movie, and cuddled, wrapping up in the blanket his mother sent along. I got drowsy and fell asleep. When I woke up, I saw David was napping too. Then he opened one eye.

"Are you ready for dessert?"

He grabbed the chocolate cherry frozen yogurt in the freezer and dished up the frozen yogurt, and we dug into creamy chocolate with cherry chunks.

He grabbed the big notebook, and we looked at our plans for tomorrow before moving to the bedroom where we listened to music before falling into a deep, restful sleep, wrapped in each other's arms. I loved this man, and he loved me. As I shut my eyes, a thought floated into my mind. Did my Great-Grandmother Mary ever experience such deep love?

Thursday, June 6

In the morning we completed our checkout procedures, gassed up, and looked at our maps. When we left here, we would drive to Alexandria, Virginia, with several stops along the way. It was about 1,160 miles or about fifteen hours of driving through Tennessee, Kentucky, and into Virginia.

I looked at David. "The largest vehicle I've driven is Uncle Rich's pickup truck. Do you think I should practice driving our RV just in case you want help driving?"

"That's up to you, Gracie. I'm doing okay, but it might be fun to let you practice and see how you do. We'll do a lot of driving in the next three weeks."

When we saw an exit for a rest stop, we pulled over. I got into the driver's seat and took a big breath. David talked me through checking the mirrors, and I drove around the back parking lot and practiced parking. I turned off the engine with relief.

"Good job, Gracie. You handled it well."

I was glad I'd done a practice drive but also happy to trade seats. I'd need a lot more practice driving before I got out in traffic.

We drove for four hours, about 250 miles, to the border of Mississippi and Tennessee. We wanted to visit Shiloh in Tennessee. When we arrived, we headed for the visitor center with exhibits I found both educational and shocking.

I wiped my tears as we left. "It's so much worse than I realized."

David squeezed my hand. "Yes, war is not pretty, and the Civil War was especially brutal."

We drove to see the cemeteries. There was a pervasive sadness—a mix of patriotism, horror, and bloodshed. We walked around to read gravestones, and David reminded me of what the National Park Service had to say about its history. Of the almost 4,000 graves, 2,359 are unknown, marked by short stones. So, I realized that more than half of the soldiers were never identified. Tears flooded my eyes.

David put his arm around me.

"What a tremendous undertaking," I said, finally. "I can't imagine what they found as they dug up those graves, but I'm sure the families of those soldiers who were identified found some comfort in knowing where their loved ones were buried."

I dug out a tissue pack from my backpack. "You must think I'm a big baby, David. I'm sorry to cry again."

"Don't apologize. You have what my mom would call a tender heart." David led me to a bench. "I've visited here before. Yes, imagine how people identified the soldiers. They didn't carry driver's licenses or other ID. It would need to be a survivor saying, 'That's Edward Jones from Madison. I recognize his beard.' Later, of course, the military began using metal dog tags to make sure soldiers were identified."

I wiped my eyes and looked up. "That makes sense. When did they start to use metal ID tags?"

"I wondered that, too," David told me. "Vendors followed the army around, offering to make engraved metal tags for soldiers during the Civil War. The War Department wasn't interested until later, when they couldn't identify forty percent of the Union Army's dead. So by 1906 the Army began requiring its soldiers to wear half-dollar size tags with the soldier's name, rank, company, and regiment or corps, and the tags were attached to a chain worn under the uniform."

I reflected on the short markers, a reminder of the countless soldiers whose families never had closure. What would my family have done if Mark had died in Iraq and was buried in an unknown, unmarked grave? It would have been devastating.

Nine

On the Road to Kentucky
Gracie

"Now we are engaged in a great Civil War, testing whether that nation or any nation so conceived and so dedicated can long endure."

~Abraham Lincoln

After leaving Shiloh, we drove another two hours, saw an RV park outside Waynesboro, and secured a spot. It was already pushing 7:00 pm, so we picked up sandwiches for supper and ate and relaxed. The next day, we planned to drive four hours to reach the Lincoln Museum in Hodgenville, Kentucky.

We ate dinner and then sat outside. When we'd watched the sunset, we folded up our chairs and walked inside. David smiled. "Are we becoming one of those RV couples with our routines down pat?"

We'd met several couples who lived full time in their RVs, but I couldn't imagine being a nomad long term. I'd rather have access to an RV for trips like this and then return home to a *real* house.

When I asked David, he agreed. "Yes, RVs are wonderful for trips, but I'm looking forward to our farmhouse. In the meantime, thank you, Uncle Rich, for this RV for three weeks."

We cuddled on the couch and went to bed early.

Friday, June 7

We checked out of our RV park after an early breakfast and headed toward Hodgenville. We wanted to see Lincoln's museum near the Birthplace National Park and the boyhood home. I read aloud from David's notebook: "The museum has a series of life-size dioramas, artifacts, and wax figures. Dioramas? Sounds kind of old-fashioned."

David grinned. "Don't forget the wax figures. I think they present scenes from Lincoln's life."

We toured the museum, and I purchased a couple of books and postcards from the park store.

"Do you mind all the books I'm buying?" I asked him.

"We're teachers—it's what we do. I've bought just as many books as you have, Gracie."

"The farmhouse basement has a lot of built-in bookcases. We could use them for our travel books."

He nodded. "Great idea."

We drove by Lincoln's birthplace and the National Park. The birthplace is a log cabin at Knob Creek, where the future president lived from when he was two and a half until he was almost eight years old. It was small and sparse and made our RV seem like a castle.

We checked into the Chimney Rock RV park nearby and determined to get a head start in the morning. David grilled burgers, and I made a salad, and we enjoyed an outdoor supper.

Saturday, June 8

We were just a few minutes away from Museum Row in Bardstown, a collection of five attractions, including the Civil War Museum and the Women of the Civil War Museum. The day flew by, and we enjoyed both museums. We capped the day with dinner at a local Mexican restaurant.

We climbed back into the RV tired but happy.

I turned to David. "Why did it take the Civil War to recognize women could excel at many professions, ranging from journalism to military service, nursing, medicine, and science?"

He shook his head. "I don't know. It makes no sense to consider half of the population less capable or strong."

"I feel even more fortunate for living now, not one hundred years ago, which takes me back to Mary and her letters. What happened?"

David gestured at my messenger bag. "Well, we have a long drive tomorrow…so why not get them out?"

"We still have battlefields we want to see in your notebook. Should I wait until the drive home?"

"No, I think it's fine to read them."

We drove back to the RV park to relax and sat outside to watch the sunset. I reflected that I'd wasted too many chances to enjoy sunsets, and David reached for my hand.

"Me, too. It's easy to get busy." He kissed me. "Let's remind each other of how much we like sunsets."

We kissed more and then walked inside for some privacy. After all, canoodling is what we do! I love that word. I heard Uncle Vern use it when I was a teenager and asked him what it meant. He chuckled and told me it meant to smooch your sweetheart. I planned to canoodle as much as possible, and David was an enthusiastic partner.

Ten

Courtship Days
Mary

"In the distance the groves of farms were softened, blurred together; the far-off rising land was swathed in blue."
~Ruth Suckow

May, 1917

Charlie came to our house last week and asked my father's permission to court me so we can spend time together. We attend church together and sit together at ice cream socials. We study at the library. Charlie comes to dinner now, and afterward we sit on the front porch swing and talk or walk out to the garden.

In a town the size of Jubilee Junction, courting couples don't have many places to go beside our church, the library, parks, the Jubilee Café, and private homes. School won't be out for a couple of months, but being engaged means we don't have to sneak notes or hide our relationship.

We visited Uncle Simon's farm a few times. This was the farm my Carlson Grandparents once owned. I always loved going out to the barn with my grandpa to see all the baby animals each spring. Once, Anna and I discovered meowing kittens in the hayloft. We begged our parents to take them home with us, but Mama said four cats were two too many cats. We compromised and took two kittens after they were weaned, while grandma assured us the mama cat and two remaining kittens would have a home on the farm.

Taking a drive on Jubilee County's rolling hills always soothed me—more so with the talk of war in the air. Charlie and I enjoyed driving down the familiar county road and seeing the family farms. We passed ponds, farmhouses, fields, and the turnoff to the family cemetery.

Two big willow trees marked the driveway to my grandparents' farmhouse and the barn and outbuildings. I remembered our family's weekly visits on Sunday afternoons when I was younger. Their collie, Shep, barked a welcome, and my grandparents came out to greet us.

We enjoyed spending time on the farm when we were little. My grandpa installed two swings on the twin willow trees in the front yard, and Anna and I loved to swing when we were younger. If we begged him, Bruce pushed us. We picked flowers and veggies with grandma and walked out to the barn with grandpa to look at the animals.

Anna and I spent the night once or twice a week during the summer, sleeping upstairs in the attic bedroom. We tried camping out in a little tent under the towering maples, but when it stormed, we got wet, so we fled to the house where grandma met us with towels and made hot cocoa.

My grandparents had forty acres of timber out past the cow pasture. One of my favorite memories was going to pick blackberries and wild strawberries. Anna and I would walk with tin buckets balanced on a sawed-off broom handle. We talked as we made our way down the path to the timber, each holding onto one end of the broomstick, avoiding the *cow pies* along the way. Mama or Grandma Carlson would go along to supervise.

The birds sang overhead in the sunshine as we filled our buckets with luscious, shiny black and red berries. We picked 100 to 150 quarts of wild berries each summer, and Mama and Grandma made jelly or jam or canned them on the big cookstove in the farmhouse. The smell of berries was intoxicating in the kitchen.

Whenever Mama opened a jar of canned berries, jelly, or jam in the winter, she'd smile. "I hear the birds sing, girls!"

Now, of course, it was my Uncle Simon's farm, but he and his wife Clara were just as welcoming. They had a large family, and I babysat their children during the summers. Grandpa's swings on the old willows were still there. I liked to go out and swing, even as a teenager, enjoying the sensation of the wind in my hair.

I told my younger cousins stories about Shep, the faithful collie, rescuing me from an angry bull that got out of its pen when I was a little girl. Shep came between me and the bull and barked fiercely until Grandpa came and grabbed the bull by its nose ring and got it back into its pen.

Now, my uncle and aunt welcomed me and Charlie. We packed a picnic lunch and walked out to the timber. We found a pleasant spot for our picnic and ate our sandwiches while listening to the birds singing. It was a memory I'd cherish.

Charlie's Uncle John also owned a farm. Charlie told me his family stories and memories, and we shared a bond as small-town kids with roots in our family farms.

We took a picnic out to his uncle's farm one Sunday afternoon and walked down to the *crick* following the path taken by the cows to pasture.

We enjoyed a beautiful afternoon, walking hand in hand, appreciating the sweet scent of wildflowers, buzzing insects, and the cool breeze. Our destination was an enormous tree near the creek and its little wooden bridge. I carried a blanket, and he carried the basket. We stopped, spread the blanket, and sat down to enjoy our lunch.

We relaxed under the shade of the tree, eating the sandwiches his mother sent along and sipping iced tea from cups I poured from a Thermos. Then we enjoyed munching on some cookies she'd put between waxed paper and folded over.

Charlie put his arm around me, and we sat back against the enormous tree trunk. We relaxed and listened as the water rippled over the rocks in the creek. Insects buzzed around us, the birds sang overhead, and from the back pasture, the cows mooed. Something in the creek splashed, and I wondered lazily if there might be fish.

I got drowsy in the sunshine and relaxed against Charlie's chest. Did we fall asleep? We realized the afternoon was almost gone. We packed up the blanket and leftovers into the basket, and walked, hand in hand, back to the barn, smiling. It was a moment in time I'll always remember.

However, several of our teachers at high school were talking about the war in Europe and how America might be drawn into it. *The Jubilee Times* was full of opinion pieces on the war and news reports on our allies. These were the pieces fueling Papa's discussions with Grandpa Carlson.

Many Americans supported President Woodrow Wilson's policy of neutrality for the past three years. Others, however, thought we should enter the war and make the world safer. Some writers complained about the financial cost of the war, while others talked about the atrocities being committed with the use of mustard gas and other terrible weapons of war. A few people thought we should forbid anyone from speaking German in this country.

I didn't want to talk about the war. I wanted to create a future with Charlie—getting married, finding a place to live, settling down, and helping Charlie decide on his career. He could work at the family newspaper, *The Jubilee Times;* however, he's also fascinated by the law and could work at his grandfather's law firm. I've told him we have plenty of time to figure it out and hope I'm right.

His big brother, Liam, is one of my older brother's best friends. They're both attending college in Prairie Falls and are roommates in the dorm. Bruce is studying business, and Liam is studying law. They take the train back and forth to college and come home some weekends.

I like Liam because he is one of the few older boys who talks to me like I'm his age, not a little child. When he and Bruce were in high school, he spent a lot of time at our house visiting Bruce, and he was always friendly to me, asking me about school and my interests.

We visited Charlie's grandparents for tea one day. They live in one of the biggest houses in town, a lovely Victorian. Mr. O'Connor took over the law firm from his uncle. His brother took over the family newspaper from their father while the youngest brother farmed. Even though he's retired, Mr. O'Connor has a home office off the parlor with a large bookcase filled with books.

Mrs. O'Connor had been the town librarian as a younger woman and loved books. She and I enjoyed talking about books, while Charlie and his grandfather discussed current events and the war in Europe.

Charlie said, "Grandpa, it is only a matter of time before America gets into the war," and his grandfather agreed.

Mr. O'Connor told us he was a young boy during the Civil War; however, one of his early memories was hearing his mother cry because her big brother had died during a battle and lay buried in an unmarked grave.

He told us, "War is always terrible, but the Civil War was even worse. It divided families into Union and Confederate and led to the slaughter of young men who should have been able to have a family and grow old. I lost an uncle who was always kind to me, and Jubilee Junction lost a dozen young men." His voice became emotional.

"The Civil war was over ending slavery, of course, and keeping the Union together. Now, the war in Europe seems remote since it's taking place overseas, but it threatens our allies. Unchecked aggression could destroy Europe, so we must do our part if the President and Congress act."

He and Charlie exchanged a serious look. I thought, *Will we ever be able to stop all this nonsense with war? Endless generations of young men going to war to kill other young men, while their mothers and girlfriends and wives waited at home. It's beyond my understanding. Women should be more involved!*

I turned back to the conversation.

"I'm ready to fight for my country, Grandpa. I'm not afraid." Charlie sounded confident.

"Oh, Charlie, I would be afraid," his grandfather responded. "There is no shame in being afraid. War is dangerous, and we keep coming up with deadlier weapons. You must trust your fellow soldiers to have your back and be alert to help them. You'll get good training, I'm confident, and let's hope that if America enters the war it will end more quickly."

Charlie thought about his grandfather's words. "Yes, I understand, Grandpa. You know, Frank, my best friend, is going to go with me."

We sipped our tea and nibbled on the delicious chocolate cake. His grandparents steered the conversation back to us, and the excitement of our high school graduation coming up, and our plans if we did not enter the war.

After we left, Charlie and I talked about what his grandfather remembered—the grown-ups crying because someone died in the war. I compared his grandfather's memories to my earliest memories. Mine were happy ones, with my parents, siblings, and our pet dogs. I remembered going to friends' birthday parties, attending school, visiting my grandparents' farm, and celebrating the holidays. I couldn't imagine growing up with Charlie's grandfather's tragic memories.

Meanwhile, as the headlines reported the status of the war overseas, some men expressed a desire to go to war for the adventure. However, I prayed we could help our allies win the war, but not send our boys overseas. Certainly, God would spare Charlie, Frank, Bruce, and Liam, wouldn't He?

Eleven

On the Road to Lexington
Gracie

"And the purpose of life, after all, is to live it, to taste experience to the utmost, to reach out eagerly and without fear for newer and richer experience."

~Eleanor Roosevelt

Sunday, June 9

The next day, David asked me, "Are you having fun? When I told my family about our honeymoon plans, my brother and sister laughed at me. They didn't think it sounded romantic to tour Civil War battlefields while driving an RV cross-country."

I beamed at him. "Yes, I'm having fun. It's making my grandfather's experience come alive, even if it makes me cry sometimes. We're very compatible. You're doing all the driving. How are you holding up?"

David grinned. "This RV is easier to drive than one of those Class A Greyhound bus-size RVs, and easier to park. We planned our trip to spread out the driving and include time to sight-see and rest."

He leaned over and kissed me. "Should we get going?"

I nodded. After Pleasant Hill, Louisiana, the troops sailed for Alexandria, Virginia. We planned to use our time to see a few Civil War sites in Kentucky, starting with Lexington.

I read aloud from David's three-ring notebook. "At least eight sons of the wealthy Todd family fought for the South, while six of their brothers fought for the North, and their sister Mary was

First Lady to Abraham Lincoln himself. So brother almost literally came to fight against brother here in Lexington."

I looked at David. "That's horrible."

He nodded. David told me about Kentucky's neutrality during the Civil War. "They didn't join the Confederacy, and thought they could be neutral, but it failed. They wanted to keep their slaves, considering them property. Unfortunately, they paid a heavy price."

Next, we headed for Camp Nelson and its National Monument, about twenty miles south of Lexington. It's over 500 acres.

David's notes said the Union Army established the camp in 1863 as a depot. It became a recruiting ground for new soldiers, including slaves, who ran away to fight on the Union side. However, loyal Union-supporting slave owners could also provide slaves to help work, getting their wages. Eventually, 3,000 black men and boys were *impressed* to work building railroads, forts, fortifications, and 300 buildings. Kentucky recruited over 23,000 black soldiers for the U.S. Colored Troops (USCT), making it the second-largest contributor of any state. Camp Nelson housed over 10,000 recruits. The Army assigned eight regiments to Camp Nelson and added five more from elsewhere.

I looked up. "Wait, a second. The Union Army paid slave owners for their workers? I thought President Lincoln freed the slaves in 1863."

David said, "Yes, it's not our nation's proudest moment. The Emancipation Proclamation freed the slaves in the rebellious eleven states of the Confederacy. The War Department allowed the recruitment and training of African Americans in these states. Since Kentucky didn't join the Confederacy, the proclamation and military authorization didn't include them."

I was angry. "What a big loophole. What were they thinking? Did they use slave labor to build this whole complex? The war was about opposing slavery, and then we used slaves to build a Union training camp."

When we arrived, David turned off the engine and leaned over, putting his arm around my shoulder. "Yes, I understand your frustration, Gracie. A lot of terrible things happened during that era.

However, Camp Nelson became a home for the refugees—and the escaped slaves' families, with a shanty town of houses for the families. After the war, this place became pretty important because the Army also gave slaves their emancipation papers and ran a soldiers' home here."

We looked around the gift shop after we toured Camp Nelson's Museum. I added another book to my messenger bag.

"I need to buy a bag to carry all these books," I told David. "My messenger bag is getting full, and so is my smaller backpack."

David grinned. "I bought us bags while you were looking at books. Here's yours."

He handed me an extra-large canvas tote bag with a snap at the top. Inside, I found a T-shirt and some postcards. "Thanks!" I hugged him.

We treated ourselves to the Copper River Grill, where we feasted on salmon and salad. Afterward, we split a brownie sundae before heading to the next RV park. After getting set up, I sat on the couch, slipped off my sandals, and relaxed, sipping my chamomile tea, and wiggling my toes. David sat beside me, stretching out his legs as well.

We'd done a lot of walking and biking over the last week, hopefully burning off all the ice cream and desserts. A storm brewed, and we watched the raindrops on the window until I yawned, and we headed back to the bedroom.

Monday, June 10

The next morning, we had a quick breakfast, checked out of our RV camp, and headed back out onto the highway. We drove in silence for a while, but I felt pensive. David seemed to sense it, and he said, "Penny for your thoughts.

"I'm glad we visited there," I told him, "it's just that, well, I get angry thinking about the horrible things done to slaves."

"You take it personally. You have a finely tuned sense of justice."

"I guess I should take it personally. After all, Samuel McDonald is part of my family—a young boy who looked white because he was the master's illegitimate child."

"I can't argue with that," David replied. "When you're right, you're right." He glanced at the RV's instrument panel and announced. "Looks like we need to fill up. And I could use a rest stop."

I kept a lookout for the next travel stop, and before long pointed out a sign pointing to the next exit. David pulled in and headed for the gas pumps reserved for trucks and RVs. He got out to gas up.

I stood up to stretch and had an idea. We were out of fruit and some snack items. I grabbed my purse and got out. "David, I'd like to go inside and grab a few things, okay?"

He had his hand on the gas nozzle. "Sure. This will take a few minutes."

I entered and picked up a small basket, but the handle was sticky. So I placed it back and spotted the nearby restrooms.

Once inside I washed my hands, still thinking about the museum at Camp Nelson. I turned off the water, reached for the paper towels, and hesitated.

A woman was sobbing nearby. She sounded young, and her sobs echoed in the bathroom. As I listened, I sensed her despair and pain.

As I dried my hands, I thought back to my assault at Iowa State and debated what to do. What if Mark and his friend hadn't come looking for me? I knew I couldn't leave without checking on the girl. Saying a quick prayer, I walked closer to the stall where the sobbing was coming from and called out, "Hello? Are you hurt? Do you need help?"

The sobbing stopped for a moment. A young woman's voice said, "Yes, I need help."

The stall's door opened, and a frightened young woman peeked out. Her face was bloody and streaked with tears.

I told myself to stay calm as I walked a step closer. "My name is Gracie. What's yours?"

She shrank back, her eyes moving back and forth to scan the bathroom to be sure no one else was around. She stared down at the floor as she stepped out of the stall and whispered, "Miranda."

I stepped a little closer to look at her injuries and put on my teacher persona. "Miranda, you need a doctor. Who did this to you?"

"My last massage appointment. He was angry about something. Some truck driver—I don't know his name."

I gestured to the door. "Come with me, Miranda. My husband and I have an RV parked outside. We'll take you to a doctor."

Miranda shook her head. "You don't understand. I'm in trouble now. I can't go with you. They're waiting for me in the parking lot. They want to drive us to the next truck stop, but I can't do this anymore. I don't know what to do."

"Who's waiting?" I asked, not understanding.

"My daddy," she sounded defeated and frightened.

I looked at her more closely. Miranda was wearing a torn cropped top and a short jean skirt that couldn't conceal bruises on her legs and torso, some of them fresh and others faded. She wore torn black fishnet pantyhose and cheap heeled boots. Her long, dark hair was pulled back in a ponytail, and I saw more bruises on her neck and throat. She didn't look old enough to be in this situation.

"How old are you?" I asked.

She looked down. "Twenty-two," she mumbled.

I looked at her again, "Miranda? How old are you?" I asked in my teacher voice.

"I'm seventeen," she admitted.

"Let me help you," I told her. "You're hurt, frightened, and under-age, and someone is exploiting you."

My heart beating faster, I sent a text to David, and a couple of minutes later, he knocked on the door. I opened it just a crack, and he handed me the blanket we kept on the couch.

Walking back to Miranda, I said, "I have an idea. My husband, David, is outside. We'll cover you up with this blanket and walk out. We're parked right by the side door—just a few steps away."

Miranda exhaled and grabbed an oversized canvas tote bag from the hook on the bathroom stall's door and flung it over her shoulder. She bent down to pick up a vibrating phone that must have fallen from her jean skirt's pocket and tossed it in her purse.

I covered her with the blanket and sensed her trembling.

"Why are you doing this, Gracie? You could have washed your hands and left."

"I can't do that," I told her. "Two men attacked me when I was in college, and I was alone, frightened—and angry. Fortunately, my brother and his friend found me, and they brought the campus police along. I can't walk away."

She was quiet for a moment.

"Ready?" I asked her, rearranging the blanket over her face.

"Yes."

I gestured. "Step behind me for now."

I opened the bathroom door to find a large man standing there beside David.

The man was in his thirties, dressed in a Nike tracksuit and expensive sneakers. He looked bored and dangerous and had the dark, sulky eyes of a bully.

"Is there a woman in there? I'm waiting for her." He demanded.

"I don't know, maybe," I lied. "My friend just threw up, so we're leaving."

He blocked the doorway.

David stepped forward. "My wife and her friend are coming out now." He stood his ground even though the other man had fifty pounds and four inches on David.

The man pulled out his phone. "The little bitch isn't answering."

Please don't call her again. Let us get her out of here.

The store's manager approached David and the man. "Is there a problem? Should I call the police?"

"No, no problem," the man backed off, still glaring at his phone.

David and the manager stepped in front of the man, creating a path. I paused, holding up my index finger. I needed to ask Miranda if she could really walk out the door.

Twelve

Saving Miranda
Gracie

"If you want to make a difference, the next time you see someone being cruel to another human being, take it. Take it personally because it is personal!"

~Brene Brown

I stepped back inside the bathroom, where Miranda was hiding around the corner, trembling. I cracked the bathroom door, adjusted the blanket, and peeked out the door. The store manager and David still stood in front of the door, giving us some cover.

"Okay, the store manager is here, and the big guy backed off. We're leaving now, " I whispered before I opened the door all the way.

The big man was muttering into his phone, ignoring us.

David moved to the other side of the young woman and led us outside.

The manager remained near the bathroom door.

I peeked over my shoulder as we walked out the side door and breathed a sigh of relief. The big man was still staring down at his phone. *What would happen when he realized she was gone?*

It was only a short walk to the RV, but I'm sure it seemed longer to Miranda who clutched my hand.

Once inside the RV, I removed the blanket and led Miranda to the couch. She sank down and crossed her arms, breathing fast, letting her big bag fall to the floor.

David locked the doors.

"Miranda, this is my husband, David MacNeill. David, this is Miranda, and I think that man was her—daddy?"

She looked petrified.

David gave her a kind look. "Hello, Miranda. It looks like you need some medical attention. Let's find the nearest hospital." He sat in the driver's seat while he looked at his phone and checked for hospitals.

I got her a bottle of water from the fridge and sat down beside her. I hadn't noticed before, but she had an unusual tattoo on her wrist that looked like a QR code.

When Miranda saw me noticing it, she flinched.

"What is that?" I asked.

"It's the brand you get—it tells others who you belong to." Her voice was matter of fact, but I remembered the big bully outside the women's restroom and shuddered.

Someone tapped on the door of the RV, and she became agitated. "Don't answer it. He'll kill me, and maybe you two."

The person outside announced, "I'm here to help. I'm from the FBI." He held up his ID to the passenger side door and announced, "FBI Agent Cal Smith."

David glanced at me. I nodded, saying a silent prayer. He opened the door.

The man outside didn't look like an FBI agent. He had brown eyes and dark brown hair streaked with gray. I recognized him as the store manager who had stepped up. "Can I come inside, please?" he asked.

David stepped back. "Yes, of course."

The agent stepped in and greeted us.

David locked the doors. Then, he and the agent sat at the dinette. I stood by Miranda.

"I'm agent Cal Smith. You've just become part of our undercover sting operation. We've been watching this group moving young women from truck stop to truck stop across Kentucky, Tennessee, and Virginia. We're part of a human trafficking task force. I have five agents on site, and backup arriving momentarily."

Agent Smith stood up, monitoring the front window of the RV

as he checked his phone. Suddenly, half a dozen vehicles arrived, screeching into the parking lot.

The big man we'd seen earlier was exiting the store. He was shouting into his phone.

Miranda flinched, rubbing her wrist with the tattoo over her other arm.

Two vans started their engines as the man walked towards them. But before he could open the car door, six FBI and police vehicles surrounded them. Police officers pointed guns at the man, who raised his hands before kneeling on the ground. The driver jumped out, pulled a handgun out of his pocket, aimed it at an officer, tried to run, and was shot.

Two men exited the other van with their hands up.

Then police officers and FBI agents opened the vans and helped the girls out while others handcuffed the three men and loaded them into one vehicle. An ambulance arrived for the man who'd been shot.

A knock at the door of our RV caught our attention. David opened the door.

An agent with short blonde hair and blue eyes, in a navy-blue suit, entered and introduced herself as Rita Clark. I stood and went into the kitchen area.

Rita sat down by Miranda and began talking to her. She explained she needed to take photos, and then we'd clean her up and take care of her wounds.

"We'll give you some privacy," I told Rita, who took the photos of Miranda's injuries.

David and I walked back to the bedroom, leaving the privacy curtain open.

We sat down on the bed, and I started to tremble. "Human trafficking? She's just a kid. And that man—he was so creepy."

David put his arms around me. "I know."

Rita asked, "Can we use your restroom to clean her up? I have an EMT here."

"Yes, of course," I said, and stood up.

Cal opened the door and greeted a young female EMT.

Rita must be a mother. She has a remarkable maternal instinct, and Miranda is responding to her soothing voice.

I handed her a washcloth and watched Rita dab at Miranda's face and then turn her over to the young EMT, who had a first aid kit with her. Backing away, I winced because now I could see more clearly the beating she'd taken. David put a comforting hand on my arm.

Cal signaled, and we followed him to the dinette. "First, thank you for your help."

"What's going to happen to Miranda now?" I asked.

"She's going to a Victims Services Division facility a short drive away, along with the other seven girls, thanks to you two. They will get good care and help. Rita will make sure of that, while I'll deal with the handlers we caught."

He continued, "The girls need medical care, counseling, support, and education to avoid falling back into such a dangerous situation. We'll work with them on job skills. I'd like to take a statement from you both and get your contact information if we need you later."

We sat at the dinette, found our college business cards, and wrote our cell phone numbers on the back.

He took out a digital recorder and took our statements. Then he handed us his card.

Afterward, Cal looked at me. "David mentioned you two are on your honeymoon. Just imagine the stories you're going to have for your friends and family."

"I'd like to say goodbye to Miranda," I told him.

He stood up. "You can. Here they are. Goodbye and thank you." He shook our hands and left.

The young EMT came out of the bathroom with Miranda behind her. Miranda had several Steri-strips on cuts on her face. She was going to have bruises and scars, but she was calmer.

Rita shook our hands. "It was nice meeting you, Mr. and Mrs. MacNeill."

The EMT exited the RV, and Rita followed.

Miranda made eye contact as she picked up her big bag.

Hugging her, I slipped one of my cards into her bag. "Here's my business card. We'd love to hear how you're doing later on."

"Thank you, Gracie. I tried to leave before, and they found me—and they beat me."

She stepped down from the RV, and Rita put an arm around Miranda. They walked to a waiting vehicle and got inside.

We watched as the vehicles left the parking lot.

David exhaled. "We need to process all of this. Did you have time to buy any snacks?"

He held out his hand to me. Together, we returned to the store and bought a few snack items—and some chunky cherry chocolate frozen yogurt.

The woman ringing us up grinned. "We haven't had this much excitement since someone spotted a retired NFL player pumping his own gas. Good job standing up to that bully." She fished in her apron and said, "The frozen yogurt's on me!" and put three one-dollar bills on the counter.

"Thanks," I said.

David shrugged modestly and bagged up the groceries.

We had a quick snack before we got back on the road. We pointed the RV toward Maysville and the Bierbower House, another two hours' drive.

The Bierbower House served as a stop for the Underground Railroad during the Civil War. Today, it's the National Underground Railroad Museum. It made me think about my ancestor, Sarah, and her bravery taking a group of slaves from Virginia to freedom with the help of four Union soldiers. The slaves included her sister's maid, Rebecca, a young man named Thomas, and Rebecca's son, Bobby. They could not have survived without the help of the Underground Railroad in Virginia.

We spent three hours exploring the museum before leaving with a bag of books and small gifts. The exhibits fired up my imagination.

As we entered the RV, I turned to David. "The museum was amazing. What did you think, David?"

"Yes, I found it extremely moving seeing stories about the people who ran the Underground Railroad, risking their lives to help slaves escape. Many of them did it because of their religious convictions, of course. Some of them were Quakers or Methodists. Others were freed slaves, like Harriet Tubman, who escaped and then returned for her family. I kept thinking about the scripture verse about faith without works is dead—from James, I think. It's one thing to believe that slavery was wrong, but it took action to show those beliefs. Sort of like my incredible wife who helped a young woman escape from human traffickers."

"I couldn't have done it without you," I told him. "I think you mean James 2:26. 'For as the body without the spirit is dead, so faith without works is dead also.'"

"Now you're just showing off, Gracie!"

I shrugged, "Six years of Bible Quiz Team. Dad was the Coach."

We stopped for Chinese food—beef and broccoli for David and sweet and sour chicken for me— then we drove to our next RV park and checked in. Once inside, David wrapped me in his arms. "Have I told you yet how amazing you are? You saw that young woman, and there was no hesitation. You knew we had to help her."

"Don't forget you stood up to that terrible bully. I hope they put him away for life. But I knew you would support me. I'm proud of you, too."

We decided it was time for our frozen yogurt and strawberries and a lighthearted movie. But I couldn't help wondering if we would ever hear from Miranda again. I whispered a prayer for her.

Thirteen

President Wilson Declares War
Mary

"This is a war to end all wars."

~President Woodrow Wilson

Late May 1917

*O*ur plans are ruined. *The Jubilee Times'* headline screams "President Wilson declares war April 2nd" in large letters. We're at war. The high school canceled our graduation ceremony and all the festivities as well.

Then Congress passed the Selective Service Act, authorizing the Federal Government to expand the military through conscription on May 18, 1917. Papa explained that our regular army only had about 121,000 and our national guard numbered under 200,000. We would need more soldiers to take part in the war in France. The President asked for an army of one million. But six weeks after we'd declared war, only 70,000 men had volunteered.

"We need the draft," Papa declared.

Many of our high school senior boys have already signed up—including Charlie. He came to ask for my hand in marriage immediately afterward. He told Papa he reports for duty June 1, but he wanted to go to war as an engaged man. Charlie gave me a simple ring and whispered he promised to return to me. My parents gave their permission, and I whispered, "Yes!"

We walked next door to our grandparents' house, where they embraced me, Mama, and Anna. They shook hands with Papa,

Charlie, and Bruce, who will also leave June 1. My stern grandma was crying and wiping her eyes with her apron. My younger brother, Aiden, looked uncomfortable.

Grandma looked at me with a hanky to her nose. "You and Anna have grown up so much, and now you're getting married! We must finish your quilt and get to work on other things."

Then we walked to Charlie's parents' house, where they hugged me and shook hands with Papa and Bruce.

His mother looked especially emotional, so I asked Charlie about it, and he shook his head. That is when I realized his mother was sending two sons to war because Liam was also going.

"Mother's upset. She worries about us."

She and my mother embraced each other, cried, and congratulated each other. They were friends, and now we'd be a family.

His parents joined us, and we all walked to his grandparents' home where we received more hugs, congratulations, and worried looks from his grandma. The men talked in low voices about the war while the women focused on the engagement.

Charlie's grandmother hugged me and told me we'd have to pray and trust the Lord. But dark clouds seem to hang over the town and all our hopes and dreams.

I was worried about Charlie, of course, but also Frank and Liam—and my big brother, Bruce. Sure, he'd teased me when we were younger, but Bruce had always been there. He'd pulled me and Anna around the block in a big wagon when we were little girls. He'd walked me to the library when I was too young to walk there by myself. I couldn't imagine not having him here, much less seeing him go to war. Even when he'd gone off to college, he was home all summer and home some weekends.

Mama told me not to be so dramatic when she saw me crying, but I caught her crying later that day as she folded laundry for Bruce.

I told her I was sorry to be so selfish, and we hugged and cried together.

A group of young men from Jubilee Junction visited the army

recruiter and signed papers a couple of weeks ago. Their orders came in today's mail. Charlie, Frank, Liam, and Bruce report to Camp Funston, part of Fort Riley, near Manhattan, Kansas, in just a few days. Mama is busy getting my brother Bruce packed up and ready to go. Mrs. O'Connor has two boys to get packed up, so Charlie and I don't see each other as much.

We stopped working on the quilt almost two weeks ago, with the announcement of war. Anna tells me she is sorry for making fun of sewing, and she'll help us with the quilt after the boys leave for their training.

We canceled my eighteenth birthday party and held a simple engagement party in late May instead.

Aunt Eva came for the celebration. She's Papa's younger sister, and she and Mama are close. Anna and I loved her because she was so much fun but also very serious about her suffragist efforts. She treated us like young adults. She stayed for a few days, and I overheard her talking to my mother the night before my party. They were murmuring, and I only heard a few words here and there, but I thought they were discussing Bruce and Charlie leaving for war and our engagement.

Mama, Aunt Eva, Charlie's mother, and our grandmothers served cake, coffee, and tea. We heard them gossiping in the kitchen and knew they were worried about the war.

The doorbell rang and soon people filled the house talking quietly, eating cake, and sipping tea or coffee. Afterward, the men walked outside to smoke and talk while the older women gathered in the kitchen.

My girlfriends admired the hope chest in the parlor, so we opened it so they could see what I'd done so far. They praised the neat stitching on my embroidered towels and liked the colors I picked for the quilt. We chatted and drank punch and nibbled on our slices of cake, but the mood was much too somber.

My best friend, Sara, admired my simple ring and told me how lucky I was. "Charlie's crazy about you, Mary. He's such a handsome boy."

Anna and one of her friends passed by. Mama asked them to pick up dirty dishes. Aidan and his best friend Roger looked uncomfortable in their dress clothes. They grabbed plates with slices of cake and escaped to his bedroom.

Bruce and Liam arrived, congratulated me, and then left to get cake and coffee. They were handsome young men who would soon be soldiers—no wonder their mothers were worried.

Charlie came back smiling and joined me, putting his arm around my waist. We tried to be happy in the moment and enjoy the time we had left together.

Charlie's father brought his camera and took a series of photos of us sitting on the bench in the garden. He promised to have them ready before Charlie left for his army training.

Mama, Papa, and I talked about a practical gift for Charlie. I thought of a pocket watch, but Papa said they would be issued one. In suggested instead, "How about a new leather wallet with a compartment holding a photo of the two of us?"

Papa talked to Charlie's father, and he promised to have pictures in several sizes for us, including one for the wallet.

Papa's friend did the engraving for the store. He put Charlie's initials on the front of the wallet and a simple message inside: "For Charlie. Love, Mary." Papa added a chain that attached to the belt on one end and slipped around the center of the wallet with the other.

Charlie and I spent as much time together as we could manage. One evening, he came to supper at our house. We helped clean up afterward, and then we sat on the porch in the swing, watching the sunset. Charlie put his arms around me, and we talked. Neighbors walked by and waved and called out hello. Several people came up to wish him luck and shake his hand.

We settled back, holding hands and listening to the neighborhood settling down for the night. I said, "Please be brave, but don't be stupid, Charlie."

"Yes, I understand. I promise you, Mary." He kissed my hand on top of my ring.

We sat there for another half hour until my mother told us I should come in. She smiled at Charlie, and he nodded. Charlie kissed me and walked down the steps. His train left in two days.

I went inside and upstairs to my room, where I undressed, put on my nightgown, and crawled into bed. I cried quietly. Anna came over, crawled into bed, and held me. She didn't say a word. We fell asleep.

61

Fourteen

Engagement & Goodbyes
Mary

*"(T)he slow inevitable progression of the seasons, the nearness
to earth and sky and weather, the unchanging processes of birth
and death, the goings of the birds in the fall and their sure return
in the spring, the coming, night after night, of the familiar stars
to the wide sky."*

~Ruth Suckow, "A Rural Community"

*T*he next day, the O'Connor family invited us
to eat lunch with them. Charlie and I planned to spend some time
together before he returned home to finish packing. The recruits from
Jubilee Junction would go to France once they completed training.

My family dressed nicely, and I was proud to walk with them to
Charlie's house just a few blocks away. We enjoyed a pleasant lunch
and conversation, and I saw how well my parents and Charlie's
parents got along. Liam and Bruce chatted with Anna and Aidan,
so they didn't feel left out. Afterward, I waved goodbye to my
parents, and Charlie took my hand.

As we walked together, we talked about our future. We discussed
the names of our four children, where we might live, and Charlie's
future occupation. He still hadn't decided between the law and
journalism.

We sat on a bench in the city park near my house. Charlie put
his arms around me, and we sat in silence. Charlie kissed me several
times. I longed to give myself to him, only vaguely understanding
what it meant.

"I love you, Mary. I will always love you," he told me.

Holding back tears, I took the wallet out of my handbag and presented him with it. "I love you, too, Charlie."

Charlie opened it and saw our photos inside: one of us together and one of me. My father had tucked a four-leaf clover made from brass inside the wallet, which made Charlie smile. He noticed the engraving and the chain for connecting his wallet to his belt, and said he liked it. He thanked me, we kissed, and then we sat side by side.

The hour passed, and we headed back to my house. His train left early the next morning.

We kissed on the porch, and I clung to him, trembling and angry at myself for acting so needy. *This man is going to war. I must show him I will be strong, waiting for him.* He held me tenderly, kissed me again, and I whispered my love for him.

He whispered it back and said again how much he liked the wallet. "I love you, Mary. I promise to do everything I can to come home to you. I'll say a prayer that we'll be together again."

He kissed me once more sweetly. And then he walked down the steps, turned and waved, and continued home just the way he'd done dozens of times before.

Inside, I fell into Mama's arms, sobbing. She held me and made soothing little sounds. I broke away, blew my nose with my handkerchief, and wiped my eyes.

I wasn't the only one crying. Mama was sending off her oldest son. "Oh, Mama, I'm sorry," I told her.

She told me the soup was still warm. Also, I should say goodbye to Bruce tonight. She wiped her eyes on her apron.

Upstairs, Bruce tucked something into his duffle bag as I greeted him. He turned with a smile. I gave him a hug and a kiss on his cheek.

Bruce hugged me back. "Don't worry, little sister. I'll look after Charlie as best I can, and his brother Liam will be someplace close by as well. Hopefully, we'll be back in a few months." He tried to make light of the situation, but I knew he was worried.

I told Bruce goodnight and slipped back downstairs to eat some crackers and cheese and soup. Sitting at the kitchen table, I pondered how life in Jubilee Junction had changed. The high school had canceled the events I'd looked forward to with graduation, and I was out of sorts.

Afterward, I crept back upstairs, put on my nightgown, and stared out the window. Anna was asleep, and the house was quiet. I cried, thinking about the boys leaving in the morning, and wondered when we would see them again.

The dawn broke, and the sunshine stabbed my heart as I realized the train was already miles down the track, taking my sweetheart and my older brother off to war. My parents had gotten up early to take Bruce to the station, but Charlie suggested I stay home. He knew his mother would be emotional, sending off her two sons.

I dressed listlessly. Anna was already up and eating breakfast. A pot of oatmeal was on the stove, and baked bread and jam were on the table. I ate a little oatmeal, drank some water, and wandered into the parlor looking for my book.

A note lay on top of my book. I opened it:

My darling Mary, I miss you already. I know you will pray for us. Be strong, dear.
Your loving boy,
Charlie.

Mama walked by and stopped. "How are you this morning, Mary? Charlie wanted you to have the note." She sat down by me on the horsehair sofa. "I'm glad Charlie suggested you stay home. The mothers were crying, and a few fathers looked like they might join us. Bruce hugged me and told me not to worry. He and Liam will look after Charlie." Mama wiped her eyes and slipped the hankie back into her apron. "I talked to Charlie's mother, and we sent our sons off with pens, stationery, envelopes, and stamps. So you should have a letter or two soon."

I wiped my tears and sat up as a horrifying thought flashed through my mind. *Would I ever see my beloved Charlie again?*

Fifteen

On the Road to D.C.
Gracie

"I saw the Vietnam Veterans Memorial not as an object placed into the earth but as a cut in the earth that has then been polished, like a geode. Interest in the land and concern about how we are polluting the air and water of the planet are what make me want to travel back in geologic time-to witness the shaping of the earth before man."

~Maya Lin

Monday, June 10

$\mathcal{A}$s we drove, we talked about our encounter with Miranda—and human trafficking.

"I can't get over it, David. We'd just toured the museum about the underground railroad and spies; then I walk into a truck stop restroom and there's Miranda, a victim of human trafficking."

David glanced over. "That was one tough guy waiting for her. He walked up, looked at me, and made me feel like I didn't belong there."

"What if the FBI agent posing as the manager hadn't come over?" I asked.

David shrugged. "I might need emergency plastic surgery. Nothing was going to stop me from getting you and your new friend to the RV, no matter what. Fortunately, Agent Smith was there."

"Do you think Miranda will be alright?"

"She's escaped that life, thanks to you. Now she's going to get help, and the chance to make her own choices."

"Thanks to you, too." I glanced at David. "I couldn't have done it alone."

I said another silent prayer for Miranda and counted my blessings that David had stepped up to the bully.

We drove almost four hours to the border with West Virginia, stopping for supper in Olive Hill. While waiting for our burgers, David reminded me of the unique nature of West Virginia, which I'd forgotten. I looked up the Wikipedia entry on my phone, and read aloud.

"West Virginia was formed out of western Virginia and added to the Union because of the American Civil War. It was the only state to declare its independence from the Confederacy. In the summer of 1861, Union troops, which included several newly formed Western Virginia regiments under General George McClellan, drove off Confederate troops under General Robert E. Lee."

I looked up just as our salads arrived.

"So, if we hadn't had the Civil War, West Virginia wouldn't exist, and Virginia would be bigger?" I asked, thanking the server.

"Yes," David replied.

"I'm sure I learned it in school, but somehow, I forgot it."

David leaned forward. "Don't feel bad, Gracie. You aren't alone. Not all white southerners owned slaves or supported the Confederacy. Some formed regiments and fought on the Northern side. Some people rely on the movie *Gone with The Wind* for their knowledge of the American Civil War."

When we arrived at our RV park across the border into West Virginia, we checked in, secured our spot, connected to the park utilities, and extended the slides. By now, we were experts and worked well together.

We gathered a couple of pillows and sat sideways on the couch, and David put his arms around me. I'd turned off the lights before sitting down, and we admired the night sky through our big front window.

"It's beautiful," I said.

"Not as beautiful as you, Gracie," David responded and distracted me with some serious kissing that led us back to the bedroom.

Later, we indulged in some frozen yogurt topped with strawberries and discussed our itinerary for the next day.

"We're five hours away from Washington, D.C. Let's head there tomorrow," David said. "We talked about doing research at the Library of Congress, visiting the Smithsonian, and taking the bus tour."

"I want to find my Uncle Patrick's name on the Vietnam wall," I reminded him.

David was quick to point out that the Smithsonian consisted of seventeen different museums, galleries, and a zoo. We had some tough decisions to make. I opened my iPad, and we looked at the options.

Tuesday, June 11

The next morning, we hustled through our routine and got on the road by 9 am. We arrived at Cherry Hill RV park in College Park, Maryland, midafternoon. The park's location made it easy to get into the city since they were near a Metro station.

We saw there was time for a bus tour, so we switched to our walking shoes and grabbed our small backpacks.

The D. C. bus made several stops at the Washington Monument, the mall, and the Vietnam Veterans memorial, where we got off. David helped me locate my father's big brother's name—Patrick Michael O'Connor, Junior. Catalogs listed the deceased alphabetically, with panel and row numbers. Volunteers walked around and helped people navigate the wall around us.

When we finally located Patrick's name and I touched it on the wall, I became emotional. I was proud of his service, sorry he died at such a young age, and suddenly understood how his death had changed my father's life. David took a picture of me holding up a photo of Dad and Patrick as teenagers while I pointed to his name on the wall. We sent the photo to my parents, brother, and grandparents.

Patrick was two years older than my father, handsome, confident, and outgoing. After being drafted, he became a photojournalist in the army, and planned to take over *The Jubilee Times* after Grandpa's retirement. Instead, Patrick died in Vietnam just days before his tour was up when he stepped on a landmine. My father changed his major to journalism and took over as the editor when I was a child.

Nearby, others wept as they located a name, took pictures, and clung to companions. David held me close and whispered sweet things until my breathing returned to normal.

The beauty of the V-shaped wall is hard to describe. The black granite slowly rises from the earthen bank, reaching its full height in the middle, then gradually recedes into the soil. Much like the Vietnam War, which didn't seem important at first, as David later mused. We sent a few military advisers, then the war became a massive disaster as over two million American young men served in Vietnam. At last, it sunk slowly into oblivion. What a great job the wall's designer, Maya Lin, did with her design!

As we learned later, the wall is especially amazing at night—reflective, shimmery, and breathtaking.

David had seen the wall before, but when he saw me find young Patrick's name, he took off his glasses to wipe his eyes, the gold flecks shining brightly. We observed other people up and down the line, finding the names of their loved ones.

"This memorial is a stark reminder of the cost of war. These soldiers—58,000—gave their lives for a war that most of them didn't understand. Every time I visit, I'm awestruck," he told me. "It's incredibly moving to watch people find their connection with the war."

We lingered and watched people leave photographs, dog tags, food, beer, and other small items by the base of the memorial.

"What happens to all of that stuff?" I asked, still holding the photo.

"National Park Service Rangers collect what people leave behind every day and take them to a storage facility. Some get displayed at the education center."

I hesitated, then left the photo of Dad and Patrick at the base. I had a copy on my phone.

By the time the bus dropped us off at the RV park, we were tired but happy. I'd heard stories about Patrick all my life, but he'd never seemed so real as today.

Wednesday, June 12

David planned to do research at the Library of Congress on Wednesday, so we took a bus to the city and spent most of the day at the library. David had reserved passes for us online. He was getting more sources for his book about German POWs working on Iowa farms during WWII. David had visited the Library of Congress before, but it was my first visit.

I took the free guided tour, including a chance to see the wonderful Great Hall of the Thomas Jefferson building. It's gorgeous, with marble floors, stained glass ceilings, enormous paintings, columns, and staircases.

Afterwards, I did research on WWI-era quilts, the Great War, and the 1918 flu pandemic. I filled a folder with photocopies, scribbling notes on them, while I emailed myself other articles and the titles of several books to find.

I was just putting the folder into my messenger bag when David came to check on me. The library closed at 5 pm, so we found a restaurant nearby. Entering, we smelled pizza and saw a large brick oven behind the counter. We sat, looked at the menu, and took in the wonderful aromas of pizza.

David and I exchanged glances. "How about the garden veggie pizza, or does the pulled grilled chicken with mushrooms and red pepper sound better?" he asked.

We decided on the pulled chicken pizza and ordered salads. As we ate our supper, we chatted about our research, comparing notes.

We got back on the bus and rode *home* to our RV with a box of leftover slices of pizza. The sky seemed brighter, with all those lights from the memorials, museums, and monuments.

Once inside, David showed me a thick folder of research and a notebook with a lot of notes. "What a great day, doing research. Thanks for giving me the gift of time. I hope you weren't bored."

"Not at all. I took the tour. I had never seen the Library of Congress. It's such a fascinating building. I did some research of my own."

"Let me guess—WWI, quilts, and the 1918 flu pandemic?"

"Yes, and I found some interesting stuff."

We put away our research, relaxed, and did a little housekeeping, washing a few dirty cups and bagging up dirty clothes. I watched him, thinking, *David picks up after himself. He sets his dirty bowls in the sink, hangs up his clothes, and just placed his dirty clothes into the laundry bag. I married a perfect man!*

I debated getting out my laptop and checking email.

Then he walked into the kitchen and hugged me from behind. "Let's watch something mindless and relax."

We snuggled on the couch and found a romantic comedy, but only watched it for a few minutes. We wandered back to the bedroom and found another way to entertain each other. After all, this was our honeymoon.

Sixteen

Leaving D. C. for Gettysburg
Gracie

"Maybe what you've written will help others, will be a small part of the solution. You don't even have to know how or in what way, but if you are writing the clearest, truest words you can find and doing the best you can to understand and communicate, this will shine on paper like its own little lighthouse."
~Anne Lamott, Bird by Bird

Thursday, June 13

*T*he next day, we took the bus tour again, with a different route. We spent a few minutes at the Lincoln Memorial, saw the Tidal Basin—without cherry blossoms–and got a different view of the Vietnam Memorial.

We debated between exploring the National Air and Space Museum or the National Museum of American History and ended up at the History Museum.

I looked at David. "There's too much to see! We should have taken an entire month off. I want to return and visit the remaining museums."

He agreed. "D.C. is one of my favorite places. I try to see one new thing each trip. Next time, we need to check out the Portrait Gallery, because I hear it's amazing."

I thought, *Yes, of course. Next time! We're married. We're going to travel and do so many interesting things together.*

At 2 pm, we took a bus back to the RV park, checked out, and headed for Gettysburg—surprised that it was just two hours away.

Once we arrived, we headed for the Gettysburg National Cemetery and battlefield but drove by Gettysburg college. David had attended the Civil War Institute, held at the college during the summer. He hoped to speak at the institute someday and told me I should come along. Participants toured area battlefields and listened to authors and military experts lecture about aspects of the war.

By late afternoon Thursday, we were both dragging. We'd walked around, driven around, biked around, and tried to cram in everything.

David looked over at me. "Whose idea was this honeymoon?" Of course, he and I'd made that decision together.

We drove to the Artillery Ridge Campground, checked in, and found our site. Then we settled down to eat taco salads and watch a movie. Halfway through, David distracted me with his kisses, and we took our canoodling to the bedroom.

Friday, June 14

After breakfast, I considered our bags of dirty clothes, and we took a load of our undies and towels to the park's laundry room. We sat to wait with David's notebook and a tablet and pen to make a list of what we needed to do.

"From now on, let's just drive by and wave at historical sites."

"Sounds good," David said.

When we got back to our RV, which we'd nicknamed *Hawk*, we had a hamper full of folded laundry to put away. We rewarded ourselves by picking up submarine sandwiches from the café next to the laundromat.

David studied his notebook as we ate our sandwiches with chips and pop. He read off the list of sites we'd hoped to visit, and I checked them off in my little notebook.

"David, we did it! We've seen most of the sites where Michael's regiment fought. We've walked through the battlegrounds, visited cemeteries and plantations, toured museums, and talked to a lot of Civil War experts."

"Yes, we accomplished our goals. Now, let's see a few places in Virginia."

We packed up, checked out, and headed for Winchester, where Sarah and Michael's story began. Her village was only ten miles from Winchester, the oldest Virginia town west of the Blue Ridge Mountains. Along the way, we saw memorials for different battlefields, including cemeteries.

"This is what we've both been waiting for, isn't it?" David asked. "The place where four Union soldiers hid in a barn to regroup and care for two wounded men, their brothers. Then a young woman named Sarah and a freed slave named Thomas found them."

I gazed at him, and my voice trembled as tears welled up in my eyes. "Don't forget Rebecca with her knowledge of herbs who cared for their injuries, and her little boy Bobby. Sarah adopted him, and he changed his name to Samuel and grew up to be a wonderful civil rights lawyer. He married Maggie O'Connor, so he's my 3rd great-uncle."

"It must be incredible to make such a connection with your family history."

"Yes, it is. Of course, we only know it now after gathering a lot of information. What do you know about your ancestors, David? I thought we could go to the library and use their genealogy databases to create your family tree."

David admitted, "I know very little. My great-grandfather died in WWII under mysterious circumstances, and his son, my grandfather, died in Vietnam."

"Oh David, " I said. "We should have looked for your grandfather's name."

"No need, Gracie. I found his name the first time I was here. His side of the family was small. We didn't see them or hear from them much. My mother's side is different. Her parents were wonderful grandparents, and my grandfather would talk to me about his days in the service during the Korean conflict. We have aunts, uncles, and cousins. But we don't have Gracie tracing our family tree."

"Um, yes you do. You married her, right? When we get home, I'm going to check out your family tree."

"I'd like that."

We drove past several plantations in Winchester until we found

Evaline. I imagined the two sisters, Sarah and Emily, walking down the steps of Evaline's white-columned plantation house. Sarah was a young, widowed teacher who went to Boston for college, where she met abolitionists who changed her attitudes towards slavery. Her older sister Emily married a wealthy plantation owner, George. Once their husbands left for war, Sarah and Emily planned to free their slaves and take Rebecca and Bobby to freedom, but Emily died in childbirth, as did her baby. Sarah kept her promise and got some unexpected help.

David and I looked for our next campground, checked in, and set up, recognizing we no longer needed Uncle Rich's checklist. We picked up burgers and ate them outside, ignoring the occasional bug, as we watched other campers arrive and settle in. The sunset was an amazing array of colors, and the mountains were like a giant canvas, with shadows moving across them.

After sunset, we stowed the table and chairs and walked inside to relax. David served up the last of the frozen yogurt, and we watched part of a movie, *The Girl with the Dragon Tattoo*. We got distracted when David's kisses were making it difficult to focus on the plot. We'd finish it another time.

Saturday, June 15

On the way home to Iowa, we started talking about the letters Charlie had written to Mary. I opened my messenger bag and found the packet of letters, setting them on the little table between us. I did a quick count of them and then opened the first letter.

Letter One
June 3, 1917

> *My darling Mary,*
> *We've arrived at camp Funston, which is part of Fort Riley, near Manhattan, Kansas.*
> *We took the train, boarding at Jubilee Junction, and it took about 12 hours to reach our destination with half a dozen stops*

along the way to pick up more soldiers. The conductor told us there are about 30 camps across the country to train soldiers and sailors. Then a bus took us to the camp.

I got acquainted with a few others from Jubilee Junction on the ride. We had a dozen recruits who lived on farms in the next county. One fellow I really like, because he is funny, smart, and quick. Jack has an older brother who left home to fight with the French over a year ago and tried to prepare him for trench warfare in France. Frank and I listened to Jack talk about the conditions in France, and wondered how anyone could survive in such terrible conditions. We're trying to prepare ourselves for war. Trading our regular clothing for army uniforms helped us think of ourselves as soldiers. Then we got haircuts. I don't think you will like mine because it's very short.

Your big brother Bruce is in our group, and he has been kind. I've always liked him. He and Liam are acting like the protective big brothers to me and Frank. Frank and I have been friends since elementary school, and I'm glad to have him by my side. The four of us sat together on the train.

We're quartered in long buildings, with a row of bunk beds on either side. Each soldier has a trunk with our number for our gear, as well as a few hooks on the wall. We're thankful it's not the middle of winter because the buildings don't seem insulated very well. However, they had to work fast. I cannot imagine the army of carpenters, plumbers, and electricians it took to put this camp together. We go to another building for classes and tests. Then we go outside to drill several times a day. We eat our meals in the mess hall, in another building which also houses the infirmary and clinics.

Bruce and Liam are in a nearby barracks and doing well. I see them in classes and at drills.

On the train trip here, we saw the latest newspaper headlines. This war has already killed many in Europe, and soldiers and civilians alike are weary of it. I pray we can help our allies win quickly so we can come home.

I'm looking at your picture in my new wallet. Thank you for that. I've enjoyed holding it and looking at the picture of us and then the one of you. I look at them and think you and I are staring at the same sky and feel closer to you. You're the last thing I think about when I go to sleep each night and the first thing I think about when I wake up.

Here is my address for the next six to eight weeks.
Pvt Charles O'Connor
Barracks B-4
Camp Funston
Fort Riley, Kansas.
Please write to me, Mary, and tell me about your day. Please say hello to your family.
Your loving man,
Charlie

David listened as he drove.

I put the letter down and opened the small album to find a picture of Charlie and Mary standing together in a garden. He was a handsome boy with dark blond wavy hair and a confident smile. Mary was beautiful, with long, dark blonde hair and lovely gray-blue eyes. I sighed.

"I'll show you this picture of Mary and Charlie when we stop. They're young and in love. It's both romantic and sad. I can't imagine being separated from you by a war," I told David.

He agreed. "I can't either, Gracie."

I put the letters back into my messenger bag. As we drove, I thought about my family tree, and all my grandmothers, and what we'd learned in the past year from the family quilts. Grandma Grace and her twin sisters went to California during WWII. They experienced love, loss, the horrors of war, and betrayal. Then there's Sarah and her arrival in Jubilee Junction in 1864. She became part of the town, teaching the children in the school and raising Bobby as her adopted son, Samuel. When the American Civil War ended, Michael came back, and they married. They had a remarkable life, fighting for universal suffrage and raising a family.

Fifty years later, Grandma Mary fell in love with her schoolmate Charlie, who got swept up in the whirlwind of WWI and sent to

France. He sounded so devoted. I couldn't wait to read the rest of the letters and learn more about Charlie and Mary.

I wondered, *What happened to Charlie in France? Why did Mary create a beautiful quilt and other linens and then hide them under a false bottom in a hope chest?*

Seventeen

Working at the Store
Mary

"Never think that war, no matter how necessary, nor how justified, is not a crime."

~Ernest Hemingway, 1946

June 1917

School ended early. Graduating seniors received our diplomas in the mail. My girlfriends and I tried not to complain, because most of us had brothers, uncles, cousins, boyfriends, and classmates on that train to Kansas. Soon, a second group of men left Jubilee Junction, headed for training.

I was going to help Papa in the store starting the following week, and I tried to take an interest. Bruce had worked in the store after school and each summer since he was twelve or thirteen. He still helped during the summer once his university classes ended. He was studying business and talked about starting his own accounting firm before the war.

Mama encouraged me to do my best because it was our family business, and my husband might well manage it someday. I wondered why neither Anna nor I could manage the store. I thought about my Aunt Eva and wondered what she would say to Mama.

Anna tried to cheer me up. "You'll get to spend time with Papa, learn about the store, and chat with customers. Meanwhile, I'll be stuck here, doing household chores with Mama, weeding the garden, and sewing with Grandma."

I exhaled. "Grandma said we would restart work on the quilt, little sister. So I'll be with you."

She grinned. "Oh, good!"

The following Monday, I woke up early, put on my good navy-blue dress, put my hair up, wore comfortable shoes, and walked downstairs to eat breakfast with Papa. Dressed in his suit, drinking coffee, he was humming when I walked into the kitchen.

"Papa, am I dressed up enough?"

"Good morning, Mary." He looked up. "Yes, you look very presentable."

After breakfast, we walked to the Carlson General Store, just four blocks away. One of his clerks was already there, opening the door. Several customers were waiting as well. Papa tipped his hat like a gentleman at the women.

Someone in the group spoke up. "Oh, is this your daughter, Mary?"

"Yes, she's here to learn about the business. She just graduated from high school. Her fiancé is in training for the army."

Papa showed me around the store. He told me I'd learn about the way he did inventory, ordered goods, priced them, and handled the money.

I sat down with Papa in his office, and he showed me his ledger with information about our accounts, vendors, and products. We sold a variety of grocery items, fresh fruits and vegetables in season, canned goods, a few tools, and hardware. We also offered fabric and sewing goods, brooms, mops, and cleaning goods.

Customers handed us a list, and it was up to us to gather their order while they chatted with others. However, women picked out their own fabric or selected fruit, and men liked to look at the tools and hardware.

Papa assigned me to check people out and handle money, but first I spent several hours standing by the regular checker, Mrs. Smith, and helping her. Fortunately, I was always good at math and could easily make change. I enjoyed bagging up purchases and greeting people.

I worked with Grandpa Carlson to unpack boxes and restock

shelves at the store. He complimented me on my careful placement of items on the shelf. "Good job, Mary. Make it easy for customers to see the goods, as well as the prices underneath."

We took turns leaving to get lunch at the diner and return to work. By six, I was tired, but I'd done better than I hoped and learned more about the business that literally puts food on the table for my family. Throughout the next week, Papa and I walked to work together. I learned about the store's inventory and when to reorder and restock.

One of my uncles came into the store with a small box of patriotic records and persuaded Papa to sell them. He brought in a gramophone and played the record for us. He said it would help to sell them if we played the record.

The song on the record was "Over There," written by George Cohan. It was a very patriotic song, and it made me cry if I listened to the lyrics too closely. Johnnie became Charlie, of course, in my mind. I bought a record for myself. Fortunately, we already owned a gramophone at home.

Johnnie, get your gun, get your gun, get your gun.
   Take it on the run, on the run, on the run.
Hear them calling you and me.
   Every son of liberty.
Hurry right away, no delay, go today.
   Make your daddy glad to have had such a lad.
Tell your sweetheart not to pine
   To be proud her boy's in line.
CHORUS (repeated twice):
Over there, over there
   Send the word, send the word over there.
That the Yanks are coming, the Yanks are coming.
   The drums are rum-tumming everywhere.
So, prepare, say a prayer.
   Send the word, send the word to beware.
We'll be over there, we're coming over.
   And we won't come back till it's over over there.
   Over there.

Johnnie, get your gun, get your gun, get your gun.
Johnnie show the Hun you're a son of a gun.
Hoist the flag and let her fly.
Yankee Doodle do or die.
Pack your little kit, show your grit, do your bit.
Yankees to the ranks from the towns and the tanks.
Make your mother proud of you
And the old Red White and Blue.

At first, it surprised our customers to hear music when they entered the store, but most of them liked it, and many of them bought the record. My uncle brought in another twenty-five records, and we sold them, too. Papa was skeptical, but he recognized an opportunity when he saw one.

Every evening, Mama greeted me and asked how I got along. Several times, she mentioned to me how Papa bragged to her about how well I was doing.

We resumed sewing with Grandma for an hour each evening. Bless her heart, Anna tried her best. Mama asked her to rearrange Mama's sewing basket and kept her busy cutting out fabric squares for the quilt.

I got Charlie's first letter. After reading it, I cried and then read it again before sitting down and writing back to him. Charlie wrote he missed me, he loved me, and he was getting along with the physical training. He mentioned that Frank, Bruce, and Liam were doing well. Charlie wrote I was the last thing he thought about when he lay down to sleep.

Later, I sat and reread the letter at my little table and placed it in a box on my dresser. He had written me love notes over the past six months. Gazing at the pictures of us, I laid them out like a deck of cards. I'd sent several of the larger photos in the last letter. A framed photo of Charlie smiled at me from the bureau, but a photograph was a poor substitute for my young man.

Anna was already asleep, so I had the room to myself. She'd been reading in bed and fell asleep mid-page. I removed the book,

Anne of Green Gables, and put it on her dresser, then covered her up. She looked so sweet and innocent in her sleep. I placed my box of letters on my dresser and returned to bed. Torn between tears and fatigue, I missed Charlie—and Bruce. I was worried about them going to France.

I lay down and prayed, "Lord, please take care of Charlie and Bruce, and Frank and Liam." As I drifted off to sleep, I imagined Charlie's kind face and asked myself, could he sense me thinking about him hundreds of miles away?

Eighteen

On the Road Home
Gracie

*"I hope audiences will appreciate the presence of World War
I in our lives today—whether it is our economy, race relations,
women's rights, xenophobia, free speech, or the foundation of
American foreign policy for the last one hundred years: They all
have their roots in World War I."*

~Historian Scott Berg

Sat. June 15, cont.

I wanted to read more of the letters in the
packet, but my planner and To-Do clipboard were also in my
messenger bag reminding me our renewal of vows was just two
months away. As we took off on our drive home, we went over
our plans and made a few final decisions, me scribbling notes in
my planner.

We reached our RV Park outside of Pittsburgh about three
hours later. We picked up some food to make dinner and relaxed.

Sunday, June 16

The next day, we drove six hours to Indianapolis, Indiana. We drove
through the outskirts, vowing to come back and explore the town.

"I've been here for a conference." David looked over. "There's a
wonderful deli here, called Shapiro's. They have some incredible
black and white cookies. Next time!"

I was impatient to dig back into the letters, so I read the second one aloud.

Letter Two

Camp Funston
    Dearest Mary,
    Training is going well overall. After we got our uniforms and haircuts, we moved through a line to do our physical exams, had our hearing and vision checked, and took a few tests.
    Frank and I are infantrymen. We drill and march in tight formation for miles. My feet are sore from getting used to the boots. My sergeant said to wear double socks for cushioning, and that helps.
    We don't all have our weapons yet, which made our drill sergeant swear something fierce. We've been carrying wooden weapons to drill with, which made me feel about eight years old again.
    Our days are long, and we only get a few minutes to eat each meal. We've learned how to get the most food onto our plates and into our mouths in the time allowed. But sometimes a slice of toast or sandwich gets carried out and eaten on the run. The food isn't bad, but I miss Mama and Grandma's good home cooking. I miss lingering at the table, talking, and waiting for dessert. But most of all, I miss you, Mary. I'm terribly homesick but trying to hide it. The only one I'm honest with is Frank, and he feels much the same way.
    We're determined to be the best soldiers possible and watch out for each other.
    I miss you, Mary. I've read your letters over and over. Thank you for writing. I look forward to each new letter.
    Love you,
    Charlie

David looked surprised. "Wooden weapons? Yes, that would turn a bunch of teens and young adults into eight-year-olds fast. No wonder the drill sergeant swore!"

We found our RV park, checked in, and put together ham and

cheese sandwiches, which we took outside and ate watching the sunset. We snuggled on the sofa to listen to music, and then we went to bed early.

Monday, June 17

In the morning, we ate a quick breakfast and left town before the worst of rush hour traffic. An hour later, we stopped to stretch our legs, then we drove to Chicago, about three hours away. David looked tired, but insisted he was alright.

"Grab me a diet coke, please. We're so close. I can rest later," he said.

We chatted about the seven years he spent in the greater Chicago area getting his master's and doctorate at the University of Chicago. Then he taught for two years at Oakton Community College in Skokie, Illinois.

We found our RV park and checked in. David called a few friends, and we planned breakfast the next day.

We picked up sandwiches and ate at our dinette. Afterwards, David took a shower, I gave him a massage, and we took a long afternoon nap.

Tuesday, June 18

David's friends were teachers, administrators, and two librarians. Four were single, joined by a couple. All were friendly, talkative, opinionated, and a lot of fun. We met at a café off campus, enjoyed breakfast, and spent an hour chatting and swapping stories about David. His former office mate, Benjamin, said they were all thrilled that David found someone like me, a normal girl, to marry him. Everyone laughed.

I looked at David in surprise.

"Am I normal?" I asked. *Is that even a compliment?*

Before David could answer, Benjamin said, "Gracie, don't worry, it's a reference to his ex. She tried to turn David into a guy who wore fancy suits and gave lectures, not the man who loves battle-fields, bookstores, and museums. She would never have visited a

Civil War battlefield or taken a honeymoon in an RV, which we all agree is a cool idea."

David's former boss, Eric, the Dean at his old college, said, "David's a great guy. He deserves a woman who accepts he's a history nerd who enjoys museums and bookstores when he isn't exploring battlefields."

I especially enjoyed meeting Cornell, a tall, handsome black man in his early thirties, one of David's closest friends. Cornell taught history at the University of Chicago, and they'd taken several trips together for history conferences. They'd been in graduate school together and shared an apartment for several years.

Everyone wanted to see the RV, so we trooped out to the parking lot and gave them a tour. Cornell walked around, checking things out. "Your husband never offered to rent an RV for me, Gracie. This is traveling in style. Actually, it might be larger than our first apartment." He eyed the bunk over the cab and estimated its length. "I don't think I'd fit up here." He and David grinned and slapped each other's backs.

Antonio and Julian, the librarians, settled in the cab and found the chairs comfortable. Julian made a joke about fitting in the bunk since he was only five foot six, and the dinette turning into a bed for Antonio. Antonio laughed, and David told them to get their own RV.

Karen, married to Benjamin, David's former office mate, took me aside. She mentioned how happy David seemed with me and how relieved they all were that he'd ditched Cynthia and all her drama. I tried not to smirk. *Oh, I love this group of people!*

They left with hugs, handshakes, elbow bumps, and promises to come to the wedding.

We waved until they'd all driven off, both of us smiling.

"What did I tell you, Gracie? They love you. I enjoyed seeing them all again."

"I liked them, too. Smart, funny, history buffs, and geeks. Did you have time to ask Cornell to stand up with you? I liked him."

"Yes. He's excited, partly because I didn't marry Cynthia, but mostly because he likes you."

Then we drove through his former community college campus.

"I made some good friends here." He showed me where he had an office near the library.

We parked on campus and caught a bus downtown to the Art Institute, where we explored the exhibits of Monet, Picasso, Gauguin, and Seurat.

David and I stopped to admire some artists. One of my favorites was "A Sunday on La Grande Jatte," by Georges Seurat. It's a lush painting depicting people relaxing by a lake, with some people in shade and some people in the sun, with several of the women holding parasols. Most of the people wear hats, a detail I especially loved.

"I love the interplay of colors with rich plums, browns, and oranges, as well as neutrals, and the blue of the water and green grass for contrast," I said, taking a step closer.

David took another look. "I like the way he paints the trees with the trunks clearly delineated, but the leaves look like they're painted with a cotton ball. And every time I see this painting, I feel sorry for the poor monkey on a leash!"

Further on, David liked Monet's "Water Lilies" because he loved the way the plants on shore reflect in the water. We stopped for a moment to enjoy it.

"The colors are gorgeous—blues and purples and greens. The combination is very relaxing. I can almost hear the insects, birds, and frogs," I told him.

After visiting the museum's shop, we enjoyed pizza, Chicago style, deep dish! We took the CTA back to the college parking lot and our RV, doggy bags in hand with surplus pizza and backpacks loaded with books and gifts.

We found our next RV park, checked in, and then consulted the checklist. By the time we were done, I was tired. We sat on the couch. I kicked off my shoes and wiggled my toes. "I feel like we walked five miles today."

David massaged my feet. "Yes, I know what you mean. We've run a marathon or two in the past few days. But I've enjoyed it."

We sat at the dinette to eat leftover pizza and talk, then moved to the bedroom, undressed, and relaxed. It was the perfect ending to the day.

Wednesday, June 19

We spent the day exploring Chicago with Cornell, who took the day off. He picked us up, and we started off with coffee and pastry at a coffee shop close to the Field Museum of Natural History.

Looking around, I smiled because Chicago was the most incredible city. I'd only been here twice, and it was a little overwhelming. But I loved the lake, the stores, the skyline, and the big hotels like the Palmer House, which had an amazing lobby. I'd stayed there once for an English Teachers' conference and enjoyed hanging out in the lobby because it was so beautiful.

David and Cornell talked like old friends who knew each other very well. I sat back and watched and listened as they joked, chatted, and caught up.

"Who imagined you'd settle down before me?" Cornell asked. "After breaking up with Cynthia, I thought you'd still be running the other way." He grinned. "But who could pass up an RV honeymoon touring Civil War battlefields with a beautiful blonde?"

I grinned, and the two men laughed. *None of his friends liked Cynthia, but they liked me!*

Cornell and David began talking about David's upcoming book. Cornell shared David's interest in the American Civil War, but his focus was on reconstruction and the great migration north. His ancestors had left Georgia for Chicago, and it was his grandmother's stories that had originally drawn him to history.

We drove to the Field Museum of Natural History, where we spent the next six hours exploring exhibits and the gift shop. We took a break to enjoy dinner at a wonderful Italian restaurant. Cornell flirted with the server to get us a table near the window with a splendid view of downtown.

Once we ordered, the men then entertained me with facts about Chicago's role in the Civil War.

"The war transformed Chicago into a hub of industry because

of its central location and access to the railroad," Cornell began.

"Chicago sent a lot of arms and food to the Union Army," David pointed out.

"Freed Blacks found a new home here," Cornell said. "Between 1860 and 1870 the black population grew over six hundred percent, and a black professional class emerged."

"Should I be taking notes?" I teased. "Will this be on the test?"

Cornell looked over at David. "Okay, Gracie, just one more. The *Chicago Tribune* was an important abolitionist newspaper before the war and became the leading Republican paper of the day."

David nodded, signaling the battle of the ACW trivia contest was over.

Cornell surprised us by reserving tickets for the Adler Planetarium's evening show. It was incredible exploring the night sky, and we enjoyed the show.

When we walked to the car, Lake Michigan was to our right and the glittering Chicago skyline to the left and the full moon was above. David and I held hands as we chatted with Cornell about the show.

Cornell drove us back to the RV park, and we said goodbye to him with promises to see him at our August wedding.

"Thank you for a wonderful day." I gave him a kiss on the cheek.

He turned to David. "See, David? It was just a matter of time. I'm irresistible to women. Gracie, I've enjoyed getting to know you. You're perfect for David. I'm so happy for you two."

He and David did a whole back slap, handshake thing that ended up in a brief embrace.

I could see how much they respected and liked each other. *I'm so glad David has you as his friend.*

We were smiling when Cornell left. David opened the side door to the RV

"What a great friend. He's funny and smart."

"Yes, he is. He's a lifelong friend who was there for me when things fell apart with Cynthia. And I was his sounding board when he went through some challenges in his career and love life."

We entered the RV and sat on the small sofa.

"Well, Gracie, we're on the homeward stretch."

"It's been wonderful having you all to myself."

"Same here," he replied.

Thursday, June 20

We got up and checked out of the RV Park. Chicago was a fascinating, world-class city, and I wanted to visit again, but it was time to go home. We had lots of work to do.

We stopped for something to eat in Galena and ended up at the DeSoto House restaurant, where we split a Chicken Quesadilla and sweet potato fries. We devoured our meal like we hadn't eaten in days.

David sat back and groaned. "We have to get home. I need to work out."

I tried to waggle my brows seductively, and he burst into laughter, rather deflating my estimation of those skills. Then he leaned over the table and smooched me.

"Sorry, Gracie. I was talking more about hitting the gym than hitting the sheets." He grinned. "But we've had a great honeymoon, don't you think?"

I couldn't stay mad. We drove towards home with so many memories. I'd taken several hundred photos with my digital camera or iPhone. We'd checked off several dozen Civil War battlefields, monuments, and points of interest. I'd filled a backpack and a canvas bag with brochures, books, keepsakes, and a few small gifts.

We'd spent an enormous chunk of time together and were still on speaking terms! Giggling, I asked David if he'd noticed any of my annoying habits after spending so much time together.

He glanced over, grinned, and looked at the clipboard in my hands. "Please tell me that isn't your list of my annoying habits?" David asked. "Of course, most of my habits are adorable, never annoying."

I assured him it was not.

"I'd like to compare your list of what you discovered about me on our honeymoon with my list of what I've discovered about you. Let's say five things?"

"Sure. You're on."

I settled into the comfortable chair, clutching the clipboard. Then, I saw signs for Dubuque and realized our trip was ending.

91

Nineteen

Reaching Dubuque
Gracie

"Here's to all the places we went. And here's to all the places we'll go. And here's to me, whispering again and again and again: I Love you."

~John Green

We crossed the U.S. 20 bridge into Iowa at Dubuque. I'd gotten quieter and quieter in the last hour.

"Gracie, what's wrong?"

"I'm not ready to go home yet," I confessed.

"Me, either. Let's go see the Dubuque Museum of Art downtown, and maybe if we have time afterward, we can go down and see the waterfront."

We wandered around the exhibits and enjoyed this last day together. I stopped, finding myself drawn to the paintings of Grant Wood, especially those depicting farm fields in the four seasons. David paused beside me.

"Did you know he was friends with novelist Ruth Suckow and her husband, Ferner Nuhn?" I asked.

He shook his head. "Ferner Nuhn? That's a rather usual name. Never heard of him or Ruth Suckow."

Was it possible that I knew something David didn't know? "Grandma Grace used to say, 'Ruth Suckow is the most famous Iowa author you've never heard of.' She wrote short stories and novels from the 1920s through 1960. Grandma Grace met her when she attended the Iowa State Teachers College in Cedar Falls in the early 1940s. One day Grandma Grace saw a poster about author Ruth Suckow giving a lecture in Cedar Falls, so grandma attended it and bought a couple of her books—*The Folks* and *Country People*. I grew up reading Suckow's short stories and novels."

I turned to him. "Do you see that portrait over there, also by Grant Wood?" *American Gothic*, the portrait of a rather sober looking farmer with a pitchfork and his daughter in front of a Gothic-style house. There are passages of Ruth Suckow's books that seem to describe Grant Wood's paintings of the fields, farmers, and hills of Iowa. Ferner's sister, Marjorie, was an artist and studied with Grant Wood at his summer art colony in Stone City.

"Grant Wood read Suckow's books and was influenced by her realistic, regional writing style. They spent some time together at the Iowa Writers' workshop in Iowa City. Ferner and Ruth were like a power couple during the 1930s, becoming friends with poet Robert Frost, James Hearst, and other notable writers, poets, and artists."

"This information is interesting. So, Ruth and Ferner were friends with the poet Robert Frost?" David asked.

"Yes, and they were also friends with James Hearst, the wonderful poet farmer from Cedar Falls. Ruth Suckow wrote the introduction for his book *Country Men* (1937), and both Suckow and Hearst had their work published in *The Midland,* a significant literary magazine in Iowa City. Hearst and Frost were also friends. Suckow also wrote stories for *The Smart Set*, whose editor, H. L. Mencken, said, 'I regard Ruth Suckow as the most promising young writer of fiction.' Ferner was a young writer and critic who wrote a review of her first book. He was eleven years younger, handsome, and persistent. They married in 1929 and spent the next thirty years together."

David nodded and grinned. Startled, I turned and saw a group of a dozen people standing nearby, staring at the painting of *American Gothic*. They'd been listening to me. "I didn't mean to lecture. My grandmother instilled a love for Ruth Suckow's writing in me. I teach literature and writing at a community college back home. The first time I read my favorite short story—"A Rural Community"—I was only twelve or thirteen."

An older woman looked over at me. "Don't apologize, dear. I stopped to listen because it interested me."

Someone else called out, "What's the story about? Why did you like it so much?"

"A man takes the train back to his hometown to see his adopted parents. He hasn't been there in many years because he's a journalist who travels the world where the stories are, including the Great War. They spend the day together, and he finds the town both changed and changeless in the sense of looking at the fields and farms. He gets back on the train at midnight and goes to his next assignment but feels connected to his family and to the rich Iowa soil. Suckow wrote "A Rural Community" in 1922, but my community college students can relate to her characters, setting, and the theme of returning home and finding it both changed, and changeless."

"They sense something magical in the story's concluding paragraphs. I've read it out loud many times, at a presentation to librarians at the Iowa Library Association, and once on Iowa Public Radio, with similar responses. Here, let me find it—it's posted on ruthsuckow.org."

I paused and then began to read,

"But he was aware that since he had stepped off the train in the morning, the current of his thoughts had been changed. He felt steadied, deeply satisfied. He looked toward the dark pastures beyond the row of dusky willow trees. They widened slowly into the open country which lay silent, significant, motionless, immense, under the stars, with its sense of something abiding.

"But all night long, as he lay half sleeping, swinging lightly with the motion of the train, he was conscious of that silent spreading country outside over which changes passed like the clouds above the pastures; and it gave him a deep quietude."

"Every time I read it, I'm amazed by the power of language to convey emotions, and my listeners can relate to Ralph's experience and sense the same powerful emotions. It's something special and lasting as they reflect on their Midwestern legacy. Suckow retains her regionalist powers even after a century since her work was first published."

"It sounds like a wonderful story," one woman said. "I love the description."

Another woman said, "I'm going to look for her books."

Someone else spoke up. "Yes, I enjoyed hearing about an Iowa author. What was her name?"

"Ruth Suckow—it's pronounced like *Soo-co.* Check out the website www.ruthsuckow.org. There are several short stories there."

We walked away, and David told me I could moonlight as a Suckow docent. "Gracie, your enthusiasm and knowledge of Ruth and Ferner, and the literary scene in Iowa, really came through. People were listening, including me. Literature can deepen our sense of history, after all."

We explored the art for another hour before stopping in the museum's gift shop. I picked up a book and snapped several photos of books I'd like to order or find at the library. As we left, I heard a woman ask, "Do you have any books by Ruth Suckow?"

David took my hand, and we left the museum full of mixed emotions, a longing for home, and a sense of wonder at our adventures together.

We enjoyed an early dinner at Catfish Charlie's out on the patio overlooking the river. There was a cool breeze as we munched on crisply fried fish and chips with salads. Everything was delicious.

David and I savored our last night in the RV, holding hands as we sat on the couch.

"This has been a wonderful three weeks," I said.

He pulled me even closer. "Yes, it has!"

Friday, June 21

After leaving the RV park, we drove to Eagle Point Park to enjoy the beautiful views of the Mississippi river. From the scenic overlook, you can see three states: Iowa, Illinois, and Wisconsin. We parked and went up to the scenic overlook.

David did an impression of his father for me. "For only one dollar per car, it's a heck uva deal.'The first time I saw this was on one of our family vacations. When my dad said it overlooks Lock and Dam No. 11, Alex and I thought he was swearing." He grinned.

I laughed. David said, "Hey, I was nine or ten years old!"

Then we headed for home. I called Uncle Rich to say we'd turn in the RV tonight. He said that would be wonderful because maybe then my mother would stop calling him to see when we were coming home.

We took a break and sat at the dinette to swap our lists of five things we'd learned about each other. David chuckled as he read my list out loud.

Gracie's list

David needs coffee and a shower to get going for the day.

David and I are both cuddlers and canoodlers.

David loves eating burgers, steaks, chocolate, cheesecake, and chocolate cherry frozen yogurt. However, he also enjoys broccoli florets, carrots, onions, peppers, fresh green beans, and sweet potatoes. We agreed we needed to encourage each other to eat more veggies and fruits like apples and berries.

David enjoys browsing in libraries, bookstores, used bookstores, thrift stores, gift shops, and book racks. When he's not driving an RV, he reads a history book a week, and more when school is out. Oddly, he won't listen to audible books while driving. Says it hurts his concentration.

David likes to have things organized, even mapped out. The three-ring notebook was a great idea. (He's also the neatest roommate I've ever had.)

Then I read his list out loud.

David's list

Gracie drinks a "cuppa" tea throughout the day—hot, cold, unsweetened, and always has a stock of Constant Comment, Green tea Constant Comment, and chamomile tea.

Gracie loves chocolate like it's a food group, but eats salads, veggies, burgers, and chicken. We must have Greek yogurt, fresh berries, apples, and nuts in the RV

Gracie's a cuddler and canoodler and so am I (and so is our cat, Agatha, ha ha).

Gracie loves her clipboards, pens, and making lists to plan her day. Juggling three different jobs, I don't think she could get it all done if she wasn't so organized.

Gracie is a very empathetic person who feels emotions deeply and is also very intuitive, as we learned from her encounter with Miranda.

David looked at me with those gorgeous brown eyes. "Looks like we're pretty compatible."

I was already moving to the cupboard for bowls and spoons. "How about the last dish of our frozen yogurt?"

Twenty

The Boys Are Away at Training
Mary

"However the world pretends to divide itself, there are only two divisions in the world today—human beings and Germans."
~Rudyard Kipling, 1915

To Feed the Nation is to Fight its Battles."
~a poster produced by the state of Nebraska, c.1917

The weeks slowly passed, and with them, the summer. I worked at the store full time, was learning a great deal, and enjoying it. It helped take my mind off Charlie and Bruce being away.

I got a lovely card from Aunt Eva, congratulating me again on the engagement to Charlie. She enjoyed her visit, said Charlie was very handsome, and was happy to hear I was working with Papa. Eva promised to visit again soon and suggested that I come and spend a weekend with her in Chicago.

Papa was getting a new cash register and thought we would open a second check out place on the long counter. I was excited about the cash register, while Mrs. Smith, our regular checker, was reluctant.

"I can write all of those prices down and add them up just fine. There's no need for a fancy machine," she protested.

Papa pointed out the cash drawer would organize the bills nicely, as well as the change. It would also provide some security.

Meanwhile, we resumed work on the quilt, and it was beautiful.

It was also a lot of work. Anna grew bored, so we invented ways to keep her engaged, sorting the squares she cut out and organizing Mama's fabrics. Later, she did an inventory of our thread so I could replenish the ones we'd used up.

Grandma seemed very tender and kind to me as we worked together. She was worried about Bruce, her eldest grandson. She wrote letters to him faithfully and helped Mama make up a little box of hard candies and cookies to send to camp. Grandpa tended the garden, relying more on Anna and Aidan's help.

I receive a letter from Charlie about once every two weeks. He liked the training, but it was physically demanding, and not everyone was doing as well. They will all serve in the infantry. After about six weeks, the group graduated from training, and he felt pleased with his performance. He sent me a photo of him in uniform, and it was shocking to see his lovely, wavy hair cut much shorter. Charlie looked more muscular, no doubt from all the training. He also sent a class photo. What a handsome group, I thought, especially those boys from Jubilee Junction.

Charlie wrote the camp was not only training the young soldiers to use weapons and how to drill. They also worked a great deal on physical fitness, military discipline, and command structure.

The next challenge, he wrote, was to prepare for the ocean voyage. Once they go to sea, his letters will be delayed. First, the soldiers travel by train to New York City. They then board one of the large ocean liners, taking them to France. The journey across the Atlantic would take sixteen days.

Once arriving in France, the doughboys—a nickname for our troops—would get more training on the advanced weapons from the British and French. They needed to learn how to use machine guns, howitzers, and other devices provided by our allies. Only after the training would they go to the battlefront.

Charlie joked he'd never been on a large body of water before—the Jubilee River didn't count. He wondered if he would get seasick. Several officers told them not to worry because their bunks would be packed close together, and they would be fine.

I worried about the German subs and ships because they'd

attacked so many ships, civilian or military. But Charlie wrote they were being escorted by smaller ships armed with weapons. The smaller ships would protect them, and he didn't want me to worry.

Sure enough, it took almost a month to get the next letter, and then I got two. We continued to correspond, and often I got more than one letter at a time and then had to wait several weeks in between.

Things were going well at the store. I enjoyed using the new cash register and was teaching Mrs. Smith how to use it, too. Papa's brothers are getting them now for the lumberyard. Bookkeeping was even more essential as the newly implemented U.S. Income Tax required excellent records.

As the summer turned to fall, I became more confident. Grandma said I was becoming a graceful young lady. I didn't think of myself as graceful, but I was happy to be working and helping Papa. When I wasn't at the cash register or stocking shelves, I delivered groceries to several of the older people in town.

I saw an empty corner in the store and had an idea. I encouraged Papa to put up some shelves and sell a few books. We've carried a few Bibles and a dictionary, but not much of anything else. I have always borrowed books from the Jubilee Junction Library, but we didn't have a bookstore in town.

Papa asked me to suggest books, and I spent several hours with our librarian to pick out some titles. We added three children's books, a children's Bible, several novels, two farming magazines, and the *Ladies' Home Journal* and *McCall's*.

At home, we continued to work on the hope chest, plan the wedding, and collect things for the troops. Our Jubilee Junction churches were sending packages overseas for the boys at Christmas.

I found the perfect wedding dress and fell in love with it. It was floor length, satiny white, with pearl accents on the sleeves and neckline, and pearl buttons. It hung in my closet and gave me great hope.

Anna's sixteenth birthday arrived, and she got her own hope chest. In our room, alone, she teased it was her hopeless chest, because she wanted to be a suffragist like Aunt Eva and have a career.

So now we were sewing for her, too. We'd finished my quilt, and it was beautiful, large enough for a full-size bed. It was turkey red and white in the wedding ring pattern.

In one of his letters, Bruce mentioned there was a group of American nurses going overseas on the same ship. Liam had a sweetheart, a pretty girl from Kansas, named Jane. A group of the nurses were going to be at a field hospital near where the American soldiers would do their final training.

When they arrived, Jane teased she didn't want Liam to get injured just to see her. But there wasn't much time for leisure in a war zone.

When I asked Charlie about it, he said his older brother was in love. His parents seemed excited at the prospect of two weddings.

Of course, we had to get through this awful war first. I wanted to meet Jane because I think we could be friends, as well as sisters-in-laws. I wondered what she was like and when we would meet.

Twenty-one

Home Again
Gracie

"There is a kind of magicness about going far away and then coming back all changed."
~Kate Douglas Wiggin

Friday, June 21

We arrived in Jubilee Junction on Friday afternoon with mixed feelings. We enjoyed traveling in the RV. As Aunt Maggie would say, it was cozy and made our cross-country trip more comfortable. But we looked forward to getting home to my little house—now *our* house—for a few more weeks.

Once in town, we gassed up the RV, packed up our clothes, cleaned the bathroom, swept the floors, and wiped down counters. We took the sheets home to launder along with the towels and our dirty clothes. David got the cooler and filled it with leftover food and then wiped out the small RV refrigerator. We grabbed our four chairs and table and the cardboard box. We thanked Uncle Rich and told him we'd be back later with clean sheets and towels.

I gave Uncle Rich a hug. "Thank you, Uncle Rich. What a wonderful experience! We had so much fun. It was incredible to see the sights through that large windshield."

David shook his hand. "Yes, I really enjoyed driving it. It was the best way to see the country, share a meal, or watch the sunset outside. Your checklists really helped us, too. Thank you, sir."

"Call me Rich or Uncle Rich. We're family now. I'm happy it worked out." He grinned.

The two of us loaded up David's car, and then I remembered our hope chest. We put the back seats down, and Uncle Rich and David placed the hope chest into the SUV.

We drove home, arranged for a pizza to be delivered, and collapsed before calling anyone to let them know we were home. Together, we unpacked the car. David dumped the sheets and towels and our dirty clothes in front of the washer. After a little rest, we sat at the dining room table and looked through the bills and mail—his and mine, now ours. I emptied the cooler, washed it, and put it out on the back porch.

Then we drove over to get Agatha, and Kathy told us to come back because she wanted to hear all about the trip. Agatha seemed happy to see us, in her own cat way. Back home, David put on our new CD for some motivational music. I cleared space for David's hanging clothes in my closet and the guest room closet. David unpacked a few boxes while I did the dishes. We retired to bed early and shut the bedroom door. Agatha meowed at the door, complaining about the new arrangement.

Saturday morning, I started a load of laundry and then ran to the grocery store with an actual shopping list. David worked on moving his essentials from the garage to the house. I explored the grocery store for a few items he added. Who knew there were so many aisles?

David worked hard while I was gone. He brought in a small dresser from the garage and placed it in a corner of the living room, near our bedroom, for his underwear, socks, and such. He put his laptop on top of the dresser along with his messenger bag.

We stacked a few empty boxes in the garage and kept a smaller one inside the house. Later, we played with Agatha, who loved hopping into the box and snuggling down. We took turns switching loads of laundry, unpacking, and reorganizing the house for two people. I had a small table I could use for a desk in my guest room and gave David my bigger one because his laptop was bigger than my laptop and he had a printer. His desk was in the garage.

It was pushing eleven o'clock before we collapsed on the couch. But the house looked great. David had moved his clothing and computer in, and there were a dozen boxes of books and kitchen things that could wait. We took a shower together. Married life was wonderful.

Later, we cuddled on the couch with Agatha jumping from my lap to David's lap and looking up at him adoringly—for a cat.

David kissed me. "That's sort of how you look when you have me to yourself."

"Are you sure?"

"I think we need to verify this."

Agatha lost interest in us, jumping down with a swish of her tail.

We laughed and went to bed.

Sunday, we got up early and decided to be heathens and skip church. We packed up things we didn't need, stacking several Rubbermaid tubs in the guest room. After calling both families to check in, we called Mark and Kathy, and found out her parents and mine were packing up the farmhouse.

We ran the clean sheets and towels to Uncle Rich, thanked him again, and looked nostalgically at *our* RV. Uncle Rich handed us the *Just Married* sign. "You forgot this, Gracie!" We walked through "Hawk" and found a couple of minor items overlooked in kitchen drawers. Then we drove out to help pack at Mark and Kathy's.

Mom asked if we would go to Aunt Violet's farmhouse and do some cleaning. She gave me the keys and loaded us down with cleaning supplies.

"Let me know when things seem presentable. I have some people and trucks available today," she said.

We loaded up the car with cleaning supplies.

David opened my car door, kissed me, and grinned. "Welcome back from the honeymoon! Now, it's back to reality."

But we didn't mind. The sooner we moved Mark and Kathy, the better. The babies would be born soon. And then we could move into their house. I couldn't wait, and David was ready to go shopping for the supplies to build that gazebo.

Twenty-two

Cleaning Aunt Violet's Farmhouse
Gracie

"Do or do not. There is no try"

~Yoda

"The beginning is always today,"

~from The Short Stories of Mary Shelley

$\mathcal{U}$sing the key for what I still saw as Aunt Violet's farmhouse seemed strange. Loaded down with cleaning supplies, we made our way inside and got to work getting the house ready for Mark and Kathy to move in, along with her parents. The twins weren't due for weeks yet, but twins often come early. We scrubbed sinks, countertops, tubs, and showers. We swept, dusted, and vacuumed. Things looked great on the main floor.

David looked around. "Something else for our resumes, Gracie!"

I groaned and said, "I love this house for its roominess, but I wouldn't want to clean it all the time, even with your help."

We went down to the basement. Violet left behind an almost new washer and dryer and a big chest freezer. The basement had four rooms: a laundry room with a counter for sorting clothes, a bathroom with a shower, a family room, and a bedroom/office with an egress window. It was all clean, painted, and ready to go. We cleaned the bathroom, wiped down counters, and mopped floors. I checked the dehumidifier and emptied it.

We picked up our buckets and went upstairs to the second floor. It had a master suite with a private bathroom, four other bedrooms, and another full bathroom. One of those rooms would become the nursery. Another would become the guest room for Kathy's parents. Two other bedrooms were empty. We dusted, vacuumed, and cleaned the bathrooms.

Mom hadn't given us any instructions about the attic. Out of curiosity, we took the back staircase and opened the door. There were several empty rooms, with two enormous trunks, a few pieces of old furniture, and a neat stack of empty boxes. We left it for now and would ask Mom later.

Next, we checked out the oversized garage for parking two cars. There was a long workbench with hooks to hang tools at one end. One door led to the deck. We swept out the garage and dusted the work bench.

By 1 pm, we sent a text to my folks—the place was "move-in" ready.

Three pickup trucks pulled into the driveway within half an hour, and some of my cousins and uncles unloaded furniture and boxes. They began carrying things into the house and piling stuff in the garage.

"That was fast. I don't see Mark. Who's in charge?" I wondered.

My parents arrived, parked, got out, and walked toward the house, Mom with her clipboard in hand.

"Thanks, David and Gracie, for getting it done so quickly. We'd lined up people and trucks, so we decided to just get going."

"I'm so glad you're here. People are carrying things in, but I don't know where they go."

Mom patted the clipboard. "I've got the plans right here." She and Dad walked into the house.

David and I grabbed some boxes marked *garage* out of one truck and put them into the garage, then found some smaller pieces of furniture to carry in.

Mom stood in the living room, surveyed things, and told people where the furniture belonged. Order replaced the chaos, as my mom's superpowers once again came in handy. Another two pickup trucks arrived, and we got those unloaded as well.

Mark and Kathy planned to use Aunt Violet's large antique

oak table and chairs in the dining room, along with a matching sideboard. Their smaller table fit into the kitchen.

The volunteers moved in couches, recliners, side tables, lamps, and a rocking chair upstairs. A small desk went into a corner of the kitchen, along with a chair. All the kitchen appliances stayed.

The main floor included a large kitchen, a dining room, a large living room, a small office, a full bath, a linen closet, and a guest room with its own half bath. For now, that main floor guestroom would become Mark and Kathy's bedroom.

The men carried in a futon for the basement. A queen-size bed, dresser, rocker went into the guestroom.

Mom looked at Kathy's neat notes. The bedroom across the hall from the master would become the nursery. The room next to the nursery would be for the grandparents, leaving two more bedrooms and a full bathroom. "So, when do we move in the rest?" I asked.

"Sooner than we thought," Mom said. "Kathy's parents are renting out their house to a visiting professor teaching summer school, and he wants to get in the first of next week. They're coming tomorrow with a load of things. So, they're buying a bed today and having it delivered tomorrow. They need to clean their house and put some things into storage. It's going to be busy for the next few weeks, but this is good. We want Mark and Kathy settled before the babies come in early August."

"Whoa." I looked around.

Mom looked up. "Yes. We'll get them settled in and then focus on you two."

"I better get some more boxes and tubs and start packing."

Mom shook her head. "We'll have some for you once they get settled in. Don't worry." She looked at her clipboard. "This was supposed to be the pre-move move, and it has gone well. The first floor is done, and so is the basement."

Dad and David walked in, smiling. "You have an amazing family," David said. "They're stacking tubs and boxes, neatly labeled, in the rooms. Five pickups unloaded and furniture put in place in under three hours. Your Aunt Delores just showed up with pop, cookies, and Wet Wipes."

Dad warned us with a grin, "The cookies are going fast. Better get them while you can."

We headed outside to see what was happening and said hello to Uncle Rich, Uncle Sean, and Uncle Joey, along with their families. Our O'Connor grandparents were also present, scattered across the large deck, enjoying soda and cookies. David and I were happy to see some cookies were still available.

Mom grabbed a cookie and then walked around, thanking people. Dad followed her with a chocolate chip cookie in one hand and an oatmeal cookie in the other.

David and I followed Dad. We munched cookies with Aunt Delores, R. J. and Allie, his wife.

"Every time I walk around Violet's house, I'm amazed," Allie said. "It's a grand house."

"Remember, this house has had a dozen additions or remodels over the last fifty years, according to Aunt Violet. She thinks it started out as a Sears Foursquare house kit," I told her.

David looked up. "You can see that the family renovated the first and second floors, but the attic is still the same size as the original house. I think it looks a little like a wedding cake."

We all craned our necks, and a couple of people near us looked up too, as if something was happening in the air. I told them, "We're just admiring my husband's description of Violet's house—like the layers of a wedding cake."

Aunt Delores looked up. "Yes, you're right. It does look like a wedding cake. Speaking of cake, how are your plans going?"

So, we began discussing the upcoming renewal of vows.

Twenty-three

Kathy & Mark's Move
Gracie

"Actually, the best gift you could have given her was a lifetime of adventures."

~Lewis Carroll

June 24

During the next week, David and I pitched in to help get the big farmhouse ready for Mark and Kathy. We painted the nursery, moved in the two cribs, two changing tables, and two dressers and found the perfect place for the rocking chair. Within the week, the family finished moving Kathy and Mark into the farmhouse.

Kathy's parents moved their belongings in and then returned home to tackle cleaning their house with the help of family members back home. Kathy was soon resting in the first-floor guest bedroom where she had a large window close to the bed. "I like the new view," she told me. "And I don't like to complain when everyone's working so hard to help us. I just wish I could do something besides sit in bed."

We talked as I worked on putting her clothing into the closet and dresser. I had several boxes to empty and a large moving box with a built-in hanging rod with things to go upstairs, but I was going to leave them for Mark and David to move.

"You're doing something important—growing two baby humans," I told her.

The two mothers put on a baby shower the following week. Afterwards, David and I took the baby clothing down to the laundry, where we washed and dried them, folded them up, and put them all away in the dressers.

I admired David's ability to fold onesies, and he chuckled. "I told you I was good at this baby stuff."

As I clumsily folded and refolded, he showed me again how to do it. I sighed. Hopefully, I got points for trying.

Others gifted them with large boxes of diapers at the baby shower. We placed some newborn size diapers on the changing tables and stored the remaining boxes in the closet.

I stared at the boxes and boxes of diapers and then at David.

"How long will this stash last?" I asked.

David grinned. "You'd be amazed at how many diapers one baby can go through, much less twins. I'm guessing eight to ten diapers per baby a day, but I read an article claiming most babies will go through three thousand diapers in the first year. Let's not tell Kathy and Mark they'll change six thousand diapers in the twins' first year."

"Why were you researching diapers?"

"My sister was looking at a diaper service for Daisy, and we were doing research together. Jack was still in diapers when she was born, so while she didn't have twins, she did have two babies in diapers."

Six thousand diapers? I tried imagining the number of boxes and gave up. I had lots to learn if I was going to be a helpful aunt. It was a good thing David was an experienced uncle and could teach me.

After getting Mark and Kathy settled, I checked in with my boss, Carl, at the museum, and Charlotte, my librarian friend. David was organizing his research with books, folders, and his laptop spread out on my old desk. Agatha was playing with one of her toys nearby. She had food and water, and he had sandwich makings and a pot of coffee. They'd be fine.

I headed for the Jubilee Public Library first because I wanted to compare notes with Charlotte before I visited Carl. I'd taken the month of June off from the museum for the honeymoon and move, but knew I'd be heading back to work soon. Grandma Mary was on my mind.

Charlotte was busy organizing materials with volunteers in the storage closet, while an assistant checked out books at the circulation desk. Two people were helping Charlotte sort, label, and inventory exhibit materials spread out on two long tables. She was checking things off on a clipboard and putting them in the tubs. I noticed several beat-up looking cardboard boxes under the table. She looked up and greeted me. "Welcome back, Gracie!"

We hugged, and she told the volunteers to take a short break.

"Looks like you're getting help organizing those lost exhibit materials?" I guessed.

"Volunteers and part-time staff have been responsible for setting up and taking down exhibits, but sometimes the materials weren't returned or organized," she replied. "We're changing that by training our volunteers. Things are shaping up."

I sympathized. "Yes, same thing at the museum. It took a year for me to do a proper inventory, assign tags to items, and create spreadsheets listing them."

Charlotte shifted the conversation. "Tell me about your trip. I saw some of your pictures from the honeymoon on Facebook."

We chatted away, and I told her about the letters I'd read so far. Charlotte was a wonderful listener. "I promise to make photocopies of everything for you. I'd like your help to get some background information about Jubilee Junction and World War One."

Charlotte nodded, grabbing a notepad. "Yes, I can do that, Gracie. I'll find a list of soldiers who served in France during the war."

I told her about our experience helping rescue Miranda from human traffickers, and she stared at me in surprise. "I'm happy you could help her, Gracie. I wish more people got involved and showed compassion. Native American women are victims of human trafficking at higher rates, and forty percent of the victims of human trafficking identify as American Indian, Native Alaskan, or First Nations."

Now it was my turn to stare at her in surprise. "Those stories about missing Native American girls are because of human trafficking?"

"Many of them are, yes. Some girls run away and end up on a bus or at a train station, and they're easy targets."

"Miranda and eight other girls were being shuttled from one truck stop to another. She tried to run away once before, but her handlers found her and beat her up."

We chatted for a few more minutes, and Charlotte told me about a couple of sources on human trafficking before we got back to discussing Grandma Mary.

"So, her fiancé deployed shortly after America entered the war," she noted.

"Yes, and it's amazing to think about how quickly they had to move to get those soldiers trained and deployed, and all without computers. I talked to Mark about it, and he told me about the physical exam he had when he joined the Army, and then the preparation to deploy to Germany. It's a lot of work, a lot of paperwork, and it requires specific training depending on your MOS, or military occupation."

Charlotte nodded, and I continued, "Mark said they had to scale up their training to get the troops ready for war back in 1917. The Army needed to recruit retired Army trainers to work with the new recruits. They had to build or update several training facilities and find the equipment and order the uniforms, boots, weapons, and gear. They needed to hire cooks, carpenters, electricians, and plumbers. It was a massive undertaking, and they didn't have the computer systems or infrastructure we have now."

Charlotte agreed. "I can't imagine how difficult it would be to organize everything without spreadsheets and the internet. I imagine they used lots of notecards and clipboards." She looked back at her volunteers and said, "I should get back to our project. Check back when you've read more of those letters."

Next, I kept my lunch date with Tiara and Shelly. We talked about sex trafficking and Miranda, the RV trip, and yes—David and what a wonderful time we'd had. I told them about our newest challenge with Grandma Mary's hope chest and showed them pictures of the beautiful red and white wedding ring quilt.

Shelly admitted, "I know very little about World War One. It kind of got overshadowed by the Second World War."

Tiara agreed. "My great-grandmother talked about it, but I don't remember studying it much. I learned more when I began putting together a series of talks on Black history and came across information about the Buffalo soldiers."

Tiara grabbed her phone and found her notes app. "You'll want to look at this article on the National Park Service website. There's a national monument to the Buffalo Soldiers. These soldiers fought hard against both racism and the Germans. They proved themselves to the Army officials, and France awarded medals and honors to multiple soldiers and regiments. I'll email you the link."

I made a note to look at that website later and thanked her.

Shelly clicked on the link and said, "These are great photographs. It really captures the era. It seems strange to have segregated regiments, but times were different."

I told them about the letters I'd read from Charlie to Mary and their story so far.

Shelly said, "Please keep reading the letters. I want to know their story."

Tiara agreed. "You've got a lot on your plate this summer, Gracie, but I'd like to know the rest of their story, too. Don't make yourself crazy, girl. It's all going to get done."

Shelly put her hand on my arm. "Yes, please let us know what we can do to help. We can pack or unpack at the new house, whatever."

I thanked them, and we made a date for them to come help me pack.

Another day, I checked in with Kathy and brought takeout from Aunt Shirley's for us.

Kathy's parents had moved in and were settling into their new routine. They loved the spacious farmhouse and had already gotten their rooms organized.

We ate our large salads with spring mix, cherry tomatoes, cut up chicken breast, pecans, and strawberries with a poppyseed dressing.

"How are you feeling?" I asked.

"Extremely pregnant," she said, as she balanced her take out bowl on a small pillow over her tummy.

"Show off!" I told her as I grabbed my phone and took a picture.

We were in her first-floor bedroom, which looked comfy with a rocker and a big wooden chest on one wall, full of vintage quilts. I sat at the small table for two, pushed against the bed.

"I just want the next six to eight weeks to go by because I want to meet my babies," she told me between bites. *Enjoy the anticipation,* I thought. *Those twin bundles of joy will keep you busy night and day for years.* I also thought, *Keep your mouth shut, Gracie. No need to be a wet blanket!*

Kathy noticed me looking at her tummy and asked, "Want to feel? They're kicking." She put down her empty bowl and gestured. "It's okay, Gracie. Mark and I lay in bed and watch my tummy at night."

I hesitated and then, curious, I stood and placed my hand on her extended belly. Almost immediately, I felt a little kick right under my hand and jumped.

Kathy chuckled at my expression.

"Wow. I felt it! There are two little babies who want to meet their mama." I sat there for the rest of my visit, talking to the babies. "Hey there, I'm your Aunt Gracie, and you're going to love spending time with me and Uncle David. Love you."

Kathy laughed again but winced when one kick seemed especially strong.

"What is it?" I asked. "That was stronger than a little kick."

"Braxton Hicks. It's the body's way of preparing for birth. My stomach gets tight with a contraction. Here, feel."

She put my hand back on her belly. I jumped again.

"Are you alright? Does it hurt a lot?" I asked.

"It hurts a little, but I'm fine, a little nervous. I worry that I'm going to pee without warning. My doctor is wonderful, and Mark and I attended Lamaze classes, so we're prepared. We're on a list at the hospital for high-risk births, so they'll be ready for us."

Her mother came into the bedroom, knocking lightly on the door. "Hello, dear. The doctor said you need to drink more water. Here you go," and she brought in a tall glass of water. "Remember, your pee should be almost crystal clear. If it's yellow, you might be dehydrated.

"Thanks, Mom. These kids are dancing on my bladder. I'm peeing constantly. I don't see how I could be dehydrated." But she drank some of the water, anyway.

Taking the hint, I picked up our takeout containers and put them back in the sack. Kathy needed to rest, so I gave her a hug and left.

Letters from the Trenches
Mary

"Arms and agriculture are the two great factors that will bring victory... Our armed forces are organized. The agricultural forces must be organized."
~a poster produced by the state of Colorado, c.1917

August 1917

$\mathcal{O}$ur Jubilee Junction boys are now overseas, and I miss them, especially Charlie and Bruce. Today, I sat down to re-read their letters to get a better idea of their lives overseas. Both mentioned they paraded through the streets of St. Nazaire when they first arrived in France. The city was unknown to me, but it houses the Naval Operating base and is where the railway guns were delivered. I wrote the name down and looked it up at the library where they had maps of France.

What were railway guns? My Uncle Andrew explained the United States Navy adapted some railroad cars to handle the large cannons needed to help the French and British troops. Their appearance was an odd mix of train car and tank, boasting powerful guns, but their effectiveness was undeniable. Seeing pictures in newspapers at the library, I shuddered, thankful it was the Americans with weapons. The French welcomed the American soldiers, thinking this would help to win the war. Many French and British soldiers had died, and the Allies had made little progress. The European people were weary, hungry, and in need of some good news.

In the meantime, when the boys arrived, their machine guns weren't there. It took another week and a half for the guns to arrive, and then it was something different from what they expected. It was a gun used by the French—a Hotchkiss machine gun. Charlie mentioned they practiced drilling with pieces of wood at first, which I imagined was frustrating to the soldiers.

Once the Chauchat machine guns arrived in France, our American soldiers needed to learn how to use them. I overheard Papa talking with his brothers about the weapons, capable of killing multiple soldiers who dared leave the trenches. Apparently, the gun delivered multiple bullets rapid-fire. They had other terrible weapons, too: tanks, poison gas, flamethrowers, airplanes, and submarines.

I learned about trench warfare from reading Charlie's letters and the newspaper articles and listening to my Papa talk to other men whose sons were overseas and fighting in opposing trenches. The distance between the Allied trenches and the German trenches varied, from fifty to 250 yards apart, and the land in between was called no-man's-land. Covered with barbed wire and filled with landmines, no-man's-land sounded like hell. For the past three years, the French and English soldiers had dealt with this deadly warfare.

Once the American soldiers made it to the front, it took time to get used to the miserable conditions of trench warfare. Sometimes the new men didn't understand how close the Germans were in their trenches and were too noisy. This scared the Germans, who sent out patrols across no-man's-land. The Americans kept saying, "You've been here for three years?"

Charlie wrote about a superstition that if three soldiers lit their cigarettes from the same match, one of them would be shot. He explained you didn't want to give away your position.

The trenches were up to twelve feet deep, with pieces of wood called duckboard laid on the bottom to keep soldiers' feet from being wet and muddy. However, the trenches were only four to six feet wide, so very narrow and crowded. The soldiers reinforced the walls of the trenches with barbed wire, sandbags, bricks, and boards.

Some trenches featured crude little caves dug into the sides, or small rooms for resting. Trenches were also part of a larger system, connecting with other trenches that led back to safety. The trenches covered over 250 miles through France and Belgium and weren't straight but zigzagged. I tried to imagine it and shuddered.

Soldiers carried their equipment with them, such as a gas mask, their weapons, and ammo. They wore boots and helmets and carried shaving kits, water bottles, and shovels. The American soldiers needed to learn not to put their heads up too high, because even a metal helmet won't stop a bullet. The living conditions were miserable and dangerous. Many soldiers developed health problems from spending so much time in a damp environment. Trench foot, usually caused by cold, wet exposure disabled many doughboys.

Mama sent socks with every box, and so did Charlie's mother, because having dry socks might help keep feet dry.

Our pastor's wife suggested we gather clothing for the children overseas affected by the war, so we began doing just that, placing a large box at our church and another at the store to collect small blankets, coats, and warm clothing for children up to twelve. Someone else suggested we could cut up old quilts and make them over for children. Several American soldiers had written home about the orphans they'd seen and the struggle to care for them.

Women in our church and every other church in the area were knitting socks, caps, and sweaters, and collecting toiletry items to send to the boys at the front. They decided they could do more and collect things for orphans.

That gave me an idea.

We put a display of socks near the gramophone with a sign: *Socks for Soldiers.* Every pair sold was placed into a big box the church would ship overseas. I also set out a box to collect things for the orphans.

Our patriotic gramophone records were also selling fast. People were coming in to listen to the music, to catch up on the gossip, to socialize, and to get what they needed.

People started asking for other songs. One of them was "America, Here's My Boy." The first time Mama heard it, she burst into tears. She wasn't the only one. We tried not to play it too often, but some people liked it, perhaps as a good excuse to cry. "America, Here's

My Boy" was written by Andrew B. Sterling. Arthur Lange wrote the musical score, and it was very popular in 1917.

America, I raised a boy for you.
America, you'll find him staunch and true,
Place a gun up on his shoulder,
He is ready to die or do.
America, he is my only one;
My hope, my pride and joy,
But if I had another,
He would march beside his brother;
America, here's my boy.

Another song, "After The War Is Over, Will There Be Any Home Sweet Home?" captures the sense of loss and looks ahead to the war's end, with its chorus:

After the war is over and the world's at peace,
Many a heart will be aching after the war has ceased
Many a child alone;
But I hope they'll all be happy
In a place called "Home Sweet Home."

These songs reminded me I wasn't the only girl missing her sweetheart or brother. It seems every family in Jubilee Junction had soldiers serving overseas—sons, nephews, cousins, grandsons, fathers, uncles, classmates, neighbors, or friends. Still, I was lonely, wondering when the next letter would come. Wondering when the war would end and our boys could come home.

I worried they would come home changed by the war—that the war would change Charlie—but the rest of us would have changed as well. It would be an adjustment for all of us when our soldiers returned to their homes and loved ones. Neither side was making progress, and for all their bluster, the generals on both sides seemed stumped. No one had fought a war like this before, with such lethal weapons, such enormous slaughter, and such terrible destruction. After three years of war, could the Americans make the difference? When would the war end and our soldiers come home? From reading the newspapers and listening to Papa, it didn't sound like that would happen soon.

I kept writing letters to Charlie and Bruce and working with Papa at the store. We all prayed that the war would end.

Twenty-five

Harvest in Jubilee Junction
Mary

"The man behind the plow is the same as the man behind the gun."

~text from poster produced by the USDA, c.1917

"No commander was ever privileged to lead a finer force; no commander ever derived greater inspiration from the performance of his troops."

~John J. Pershing

Summer ended, and the fall began. But instead of stocking up on pencils, paper, and erasers at the store, my family was pitching in on the family farms. We needed to work extra hard to make up for the missing family members at harvest. We helped my uncles at harvest. I'd always looked forward to it, because we got to spend time together as a large, extended family. This year, they needed our help more than ever, because several cousins and uncles were overseas and so were their neighbors.

Our work this year was especially patriotic since the government was urging citizens to help grow their own food. We took that message to heart. Our farms produced corn to feed the hogs, to be ground up to make cornmeal, or be made into other products. And the large farm vegetable gardens, fruit trees, and berries produced more than one family could eat.

City cousins brought empty glass jars and buckets and contributed their labor. They helped plant and care for the large farm gardens and then helped with the harvest. We sent a group of people out to gather berries in the timber—wild strawberries, a patch of blueberries, and other berries that grew there and had for several generations.

Not every farm family was as fortunate, and one poster produced by the Iowa State University Agricultural college in Ames, Iowa, was titled *War Food Volunteers*. A General stood in an Iowa field, where an Iowa Farmer saluted. The Ghost-like apparition at the left was titled the *Hunger of the World*. Behind the farmer stood a line of workers. The general commanded, "General, your division will attack at once!" Underneath it said:

"Boys, Girls, Men, Women Needed in Each County.
To help meet farm labor shortage.
To promote economy and thrift.
To prevent the waste of food.
To increase the food supply.
Get enlistment blank from your editor, school superintendent, club
leader or county agent. Enlist today. Don't Delay."

I hoped that others in Jubilee would offer their help to several farms that were short-handed and didn't have extended families in the area.

Another poster from the U. S. Department of Agriculture urged everyone to;

"HELP FEED YOURSELF
and Make Backyards and Vacant Lots Productive.
WORK A GARDEN—RAISE CHICKENS.
Grow Vegetables and Fruits, Can or Preserve Surplus Perishables,
and Keep a Flock of Hens.
SOMEBODY HAS TO RAISE OR PACK
EVERYTHING YOU EAT.
DO YOUR SHARE.
Make every jar help feed your family."

Papa left the store open with Grandpa and Mrs. Smith in charge. The rest of us headed out to help at the family farms. We started with my Uncle John's farm where he had a large garden. Women focused on staying in the kitchen where they washed fruit and vegetables and chopped them up. Others canned them and labeled the jars they would share. They pickled vegetables and fruits. Others made preserves and jellies on the old cookstove, using the enormous old kettles and pots my grandmother left behind. Children helped gather vegetables, wash them, sort them, and then headed back for another load with their small wagons.

Teens and young adults helped in the fields, and Papa supervised their work. They harvested hay, wheat, barley, oats, and corn.

The threshers—men who had not been drafted—did the heavy work of threshing grain. This year, several of my great-uncles helped because their sons and nephews were deployed. Their rigs were horse or steam powered. The *huff puff* of the steam tractors was mesmerizing. The women of the family were also cooking meals to feed these workers.

This year, we were all keenly aware of those missing family members. We worked together, chatted about our boys overseas, and tried to remain cheerful for each other. Women made gallons of coffee and lemonade and platters of sandwiches for workers. Underneath the chatter, however, was an undercurrent of worry, because we were all reading gloomy headlines and subdued letters.

Grandpa Carlson always claimed we honored our ancestors at harvest. They came to Iowa for its rich soil, and to Jubilee Junction for access to water with the Jubilee River. Reaching into the good Iowa soil, planting seeds, and caring for the young plants, weeding, and watering as needed was very satisfying to him. Harvesting the crop made it possible to feed his family and take products to market. He thought there could be no higher calling than to be a farmer.

Grandpa also loved caring for the animals, helping animals give birth to little ones in the spring, and seeing them grow. With gentle hands, he once considered a career as a veterinarian, but lacked funds for formal training. Other members of the family asked him to help with difficult births, and he saved many animals.

He owned a beautiful black horse he loved named Prince, and he rode Prince around the farm or hitched him to the small buggy he and grandma used. As Prince got older and gentler, Grandpa took turns putting us grandchildren up in the saddle, told us to hang on, and walked the horse around the farmyard. We loved it.

I remember putting my little arms around Prince's neck and holding onto his mane. I smelled his earthy, horsey smell, and marveled at the view of the farm from such a height. The horse lived a good long life, and when he died, Grandpa buried him down by the creek close to an apple tree.

Even after he retired, Grandpa liked to walk down to the pastures to see the cows grazing and sit by the tree and eat an apple with his grandchildren. I wonder if he sat there, thinking about his beloved Prince.

He told us stories told to him by his grandfather, about the three founding families and how they worked together in the first sixty years of Jubilee Junction. They broke ground together, and it took the first four generations to clear land on the thousand acres on the five farms. Since then, the three families had gained more land, but we still worked together in the spring and fall to plant and harvest.

City cousins helped with chores when someone was sick. When a family had a baby, we celebrated and brought food, and made sure the new mother and child had what they needed. When a couple married, someone gathered home canned vegetables, fruits, and jams and filled a bushel basket with towels and utensils and put the food on top. When someone died, we held a visitation before the funeral, brought the grieving family food, took care of children, and did chores. As a close-knit family, we supported one another through war and peace.

Now we were dealing with yet another aspect of the war—reducing our consumption of wheat, beef, pork, butter, and sugar so we could feed the troops. President Wilson appointed Herbert Hoover as the food administrator to control the production, distribution, and conservation of food. Europe couldn't produce enough food. The war had gone on for several years, farmers had become soldiers, and those left behind lacked fertilizer and machinery. Food had to come from North America.

Every family got a card that was to be hung in the kitchen titled: *"WHAT YOU CAN DO TO HELP WIN THE WAR."*
It presented the problem of the starving Allies and needing to

feed our soldiers. The solution was for us to eat less of those foods. We wanted to send them as much wheat, beef, pork, butter, and sugar as possible.

Posters from the Food Administration hung everywhere, including our store, the courthouse, post office, school, and other stores and offices around town.

The Jubilee Times printed a poem about Food.

FOOD

Buy it with thought,
Cook it with care,
Serve just enough,
Save what will keep,
Eat what will spoil,
Homegrown is best."

This meant that our store would not be selling meat or meat products on Tuesdays. In addition, we were being asked to cook with olive, cottonseed, or corn oil instead of butter, and to replace sugar with syrups—corn or maple—and honey.

My uncle raised hogs and cattle and butchered some himself. He had a smokehouse where he cured hams and ribs with hickory smoke. I didn't like being there for the butchering, but when we visited, we could smell the hickory smoke and picture the tasty Easter hams. Now, that meat was being sold to the government to feed the troops.

The women in my family worked hard to put together things for the boxes they shipped overseas. They knit socks and scarves and gathered foodstuffs like crackers, tins of fish, and small jars of jam. We added writing paper and envelopes, bars of soap, and other toiletries. Between the three big families, almost a dozen boys and men were serving overseas. As we worked, we chatted and comforted each other.

They considered me a woman this year, so I was working in the house with my mother, grandmothers, and aunts. It was a strange threshold to cross over. Last year, I helped in the fields, and in previous years, I'd overseen the children in the garden as they picked the vegetables. I had been a young woman then, a teenager still in high school.

Now, I was an adult, an engaged woman. Anna patted my arm before she walked out to oversee the children in the garden. I felt like an imposter. *Will Charlie return before next year's harvest—will we be married by then?*

I hesitated at the kitchen door, shy. Did I belong with the grown women? But Mama smiled, handed me an apron, and put me to work sorting and cutting up fragrant strawberries for jam from grandma's everbearing berry patch. I relaxed and listened to the surrounding chatter.

By the time I had filled two large bowls with berries, I'd learned more than I needed to know about my uncle's snoring and my great-aunt's memory problems. I'd also heard updates on several of our deployed family members. I resisted the urge to giggle and looked at my berry-stained hands and wondered if I'd ever get clean hands again, but they smelled heavenly.

Mother came over to check on my progress and patted my shoulder. "Nice work, Mary. It's good to have you working here this year."

I warmed to her praise as she set me to work sorting other kinds of berries.

My mouth watered, thinking of the jam, jelly, and pies these berries could create as I washed them, sorted out the good berries, and filled yet more bowls. Then one of my cousins came in the back door with another load of strawberries.

"Here you are, Mary!" she said.

I sighed and got the big strainer and began filling it with the fragrant berries. As I walked to the big farm sink, I saw Grandma washing out her canning jars and smiled. I'd remember this day when I put strawberry jam on my toast.

We took a break for a sandwich and then it was back to work. By supper time, we were all tired, but we'd accomplished a great deal.

Twenty-six

The Forgotten War
Gracie

"I was once again struck by the key to genealogy: stick-to-itive-ness. Yes, it takes creative thinking and knowledge of available resources, etc., but basically it takes a willingness to just keep at it and never give up. Being an optimistic idiot helps."
>   *~Buzzy Jackson*

"The First World War was a horror of gas, industrialized slaughter, fear, and appalling human suffering."
>   *~Nick Harkaway, 2012*

Late June

$\mathcal{I}$ sat down with my notebook to ponder the hope chest and my family during the first world war. I'd only read the first couple of letters from Charlie and had more questions than answers. So I did what I always do when I'm stuck—I asked for help.

Over supper I commented, "Of course, I need to find time to read the rest of the letters once we're moved."

Mom assured me, "You'll get a break, I'm sure of it. Don't be discouraged."

Dad leaned forward. "World War One was supposed to be *The Great War* and *The War to End All Wars*, but within two decades, there was an even bigger war. During the 1930s and 1940s, technology progressed in the realms of weaponry and medical care. Journalists got an upgrade on their tools, too, with better cameras and later, video cameras. Suddenly, the audience back home could see the devastation of war up close. Communication improved, with telephones and cables under the ocean, so reporting on the war increased."

He continued, "During World War One, trench warfare was brutal, and the use of mustard gas was terrible. It burned men's lungs. I read about cases where those soldiers survived the war, but their lungs gave out after they came home. Soldiers were reluctant to talk about their friends who were terrified of climbing out of the trenches to attack, and this was before doctors understood Post Traumatic Stress Disorder. Cemeteries in Iowa are full of World War One soldiers, but World War Two overshadowed it."

David said, "Matthew, you sound like my history professor in Chicago, who called World War One *the forgotten war*. I've visited many of those Iowa cemeteries, and it's humbling to see the tombstones of veterans of both World War One and Two. I've heard all those stories—about the mustard gas destroying lungs, and the terrible conditions of trench warfare."

David and Dad turned the conversation toward the Civil War. That made me think about Mary's family, Jubilee Junction, and how her generation of women had stepped up. They kept the shops open, harvested crops, and took care of injured soldiers.

I continued my research with a deep sense of commitment. I needed to find answers, not just for Angela and Vikki, but for myself and my whole family.

Meanwhile, Aunt Catharine asked Mom again if Grandma Mary's hope chest and World War One quilt were going to be in an exhibit at the museum. Mom said, "No, I don't think Gracie has any plans to use the hope chest or quilt in an exhibit. Don't worry Aunt Catharine."

"You would think she would be more trusting after we helped figure out the Civil War quilt and its legacy. Why is she so fixated on it?"

My father admitted, "I worry about her, living in that big house by herself. She's lonely and has too much time to brood."

My mother nodded. "I think you're right, dear. Vikki and Angela have talked to her about moving, but she's very resistant to the idea."

A few days later, I talked to Aunt Violet and Grandma Molly about any stories they knew regarding the flu pandemic of 1918.

"Oh, my. That happened only a few years before Grace, Vera, and I were born. Our mama told us stories about whole families being sick, and relatives finding all of them in one bed, in dire shape," Aunt Violet recalled. She continued, "In the past, we didn't have visiting nurses. However, we had compassionate women who looked after their neighbors and relatives. They hitched up a buggy to check in on them and cook, clean, and care for those who were ill." They recruited others to help with chores. Fewer than a hundred people died in Jubilee County, but it hit our soldiers hard here and abroad alike."

Grandma Molly nodded in agreement. "I heard a few stories from my grandmother. I think she and her two sisters got it, recovered, and then took care of other families, including one with a baby. Let me talk to my sisters-in-law and get back to you, Gracie."

The next time I stopped at the Jubilee Café, I asked Aunt Shirley about any relatives who might have more information about Mary Carlson.

"I heard about your new quilt mystery," she told me. "I'd like to see that quilt sometime. Let me check around. My great-aunt Lila Carlson lives at the senior living place where your Aunt Violet lives."

I went back and looked at the cardboard box from Angela and found several pieces of paper on the bottom, including a poem. I don't think it had ever evoked such a sad and bittersweet emotion in me. I'd read it before, but forgotten it was from the World War One era.

In Flanders Fields

by John McCrae

In Flanders fields the poppies blow
Between the crosses, row on row,
*   That mark our place; and in the sky*

> *The larks, still bravely singing, fly*
> *Scarce heard amid the guns below.*
> *We are the Dead. Short days ago*
> *We lived, felt dawn, saw sunset glow,*
> *Loved and were loved, and now we lie,*
> *In Flanders fields.*
> *Take up our quarrel with the foe:*
> *To you from failing hands we throw*
> *The torch; be yours to hold it high.*
> *If ye break faith with us who die*
> *We shall not sleep, though poppies grow*
> *In Flanders fields.*

The poem reminded me of the sweet old veterans standing by the door of our grocery store with donation cans and red poppies. They were once young men, in the military, deployed, defending this country. Too many of them lay in graves overseas.

The other piece of paper I found was a list of three things, with notations after them:

Over There—35

America, Here's my Boy—25

After the war is over, will there be any home sweet home?—18

I showed the paper to David, and we looked at the numbers together. "A rating system? Scores? Sales? It could be a lot of things."

Then I remembered something. Mary's father owned the general store in Jubilee Junction, so it could well be sales.

Curious, I googled them and discovered all three were WWI songs, and thanks to YouTube, someone had uploaded recordings of them. I listened to the songs on YouTube and was in tears when David walked in from mowing the yard. I played them for him, and he listened intently.

David helped me get the hope chest into my Subaru so we could take it to the museum. I wanted Carl and Charlotte to see it for themselves. The false bottom was partly open when we arrived, and we found one more object underneath it: an old leather wallet with a chain. I wasn't sure how Angela had missed it until we removed the false bottom and saw that the chain snagged on the underside.

Inside the wallet we found several faded photographs of Mary and Charlie, as well as a green, copper-looking, four-leaf clover, and an old, faded envelope. The envelope was too fragile to remove. Someone had engraved the wallet with Charlie O'Connor's name. I donned gloves to examine the wallet further and then put it into a zip-lock bag.

I made photocopies of all the letters and showed them to Carl, who scanned them. Charlotte and I did research on Mary on Ancestry and Find a Grave. We found an engagement photo and article. Mary Carlson got engaged to Charles (Charlie) O'Connor on May 15, 1917. Unfortunately, Charlie died March 21, 1918, in France, fighting in the trenches.

As we looked at the family tree, we found Mary's name again. She married Liam O'Connor on June 17, 1922. I glanced up at Charlotte. Liam was a WWI veteran and Charlie's older brother. He also served in France.

Charlotte looked thoughtful. "This story keeps getting more interesting. A girl gets engaged, her fiancé dies, and then she marries his older brother."

She promised to check the library's special collections for WWI artifacts.

I nodded. "I'll check *The Jubilee Times* archives tomorrow."

The next day, I climbed the steps to the second floor, which held digital equipment and workspace. Some archives were digital, and I found a half dozen articles from 1917 to 1920.

Several articles were about the sendoff of two groups of boys from the Jubilee Junction bus depot, complete with photos. Both O'Connor boys were handsome young men.

There were stories about the Jubilee boys who'd died, including Frank, Charlie's best friend. He died when enemy fire hit the trench while Frank and a medic were trying to rescue a wounded soldier. The trench collapsed, burying all three in hundreds of pounds of dirt and boards. I printed the article, but reading it was awful. I had to sit down suddenly, feeling dizzy, trying to ignore my overly active imagination. Mom was on the stairs and rushed over to check on me. I waved her away, my head still down, and handed her the article. She sat beside me and read it, then put her arm around my shoulder. Still holding me, she murmured, "How terrible. Mary's family must have been upset as well."

I nodded, in tears because WWI and trench warfare had never seemed more barbaric. I couldn't imagine how Mary had endured getting the news of Frank's death and then Charlie's. How had the other soldiers from Jubilee Junction handled combat under such primitive and dangerous conditions? My heart hurt for all of them.

Twenty-seven

Visit from Ben Carlson
Gracie

"A kind gesture can reach a wound that only compassion can heal."

~Steve Maraboli—Life, the Truth, and Being Free

Saturday morning, we lingered over tea and coffee after breakfast when there was a knock on the door. David answered it and walked back in with Lt. Ben Carlson of the Jubilee Police Department. "Hello, do you two have a minute?"

We sat down, and David offered him coffee which he accepted.

"First, congratulations again. I heard a little about your RV honeymoon. An FBI field agent by the name of Cal Smith contacted the Omaha office. He praised both of you for assisting with a covert operation in Kentucky where you rescued a young woman, a victim of sex trafficking, from a restroom at a truck stop."

I sat up a little straighter, remembering that day. "Miranda needed our help to get away from that terrible man."

David smiled at the young officer and said, "And were you surprised by the report, Lt. Carlson?"

Lt. Carlson grinned. "No, not at all. Knowing Gracie, she'd help someone in trouble. I'm proud of both of you. Agent Smith wanted you to know that Miranda is doing well. She sent you a postcard—here it is." He handed it to me. "Officially, she can't have contact with anyone for a few months, but she wanted to thank you both."

We discussed sex trafficking in Iowa.

I admitted, "I'm a little naïve or sheltered, I suppose. I thought it happened on the coast, but not in the Midwest."

Lt. Carlson sipped his coffee. "You aren't alone, Gracie. They use the internet to arrange things now. And they take advantage of runaways, immigrants, Native Americans, and young women who are desperate to get away from home. Any big football game or holiday they're bringing in vans or RVs with young women. We need more people like Gracie to help us spot them."

"I was proud of her but also worried. The thug outside that bathroom didn't want a scene, but I'm sure he was packing a gun," David admitted.

I shrugged. "Thank you both. I'd do it again."

Lt. Carlson shifted in his chair. "There's something else you should know. Someone vandalized the Carlson cemetery sign earlier this summer, and it appears to be the work of someone with white nationalist tendencies, judging from the spray-painted words. Then, to make their point, they added a couple of bullets."

David asked, "Any idea when?

Lt. Carlson shrugged. "Someone saw a white Ford F150 pickup with Confederate Flags painted on its doors driving around the weekend you two left on your honeymoon. A farmer was out checking on some cattle and spotted it near the cemetery. He didn't get a license plate, so we don't know who's behind the wheel. My question is, what do you want to do?"

David looked determined. "We need to let the rest of the family know, and I'd like to go out and look. We should set up some cameras. I wanted to think we'd gotten the white supremacists out of the area, but that was wishful thinking."

Lt. Carlson nodded. "Talk to your family. I told Matthew, but I wanted to wait until you returned before taking any additional steps. Without a license plate number, we can't do much of anything. We need to be vigilant, because I think it's likely this person, or persons, will escalate from vandalizing signs to posing a threat to those who stood up against the Proud White Boys."

He stood up and shook hands with us. "Mark mentioned you're moving to his old place soon and planning to build a gazebo. When you get ready to work on it, call me. I like to build things. It helps me unwind. And you can call me Ben. If we're at the Police Station, you can call me Lt. Carlson." He smiled, and I thanked him. David walked him out, chatting about tools and gazebo designs.

When David returned, I called my folks and put it on speakerphone." Ben just left and told us about the sightings of the big truck and the damage done to the pioneer cemetery's sign. We need to get some security cameras out there."

"Rich and I drove out, took pictures, cleaned up the sign the best we could, and looked around. There doesn't seem to be any permanent damage to the stones, but several had graffiti scrawled on them with magic markers," Dad replied.

"Any leads on who did it? I thought all our Proud White Boys were in jail," David asked.

"Not yet. We put out the word, and Ben's on the case, of course."

"Matthew, let me talk to my dad. He'll give us the family discount on any security cameras we need. I'd like to post a couple around town, including at the farmhouses." David reached for my hand as he spoke.

Dad agreed. "Thanks, David. That's a good idea. We need to coordinate our efforts. Let's talk more after you talk to your dad."

Mom spoke up. "Once your cameras are in place, we'll put out the word on the cousins' network to look for this truck. Maybe we can capture video so Ben can figure out what the driver is up to—and who he is, hopefully."

After we said goodbye, David called his father and talked about the situation. His father was concerned and promised to bring over half a dozen motion-activated cameras and other equipment.

David and I continued doing research into Charlie, Mary's fiancé, who died during WWI. I found an article from *The Jubilee Times* archive that talked about Charlie's bravery. He rescued a medic and a wounded soldier and was awarded two medals after his death. I located the obituaries for Frank and Charlie, as well as those for other young men from Jubilee Junction and surrounding farming communities.

David made a copy of an article about trench warfare that talked about the health risks soldiers faced, like trench foot and lung damage from mustard gas. He brought it up to my attic study with several books. "WWI was the first war where battle casualties were greater than those caused by illness. Sixty-five million soldiers were deployed, and over eight million soldiers died along with about six million civilians died."

He also found an article about the 1918 pandemic. While it started in soldier training facilities, both locally and abroad, it spread to the civilian community.

I made photocopies of all the articles to add to my collection. Then I sat down and read the photocopies of the letters, which were love letters to Mary from Charlie.

Letter Three

> *Dear Mary,*
> *We did a practice battle drill today, breaking into two groups to simulate battle. It was a lot of fun, especially with the wooden weapons, until our sergeant told us about the dangers we would encounter in France, such as the perilous trenches and no-man's-land. That sobered us all up to where no one said much of anything for the rest of the exercise or at the evening meal.*
> *I received your letter and tried not to weep, for the sight of your handwriting moved me so. We are working hard, and I'm tired. But I miss you, Mary.*
> *Our bunks are close together, and I can hear the snores all around me at night. A few good boys are saying their prayers and so do I. If my handwriting looks worse than usual, I'm trying to finish this letter in my bunk and fighting sleep.*
> *Our sergeant said we may leave for France in another week or two. I hope we are ready and that I can make you and my family proud of me.*
> *Your loving Charlie*

Letter Four

> *Dear Mary,*
> *Don't worry because we have all our gear now. Uniforms, side*

arms, and duffle bags. We will get rifles once we arrive in France. We're doing better with our drills, but we're a somber group compared to the carefree boys who had just arrived.

Frank and I talk about our fears about the war. No one relishes being stuck in the trenches, killing, or being killed. We want to come back to our loved ones. Marry, raise children, and start our careers. Have a life and die as old men, not in a muddy trench.

I've made friends with a boy who serves food in the cafeteria.

We sat and chatted twice. He says they built this base in a matter of weeks.

He could believe it. His father works here. He's only 16 but wants to be a soldier.

I told him we would try to wrap up the war, because I don't want him to end up in a trench.

Please keep writing, Mary.

Your loving man,

Charlie

I exhaled thinking of Mary and Charlie writing letters back and forth, hoping against hope Charlie would survive the war.

I thought of something from our RV honeymoon. I put a sticky note on my day planner. *Research David's family tree.* It would have to wait until we moved, renewed our vows, and started the new semester, of course. But I wanted him to know his family history, and to understand what happened to his great-grandfather in WWII. Right now, we had our hands full. We needed to finish solving the puzzle with Grandma Mary before we took on anything new.

Once Mark and Kathy had settled in at Aunt Violet's big farmhouse in late June, David and I took a tour of their farmhouse, now empty. We inspected it, going room by room. I brought my clipboard, and we made notes of what we needed to do, or what we would need to buy. Upstairs, there were two bedrooms, a walk-in linen closet, a bathroom, an attic entrance, and a small storeroom for boots, luggage, and other items.

David entered the guest room and decided to use it for his office.

He agreed the upstairs attic room would work well for me. The guest room was just around the corner from our master bedroom, which I reminded him resulted from combining two smaller bedrooms into one.

My cousin R. J. and his wife Allie spent a Saturday with us, and we painted my attic office pale blue and removed the door at the bottom of the steps.

We bought a king-size bed and bedding, and new dressers and side tables for the bedroom. Grandma Grace's little vanity table and bench fit in the corner for my makeup and jewelry. We agreed we could share the double closet, and there was another one in his office, which would hold a lot of off-season clothes.

Mom gave us a stack of empty boxes and tubs, and we got to work—with help. David's family came one weekend and helped us pack. Both families helped move us into the farmhouse, and our uncles and cousins helped as well. Mom found a large desk and office chair for my office upstairs, as well as a loveseat and a rocking chair. David's parents gave us a couch for the living room. Our old couch found a new home in the basement family room, along with a recliner and my small desk and a chair.

David settled into his office in the guest room. His parents gave us a pair of matching tall bookcases, and they fit. He brought his desk, chair, floor lamp, and comfy recliner from his apartment, and the chair fit in the corner, giving him a spot to watch the field across the road.

By the second week of July, we were calling the farmhouse home. We focused our energy on cleaning the house in town so we could return the keys.

We celebrated my twenty-sixth birthday on July 1st with a family meal at Mark and Kathy's house. Great-Aunts Violet, Vera, and Maggie were there with Uncle Vern. Aunt Vera's daughter, Donna, and son-in-law joined us. Uncle Rich, Aunt Delores, and their children were there as well as David's family. We grilled brats and burgers, loaded up our plates with beans, coleslaw, and chips, and spread out across the deck and yard. We chatted as we ate, washing it all down with beer, tea, and pop.

Kathy, still on bed rest, enjoyed her lunch in her bedroom with Mark. Her window looked out on the festivities, and people went up to the window to chat with her. "So, I'm the entertainment?" she asked, as I came up to chat.

"Yes, you should never have shown me your party trick of balancing your plate on your tummy," I told her.

Mom and Aunt Delores brought out a small chocolate birthday cake and several trays of cupcakes to feed the crowd. We cut the cake, and I ate a slice to applause as we passed around slices and then cupcakes to feed the crowd.

Uncle Vern told the story of Grandpa Richard giving me my first bite of cupcake when I was not quite two years old. "She had chocolate frosting smeared all over her face, and begged for more," he chuckled. "He gave her the rest of his cupcake."

Mom got out the photo album and passed it around, with lots of laughter. Dad had captured the moment, me sitting on Grandpa's lap and leaning forward eagerly to get a bite of cake. Then the look of rapture as I tasted chocolate for the first time.

Mark looked out the window from Kathy's bedroom, "Wasn't this at my fifth birthday party? I think I've heard this story two ways."

Uncle Vern looked thoughtful. "You might be right, Mark. Maybe it was her first taste of chocolate ice cream that I was remembering."

Everyone laughed, and I realized again how lucky Mark and I were to have Great-Uncle Vern, and Great-Aunts Violet and Maggie with us still. They carried the stories of our grandparents and great-grandparents. They represented our family's legacy, our deep roots in Iowa. Mark's children, and one day our children, would carry that legacy into the future.

I realized I wanted to have a baby with David someday. Not just yet. But I wanted our children to grow up with Mark and Kathy's children, just how Mark and I had grown up with R. J. and James. I snagged a second piece of cake and split it with David.

Twenty-eight

The Carlson General Store
Mary

*"Have you eaten your pound of potatoes today? Save Wheat
by Eating Potatoes. We are doing our part in moving the large
surplus of potatoes by serving liberal portions at low prices."*
*~U.S. Department of Agriculture and the U.S. Food
Administration*

*I*m feeling quite grown up, working at the
store with Papa. He says I'm doing well, and I enjoy the challenge
of learning new things. I've been carrying a small notebook and
jotting notes in it with questions to ask Papa, and recording things
he tells me, reminders and other information.

Being the largest store in Jubilee County, we attract orders from
all over. The store sells bakery items like cinnamon rolls and oatmeal
cookies, but we also sell baked, sliced bread. Not everyone wants
to bake their own bread these days. Across the street from us, we
have a bakery with a large kitchen, and four women work there
making bread, rolls, and pastries. Of course, we also sell all the
ingredients one would need to make their own bread: flour, yeast,
sugar, and other items.

Grandma Carlson says she baked bread every day when she
was out on the farm. Every generation before her, including
her mother and grandmother, baked bread daily. Large families
could go through several batches of bread and rolls each day.
But she admits she doesn't miss those days, especially in the
heat of summer.

Last week, she came into the store and picked up one of the nice loaves of freshly baked wheat bread. "I baked enough bread in my lifetime for a small army," she told me.

After we entered the war, things changed. We began selling lots of potatoes and other vegetables. We put up posters about *meatless* and *wheatless* meals because the government was sending massive amounts of wheat, beef, and pork to Europe.

Papa reminded us, "We aren't only feeding our troops; we're helping to feed Europe." Their people were starving after three years of war and many of their farmers were deployed as soldiers.

We encouraged customers to buy less wheat and more corn-meal—to use oats, rye, and barley products in place of wheat. We distributed booklets from the U.S. Food Administration that included recipes and suggestions for making *war bread,* which often included potato flour and other types of flour.

Meanwhile, farmers brought produce to the store for at least three seasons. We stock fresh fruits and vegetables in spring, summer, and fall, and winter squash, onions, potatoes, pumpkins, and apples in the fall.

One of my tasks was to go out twice a day and tidy up the produce aisle. Grandpa hated seeing the fruit displayed in a messy manner, so he wandered off from stocking shelves to rearrange the bananas or apples. I looked at the various vegetables that I don't like and wonder why anyone would eat okra, parsnips, kohlrabi, or some of the other vegetables we sell. Papa assured me that other people liked them, and with the war on, we needed to eat more vegetables, especially potatoes.

We arrange the food products in the middle. Shoppers could find jars of pickles, boxes of crackers, jars of mincemeat, candy, and bins of potatoes. One side of the store featured housewares like pots and pans, dishes, kitchen products, towels and sheets, clothing, socks, shoes, and boots.

We displayed jewelry on the long counters, along with watches. Beside the cash register, we kept a coffee mill, scales for weighing grocery items, and a contraption for wrapping goods with brown paper and string. Close by, we had candy jars filled with different types of candy like peppermint sticks, licorice, jellybeans, lemon drops, and chocolate drops.

Our store provided a gathering spot for farmers who visited town weekly for supplies. A sturdy table with a checkers board and four chairs where people could sit and talk was tucked in a back corner, making the store something of a social hub. A large bulletin board hung in the back of the store gave customers a place to post notices of things for sale, for rent ads, and flyers advertising events.

In ordinary times, an uncle and his sons butchered hogs and cows as needed, and we let our customers know when he was going to have fresh meat. As people needed chickens or turkeys, we took orders. But these days, our cousins and younger uncles were deployed, and we had posters urging people to eat meatless meals so we could send that meat overseas to feed our troops and help feed starving European Allies. Instead, we were urged to eat fish and other seafood, poultry, rabbits, and beans instead of beef, mutton, and pork.

We had copies of a cottage cheese recipe book on the counter and recipe booklets about corn. Mama and Grandma were trying them out.

The porch on the front of the store featured four big rockers, so people often lingered there to chat with neighbors. Anna says it's old-fashioned, but no one seems to have the heart to change it. When Anna and I were younger, we would play on the porch with a young aunt or Grandma supervising us while Mama shopped.

Some customers still came by buggy. Others walk to us, and we deliver groceries as well.

There are at least a dozen automobiles in town. Papa bought a truck for the store and a car for us. We also have a few parking spaces.

Papa says we have a great location close to Jubilee Junction's bank and post office, and the Jubilee Café was across the street. The courthouse, jail, county sheriff's office, and police department were a block over. There was also a law office nearby, and the doctor's office and clinic. The new gas station was two blocks away.

Our house was four blocks away, which made for a pleasant walk during spring, summer, and fall. During winter, walking could be difficult if the roads weren't plowed. When he was younger, Papa used to ride a horse to the store and tie it up outside if he were doing deliveries or take him to the nearby livery stable. Now, we took the car or walked.

Grandpa loved his horse and buggy, but drove the big truck for the lumberyard in town. He told me someday we won't need horses at all on the farm because tractors will replace them.

I asked him if he thought farmers would keep a few horses in the future.

Grandpa thought about it. "I want to say yes," he said, "but horses take a lot of work. They're social animals, so you need several, and they want something to do, not just wander around a pasture." He shook his head. "No, I guess not." He looked sad, thinking of his beloved Prince.

I asked Grandma the same question.

She also thought about it. "For most of my life, we depended on horses for transportation. I loved to ride horses when I was a girl. But I think your grandfather is right. Someday, tractors will replace horses. You can get more done, and you don't have to pay vet bills for horses or feed them. So, yes, I love our new car. We can travel in a fraction of the time it took by horse and buggy."

I realized that something had changed. My grandparents treated me more like a grownup since I'd graduated high school and started working at the store. I was now an engaged woman, of course. I liked it. I was also seeing things from their perspective.

I was thinking more about the world and how things worked. Using a cash register made sense for the store, and I wanted to teach others how to use it. I wanted to contribute something to my family. Our boys were fighting in France. Surely, I could do my part here.

Twenty-nine

Settling into the Farmhouse
Gracie

"When people live in Iowa, they are rather apt to like it."
~Ruth Suckow

$\mathcal{D}$avid and I were especially pleased with the basement in our farmhouse, which had a room for the furnace, water heater, and shelving. I stored my holiday decorations there, and David added some boxes that could wait to be put away. The basement also had its own bathroom and a walk-in closet in the laundry room where Mark and Kathy had left appliances.

Next to it, there was a family room with a cozy electric fireplace, built-in bookshelves, and an entertainment center for David's TV.

We sat on the couch downstairs one morning, and he looked around. "This is a perfect place for reading, working, or watching TV. Remember, I've lived in a series of studio apartments since I left home. Your house in town would have been big enough for me if I didn't have a home office or all my books and things. This farmhouse is a mansion, with lots of space." He stretched his arms wide on the back of the couch and surveyed his domain with a satisfied smile.

David also liked the large garage with its long workbench and the pegboard above. We had ample space for two cars and more, thanks to shelves along one wall.

Our minimal rent, a fraction of his Chicago apartment's cost, amazed him. "It pays to have family connections," I quipped.

I explained why there were so many farmhouses connected with my family. Multiple generations often lived on farms in the past. As the grandparents got older, they moved into their own little house. Some farmers might build a couple of houses for tenants—or for their three daughters, so if they did not marry, they would have a place to call home.

Grace, Violet, and Vera were each given a house on the family farms when their parents were still living. Vern lived in the same farmhouse where they were all born, and he raised his family there. Uncle Rich, Mom's older brother, lived in what was once Grandma Grace's house.

Mark and Kathy had first lived in Vera's old house, which sat vacant for a few years—where we were now living. David looked a little shocked when I told him we were living in Aunt Vera's old house, but he got over it quickly. Mark and Kathy were now living in Aunt Violet's old house. It was the largest of the family homes and therefore our social hub as a family.

We found a tiny desk for the corner nook in the kitchen, and it became our wedding planning hub, with a calendar, list of phone numbers, and clipboard with to-do lists.

While David liked his second-floor office with a large window overlooking the cornfields, I thought, *I got the best spot in the house.* I loved the attic room and the built-in bookshelves, and closet gave me plenty of storage.

We started completing plans for the wedding. With Tiara and Shelly, I drove to Mom's to check out the nine long dresses. We decided on one with a late 1940s vibe with satiny, silky fabric, a sweetheart neckline, and a short train. We sent pictures and videos to Kathy, and she agreed with our choice. Katie had her iPad, and my mom did Facetime with her, letting Kathy watch our session of trying on three gowns.

"I love it. You look very glamorous." Kathy dabbed at her eyes and so did Shelly as I stood before the full-length mirror.

Shelly sighed. "Remember playing with Barbie dolls? You married Mr. Potato Head at least once, if I remember correctly. Now, you have the perfect dress and the perfect husband."

Tiara stood behind me to zip up the dress and agreed. "It's a gorgeous dress, and you're already radiant without makeup, fancy hair, or jewelry."

My reflection smiled back at me. It was the perfect dress.

Once or twice a week, we drove over and checked on Mark and Kathy. Her parents, Ken and Katie Daniels, had moved in and seemed pleased with their new living situation and the chance to be useful. Ken and Katie set up their bedroom in one room, and they took over the other empty bedroom for a small office, with a desk and laptop, printer, matching recliners, and TV. They wanted Mark and Kathy to have some privacy downstairs.

Ken and Katie brought along their two dogs, two-year-old golden retrievers. Littermates, they were handsome animals. Chewie's coat was yellow, while Han Solo's coat was chocolate brown.

Katie explained that when their next-door neighbor's dog had puppies, she asked to buy one. Katie wanted a dog to encourage Ken to be more active, and when they couldn't decide between the last two puppies, they got both. Now that they'd moved to the farm, the dogs had plenty of room to run and get their fill of exercise.

The dogs had their quieter moments too. They liked to visit Kathy and check on her, and if given permission, they'd keep her company on the bed.

Ken spent a couple of hours a day keeping in touch with his manager at the small marketing company he'd built. He'd taken a six-month leave of absence. Katie was a retired elementary teacher, with lots of energy and a cheerful disposition. My parents liked Kathy's parents, and I saw them becoming friends.

One afternoon, David sought advice on tools. Mark and Ken joined the conversation, discussing their own tools. They walked out to the garage as Katie laughed and the three of us women chatted.

Kathy asked about the honeymoon when her mom left to check on lunch.

I told her about our RV trip, some places we'd visited, the drama with Miranda, and the experience of taking our hotel with us.

"We'd take another RV trip," I said. "It was wonderful."

Kathy assessed me from the bed. "And how was the honeymoon?" she asked.

I smiled. "Wonderful. David's very romantic. He was gentle, kind and very patient with me. I'm not a prude, but it was amazing to compare what little I'd experienced before with Steven, of course, to being with David. So don't worry. I love being married."

Kathy grinned. "It shows."

She asked about the new mystery quilt, and I told her about the hope chest and showed her pictures from my iPhone.

David came back to give me a kiss and say they were running to Menards with her dad, so the dogs came in and hung out with us. They lay down on the floor for a moment before Han Solo whined and got permission to get up on the bed.

"How is Felix getting along with these two guys?" I asked as I petted Chewie.

"They're settling in, but when he's tired of them, he comes in here and hides under the bed." Kathy scratched behind Han Solo's ears, and he cuddled up to her.

As we chatted, I realized we'd read the first few letters, but the box from Angela was in the basement, and the hope chest was in my museum work room. We'd gotten no further.

Kathy laughed. "Well, it's been a crazy, busy summer. You got married and took off on a honeymoon in an RV, helped us move, you moved, you got your house in town ready for someone else, and you're planning a wedding."

When the men came back, David was excited. "I got some tools!"

Kathy and I tried not to smirk.

Once home, David and I completed some chores and crossed items off the wedding list.

He wanted to hang up his new tools in the garage, and I walked down to the basement and laid out Grandma Mary's quilt and the linens that Angela found in the false bottom of the hope chest. After taking photos with my iPhone, I grabbed a notebook and did an inventory of them.

Afterwards, I walked out to the garage and admired David's new tools. They were hung on fresh hooks on a pegboard over the long workbench. He looked like a kid after Christmas; excited to play with the new toys. I wasn't sure what he planned to do with them but decided it wasn't important. He was settling in, and I admired his new square organizer, with drawers for nails, screws, and bolts, next to a small toolbox.

I kissed him. "Looking good, sweetie."

"I'm going to talk to Vern and Mark more about tools. Kathy's father, Ken, is a great guy," he told me. "We have a few ideas for projects." Then he picked up a copy of *Popular Mechanics* and started looking through it.

I'd never seen David looking at the publication before now. I headed back to the house.

Farmhouse settled, it was time to prep for fall classes and find out more about Grandma Mary. I spent more time in my attic office, thankful for the ceiling fan and the windows letting in natural light. Agatha came to visit me from time to time, curling up on a sunny window ledge.

David wasn't the only one to have ideas for a project. Looking at the prints from our honeymoon trip, I'd found about two dozen pictures of us I liked. I laid them out on my desk in my office one afternoon. I narrowed it down to twelve, then found a calendar template online. We'd taken selfies at half a dozen battlefields and museums. Kind strangers took the rest. I created a calendar for David and got a copy for myself to preserve some memories of our trip.

David liked it so much that I ordered copies for both sets of parents, grandparents, and Violet, Vern, and Maggie.

I'd taken the summer off from college—typically, I taught a class or two. I took time off from the Museum in June and part of July for the honeymoon and moving. But I was still writing my columns on our travels, staffing the reception desk, and writing news stories for *The Jubilee Times.*

Normally, David taught several classes. He decided he needed the summer off as well, for the honeymoon, moving, and a book he was writing about the German POWs in Iowa. Thankfully, he got paid during the summer from his full-time teaching job. Once, I'd been worried about health insurance and other benefits, but now I was covered by David.

We were blissfully happy. Agatha enjoyed the new house with ample space for running, exploring, and hiding. However, Agatha hid from us several times, and I worried she had escaped outside and was lost in the cornfield. After more frantic searching, we'd find her each time. David threatened to put her on a leash. With a bigger house, I wondered if she'd landed on *her spot* yet.

I'd gotten her a cat bed when Mark first brought her to me as a kitten. Now we dragged it from room-to-room downstairs, trying to tempt her. She'd gotten kicked out of the bedroom when David and I married. We found her sleeping on the rug outside our door, on the couch, under the kitchen table, and once, right beside the cat bed. I was getting the idea she didn't like her cat bed.

What were we going to do?

Thirty

Agatha's Cat Tree & Wedding Drama
Gracie

"A cat has absolute emotional honesty: human beings, for one reason or another may hide their feelings but a cat does not."
~Ernest Hemingway

*D*avid, Mark, and Ken conspired in the garage after bringing over some more tools and wood, and they made Agatha a cat tree one Saturday afternoon. They covered parts of it in remnants of carpet, creating a couple of little boxes with entrances, a short tunnel, and some other cool features. We placed it on the first floor, in the living room but near the kitchen.

Agatha was in cat heaven, crawling, leaping, exploring, meowing, and having a good time. We all laughed at her antics.

I had tears running down my face. "Are you sure you didn't put catnip in this cat tree?"

All three men tried to look innocent and shook their heads. Mark took pictures and sent them to Kathy.

Mark brought Felix the next afternoon and the two cats were hilarious, chasing each other around the tree. We took photos and some video clips, and the whole family enjoyed the fun.

But we couldn't have a jealous cat brother, now, could we? So, the men made a cat tree for Felix, too, and he loved it. Felix could retreat to the cat tree while the dogs roamed the house, getting used to their new home.

It became a fun hobby, and several other people wanted one too. Aunt Violet was the next in line, of course. The boys asked for carpet leftovers, and with the help of Uncle Rich, Uncle Vern, and Ben, they made twelve more cat trees. I could see Mark and David becoming fast friends.

My parents were visiting one afternoon as the boys finished up another batch of cat trees. Dad observed, "David's typically an intellectual, scholarly type, but look at him over there with Mark. He's become a real macho man this summer, driving an RV and building things with other men."

"Macho man?" I asked, wondering why Mom looked so amused.

Dad got out his iPhone and googled "Macho Man" and found a YouTube video of The Village People from 1978. The song made me giggle, but I couldn't get the lyrics out of my head about every man wanting to be a macho-macho man.

David and Mark walked over to see why we were all singing and dancing around. They watched the video and joined us in the chorus.

Summer was going by too quickly, and July was nearly gone. Wedding plans were all set for Saturday, August 17th. We were getting married at our family church, the large Methodist church the founders established in Jubilee Junction with Rev. Luke Carlson in the 1860s. We had several premarital counseling sessions with the pastor.

Then, just five weeks before the wedding, we hit a snag. The church secretary called me, apologized, and said we needed to find another venue. I got off the phone, shaken, and on the verge of tears. What were we going to do? I plopped on the couch, my phone on my lap, tears now running down my cheeks.

David saw my face. "What's wrong?"

"They made a mistake. The church got double booked, and that was the church secretary calling to apologize. We can't get married there. The wedding is off, I guess."

He put his arms around me. "We'll figure it out. Don't worry."

My parents had stopped over for a quick visit. Dad looked at Mom, who told me, "Don't panic, Gracie. Let me make some calls." She grabbed her purse and headed for the kitchen.

David and I sat on the couch, his arm around my shoulder. Agatha came to check me out, mewing until I told her, "Okay, Agatha, up," and she jumped on my lap, sensing my distress.

Dad paced around, frustrated. "How did they get double booked?"

I tried to speak between sobs. "The secretary told me… she wrote it down on a sticky note on the paper calendar but entered it on the wrong date on their church… calendar. Bby the time, they caught the error, they already had another wedding booked."

I looked around for a tissue, realizing I'd meant to put a box downstairs, so I dabbed at my tears with a takeout napkin from my jeans pocket and clutched Agatha.

Dad paced some more, looking concerned and muttering to himself.

David patted my back, and then rubbed it with circular motions, murmuring sweet little things. "It's going to be alright. I love you, Gracie. Don't cry."

Agatha could only deal with a certain amount of drama. She jumped down to go to her cat tree.

I sat up, dried my eyes on the takeout napkins, which were not a suitable substitute for tissues, and tried to joke, "Dad, should we boil some water?"

Dad stopped pacing. David stopped murmuring and rubbing my back. They looked at me.

"This is like a scene from an old movie, where someone goes into emergency labor," I explained.

David sighed, and Dad tried to smile.

"It's okay," I patted David's leg. "After all, we're married, right? So, we don't get the big fantasy wedding with all our friends and family. We're married."

I was trying to convince myself. "So we don't get married in the wonderful old family church. I don't get to wear the beautiful family wedding dress and have my friends stand up with me. We're still married, right?" Now I was working myself up into a frenzy, and still no tissue in sight.

David looked more alarmed than amused and hesitated, trying to figure out if he should start rubbing my back again or murmuring sweet nothings. He looked to Dad for direction as I repeated my litany.

Dad sat down in a recliner and hesitated before he spoke. "You're right, Gracie. No one's having a baby here. Yes, you two are already married, but we wanted to see you walk down the aisle, and I wanted to give you away."

I looked at him in alarm. Dad was getting a little teary. I didn't know what to do—we couldn't *both* be losing it.

I stopped, sniffled, and glanced up at David.

David sat up, ignoring my teary, snotty face, and said, "I'm not a gambling man, but my money is on your mother, Gracie. If anyone can find us a place to get married, Becky can. Right, Matthew?"

Dad perked up.

We sat there, gathering our thoughts. Just as I was getting up to find a tissue, my iPhone buzzed with a text. I sniffled.

The text was from Jubilee Junction Community College.

```
Confirmation of Founder's House and
Gazebo rental, David and Gracie MacNeill,
August 17-18.
```

I showed the text to David and read it aloud to Dad. He and David exchanged a grin.

Mom sauntered back in, looking smug. "Okay, we're set. We get the Founder's House, patio, gazebo, and the whole works for Friday afternoon and all day Saturday. Since you work at the college full-time, David, and I have connections with the foundation, it won't cost you anything. We just need *The Jubilee Times* to give them a break on advertising for the next year. Now we need to let the catering people know, and the cake people, and the flower people."

Bless her heart, she found a box of tissues, which she offered the bride with a glass of iced tea. I blew my nose, took a slug of tea, and stared at my family in awe. David and I exchanged surprised glances. *Really? My mother has superpowers.*

She admitted, "My cousin works in the scheduling office at the college. I sent a text asking if they had that date open."

I stood up, still teary-eyed, and hugged her hard. She patted my back and made little soothing noises while I sobbed the last of my hysterics out.

"Thank you, Mom."

David gave her a wonderful smile. "Becky, you're a dangerous woman. Did you know that? I believe you can persuade anyone to do anything."

Dad snorted. "You got it, David."

Mom crossed her arms and gave a contented smile.

I left the room to blow my nose and wash my face and hands. On my way back to the living room, I grabbed several clipboards from our wedding desk in the kitchen. I gave one to Mom and Dad, one to David, and kept one for myself.

David and I walked into the kitchen to make calls, while Mom and Dad were in the dining room and living room. We called the folks doing the flowers, catering, and cake with the new arrangements. Then we split up the list and called the wedding party. We sent out an email blast to our family and friends. Mom told us that the Founder's House was ideal for weddings and receptions. It had a spacious dining room, a sunroom that led to the patio for receptions, and a gazebo for weddings. Fortunately, Judge Nelson was available. Our pastor apologized for the church being double booked and expressed gratitude for our understanding.

David asked his younger brother Alex, Mark, and Cornell, his old friend and grad school room mate from Chicago, as his groomsmen. He called each one to give them the new details.

Kathy talked me into dropping her as an attendant, so I asked David's sister, Joanna, to stand up with me. Her children were going to be the ring bearer and flower girl, so it made sense. Jack and Daisy were excited about the wedding. They looked forward to dressing up and being responsible for something so important as the rings and rose petals. My other two bridesmaids were Shelly and Tiara.

We were going simple—no tuxes. We found dark gray dress pants, light gray dress shirts, suspenders, and bow ties. The girls and I found a dress with a 1940s vibe. It was a simple gown, a long A line with short, fluttery sleeves, a high gathered waist, and a simple sweetheart neckline mimicking the wedding dress. We debated between a lovely mauve rose to a steel blue-gray for the dresses. In the end, we chose the steel blue-gray because we found matching bow ties.

A Nelson cousin owned a floral shop and was handling the decorations. We used mauve rose and steel blue-gray for our colors.

Once again, family connections had saved the day. We were going to get married—again. Now, if we could just put the puzzle pieces together about Grandma Mary.

Thirty-one

At the Front
Mary

"Let us, while the war lasts, forget our special grievances &
close ranks shoulder to shoulder with our white fellow citizens
and the allied nations that are fighting for democracy. We make
no ordinary sacrifice, but we make it gladly & willingly."
~W.E.B. DuBois, *The Crisis, July 1918*

Fall 1917

Charlie and the boys have arrived in France.
My last letter was three weeks ago, and Charlie wrote they'd
completed three weeks of training, and would head for the front
soon. Charlie sounded anxious, which is normal because war is
not normal. Killing is not normal. I cannot imagine what he is
about to experience.

The Jubilee Times published a poem, "In Flanders Fields," written
by Canadian officer and surgeon John McCrae in 1915. It is a
solemn, sad poem and brings me to tears. I clipped it and put it in
the wooden box Grandpa made me where I store Charlie's letters
and a few newspaper clippings.

Fall has come to Jubilee Junction, with the leaves turning brilliant
colors. Grandpa, Grandma, Mama, and Anna are busy with the
garden, harvesting vegetables, canning, storing, and sharing produce
with family members. Our squash vines quite overtook the yard,
and we enjoyed a bounteous amount of produce.

We're eating lots of sandwiches with fresh sliced tomatoes and lettuce and enjoying lots of roasted vegetables. When I'm enjoying a meal, I often stop and wonder what my sweetheart and big brother are eating overseas. Is it soggy biscuits, canned stew? Are they cold, wet, able to sleep? Are they safe?

We keep seeing posters, some geared for farming states. One featured troops charging forward and read:

Your Country Calls
Save Food with a Silo
40% of the crop is wasted when left in the field. A Silo saves
10 cents on the production of one pound of butter
$1.50 on 100 pounds of beef
$1.50 on 100 pounds of mutton
40 cents on 100 pounds of milk
It's to your interest to buy early & put it up early.

Another poster features Uncle Sam pointing to a silo.

Help Uncle Sam put your corn in a Silo
and save millions of dollars.
A silo saves good for stock
as the can saves for man.
We have posters all over the store.

I've been working at the store for three months now. Papa says I'm doing well. My book section has become quite popular, and we now carry three farm journals and three magazines for housewives, as well as a dozen books, a children's Bible, and some children's books.

Charlie's mother came in last week to shop, and her face lit up upon seeing me. She walked over and gave me a warm hug. It was good to see her. We compared notes from the boys' letters, which are shorter and less frequent since their arrival in France. Liam's girlfriend works at a hospital a few miles from the front, and they're quite fond of each other, even though they haven't been able to see each other.

Underneath our chatter, I see the worry in her eyes reflected in mine. How long will this war last? Can the American soldiers make the difference and end it? How can our boys survive in such a hostile environment? We assure each other that they're doing well and hope we're right. The newspaper headlines are anything but encouraging, but I tell myself not to worry.

Papa took me to the bank to open an account for my earnings last week. I feel very grown up. By the time Charlie gets back, I could have several hundred dollars saved. I make $12 a month, deposit $8, and allow myself $4 a month for spending or a dollar a week.

When I'm not at work or helping with chores for Papa, I join the ladies at our Methodist church who roll bandages and gather supplies for the Red Cross. Mama and Grandma are there several times a week. There's an African Methodist Episcopal church in town, too, and they also help with our efforts, rolling bandages and gathering supplies. The store put a donation box with a list of things needed, and people are helping us fill the box. I like to think we're making a difference.

At least once a week, I stop at the Jubilee library after work and read newspapers from around Iowa. France is a dangerous place, and it seems to have gotten more dangerous with our boys over there. I stare at the photographs of the ravaged trees and see the ground broken by trenches and explosions. It seems otherworldly. Fire and smoke cover part of the battlefield. Soldiers advance through what looks like hell, with bombs exploding, and canteens, helmets, and personal gear thrown around.

I don't know how anyone can survive those harsh conditions. Then I discover a group of soldiers who have it even harder, if you can believe it. There's an African American division deployed, the 93rd, and they've fought racism and the Germans, according to my friend Ruby Collins. She has two cousins serving in the 93rd. Despite the prejudice, the unit has developed a reputation as fierce fighters and earned them the nickname of the *Hell Fighters.*

Others call them the *Buffalo Soldiers* for their dark, curly hair and fierce nature. As Ruby shows me their pictures, I'm grateful that we have such outstanding soldiers. It's disheartening to see some white people being mean to fellow Americans, so I'm committed to teaching my children to accept everyone.

Ruby and I have been friends since we were little children. Our maternal grandmothers are friends and working together for women's suffrage in a group that met at her church. Ruby's my age, smart, and active in the African American community in Jubilee. My mother and father brought us up to respect all people. When we see each other at the library, she and I compare notes on the war and what we're hearing from our soldiers. Her aunt and mother are close and her aunt shares tidbits from the boys' letters home.

Ruby told me stories about the prejudice the Buffalo Soldiers faced during their training, and how differently the French people and soldiers treated them, since they had Black soldiers from their colonies. Her cousins wrote about their hope that once they've proved themselves, they might experience less racism when they return home.

"I'm the great-granddaughter of a slave, and even here in Jubilee Junction, I sense people look down on us. Not you or your family, Mary."

Ruby considers herself a suffragist. She's educated me on the brave African American women who were fighting for the vote and for equality, like Ida B. Wells, Mary Church Terrell, and Mary B. Talbert. She recommended several books, and we made it a point to meet weekly at the library to chat.

I'm ashamed of the treatment towards her, other African Americans in Jubilee Junction, and the soldiers fighting for our freedom in France. When can we learn to live together? When will women be seen as equal to men and able to vote? I'm not content to sit back and wait any longer. I want to make a difference.

Thirty-two

Trip to Chicago
Mary

"The vote is the emblem of your equality, women of America, the guarantee of your liberty. That vote of yours has cost millions of dollars and the lives of thousands of women. Money to carry on this work has been given usually as a sacrifice, and thousands of women have gone without things they wanted and could have had in order that they might help get the vote for you. Women have suffered agony of soul which you can never comprehend, that you and your daughters might inherit political freedom. That vote has been costly. Prize it! The vote is a power, a weapon of offense and defense, a prayer. Understand what it means and what it can do for your country. Use it intelligently, conscientiously, prayerfully."
~Carrie Chapman Catt

Aunt Eva called and invited me to come to Chicago for a weekend. I asked if Ruby could come along, and she said that was fine. She knows Ruby and her family. We took the train on Friday afternoon. I thought Ruby was a little quieter than usual when we boarded the train in Jubilee Junction, but I chatted away and led us to a pair of seats. Both of us brought along books, and we read, talked, and watched the changing scenery. About midway, she seemed to relax and explained to me her relatives down south told stories about having to ride in the *colored* car.

I looked at her. "Well, we need to get rid of such old-fashioned and prejudiced ideas. I'd like to see someone ask you to move, because they would need to deal with me, too."

She smirked since I'm barely 5' 3" and not the most intimidating person. I tried not to giggle as I dug out the waxed paper container of oatmeal cookies Grandma sent along, and we chatted and munched away at the cookies.

Aunt Eva met us at the train depot in Chicago and took us for a late supper of pasta and crusty bread at a small restaurant in her neighborhood. As we walked into the restaurant, all three of us took in the sauce's fragrance. We sat down, and Ruby and I put our small suitcases underneath the table. Menus were on the table, so we opened them.

"I'm paying, girls, so get what you want. However, I recommend the lasagna or the spaghetti and meatballs here. The meals come with a salad and bread, and the bread is crusty with garlic and butter."

Ruby looked around and relaxed because there were several African American servers and diners. The two of us looked at the menu.

"What sounds good to you, Ruby?" I asked.

She grinned. "Lasagna, I think. I keep changing my mind, but maybe it's because I'm hungry."

Aunt Eva said, "I get overwhelmed with too many choices, so I don't look at menus as much as I used to. You can't go wrong here. And yes, I'm getting the lasagna."

That settled it. "Me, too."

The server, a young African American girl with a big smile, took our orders. She brought out beverages and a plate of crusty bread and butter, then the salads.

When our food came, we were in awe of how this girl carried three large plates.

She made another trip to refill the breadbasket.

We ate, chatted, ate more, and each one of us ended up with a packet of extras to take with us for the next day.

We walked to Aunt Eva's apartment, just two blocks away, and settled in for the night. Her apartment was small but cozy, filled with books, art, and knickknacks from her trips around the United States. A large sign, "Votes for Women," hung behind the sofa. We wrote our names on our leftover packets, still groaning from our meal, and put them in her icebox.

Her guest room served as her office, equipped with a wall-mounted Murphy bed. Ruby and I made the bed, giggling a little about the prospect of the bed folding up with us inside during the night.

As I put the fitted sheet on one corner, I asked, "Can you imagine the headlines? Girls squashed in a Murphy bed, flatter than a pancake."

Ruby giggled. "I wonder how fast it goes back up?"

Aunt Eva assured us with a smile that she hadn't lost a guest yet. "Please ignore the clutter in here. I have too many projects going on. But I'm so delighted you could both come this weekend. Here's an extra blanket if you get cold. If one of you is restless or kicks the other, there's always the couch."

After making the bed, we returned to chat with Aunt Eva, who was looking at her mail at the kitchen table. "Tomorrow, I'm taking you to a big meeting of suffragists. Then we'll have lunch out and go see a museum afterwards. But now, I want to catch up on Jubilee Junction gossip. What's going on? How is your handsome young man, Mary? Ruby, how is your family?" We sat and chatted until I couldn't help but yawn.

At bedtime, we got on our pajamas and enjoyed chamomile tea and scones. Then Ruby and I said goodnight and retired to the guest room, where we talked more like two teenagers at a sleepover. City lights gleamed through the curtains, filling us with excitement. We fell asleep.

In the morning, we dressed and headed off for a busy day. We ate waffles at a nearby restaurant before leaving for our meeting. Aunt Eva was excited as we ate. We later learned why, as we took a bus to a large downtown building. There she led us into a large auditorium filled with women and girls, white and African American, young, and old. Several women made a beeline for Aunt Eva, chattering about a program they'd all attended. Ruby and I smiled. Then her eyes got bigger as she noticed a sign for the Alpha Suffrage Club.

We found our seats, people quieted down, and an African American woman took the stage. Beside me, Ruby whispered something under her breath.

I whispered back, "What?"

"That's Ida B. Wells!"

Ida B. Wells-Barnett's demeanor was a mix of a schoolteacher and a southern preacher. She wasn't a tall person, but somehow, she commanded a presence unlike anyone I'd seen before.

She spoke for half an hour, and I sat almost motionless, drinking it in. I wasn't the only one. Ruby sat beside me, sitting up straighter, smiling as she listened.

The meeting broke up, people greeted us, and we left after half an hour of visiting.

Aunt Eva explained the Alpha Suffrage Club held many beliefs and ideals other suffrage groups lacked. The group believed that all women, regardless of race, should have the right to vote alongside men.

Then she told us a story about Ida B. Wells as we began walking towards the bus stop.

After being elected president of the Alpha Suffrage Club, she took a group of sixty-five African American women from Illinois to march in a big parade in Washington. However, the National American Woman Suffrage Association didn't want to offend southern suffragists. They told Ida B. Wells to go to the end of the parade, in the segregated section for black women. She refused. No one listened to her except for two of her white colleagues, Belle Squire and Virginia Brooks. She waited until the Illinois group marched by to step out and take her place with Belle and Virginia."

Ruby sat up a little straighter. "She's a wonderful woman. I never thought I'd get to hear her in person."

I agreed. Ruby had spoken about Ida B. Wells several times.

Aunt Eva said, "Ida has spoken out on lynching, giving lectures all over Chicago. She says lynching killed 3,500 men, women, and children between 1885 and 1912."

I gasped. "People lynched women and children in the 1900s? And someone has been keeping track?" I asked, horrified.

Aunt Eva nodded, "Yes."

Ruby sighed. "I doubt you've read about it in your history books, Mary. Lots of bad things happen to people who look like me."

I didn't know what to say. Aunt Eva looked sad and angry as well.

We headed to one of Aunt Eva's favorite restaurants, called Frinches. As we walked into the small family diner, we saw a mix of races and ages. I recognized some faces of women who'd attended the meeting. They pushed together several long tables for us, and we enjoyed another good meal and lively conversation with Aunt Eva's friends.

Ruby and I enjoyed talking to women who believed what we did—women not only needed the vote, but they also needed to have more of a say in our government. Aunt Eva later told me that Frinches restaurant in Chicago was owned by an African American family and was one of the first integrated restaurants.

We took a bus to the Art Institute of Chicago. For three hours we admired sculptures, paintings, and a collection of war posters. Then we stopped at the museum gift shop and spent another half an hour there. Ruby and I had a shopping bag of books and gifts when we left.

I'd visited Chicago before. The noise of downtown traffic and the hustle and bustle of people going to shops, restaurants, office buildings, and museums overwhelmed me. It was difficult to ignore the sense of excitement being downtown. I preferred Jubilee Junction, but it was fun to spend time with Aunt Eva and Ruby. And I'd enjoyed meeting other women like Aunt Eva who believed women should be able to vote.

Thirty-three

The Twins interrupt Wedding Prep
Gracie

"We have a secret in our culture, and it's not that birth is painful. It's that women are strong."

~Laura Stavoe Harm

July 25th, Thursday

Almost three weeks before her due date, Kathy's water broke. Mark rushed her to the hospital, with her mother following them in her car. Fortunately, they'd packed Kathy's Go-Bag the previous week at her mother's urging. Her father, Ken, called us, trying not to panic, because Mark gave him a list of chores needing to be done.

My parents, David, and I drove over to help. There we waited for word on Kathy and the babies. Uncle Vern and Aunt Maggie drove over to see if they could help. We fed and watered the animals, watered the extensive garden, and checked chores off the list. The dogs followed us around the farm and reminded us to feed them.

We knew Kathy would most likely have a C section. No one knew the gender of the babies yet, so there was a stack of neutral onesies upstairs. The last sonogram showed a girl, with the second baby hiding, so would she deliver two girls? A boy and a girl?

Aunt Maggie, Mom and I walked up to the nursery and fussed around. Mom and Aunt Maggie put sheets on the crib mattresses. I grabbed packages of baby wipes for the two changing tables and made sure the newborn size diapers were handy. We'd painted the nursery a very pale green with a fun mural on one wall with trees, birds, squirrels, dogs, and cats. It was a scene from a park, adding Chewie and Han Solo. Kathy had sketched it on a large piece of poster board, and Katie had drawn it on the wall and painted it.

Mom got a text from Mark. "The babies are here!" she announced, and we walked downstairs to share the news.

The men were sitting around the kitchen table drinking coffee. Chewie and Han Solo rested beside Ken's feet. They looked up, sensing our excitement.

"Mark just sent a text," Mom announced, a little out of breath. "The babies are here. A boy and a girl. They're debating names. They were almost five pounds each, and they're breathing just fine. Kathy is recovering from the C-section, and she's resting."

The rest of us sighed, expressing our relief. The grandparents grinned and congratulated each other. Chewie got up, yipped softly, and moved closer to Ken, who reached over and patted him. Han Solo, not to be outdone, crowded Chewie and begged for attention. Ken chuckled and patted Han Solo.

Mom's phone pinged with pictures of the babies. Mark held them near Kathy, and they seemed tiny but sturdy. One of them was howling and one looked sleepy. Both had dark blonde hair. Kathy's face was pale, and her facial expression made me take a second look. Where was my sister-in-law who wanted to meet her babies?

We all looked at the picture and said "Ahhhh," the typical nonsense you see when adults admire newborns.

David spoke up as the experienced uncle. "They'll get better looking, you know, and better behaved. It's traumatic to leave their safe place and be pushed into this noisy, bright world."

Mom and Aunt Maggie beamed at him. My Uncle Vern, Dad, and Ken looked at each other and chuckled.

The next text offered us a better photo of the babies and their names—Sophie wrapped up in a pink blanket and Sean wrapped in a blue blanket. We could see little wisps of golden red curls.

David informed us that swaddling soothed newborn babies.

The staff requested we wait until the following day to visit. The babies were being monitored overnight since they were premature.

Kathy was exhausted and didn't want to see anyone yet. Mark was spending the night. My dad drove with Ken to the hospital to pick up Katie and took a few things for Mark. In the meantime, Mom ordered several pizzas and put together a simple salad.

Dad and Ken returned with Katie and the pizzas. She showed us several more pictures of the twins. Mom pronounced them to be beautiful, hearty, healthy, and photogenic, even though they were not quite six hours old.

Katie told us they made Mark change into scrubs and wait until they'd settled Kathy in the OR. When he came in, he stood by Kathy's head, behind a screen that separated him from the sterile area where the Cesarean was being performed.

"As a farmer, he'd witnessed lots of animals give birth, but seeing Kathy go through this experience was moving. Given her previous history, they didn't want to try a vaginal delivery, so they got her prepped and into surgery within half an hour of arriving. After giving her a spinal block, the doctor made a small incision and lifted out the babies, the little girl first, and then her brother." Katie said.

Mark was proud of Kathy for the ordeal of the bedrest and putting her teaching career on hold to have these babies. He told Katie he was sure the twins would be their only children. And "Yes," she said, "He'd cried when he held the twins."

Soon, both grandmothers were embracing, laughing, and crying. Dad and Ken shook their heads and then shook hands. Uncle Vern and Aunt Maggie came over and hugged me. The dogs joined in the excitement and ran around the room.

Mom surveyed the cheerful group. "We'd better eat and then do those chores, folks."

During our meal, Katie informed us that Kathy and the babies will probably be in the hospital for three days. Kathy wanted to breastfeed, so the time in the hospital would give her some time with experienced lactation coaches.

We cleaned up and headed out to do some farm chores.

The following day, we visited Kathy and the babies. My parents were first in line, then Ken and Katie. Great-Grandma Molly and

Great-Grandpa Patrick arrived. Later, Aunt Violet, Aunt Maggie and Uncle Vern visited. Then it was our turn.

Kathy sat up in bed with Sophie in her arms, resting on a pillow, and Mark sat beside her, holding Sean. The babies wore ridiculously tiny onesies and were swaddled. Sophie wore a tiny pink bow in her hair, which was maybe two or three wisps. Sean was a feisty little guy, and both babies were very cute.

David and I didn't stay long because we could see the fatigue on both their faces. Kathy looked away when I tried to talk to her, answering in a monotone. I'd never seen my practical, cheerful sister-in-law like this before.

Like good soldiers, we drove out and did Mark's farm chores, along with both sets of parents. Thank goodness for clipboards and Uncle Vern, who supervised us. Our family had expanded, not only with the twins' arrival, but with Kathy's parents—good people.

However, Mom confided she was worried about Kathy, who seemed overwhelmed, weepy, and emotional during their visit. Katie was also worried. She reported Kathy struggled to hold the babies to breastfeed because her incision hurt, and she felt weak. Katie said Kathy worried she would drop the babies, didn't want to be alone with them, and worried she might not have enough milk to nurse them both.

Mom added, "It was unnerving to see her so upset. And of course, it rattled Mark."

David and I stopped by to check on them the next day. Kathy and the babies were sleeping. Mark stepped out to talk to us. He'd declined the offer of a cot and slept in the recliner in her room, but Kathy had been restless during the night, and the twins had come into feed several times. David left to get coffee to give me a minute alone with my brother.

Mark told me, "She's feeling overwhelmed, like it's all on her, but she has me and her parents, and others are going to help. I read up on postpartum depression and the baby blues last night, but I'm worried. We've waited for four years to be parents. What if she doesn't get better once we get them home?"

"Then we deal with it, Mark. Don't borrow trouble, as Grandma

Molly would say. Kathy's been through a double whammy. She carried twins through a high-risk pregnancy, and then she endured a C-section, which is a big deal. She's healing up from surgery, in pain, and weak. Kathy needs rest and time to recover from surgery. If she needs help, we will find someone who knows more about postpartum depression."

David brought coffee and a pastry for Mark, who accepted both. David heard the tail end of the conversation.

"Gracie's right. We're all going to help. My sister got depressed after her youngest child was born, and it was quite unexpected. I'm sure she would be happy to talk to Kathy when she's feeling up to it. Doesn't Kathy have a friend who's a counselor—Charlene?" He looked at Mark. "When was the last time you ate a hot meal? How about Gracie sitting with Kathy and I take you down to the cafeteria?"

I nodded and Mark gave in, thanking us and looking close to tears. I hugged him hard and whispered, "It's going to be okay, Mark," hoping I was right.

David and Mark headed for the cafeteria. David said, "I think the cows miss you. They mooed extra-long yesterday, and I was glad Uncle Vernon was there."

I sat in the chair by Kathy's bed and watched my sweet sister-in-law sleep. The twins were back in the nursery. Several times, she moved around and seemed in pain, her hand cradling her abdomen. I wondered how long it would take for her to recover from the C-section and baby blues, and be able to enjoy her babies? What would we do if she didn't get better?

Thirty-four

Collapse of a Trench
Mary

"We're telling lies; we know we're telling lies; we don't tell the public the truth, that we're losing more officers than the Germans, and that it's impossible to get through on the Western Front."
~Lord Rothermere, 1917

"As I watch'd the ploughman ploughing,
Or the sower sowing in the fields, or the harvester harvesting,
I saw there too, O life and death, your analogies;
(Life, life is the tillage, and Death is the harvest according.)"
~Walt Whitman, Leaves of Grass

Winter 1917

The women at the church put together holiday boxes for our soldiers. They'd been busy for months, knitting warm woolen socks, gloves, and scarves. Others donated bars of soap, washcloths, hard candy, tins of peaches, and candy canes. Our donation box at the store grew into four boxes. We boxed them up in October, to be sure they would get to the soldiers overseas.

Winter has overtaken fall, with light snow on the ground and Thanksgiving next week. Few of us are in the holiday spirit, but we've stocked red and green streamers at the store, a few Christmas decorations, and candy canes and ribbon candy.

The lumber yard has a few Christmas trees for sale, but so far, sales are down. People aren't sure that it's appropriate to celebrate.

Our butcher will have turkeys, chicken, and other meats next week.

The Jubilee River is frozen, but no one is ice skating. The town seems subdued. Many families have loved ones overseas and some families have two. Unfortunately, several families have already gotten a telegram with news of someone injured, missing, or dead.

The church choir plans to carry on without our missing members, but all the normal holiday festivities seem frivolous this year, and wrong. Pastor John says we must carry on, for the sake of the children. Even the children know this is not a normal holiday season, though.

We got through Thanksgiving with a family gathering, everyone bringing food. We exchanged many embraces and shed tears and sensed the comfort of getting together, but there were empty chairs and lapses in conversation. I missed my older brother's teasing, and I missed Charlie.

I felt guilty for having a good meal, a warm blanket on my bed, the calm of a winter snowfall, or the birds singing in the meadow. After all, why should I sleep in a comfortable bed while they huddle in a trench? Knowing they are almost certainly cold, wet, and miserable left me sad. But I knew I wasn't alone. Every mother, father, and sweetheart in the city was crying out for their loved ones.

Christmas was unbearable. Aidan was quiet as we continued our usual Christmas traditions, like decorating the tree, caroling, hanging stockings, singing hymns at church, and opening small presents. I talked to several of my friends, and our experience was typical across the city. There were too many empty chairs at the tables across Jubilee Junction, and too many broken hearts.

Then, early in 1918, we got bad news from France. Charlie's best friend, Frank, died while trying to help rescue a wounded soldier from a nearby section of the trench. The medic thought it would be safe, and Frank offered his help. Unfortunately, the shelling which injured the soldier also damaged the trench, and it collapsed on all three of them during the rescue efforts.

Hundreds of pounds of dirt, sandbags, wood, and debris rained down. Soldiers rushed to their rescue, but the men were lifeless by the time they'd dug them out. Charlie heard the commotion, came to help, and tried digging out his friend with his bare hands, but it was too late.

The news of Frank's death arrived in a telegram to the O'Connor's, and they came to see us that evening, to assure me Charlie was alright, but his best friend Frank was dead. They were going to visit Frank's family before publishing any information about his death in *The Jubilee Times*.

Mr. O'Connor described the incident to my parents as we sat in our living room. Shocked into silence, twisting my handkerchief in my hands, unaware of the tears streaming down my cheeks, I listened in horror. Charlie and Frank grew up together and had been best friends since they were little boys. Frank was a good young man and was always kind to me. This was a terrible blow for Charlie and all the boys from Jubilee Junction. But it was unbearable for his family.

"I know he's at war," Mrs. O'Connor said and shook her head. "But this is the first death Charlie has witnessed, and it's almost certainly not the last."

Anna and my younger brother listened from the landing on the stairs to the second-floor. Anna was a sensitive girl with a vivid imagination, and I knew she was imagining the nightmarish scene, as I was. Reaching out to touch a wounded soldier's arm, to help him to safety, only to unleash an avalanche of dirt, sandbags, wood, and other materials. Hopefully, it happened quickly, so he couldn't scream. Then, his mouth and nose clogged shut with dirt. Mercifully, the pressure pushed him down, down, down, into the collapsed trench, until there was no breath, no life. "Oh, dear Lord, please let it be quick. Let them not have suffered." Suddenly, I was breathing hard.

Mama looked over at me, concerned.

Anna gasped from the stairs, just as I restrained a gasp myself. My eyes filled with tears, and I nodded to Mr. and Mrs. O'Connor. "I'm so sorry."

I rushed up the steps to comfort Anna, who was sobbing, while Aidan, stricken, stared around, not sure what to do.

I led them into our bedroom, where I wrapped an arm around each one and drew them to me. "Hush, it's going to be alright."

Aidan cried, "What a stupid way to die! I hate this war." He liked Frank, who was a kind young man.

Anna sobbed. "He was helping the wounded soldier. He wasn't supposed to die."

Eventually, they calmed down, and Aidan became self-conscious. "I'm all right. I'm not a baby." He stood up. "Thanks, Mary."

Anna and I lay on my bed, not talking, taking comfort from each other like two small kittens. She got up, undressed, put on her nightgown, and crawled into her bed. Her tear-streaked face was still stricken.

I sat at my little table and took out the pictures and letters from my box. I read the letters and looked at the pictures. The man I loved was in harm's way, but he'd promised me he'd come home. I clung to the promise, even as my mind screamed I was foolish to believe it.

I put on my nightgown and lay in bed, where I pondered all the ways my Charlie might die. He might get shot going over the top of the trench to attack. He might get stabbed by a bayonet, or he might get sick from the foul air and soil. Charlie could get blown up by a bomb or gassed. He might get trench foot. Now I knew to add that Charlie could die in a trench collapse. Somehow, I'd never imagined the trenches themselves could kill our soldiers.

I prayed my nightly mantra, "Dear God, please protect Charlie, Liam, and Bruce," until I fell asleep. Tonight, I added prayers for the comfort of Frank's parents. I also prayed for Frank, hoping his last moments were brief, and he died without too much suffering. Would Charlie be alright? Would I ever see him again? My pillow was wet, and sleep would not come.

I willed myself to fall asleep. Then I felt a stab of fear in my gut, followed by a sensation unlike anything I'd felt before–the ground trembled beneath my feet. I thought I heard the roar of rushing dirt, boards, and men as I staggered backwards under some of the dirt that had spilled onto me. I smelled the packed earth and felt its grit on my body. Other soldiers hunkered down beside me, digging frantically in the dirt. I heard the whistle of ammunition in the air overhead. They were dragging out the bodies, now lifeless. Someone sobbed as I searched for Frank, for Bruce, Liam, and Charlie, but the air was smokey and I couldn't find them.

I called out their names over and over—

"Mary, are you alright?" Anna was leaning over my bed, her eyes enormous and bright blue, as she shook my shoulder.

When I woke, it was with the groggy sense of waking from a nightmare.

"You were calling out for Bruce and Liam, for Charlie–and for Frank—" Anna gulped. "And you were muttering about digging people out of the trenches."

I sat up, leaving the nightmare behind me. I shuddered and rubbed my forehead. Did it feel gritty? Trembling, I remembered the dirt shower, trench collapse, and three men's deaths.

Anna crawled into bed with me and lay down with me until I fell back asleep. I assured her I would be alright, but I was shivering. She grabbed the quilt and blanket off her bed, and lay back down and held me, covering us up. The extra blankets warmed me, and I fell into a deep, dreamless sleep.

Thirty-five

Families & Wedding Plans
Gracie

Love is always bestowed as a gift—freely, willingly, and without expectation…We don't love to be loved; we love to love.

~Leo Buscaglia

Some people go to priests; others to poetry; I to my friends.
~Virginia Woolf

The family was officially worried about Kathy. It had been three days, but Kathy cried whenever Mark left for coffee, when they brought the babies, and when they took the babies away. Kathy wanted Mark there, or her mother, or my mom, because she said she couldn't handle being alone with the twins. Kathy cried, saying she might drop a baby, and she worried she didn't have the milk to feed both twins. She cried because her incision hurt. She wanted Mark to leave, to go home and rest, but when he stood up, she cried, "No, don't leave me here, Mark."

The medical staff told Mark it was typical baby blues but times two, with the twins, and not to worry. However, Kathy was the most balanced, practical, optimistic person, and this was upsetting to Mark and both mothers.

Kathy and the babies came home a week after her C-section, but she was still healing. Her postpartum depression was now more evident. Kathy cried easily and struggled to lift the babies to nurse them, so having her mother there was a godsend. A visiting nurse/

lactation consultant came three times a week to check on her and the babies, who were gaining weight.

Mark was tired and discovered it was a full-time job managing the farm and taking care of Kathy and the babies. He was thankful for his parents-in-law, who had stepped up. People from both sides of the family brought evening meals for the first six weeks, and my Aunt Delores was the liaison with a list and worked with Katie to plan meals. Other people delivered groceries, helped clean and keep up with laundry, or held a fussy baby and let the caretakers have a nap.

Mark talked with David. He'd decided he needed to step back from the wedding. We turned to a candidate who was about the same size as Mark, Carl, so we didn't have to find pants, shirt, and bow tie at the last minute. David called him, and Carl readily agreed to help us.

Somehow, it was Wednesday night, and the wedding was this weekend.

Cornell arrived in Jubilee Junction on Thursday morning and checked in at the Jubilee Junction B & B. He and David had lunch that day, and he came over Thursday evening, along with the wedding party and our families, for a cookout instead of the traditional bachelor party and bachelorette party. The men took care of grilling, and we ordered salads and desserts from Aunt Shirley's.

David took the men to his garage to see his tools. They chatted before getting to work at the grill.

Meanwhile, Shelly and Tiara were up in my attic office admiring my workspace and the view from the windows. They came early to help.

Tiara mused, "It's still hard to believe you're living in your Aunt Vera's old house."

Shelly agreed. "This is nice up here. I wonder why Kathy didn't use this room. Of course, I liked the little desk in the kitchen, too."

"I like it up here," I told them. "Kathy kept busy with gardens and helped with the high school speech and debate program. She had very little free time."

While they were there, I showed them the red and white quilt

Grandma Mary made with her family. I passed out white cotton gloves, and we unfolded the quilt to admire it.

"It's lovely," Tiara said. "Doesn't look like it ever got used."

"That's what I thought," I told them.

Shelly examined the quilt carefully. "We have one like this in my family, made about the same time. It shows considerable wear and tear compared to this one. Sad to think it might have stayed hidden if your cousin hadn't been cleaning the hope chest."

My mother came upstairs then. "People are arriving, Gracie. Why don't you girls come downstairs now?"

She saw the quilt, walked over to admire it, and looked thoughtful. "It's a shame to hide it back in that hope chest. I wonder what Angela plans to do with it? She never had children, so there's no daughter to pass it down to."

Shelly and Tiara nodded in agreement.

I realized then that I hadn't thought about giving back the quilt. It was so lovely. Shelly was right—it shouldn't go back to its hiding place in the hope chest's false bottom.

Mom watched as we folded it up and put it back in its protective case. Then we went downstairs.

People wanted tours of our farmhouse, admired the cat tree and Agatha, of course, and loved David's office and my attic study. Agatha decided she didn't want to be petted anymore and retreated to the top of the cat tree.

Tiara and Cornell talked with Carl and Shelly. Shelly's husband, Seth, chatted with David's brother, Alex, about sports as they tended the grill with David. David's sister, Joanna, and her husband, Jared, acted as bartenders, although most people enjoyed beer, soda, or wine coolers. We weren't a hard liquor crowd.

A new Suburban pulled up, and Mark, Kathy, her parents, and the twins arrived. The two grandfathers helped unload several contraptions from the car, and soon Kathy joined us, seated on a folding chair with a padded seat.

Mark carried one baby car seat and his mom-in-law, Katie, carried the other one. Ken and Dad set up a portable crib near Kathy and placed several diaper bags nearby. Mark and Katie took the babies out of the car seats and placed them in the portable crib on a blanket.

Everyone gathered around the babies except for the men tending the grills, and there were the predictable "ohs" and "ahs" at the three-week-old twins and congratulations for their tired but happy parents and grandparents. Sean wore an adorable blue onesie, and his sister Sophie wore an equally adorable pink onesie.

I walked back in to grab some tongs and a platter for the cooked brats and burgers when I saw Mom and David's mom in the kitchen talking with Grandma Molly, Aunt Maggie, and Aunt Violet. Their backs were to me as they walked toward the living room.

I grabbed the tongs and reached for the platter from the island when I heard Mom say, "Of course, when they have a baby, David's office would be a great nursery, and then he can use the basement room for an office." David's mom agreed, and Grandma Molly and the aunts murmured.

I thought, *What? A baby?* I stood there, holding the tongs and platter for a moment, flustered. *Yeah, technically, I want a baby with David, but we just got married.*

I stepped back outside, caught David's attention, and mouthed "Baby," and he looked puzzled. I handed him the tongs and platter, and told him, "Our moms, Grandma Molly, and the aunts are taking a tour and deciding where to put our future baby—and your office—someday." My voice came out higher than normal, almost squeaky and in a scandalized tone.

David grinned. "So? You're surprised?"

Shelly's husband, Seth, and David's brother looked up.

"You got news for us, bro?" Alex asked as he flipped burgers.

"No news. The mothers and aunts are just plotting where we'll all fit someday," David told him.

The men snorted.

David chuckled. "Don't stress, Gracie. This is fun, right? Our families and friends are here and we're going to renew our vows this weekend." He gave me a long kiss that had Alex hooting and Seth protesting, "Hey you two, get a room."

It must have been some kiss because I relaxed.

We had plenty of food. Aunt Shirley sent big pans with ice for the three-bean salad, potato salad, and coleslaw. She'd piled fresh fruit on another platter. The condiments, plastic plates, napkins, and silverware were all in place.

David yelled, "Hey, come on and eat, folks." He raised a spatula and greeted Mark and Kathy, Ken, and Katie.

The men had set up several long tables and chairs, and Kathy's father, Ken, walked back to the Suburban and produced a small side table for Kathy. Mark came to check on Kathy, leaned down, and gave her a kiss.

"I'll be back with food," he said. The dogs had been checking out the guests, collecting pats and scratches behind their ears. They sat down beside the twins and Kathy protectively.

I leaned down to talk to the babies. "As the beautiful bride-to-be, how do I compete with your cuteness?" I touched Sophie's little foot and then Sean's. They burbled up at me.

I touched Kathy's arm. "How are you today? I'm so glad you came."

She tried to smile, but I could see the fatigue—and something else—in her eyes. "I'm tired, but my parents and Mark have been incredible. I'm breastfeeding, and everyone else changes diapers, even Dad. With two babies, you wouldn't believe how many diapers and onesies we go through in a day. The family has helped so much with meals, groceries, and I don't know how we would have done it without them."

Kathy glanced over at the babies and brushed away tears. She looked around to see if anyone noticed. I handed her a tissue pack and shifted so I blocked the view and talked to the babies, who were quiet and wiggling around. Han Solo whined, stood up, and moved over to her, nuzzling her hand. She looked down and petted him.

After a minute, Kathy told me, "Right now, it seems like all I do is sleep, feed, and cry. My mother tells me it's going to be okay and so does Becky." She paused. "Did you know some women can feed both babies at one time? Can you imagine? It's like holding two footballs. I haven't mastered it yet. Anyway, go eat. Mark promised to get me food." It was the most I'd heard her say in weeks.

I shook my head. "I don't know if I can get the image out of my head. I'm imagining you in football gear, running onto the field, carrying the twins while you nurse them. It sounds like a competitive sport. Seriously, are there support groups for breastfeeding?"`

"Yes, a volunteer at the hospital belongs to a group called La Leche League, and she gave me her number, and I've talked to her a dozen times. She's wonderful. I also have Barb, a lactation counselor, checking on me. And Charlene stops over to check on me, so I'm okay. Go get your food."

I joined the line, and someone called out, "Hey, you're the bride. You can go to the front of the line." Soon, I was standing next to David, who beamed. A couple of people yelled, "Kiss her!" And he did.

We all grabbed food and then found places to sit. Grandpa Patrick said the blessing, and we dug in. Mark brought food over to Kathy. One table was right next to her, so she wasn't eating alone. I noticed Shelly sat down next to Kathy and gave her a small gift bag, and then slipped away. Everyone wanted to check out the twins and say hello to Mark and Kathy and meet her parents. The twins fell asleep, but still looked adorable. The dogs ate one or two hot dogs that fell to the ground and stayed by Kathy's side.

People hugged and congratulated us.

Mark talked with David and reported Kathy was doing somewhat better. Her crying jags were fewer, her counselor Barb was very helpful, the babies were thriving, and Kathy's parents were helpful. He said having evening meals delivered was a godsend.

Kathy and Mark were the first to leave, after many quiet hugs. They had lots of help to carry things to the car. Grandma Molly and Mom loaded them down with food. The babies woke up and cried when put back into their infant car seats and then surrendered to sleep. Their parents and grandparents seemed tired but cheerful, except for Kathy, who seemed drained.

Mom hugged Katie, and they talked before she got in the car. The fathers loaded the baby things in the back of the Suburban, and the dogs jumped in too. Ken was last. He smiled and said, "Congratulations, you two! We'll enjoy the leftovers tomorrow."

I leaned down to talk to Kathy once she was in the car and told her, "Thanks for coming." She didn't make eye contact. Mark grabbed her hand from the driver's seat. We exchanged glances and then he started the car. "Thanks, Gracie. Talk to you soon, sis. Great party, David."

Thirty-six

The Wedding
Gracie

"Love is patient, love is kind. It does not envy, it does not boast, it is not proud. It does not dishonor others, it is not self-seeking, it is not easily angered, it keeps no record of wrongs. Love does not delight in evil but rejoices with the truth. It always protects, always trusts, always hopes, always perseveres."

~1 Corinthians 13: 4–7 (NIV)

"The dress only means something if you want it to. What is important are the people behind it. When it comes to these things that are handed down from generation to generation, each woman leaves her own mark on it, so that it tells our story, stitch by stitch."

~Brenda Janowitz

After Mark and Kathy left, David and I discovered people had a fire going in the firepit that Mark built when they lived here. We sat by the fire and chatted, relaxed, and looked at the clear, beautiful sky together. Then we split up to talk to friends.

I saw David talking to his friend Cornell and gesturing and smiling. He was showing him where he and Mark planned to build a small gazebo, with a bigger one at Mark's new place.

A group of people had already gone inside to tackle cleaning up. The top priority was to take care of the leftovers so we could return Aunt Shirley's platters and bowls. We also wanted to send a few things home with my grandparents, Aunt Violet, Uncle Vern, and Aunt Maggie, who wouldn't be at the rehearsal dinner.

Grandma Molly, Aunt Violet, and Aunt Maggie sat at the big kitchen table dividing up leftover burgers, hot dogs, and salads.

Aunt Maggie looked over at me. "Kathy will be alright. Give her a few weeks. Your aunt and I have seen this before. In England, they kept a close eye on young mothers throughout pregnancy because some women started showing signs then."

Aunt Violet agreed. "We take pregnancy and childbirth for granted, but postpartum depression is more common than we think." She exhaled. "It's something else we stay too silent about. Kathy's one of the lucky ones, dear. She's getting help."

Grandma Molly nodded. "Violet's right. We need more funding for mental health services. Women have struggled with this for generations and relied on family. But some have suffered alone in silence. The League of Women Voters continues to advocate for increased funding for women's health and mental health."

Cornell and David were doing dishes and putting things away with Shelly and Tiara, who seemed to sparkle around Cornell. He was six foot two and a very handsome man.

Shelly came over to me. "I had an idea, and I hope you'll approve. I bought a copy of Brooke Shield's book about postpartum depression several years ago. Have you seen it? *Down Came the Rain: My Journey Through Postpartum Depression.* I'd gotten it for a book club. I thought it might help Kathy."

"That's what was in the gift bag? I wondered. Yes, great idea. Thank you."

"The twins are cute, but she wasn't herself." Shelly gave me a kind look as she handed me serving platters to put aside for Aunt Shirley. Tiara came to help, and soon we had an assembly line and finished. My parents would return them.

David and Cornell sat at the table having one last piece of chocolate cake. Cornell asked, "David told me your family is one of the founding families of Jubilee Junction. I can't imagine that. But how are you feeling about the change of venue for the wedding?"

"Yes, it's fine. I'm an O'Connor, but I have Carlson and Nelson cousins. The Founder's House is the next best place for our wedding. The three founding families of Jubilee Junction valued education and wanted their children and grandchildren to have more education than they did. Nelson Hall started as a teacher's normal college and became a general education two-year college. Carlson Hall started as a nursing school and offered other hands-on courses in the medical field. O'Connor Hall offered metal working/blacksmithing back in the day, as well as agricultural courses, auto repair, and welding."

After everyone left, David and I collapsed on the couch and kissed. I cuddled on his shoulder as Agatha jumped down from the cat tree, running around as if to say, "Oh, good, they're all gone." We laughed at her and went to bed.

The rehearsal dinner Friday night was for the bridal party, parents and immediate families, and Judge Nelson. We walked through the rehearsal at the Founder's House before enjoying a simple salad bar and soup meal. Then our wedding party came over to our house to play board games, talk, and have fun. Joanna's husband, Jared, came along as well as Shelly's husband, Seth.

We set out a stack of board games: *Ticket to Ride*, *Settlers of Catan*, *Madeira*, *Francis Drake*, and *Apples to Apples*. Groups played at the kitchen table, the dining room table, the kitchen island, and the coffee table. We served popcorn with M&M's, brownies, assorted soft drinks, and beer.

Saturday morning, I got up, showered, and did minimal fussing with my hair, knowing Shelly or Joanna would help later. After sending a text to our mothers, we left food and water for Agatha who was up in the cat tree looking out the window for birds.

We packed up our wedding gear, looked at our checklists, and drove to the college around 1:00 where we met our crew at the Founder's House. The women and I headed in one direction, and David and the men went in another one. The wedding started at 3:00.

David kissed me passionately before he followed Alex, Cornell, and Carl. "See you later, Gracie. I'll be the one waiting at the altar."

"I'll be the one in the wedding dress."

My cousins from the floral shop were there, putting final touches on the gazebo in the courtyard. They had lined up chairs with an aisle in the middle.

We'd found an adorable little flower girl dress for Daisy, and Jack wore a nice shirt, tiny bow tie, dress pants and suspenders. Both children were super excited. All too soon, it was time.

Shelly was fluffing out my curls and repositioning the veil when Mark and Kathy and their entourage arrived. Someone brought along an old-fashioned baby buggy big enough for the babies. The grandmothers hovered, and David's mother joined them, as Ken and Mark got the babies out of their car seats and into the baby buggy. Kathy still looked fragile, not making eye contact with anyone.

The photographer took a lot of pictures, and I hoped Dad could keep it together for the ceremony. He'd teared up during the rehearsal the night before.

The music started, and Dad and I watched Cornell, Alex, and Carl take their places in front with David and Judge Carlson. Tiara, Joanna, and Shelly walked down the aisle. Daisy and Jack walked behind Joanna and in front of Tiara, who tried not to giggle. Daisy sprinkled flowers here and there on the aisle and hummed along to the piano music. Jack carried the pillow with the rings, and stage whispered, "I have the rings," showing them off to people on either side.

Dad whispered to me, "Vaudeville actor W. C. Fields said never work with children or animals. He may have been right." The crowd loved it, however.

By the time "The Wedding March" played, I was ready to run down the aisle, too, but forced myself to walk sedately with Dad. I loved the way the 1940s gown felt, with its sweetheart neckline and satiny fabric. The dress had a short train and was elegant and swishy against my legs.

I saw Mark chuckling while Kathy gently rocked the buggy from her chair. Her parents stood nearby, poised to help, and David's parents sat beside them with Mom. The dogs were there too, and Chewie kept his snout up on Kathy's lap. Our parents were smiling, and our friends laughing at Jack and Daisy's antics. Uncle Vern, Aunt Maggie, and Aunt Violet sat in the second row, behind my parents, along with Grandma Molly and Grandpa, and his three sisters. They were all smiling or chuckling.

Dad and I reached the front, inside the gazebo. Joanna now held her daughter's hand. Jack hopped around until Uncle Alex reached out and took his hand.

David smiled and mouthed, "You look beautiful. I love you."

Judge Nelson smiled at us and began the ceremony.

David and I said our vows and exchanged rings, which depressed Jack, since he was no longer needed. He held the empty ring pillow upside down, looking dejected. Then he saw his sister still had some rose petals left in her little basket.

Daisy saw he was sad. She handed him a handful of rose petals. "Don't be sad, Jack. You can help me with the rest of the rose petals," so they flung the remaining petals all over the wedding party, including the Judge, and that cheered them up. More laughter erupted from the crowd, some from the wedding party, and I was giggling, too.

Then it didn't matter. Judge Nelson ignored the giggles. "You may now kiss your bride," he told David with considerable dignity, and I noticed a rose petal or two on his robe.

David kissed me passionately and whispered, "I love you, Gracie. Here's to more adventures."

"I love you too, David," I told him.

As we walked down the aisle, man and wife—again—I realized I was the happiest I'd ever been.

Aunt Violet came up and embraced me while David and his parents exchanged hugs. "You're a beautiful bride, Gracie. The dress looks just as pretty on you as it did on my sister, Grace."

"This was Grandma Grace's wedding dress? Why didn't anyone tell me?" I asked her, taken aback. Then I remembered my first sight of the dress—trying it on—and knowing it was the right one. Tears glistened, and David, turning towards us, noticed.

"We wanted you to pick the one you liked and felt special wearing," Aunt Violet replied.

I hugged her as Grandma Molly, Aunt Maggie, and Mom walked up, then David's parents. Grandma Grace had died three years ago, but I sensed her spirit with us today, and her blessing. She would have loved David.

Thirty-seven

Charlie Dies
Mary

"Only the dead have seen the end of war."
~George Santayana, 1922

March 1918

New Year's Eve came and went, and 1918 brought fewer, and shorter, letters from Charlie and Bruce. The warfare became intense, as the newspaper headlines reminded us.

My family carried on with our usual daily routines, eating meals together and discussing local news, all while pretending that everything was fine. However, we've lived with uncertainty and fear for months and months, since the boys deployed. As February turns to March, something changes inside me.

I wake up day after day, feeling terrified. I go to work, answer questions from customers, ring up their groceries, and try to put a smile on my face. Food tastes like sand to me. Not even the chocolate drops I love can bring any pleasure. Somehow, I know bad news is coming.

The hammer hit on a dreary day, March 21, 1918. A young teenage boy with a serious manner comes into the store, holding a small envelope. He looks around, finds my father, and hands it to him while I'm ringing up a sale and bagging groceries for Mr. Phelps. He pays me, thanks me, and walks towards the doors.

Papa opens the envelope and reads the telegram inside. He thanks the boy, gives him a coin, and goes into his office, and sits down. He calls me over and says, "We must be strong," while he hands me the telegram.

My heart pounds and I think something has happened to my beloved older brother. Then I stare at the telegram, trying to make sense of its message. I cannot comprehend the words. If I read these words, they are real—and my Charlie is dead.

I hand the telegram back to him and turn to go back to work.

Papa stands and draws me to him in a hug. I break—I sob—I scream. I would have fallen to the floor had he not been there, holding me up. The telegram makes no sense. How could Charlie die like that—running out into no-man's-land and being shot?

Grandma rushes back to us. Grandpa, who was stocking shelves, turns and looks at us in concern. My father shakes his head. I fall sobbing into Grandma's arms. She sooths me.

My father says quietly, "I must go check on the O'Connor family. I will be back." He takes back the telegram I have been clutching in my hand.

Our other checker, Mrs. Smith, looks concerned. He tells her he will be back, and she and Grandpa are in charge. A customer walks in the store, and Grandpa goes to help her.

My grandmother shuts the door to my father's office. She calls my mother, and she and Grandma take me home in Grandma's big buggy. I lie in bed and weep, unable to be consoled. My universe has been shaken, torn apart, and destroyed. I cannot stop weeping.

Every night, Anna comes to my bed, crawls in, and holds me, saying nothing. There are no words left to say.

Pastor John visits. He and his wife read me scriptures, prayed with me, and told me I am young, and Charlie is in heaven, and someday I will see him again.

Of course, I don't want to listen. I want to scream at them, "I want Charlie back now. I don't care about heaven," but I don't dare say such wicked things out loud. I nod and try to endure their visit, and not cry until they are gone.

My faith has been shaken. I am on a floating island of grief, with enormous waves threatening to take me under. God may exist, but I trusted Him with Charlie, and see how that turned out.

People come with food, flowers, and sympathy. My girlfriends from high school come up to my bedroom and try to comfort me. My best friend, Sara, tries to lure me downstairs to see people here to pay their respects. They can't reach through the fog of grief that envelops me. Nothing matters. I'm on the island. Can't they see? Sara leaves but promises to come back. I can see the confusion and hurt on her face because we've been best friends since sixth grade. But she can't reach me through my grief either.

Charlie's mother and father come over, and she comes up to my room and we weep together. She is the only one who understands the depth of my emotions. I love her, and she tells me she already thought of me as her future daughter. Now what?

We comforted each other for maybe an hour. It is as if she can walk onto the island and join me. My grief senses her grief. I loved Charlie for two years, when she loved him for almost two decades. I cannot imagine a mother's grief. We cry together over all we've lost—a wedding, anniversaries, babies, watching them grow up, and growing old together.

They're holding a memorial service, not a funeral, because the army has already buried Charlie in France. I won't go to the memorial because I cannot stand the thought of my grief laid bare in front of the town. I haven't dressed, combed my hair, or left the house in days.

My family attends the service, but Grandma stays home with me, bringing me tea, patting my back, and wiping my tears. My stoic, stern grandmother reveals her tender side, and it's comforting. I'm still on the island, in my fortress, but she is standing on the drawbridge, at least.

All I want is the impossible: turn back time and let Charlie stay in the trenches. Let him not do the stupid but brave thing and save him for me.

After a week of not leaving bed, sobbing constantly, and not wanting food, the doctor comes. He tries to talk to me and checks me over. I'm not interested in talking to him. He can't bring my

Charlie back. *Go away.* I turn my back, weeping, retreating to my fortress.

He leaves, and I hear murmuring in the hallway as he talks with my parents, grandparents, and Anna. Later, I find out he tells them I'm suffering from severe depression, and there is little they can do. He'll check back on me in a few weeks.

After two weeks, I'm pale, shaky, and thin. I'm not sleeping much. Mama and Grandma try to make me eat, fixing my favorite dishes, and I have no interest. They come upstairs with a bowl and spoon, and a hopeful look on their faces. "Just try this, Mary. You've always loved it."

When I taste it, it tastes like the sand surrounding me on the island. I'm confused. How did the sand get into my mother's kitchen? I try to be polite, but after a bite, I'm done. I don't want to dress, wash up, or leave our room. It is my sanctuary.

The only thing I tolerate is tea because it doesn't taste like sand. I drink cup after cup of tea.

When I sleep, sometimes Charlie comes to me in dreams, holds me, comforts me, and tells me not to cry. Then I cry when I wake up because he's gone. He's dead again.

One day, almost three weeks after Charlie died, Anna goes out to check for mail and returns with a handful of letters. I hear her steps on the stairs. As she enters the room, she examines me, judging my mood.

"I didn't know if I should hide these," she confesses.

I held out my hand.

Three are from Charlie, delayed. I set them aside, knowing they will make me cry. Another letter has an unknown name on the return address. I held it for a moment. Reaching over for my letter opener, I slit open the envelope and removed a single sheet of paper.

Dear Mary,

You should hate me. You probably do. Your fiancé, Charles O'Connor, died saving my life and the life of my patient. I'm a medic and was assigned to a field hospital close to the front. We got a message saying a young soldier panicked, climbed over the top of the trench, and ran out onto no-man's-land. The Germans shot him, but he was still alive. I saw him struggling to crawl back to the safety of the trench.

So, I ran out, hoping to drag him to safety. I nearly made it, and then someone shot me in the hip. We were at the mercy of the Germans in no-man's-land. Then, a young man was there. He put the patient over his back and grabbed me. "Let's go." We did, thank God. He lifted the young man up and several soldiers reached for him, bringing him to safety. He lifted me up, and soldiers grabbed me. Then, a shot rang out and hit the young man as he climbed back over the top of the trench.

He collapsed once inside and gestured to me. I leaned down. "Tell Mary I'm sorry." He handed me something—a leather wallet on a chain. There was a photograph of the young man with a beautiful woman inside. He smiled, and I bent down and examined him, starting first aid.

I stayed with him while they moved the young soldier he'd saved and taken him to the field hospital. They came for Charles, but he was too far gone. So, I talked to him, telling him he was loved and thanking him for saving my life and the life of my patient. I tried to stop the bleeding and stabilize him, but he died a few minutes later.

I found your letter and an envelope in the wallet, with a return address, and had to reach out because I owe you a debt I can never pay.

Charles loved you. He died with your picture in his hand, and your most recent letter. Please give his family my condolences as well.

I am truly sorry for the pain you are suffering. Charles was a hero, and a remarkable young man.

Yours truly,
Gregory Barrons"

I read the letter over and over. "Anna, come here." I handed the letter to her. She read it, paled, sat down on her bed, and read it again.

She looked up at me. "Charlie wasn't alone when he died. And he died thinking about you…"

She burst into tears, and I went to her, and we embraced and cried together.

Charlie hadn't died alone. Gregory had been there with him.

Thirty-eight

Letters from Gregory
Mary

"Our silence about grief serves no one. We can't heal if we can't grieve; we can't forgive if we can't grieve. We run from grief because loss scares us, yet our hearts reach toward grief because the broken parts want to mend. C.S. Lewis wrote, 'No one ever told me that grief felt so like fear.' We can't rise strong when we're on the run."

~C.S. Lewis & Brené Brown

The island stopped moving. I saw solid ground ahead. I stepped forward, waiting for the land to rock back and forth, for waves of grief to follow me onto shore. Anna urged me to put on a robe and my slippers, and I did, feeling shaky.

We walked downstairs and showed the letter to my parents, who were surprised to see me outside my bedroom. My father stood and put down the newspaper.

My mother came towards me, seeing my face, concerned.

They read the letter together then, and my father sighed.

"I would like to show this letter to Charlie's parents." He reached for his coat and hat. I was too numb to respond. He folded the letter back up, put it in the envelope, and put it into his inside jacket pocket.

My mother sat me down, heated soup, sliced bread, and put butter and jam on the table, and she and Anna sat and watched me eat it all. I was calmer, wondering if I'd cried all my tears. But the food still tasted not quite right, and I ate mechanically, knowing I needed to eat.

Afterwards, I washed my face and looked with disinterest at the dull young woman in the mirror, who looked like she'd lost her love and had no purpose in life. Anna stood behind me. She brushed my hair and handed me my toothbrush.

She led me into the parlor, a strange place to me now since I'd barely left my room in three weeks. I picked up my book, saw the letter from Charlie tucked inside, and tears trickled down. I tried to read it, but couldn't focus, rereading the same paragraph over and over. I laid it down.

Anna pretended to read, glancing up at me.

I realized I hadn't seen my younger brother Aidan in weeks and asked Anna about him. She hesitated and told me he was upset, and Grandma took him home with her.

Papa returned, handed me the letter. His eyes were red, and he looked tired, as did Mama and Anna. Had I ignored their grief and driven Aidan out of our home? I stood up, held out my arms, and said, "I'm sorry." My parents, Anna, and I embraced for a long time. Then we all sat down at the kitchen table.

Papa took off his glasses and wiped his eyes. "Dear girl, you've received a blow that would destroy many of us. But you're young, and you will go on."

I nodded dully, not convinced.

He cleared his throat. "The O'Connor's were very grateful for the letter, and to know Charlie died with someone so kind as this young medic. They wanted me to convey their thanks. It's been a difficult time for them."

I saw then how I'd surrounded myself with grief, built a fortress, walled myself up in it, and withdrawn from those who loved me. Looking back, I remembered grieving with Mrs. O'Connor and trying to imagine how my grief compared to hers as a mother. I thought of Charlie's father and saw how the grief might wreak havoc with their home, relationship, and family.

I decided not to be a burden to my family and loved ones. I'd lost Charlie, but he would always be with me.

The following week, I returned to the store to work. Everyone treated me kindly, but I couldn't respond. There was a wall between me and the rest of the world, and few could get through, except for Anna, Mama, Papa, and Grandma. Aidan came home, and I hugged him, apologizing for driving him away.

I got a second letter from Gregory. I'd written back to him and thanked him for his letter and telling me about Charlie's last moments. He wrote to me about his rehab in England. He also wanted me to know the patient that Charlie helped rescue had survived after several surgeries.

I thanked him for this news and his letter. Gregory wrote back, and for the next four months, I wrote to him once a week, and he wrote to me once a week. It was one of the few things I looked forward to, because Gregory was with Charlie when Charlie died.

Then Gregory wrote to tell me he was coming home and wanted to come see me, to pay his respects in person. I agreed, and we set a date. He'd arrive on the train to Jubilee Junction and only be in town for a few hours before the next train took him home.

My parents looked intrigued and puzzled.

"Why does he want to come?" Papa asked.

"To pay his respects in person."

They looked doubtful.

By now, I was tired of thinking about it. "I think he just wants to meet me."

I walked upstairs to bed but overheard them talking.

"Do you know if this is a romantic thing?" Papa asked.

Mama replied, "No, I'm sure it is not."

Upstairs, Anna and I overheard our parents talking and stared at each other. She'd matured over the past half year. Her sweet, compassionate nature manifested itself many times.

She came over to my bed, sat beside me, and leaned her head on my shoulder. "Don't worry. They'll be kind to Gregory. It's interesting he's coming all this way to see you. However, from everything you've told me, I think he feels guilty for Charlie's death and wants to comfort you."

I put my arm around my little sister.

"That's what I think too," I replied. "Thanks, Anna."

I was too tired to think about it further. Gregory was the last person to see Charlie alive. He was my last link to Charlie, who lay buried in a grave in France that I would never see; a grave that I could never visit and lay flowers on each May. I would never again embrace Charlie, kiss Charlie, or walk with Charlie. But I could visit with the man who was there with Charlie in his last moments. That would have to be enough.

Thirty-nine

Back to College
Gracie

"Bareness is often the first outline of strength not yet developed, holding within it the seeds of abundance."

~Ruth Suckow

David and I had been getting ready for the fall semester for weeks, as we updated syllabi, ran to the college with print jobs, and got ready for classes. Classes began after the wedding, but the semester started slowly in terms of committee meetings.

We compared notes the Sunday before classes began, posting a printout of our class schedules on the bulletin board hung above the little kitchen desk. It was bittersweet to clear off all the wedding to-do lists I'd thumbtacked to keep us on schedule. Now, we mused about posting our weekly menus there and putting mail and bills on the desk.

"I feel so grown up. I don't think I've ever thought ahead to what I would eat all week before," I confessed.

David looked reflective. "Yes, and it would help us generate a shopping list and a budget for groceries and eating out. We could eat at Aunt Shirley's once, have pizza or Chinese once a week, and actually cook the other nights."

I thought out loud. "Soup and salad, grilled cheese and soup, meatloaf, tacos, chili, burgers, and chicken fajitas. Yes, that sounds good. We can do this!"

I put my two small clipboards on the table, and we wrote out our first week of menus and shopping list.

I'd worked at the museum twenty hours a week since mid-July, and Carl and I were exploring a couple of ideas for the next exhibit. The 1920s hope chest and quilt seemed too personal, so I rejected the idea of using them for an exhibit of WWI era quilts. Besides that, we'd only located a handful of WWI quilts. I wanted to solve the puzzle, but not share it with the whole county.

I suggested telling the story of Jubilee Junction through an exhibit of wedding dresses over the past 150 years. We'd add audio clips of brides and relatives talking about the women who wore them. We might have enough quilts for an exhibit later of WWI quilts, but I didn't want to focus only on quilts, and Carl agreed.

I had been doing research about WWI and saw a great deal of potential for an exhibit down the road. Many stories emerged during the pandemic, the 19th Amendment, and the Great War. They showcased the courage of the Buffalo Soldiers, but also shed light on the ongoing discrimination faced by women and minorities. We would come back to that later and decide on our focus.

I wrote a column to explain my idea. I asked people to loan us wedding gowns for the exhibit. We needed a letter about the person who wore the dress, the approximate date, and any other details that would be useful. My family members told me I could use the dresses Mom had collected, and they would compose the histories of each one.

A few of my students from last semester showed up in another class I taught or caught me in the hallway to say how much they'd enjoyed the class. There were one or two fresh faces in the adjunct office. Tiara and I chatted a few times between classes, and Shelly and I talked a few times. The first few weeks of the semester were always a little more hectic as we figured out our new routines.

David and I were settled in by now, and enjoying the comfort of the farmhouse. And Agatha was happy with her new cat tree. Kathy and Mark were doing better with the help of her parents and our extended family. David was working on editing his book, so he was busy in his office. It was time for me to get back to work on Grandma Mary's hope chest and letters.

I remembered Great-Aunt Catharine had given me two boxes

of old family papers, and I'd only started looking at them. I found them down in the furnace room, carried them upstairs, and spread them out on the dining room table, to get an idea of what else was there. After an hour, I came up with several promising items—what looked like a diary and some additional letters. The other box was full of more contemporary things on top, and I would come back to it later.

I grabbed everything that seemed to be about Mary and her family. I put those documents into a large folder and put the rest of the box aside. For now, I wanted to read and scan the documents I'd found and share them with David, Carl, and Charlotte.

With the folder in my hand, I walked up to my attic office, where I found the packet of letters fanned out on my desk. I began reading them, starting from Letter Five.

Letter Five

> *Dearest Mary,*
> *This is my last letter from our training camp. We're all excited and trying to prepare ourselves for the next thing. I passed all my tests and so did Frank, Liam, and Bruce. We're still drilling twice a day and getting ready for a lot of travel. The doctors did another physical exam to be sure we were all fit for duty, and we all got a typhoid vaccine.*
> *We leave tomorrow morning on a train bound for New York City to board an ocean liner for France. It'll take us a day or two to get to New York and then the ocean voyage will take 16 days. Don't worry! We're going to be part of a large convoy of ships for protection.*
> *Our sergeant warned us we may get seasick on the ship. I hope not but it will be a new experience.*
> *But my letters will be delayed coming to you and your letters won't get to me for several weeks, so don't worry. We've learned how to put our gear together in the duffle bags, so I've just packed up everything for the trip.*
> *We'll see the country from onboard the train, which would be*

fun under different circumstances, especially if you were along. I've never taken a long train trip across the country. I've never been on such a large ship, so I'm trying to look forward to it. Frank agrees! We're going to have an adventure to talk about for the rest of our lives.

I'm taking my messenger bag along with stationery and pens to write to you on board the train and ship. Sorry for the quick letter. We're working hard, and I'm tired.

Thinking of you. I love you!

Your loving man,

Charlie

Letter Six

Dear Mary,

We're on the train, and I am scribbling this letter on my lap. So, I hope you can read it.

Traveling across the country by train is such an interesting experience.

In other circumstances, I would want to get out and explore a dozen places we've passed.

People are reading, napping, staring out the window, and talking around me.

Others are playing endless rounds of cards. Frank's half asleep from the rocking of the train.

We're someplace in Illinois or Indiana right now.

Some of my traveling companions are saying nothing, worried about what we'll face in France.

Frank and I are sitting together with Liam and Bruce.

They all send their greetings to you and your family.

We're looking forward to seeing New York City, even if just from the train.

We alternate between looking outside and chatting.

But for the past hour I've been half asleep, rocking with the train.

I close my eyes and I'm on the porch swing with you.

We're in the library, and I'm kissing your hand.

We're at your house, at our engagement party.
My imagination is a powerful weapon against despair.
I believe I will see you again.
We will marry, have children, and grow old together.
I promise.
They say our crossing the Atlantic will take about two weeks.
Thinking of you,
Love from your man,
Charlie

I sighed as I laid the letter down, my eyes filled with tears at the passion in those lines.

What would it be like to find such a wonderful young man, and then lose him? I think I knew why my Great Grandma Mary was sad. She'd lost her first love. Charlie died in the Great War.

Forty

Visit from Gregory
Mary

"Grief is not a disorder, a disease or a sign of weakness. It is an emotional, physical and spiritual necessity, the price you pay for love. The only cure for grief is to grieve."

~Earl Grollman

"I wish those people who talk about going on with this war whatever it costs could see the soldiers suffering from mustard gas poisoning. Great mustard-colored blisters, blind eyes, all sticky and stuck together, always fighting for breath, with voices a mere whisper, saying that their throats are closing, and they know they will choke."

~Nurse Vera Brittain, 1933

August 1918

The following week, Gregory came to visit.

We met him at the Jubilee Junction depot. As he stepped off the train, Gregory looked up and waved to me. He used a cane and walked slowly. My parents stepped forward and introduced themselves.

Gregory shook hands with my father, tipped his hat to my mother, and then looked at me. He was a handsome man, with dark blond hair and blue eyes filled with compassion and promising stories.

"Is there a diner or someplace we could sit down to talk?" He asked.

We walked around the corner to the Jubilee Café, where we ordered coffee and tea and chatted.

After taking a few sips of their coffee and making small talk, my parents got up to go see friends at a nearby table. Only Anna and I sat talking with Gregory. Aidan was spending the day with friends.

Gregory leaned forward.

"Mary, thank you for seeing me. I have something for you." He bent down, reached into his messenger bag, and put something on the table.

I gasped and reached out to touch it. It had survived the trenches, the battles. It was Charlie's wallet, complete with the chain. I opened it, and there were our pictures, a little folded, and inside the wallet was my last letter to Charlie. The wallet was battered and smelled of the earth. I held it close and tried not to cry in public. Anna put an arm around me.

Gregory said, "I thought you'd want this back, Mary. I didn't realize I had taken Charlie's wallet until I unpacked from my stay in rehab. Of course, I'd been shot, too, and was in shock. But I don't remember taking the wallet with me. I looked for ID, realized it was Charlie's, and found the letter with your address on the envelope. I debated about mailing it to you, but I decided bringing it to you in person was better because I wanted to meet you."

I couldn't speak for the tears filling my eyes.

Gregory looked at me with those kind eyes. "I heard they awarded Charlie two medals for his bravery."

Anna stepped in to give me the chance to compose myself. "Yes, a chaplain and a captain brought them to his parents' house. Mr. and Mrs. O'Connor asked Mary over to see them."

I took a big breath, wiped my eyes, and looked at Gregory. "Thank you for bringing this back to me. It means a great deal."

looked at his cane and asked, "How is your recovery coming?"

Gregory shifted his position in the chair and winced. "I'm doing much better, thanks. I can't return to the military as a medic, so I'm returning to medical school. I promised my father I would go back to medical school after the war. He's a surgeon."

At the mention of the word, *promise,* my eyes welled up with tears.

"Charlie promised me he would come home," I sobbed. Anna handed me a hankie.

Gregory didn't seem upset or surprised. He would make an excellent doctor. "Every soldier makes promises, knowing there's a chance he'll break them, because no one can guarantee he will survive war. I promised to return to my wife, Elizabeth, and because of Charlie's sacrifice, I'm on my way home to her."

He cleared his throat. "I wanted to give you the wallet in person, because I promised Charlie I'd find you. We gave him first aid until we could get him back to the field hospital, but it was clear he was dying. I held his hand and told him what a brave thing he'd done, and how much his family loved him."

My eyes filled. I clutched the wallet. Anna's arm around my shoulder comforted me and reminded me I was not alone.

I exhaled, held out my hand, shook his, and thanked Gregory for bringing me Charlie's wallet.

We sipped our tea and made small talk while I composed myself.

My parents came back, and we chatted until it was time for Gregory's train, and we walked him back to the station.

He seemed lighter, as if he'd fulfilled a promise and been relieved of a burden. Gregory thanked us for meeting him and lingered, shaking my hand. "Remember, Mary, Charlie loved you. He didn't break his promise. He tried his best, but he died a hero. I will always be grateful to him—and to you. Your letters helped me through my rehab overseas. Goodbye." He turned back to board, tipping his hat to us from the steps.

As we watched the train leave the station, I showed my parents the wallet, unable to speak.

"In all the confusion, he didn't realize he'd taken it," Anna explained. "He's married. The patient who Charlie saved made it, too. So two men go home to their families, because Charlie ran out into no-man's-land."

My father bent his head. "What an honorable young man."

But I withdrew to my fortress, clutching the wallet and putting it into my pocket, where I could touch it. It was the only piece of Charlie I had left, and I would cherish it always. I was quiet while

Anna remarked on the good fortune of Gregory finding my letter and writing to me.

Later, she and I walked out to the garden to pick flowers for the table. I watched her walk around, gathering blooms, and realized she had grown into a graceful young woman.

We still sew with Grandma, filling up my sister's hope chest with generous help from Mama and Grandma. I contribute pieces as well, but have given up on adding anything to my old hope chest. Charlie's dead, and I have no hope.

Then Papa brought my hope chest upstairs. I hadn't seen it for many months. He showed me something he's done. He created a false bottom, with a space below large enough for my lovely quilt and all the linens I'd worked on.

"Mary, keep your memories of Charlie, just like you'll keep your lovely quilt and all the other things you made with Grandma. But you must think of the future and not stay locked in the past," he told me.

I stared at him blankly. *What future? My future is gone. I'll die an old lady, alone, except perhaps for Anna, who will marry and have lots of babies I can hold and love.*

I stared at my hope chest again, resisting the urge to rub my hands across its lid. It seemed to emanate hopelessness now, emptiness, abandonment, and loneliness.

"He promised to come home to me, Papa." I sobbed like a small child.

Papa held me. "Dear girl, if he'd stayed in the trench, how do we know he wouldn't have been shot another day?"

I couldn't answer him. His truth shattered my fortress, however. My island was gone. I could no longer ignore the harm my isolation was causing those I loved. My hope chest stayed upstairs, next to Anna's, in the parlor. But I doubted I would put anything else in it, for fear it was cursed. After all, I'd used it to collect linens for my marriage to Charlie, and see how that turned out?

Forty-one

Tiara has Emergency Surgery
Gracie

"It is love and friendship, the sanctity and celebration of our relationships, that not only support a good life, but create one. Through friendships, we spark and inspire one another's ambitions."
~*Wallace Stegner*

Six weeks into the semester, I was in the adjunct office, preparing for my next class. A student ran in and said to come because Miss Tiara was in horrible pain and had collapsed in class.

I called 911 as I rushed into the classroom and found my friend on the floor, struggling to sit up, gripping her abdomen on one side and moaning.

Her students looked panicked. Several were kneeling on the floor near her.

I asked, "What speech are you working on? Go to the library and do research."

They left except for the young woman who came to get me. She was in tears.

"Miss Tiara, please don't die. You're my favorite teacher," she blurted out, and ran out of the classroom.

Tiara was in pain, but said, "Did you hear that girl?" She winced and panted in pain.

I held her hand and stroked her forehead, checking for a fever. "Tiara, hang in there. I called for help, and they're on their way. We shouldn't move you until the EMTs get here."

"Get my purse and go for your purse," she said, breathing hard. "I'm not going anywhere."

I ran back to the office and grabbed my purse and bags, tossing my travel mug in my tote bag. I saw Tiara's messenger bag, grabbed it, and went back into the classroom to check on her.

"How are you? I have your messenger bag. Where's your purse?"

Tiara pointed. I found it by the teacher's station at the front of the room, along with another messenger bag. I found her lesson plan on the podium, put it in the bag, and regrouped.

Tiara moaned. "You're a good friend, Gracie."

I called our department office to let them know what was going on and asked them to send my students to the library to do research. I sent a text to Shelly and David. Then I held Tiara's hand again, and we waited.

She shut her eyes against the pain and clenched my hand. I tried to make small talk but gave up, murmured a prayer, and hoped my hand would function later. She had an impressive grip.

The ambulance arrived and two EMTs loaded her onto a stretcher. They moved her to the ambulance, where they lifted her into the vehicle. She held out her hand to say goodbye, but I shook my head. "You aren't going anywhere without me." I attempted to step up to join her in the ambulance.

Unfortunately, carrying three messenger bags and two purses threatened my balance—and dignity—until one of the EMTs took the bags in one arm and lifted me up with the other. The doors closed, and I held onto my perch.

I watched as the young man and woman got an IV going, checked her vitals, and relayed the information to the hospital. Once there, they did a few tests, determining that it was her appendix.

She handed me her phone, told me her passcode, instructed me to not bother her daughters unless she was dying, and to call her Auntie Phoebe. So I did just that, and they wheeled her away. Tiara went in for emergency surgery, and Auntie Phoebe came to the hospital to sit with me. She was a spry elderly woman who was best friends with Tiara's grandmother. We sat in the waiting room together before she left, searching for coffee.

Meanwhile, I clutched Tiara's phone, her purse, my purse, and three messenger bags while trying not to cry. Shelly and David arrived. I'd been worrying about Tiara, and it seemed like I'd been at the hospital for hours.

They gave me a hug. Shelly found a tissue, and they both chuckled when I described the student telling her not to die because she was her favorite teacher.

Auntie Phoebe came back with coffee for us, and I gave mine to David. Shelly took Tiara's bags. My arms were numb from dragging two purses and three bags all over the hospital. We made introductions and sat down, and Auntie Phoebe took care of me, patted my hand, and told me it was going to be alright.

"Thank you," I said. "She's special, and I can't lose her."

Auntie Phoebe grinned. "Yes, I remember now. You're Gracie? The young quilt lady? And this must be Shelly? I've heard some stories about you three girls and your handsome husband." She smiled at David.

David perked up. Another woman over eighty had fallen for his charms.

Shelly smirked and handed me what I craved—a cold diet Dr Pepper.

We sat and talked and heard stories about Auntie Phoebe's best friend, Tiara's grandmother. They'd been friends for sixty years. I got out my notebook and scribbled a few notes.

Later, we visited Tiara in her hospital room, where we saw a tall, black man wearing scrubs talking to her.

I let her auntie go in first, then Auntie Phoebe waved us in.

The surgeon smiled. "You must be Gracie." He shook my hand, and I introduced David and Shelly.

"I'm Dr. Davis. She's going to be fine, but we're keeping her overnight," he said.

Tiara beamed up at him, and we could see she was still a little dopey from the anesthesia.

Tiara gestured for us to come closer. "Gracie and Shelly, I have to tell you this before I forget. After surgery, I woke up thinking, *I'm in God's hands,* and then I saw this little gray dove coming down to rest on my arm. My brain said, *those are the drugs*, but I swear, I sensed the pressure of its little feet. It cooed at me and then flew off, but I had this real peaceful feeling. When I woke up, the nurse was calling my name."

She asked the surgeon. "Do you hear this kind of thing often, Doctor Davis?"

He grinned. "No, can't say I do. Of course, my patients are unconscious while I'm doing surgery. I'll be back in the morning, Miss Tiara."

She waved to him, and he took his leave. However, I couldn't help but watch him walk away, along with Shelly, Tiara, and Auntie Phoebe. David pretended not to notice.

After the surgeon left, I handed Tiara her phone. "Wow, Dr. Davis—"I noticed her auntie listening—"looks, ah, very competent." Tiara grinned but winced.

David and Shelly glanced at each other. David ventured, "Would you classify him as a medical hottie?"The four of us women giggled like teenage girls in church, and David looked pleased.

"I'll see you tomorrow. Do you want a ride home?" I asked.

She nodded. "That sounds good. We can drop Auntie Phoebe off, too."

Her auntie told us, "I'm going to spend the night here, so I need to ask for a cot." She pressed the call button, and a young aide came in. They left together to get a cot.

"I thought it was Cornell at first. Crazy," I said.

Tiara said, "Cornell's a great guy. I liked him. He reminded me of Benjamin, my late husband. Cornell's called me a few times. But Cornell's in Chicago, and I'm here. I know nothing about this surgeon beyond his good looks, charm, and people skills, but I'd like to get to know him. Apparently, he's new to town and the hospital."

"Okay, get some sleep. We'll talk more later." I gave her a little kiss on the cheek. "A little gray dove, huh?"

Shelly patted her arm. "Yes. Get some rest."

David and I walked out, hand in hand, with Shelly, each of us carrying a messenger bag. "Good job, sweetie. You're one of the girls, now," I told him. Shelly hooted softly, and David grinned.

Forty-two

Gracie's Discovery
Gracie

"Friendship improves happiness and abates misery, by the doubling of our joy and the dividing of our grief."
~*Marcus Tullius Cicero*

*D*avid drove me back to the college to get my car. I followed him home. Once inside, I relaxed for a moment in David's arms.

"How are you doing, Gracie?" David asked.

"I'm worn out from sitting in the hospital. However, I needed to be there. Thanks for coming," I told him, lingering. He nodded and broke the embrace.

David set the table before he heated some soup. It was my job to make the salad, so I got to work. I filled two bowls with salad greens, baby tomatoes, chopped up green pepper, some cheddar cheese, and a few cucumber slices. I grabbed the dressings out of the refrigerator and the container of saltine crackers out of the cupboard.

David put two mugs of potato soup on the table, and I poured us each a tall glass of iced tea. We sat down, joined hands, and David said a simple blessing. Planning our week's meals together, making the shopping list, and preparing simple meals together had become part of our ritual.

After cleaning up, he gave me another hug and headed for his office, and I went to my attic office. I needed to finish a stack of student essays, but I reached for the big three-hole punched notebook with the letters. I read the next three, looking for clues.

Letter Seven

Dearest Mary,

We're onboard the most enormous ship that I have ever seen. It's magnificent, and I'd enjoy exploring it if we weren't on our way to war. We're on our way to England first and then to France.

This cruise ship is like a floating city with restaurants, shops, and a clinic. The Army converted it to a troopship with the restaurants made over into cafeterias. We have a commissary that sells things a soldier might need, like socks, stamps, chocolate bars, writing paper, and pens. The clinic is our Military Treatment Facilities, and we have a full staff of doctors and nurses, and they're needed.

Many people are seasick. Fortunately, so far, I am not. I take several walks on deck a day to breathe in the sweet smell of fresh, salty air. Frank is fine, but Bruce and Liam both struggled to keep down their lunches several times.

The Army converted the passengers' quarters into several large rooms on multiple decks. Our bunks are numbered at the end and stacked in the spaces below decks. People on top must scramble up a ladder to reach the bunk, but they can breathe a little more easily, not having someone on top of them. I'm on top. People on the bottom can just roll into their bunks, but must deal with a more constricted space.

All of us have small lockers at the end of the rows with our number and name. Your letters are with me, my darling girl, and I read them every day.

Thank you for the box with socks, crackers, writing paper and pens, jam, tins of fish, chocolate bars, soap, and washcloths. Liam, Bruce, and Frank all got boxes as well, so I suppose the church ladies were involved. Tell everyone thank you!

Love, Charlie

Letter Eight

My darling Mary,

It's been three days on board this ship, and when we get up on deck, it all looks the same to me.

Water, water, water. There's too much ocean, and no sign of land.

I strain my eyes but cannot see anything but water.

Frank comes up on deck with me. He laughs at me, but he's also eager to get off the ship.

We see other ships not far away, carrying more soldiers to war, so we know we aren't alone on this vast ocean and that is comforting. We're part of an enormous convoy of ships.

But you and home seem a million miles away.

Most of the men are over the seasickness, thank God.

But the smell of sickness is hard to ignore and lingers.

And, sometimes we hit a wave more roughly and must hold onto something.

The ship is enormous but no match for the ocean. It's humbling to experience the raw power of nature. Our officers look after us as best they can. Several of them have become ill as well. The more experienced men try to act professional and calm, while the rest of us are struggling to walk around the deck during rougher seas.

We eat, drill, attend classes, drill again, and spend the rest of the day reading, writing letters, and walking around the deck.

There's a library below deck, and I go there to read to pass the time. But I prefer to reread your letters and shut my eyes, pretending I'm just waking up and going to walk over to your house to see you.

Love, Charlie

Letter Nine

My darling Mary,

I'm now convinced I chose well in joining the Army.

I am sick of the ocean after more than a week at sea.

It's so vast, and it's taken so long to cross it.

I'm thankful to have a little more time to spend with my Jubilee Junction friends and our older brothers. But I'm ready to see land, instead of the endless stretch of ocean.

Frank and I are rather proud of our sea legs having taken many strolls on deck.

Classes continue, drills continue, and our officers promise us we'll see land soon.

Did I tell you that the Army sent us to war without our weapons? We're still drilling with long pieces of wood. They say that the manufacturers can't keep up with the demand. I guess war is good for business if you make guns and ammunition.

At night I hear others saying their prayers, and I do as well, of course. But every night I close my eyes and pretend I'm holding you in my arms under that tree out on the farm.

I've just kissed you and you're smiling at me, Mary, even if I'm just kissing your photo.

Love, Charlie

I sighed and looked at my stack of student essays. I wanted to read the next letter, but I needed to get busy with grading, so I turned on some music and lifted the first essay onto my desk.

Two hours passed, and I heard some meowing. Agatha was at the entrance to the room, looking around. I wondered why, because she had been in my office countless times since we'd moved in. She wandered around, making a funny noise deep in her throat, and stopped at the closet in the corner. I'd put a couple of small boxes on the floor in there but hadn't had time to do much more.

Now, curious, I walked over to the closet, looked down at her and said, "Okay, I'm not doing this for you. I've been meaning to organize this space," and opened the door. It was a simple closet with a hanging rod and a shelf above and a row of short shelves along the left side. Agatha walked inside and headed for the lowest shelf on the left side. She pawed at something, but I couldn't see what it was.

Curious, I got down on my knees to look and ran my hand along the length of the shelf. My fingertips brushed against something, so I leaned in more and grabbed it, wondering what it was.

I drew out a small photo. Intrigued, I turned it over and found an old-fashioned picture of a baby girl. *How long had it been stuck in a crevice in the closet? That must be my cousin Donna from the 1940s.*

This was her mother's house, after all. I put it on my desk and played with Agatha, who seemed pleased with herself. *So now my cat has some kind of detective skills?* But it gave me an idea. I wanted to search the hope chest again, and I wanted to look at the cardboard box. Had I missed something?

I walked downstairs holding the old photo and told David what had happened. Agatha followed me, heading for her cat tree.

David looked thoughtful. "I wonder if the false bottom comes out. All we did was lift the lid when I found the wallet. I didn't get a flashlight and look inside."

The next day, I went to the museum and examined the hope chest, getting help from Carl who carefully removed the false bottom. At first, I thought I was being foolish because the bottom seemed empty, but then we found a letter that had gotten separated from the packet, wedged in a corner.

Carl handed me a plastic protective sheet, and I slipped on my cotton gloves to pick it up, unfold it, and insert it into the sheet, my heart beating faster with the discovery.

I read it out loud.

Dear Mary,

I hope you will continue with the things we discussed.

When you get anxious, remember the breathing exercises we did together for anxiety.

Whenever you can, reframe your thoughts into positive statements.

Not, Emma is so little. What if I drop her?

But, Emma is growing bigger every day and I can take care of her. I'm her mother.

Remember, Mary, there is room in your heart for LOVE. Liam is steadfast.

Charlie would not want you to grieve him any longer.

He gives you permission to move on. He'd want you to be happy and to have someone love you.

Your body worked hard during your pregnancy and your mixed emotions are normal.

Feel the sadness, but don't welcome it into the room.
Speak it out loud and then add a sentence or two.
"My body is recovering from the hard work of making and having a baby.
What I'm feeling is normal.
I'm not crazy and I will not feel like this forever."
I'm praying for you, dear girl. I stopped by to say hello to Ruby at the Community Center and she's praying for you, too, and so is everyone else there.
She misses you and plans to stop by to see how you're doing soon.
I'll be back in a few weeks to see for myself how things are going.
Till then, be gentle to yourself and kiss that baby for me.
Hello to that handsome husband of yours.
Love, Aunt Eva

All of this was news to me. Mary suffered from postpartum depression? I knew her Aunt Eva was a nurse and visited when Mary was grieving Charlie's death, but nothing about this situation. I looked for a date and didn't find one. Apparently, her Aunt Eva worked with pregnant and young mothers in Chicago and was ahead of her time in understanding the disorder.

So, Mary had two reasons for being sad. She'd lost Charlie, her first love. Later, she married his older brother and had a child with him but sank into depression after giving birth.

I sat down, thinking, *Agatha's getting some extra treats tonight.*

Carl looked at me. "From your expression, this is a significant find?"

I was just about to explain when my phone rang. Lt. Carlson's voice was professional but concerned. "Gracie, we found another confederate flag planted in the pioneer cemetery with a note. 'This cemetery should be reserved only for real Americans–white men.' We're checking video footage and running license plates. For now, be careful. I'll get back to you when we know more."

I put the phone down, my heart thumping.

"Gracie? What's wrong?" Carl stood up.

"Someone—more White supremacists in the area—left a

confederate flag at the pioneer cemetery earlier this summer, when David and I were on our honeymoon. Ben Carlson contacted my father and Uncle Rich, and they cleaned it up. He or she, or they are back. This time they left a note complaining about Blacks being buried there."

Carl exhaled, sitting down. "Yes, I knew about the incident right after you left. But I didn't expect they'd be seen again. We need to take precautions, Gracie. I don't want you to be down in your workroom alone. You should take precautions at college, too."

And then I explained what I'd just realized. I knew why Grandma Mary had written her note. "Carl, I understand what happened to Mary now. She had two reasons for being sad. Yes, she'd lost her first love, Charlie. Later, she married his older brother and had a child with him, but sank into postpartum depression after giving birth. Her Aunt Eva, a nurse, helped her."

I grabbed a sheet protector, placed the letter inside, scanned it in, and then made several photocopies. I couldn't wait to show it to David, Mom and Dad, Charlotte, and Great-Aunt Catharine. This was the big break I'd been waiting to get. I pushed aside my anxiety at the idea of confronting more White Supremacists. There would be time to discuss that more with David.

While I worked, Carl called Ben to arrange for someone to patrol the museum in the afternoons. Next, he called David to check if we had any images of the big truck yet.

David's father had driven to Jubilee Junction with half a dozen surveillance cameras a couple of weekends earlier. He, David, Mark, and R. J. installed cameras at the cemetery, the newspaper office, at both farmhouses, and near the big sign, "Welcome to Jubilee Junction." Then David, Mark, or Dad could see the resulting video feed with a smartphone app or laptop. Unfortunately, Ben didn't have a readable license plate to run yet. Mud covered most of it.

Could anything else go wrong?

Forty-three

The Great Pandemic
Mary

"However, as bad as things were, the worst was yet to come, for germs would kill more people than bullets. By the time that last fever broke, and the last quarantine sign came down, the world had lost 3–5% of its population."

~Charles River

Life took on shades of gray, black, and white. I was working at the store, doing volunteer work, and determined not to be a burden to my family, my church, or my community. I only let myself cry at night.

My island was like a boat moored to the mainland. Each night, I went back out to sea, grieving for Charlie. I read and reread Charlie's letters. Six months had passed since he died, and my heart still ached, but he came to me in my dreams less and less.

And we had worse problems than grieving those we'd lost to the trenches.

A strange new sickness spread among the soldiers who were preparing to go overseas in 1918. While it was called the Spanish Flu, no one knew what it was or where it came from. During September and October 1918, several of our Jubilee Junction boys got sick at two training camps in Iowa and Kansas, even before leaving for France. A flu-like illness, it turned into pneumonia for some. Doctors were surprised by how quickly it progressed and had few tools to fight it. Two local boys died from it before they could set foot on the ships taking them to France.

Many of our soldiers deployed overseas got the flu, but we were shocked when Liam's girlfriend, Jane, an Army nurse, died of pneumonia. She'd worked overtime, trying to help staff the field hospital overrun with soldiers who were sick with the flu when she began coughing herself and collapsed. It was sudden, shocking, and devastating to Liam.

Charlie's parents came to our house with the news, the telegram in Mr. Connor's hands. They were deeply saddened.

His mother wept in my mother's arms. "Liam wrote this was the girl he would marry. He just knew it."

My mother comforted her. The two fathers exchanged silent glances. The war had taken this victim before we got to know her. Jane sounded like a lovely girl.

Later, we found out the flu killed more of our American soldiers and sailors than the bullets and weapons of the Germans.

The Jubilee Times would later report almost one million men in the army got sick with the flu, and 30,000 died.

Then the flu was no longer something only over there. People contracted the flu in this country, and doctors were baffled. There was little they could do beyond keeping patients comfortable with rest and a mild diet and hope their patients would not develop pneumonia.

During the fall of 1918, the Iowa Board of Health quarantined the state, forcing the closing of public gatherings at churches and schools alike. The store stayed open, but customers put their grocery orders into a box we'd installed on the front door.

My brother Aidan stepped up to help us at the store and make deliveries. Everyone wore masks. By mid-December, it was over, but it took a toll and left us all changed.

The state reported that almost 100,000 Iowans sickened, and 6,000 died in Iowa. However, medical authorities suggested the number of deaths was probably much higher. Besieged local doctors weren't required to report cases and lacked tests to verify the diagnosis. Doc Wilson was busy but credited the many local volunteers--women—for their help caring for the sick in Jubilee County. Even so, Jubilee Junction lost a dozen people, and the town was grieving.

The unsung heroes were the courageous women who visited house to house to check on neighbors, took them soup, washed their clothes, and tended their babies. One of them was our faithful clerk, Mrs. Smith, who died after taking care of her relatives. Now I handled the cash register by myself. Mrs. Smith was my mother's age, but she'd been kind to me, and I grieved for her passing.

Mother, her sister, her aunts, and her cousins checked on families, neighbors, and friends. The stories they told later were shocking, but they refused to see themselves as heroes. They cooked, cleaned, aired out houses, took care of babies, and found someone to do the outside chores. Doc Wilson joked he would like to kiss them all, but he would get in trouble with his wife—or their husbands.

In our household, Anna and Papa got sick, but thank God, both recovered—Anna first, but Papa was sick for several weeks. Aidan and I took care of them. Mama was away helping with a newborn and a sick mama. Our grandparents drove out to the farm to help with sick children and do chores. When they returned to town, Grandma got sick herself, and Grandpa cared for her.

The Pandemic hit us in two waves, and both times it exhausted our medical staff, filled our hospitals, and kept the funeral homes busy. Medical authorities declared it unsafe to hold traditional funerals, so families grieved alone. We heard stories about people dropping dead on the street in the bigger cities like Des Moines and Chicago.

It was hard for me to hold back tears when we could finally remove masks, go back to church, welcome shoppers, eat at the Jubilee Cafe, and greet each other on the street. We'd all been through such a terrible ordeal and were exhausted.

In the end, the Pandemic was just one more bad thing in a terrible year. It seemed cruel for so many soldiers and sailors to die before they made it to the battlefield. We learned how much we needed each other, how interconnected our lives were, and how much we took for granted.

As time passed, and Charlie came to me in my dreams less frequently, I tortured myself wondering if I could still remember his voice, his kiss, and his smile. I grieved, wondering how could I could love a man and yet forget his face and voice?

Forty-four

Visiting Aunt Catherine
Gracie

"After a good dinner one can forgive anybody, even one's own relations."
~Oscar Wilde

"I sustain myself with the love of a family."
~Maya Angelou

My mother called me into her office one morning at *The Jubilee Times.*

"I don't want to upset you, Gracie, but Aunt Catharine called us last night, and she claims she never expected Angela to give you her grandma's old hope chest and quilt. She wants to make sure that you won't parade them in an exhibit. Apparently, it came up in conversation after your wedding. Angela and Judd came back and were chatting with Vicky about it, and their mother got very upset."

"Paraded? So, what do you want me to do? Should I call her?" I asked.

Mom sighed. "Your father thinks we should go see her before she gets more riled up."

We left the office with Aunt Delores in charge. She raised her eyebrows and said, "Good luck."

We arrived at Aunt Catharine's beautiful Victorian home. Dad had called, so she was expecting us.

Aunt Catharine came to the door and welcomed us in. We sat

down in the living room. Her eyes were red-rimmed, and she was clutching a handkerchief.

Mom put her hand on her aunt's shoulder, trying to comfort her. "Aunt Catharine, we don't want you to worry about Grandma Mary's old hope chest. Gracie wants to explain what happened."

Aunt Catharine was upset. "I know what happened. My addled daughter gave Gracie the hope chest."

My parents exchanged worried looks.

I kneeled beside her chair. "Aunt Catharine, I would love to use Grandma Mary's wedding dress in the wedding dress exhibit. I loved wearing it this summer—but the hope chest and its contents are more personal, and I will not use them in any exhibit."

I took a breath and continued. "Angela asked me to find out more about the hope chest, so I've done some research and learned a great deal about Great-Grandma Mary. I don't have all the answers yet, but it has been interesting, and it's part of our family history."

Aunt Catharine looked at me. "You can use her wedding dress, but I want you to be respectful. My Great-Grandma Mary is dead and can't defend herself. Do we need to dig into all the unpleasant circumstances of her life? Do we have the right?"

I looked at my parents. "Aunt Catharine, Mary lost her first love, Charlie, in World War I. I wouldn't call her loss *unpleasant*. She grieved for him, and it sounds like she suffered from severe depression, which is a normal response to grief and nothing to be ashamed of."

Aunt Catharine persisted. "Do we need to tell everyone about her episode and every little detail of her life? Is it anyone's business? She was sad after Charlie died. And she was sad after her baby." She stopped talking and looked at me. "Do you know about her first child with Liam?"

"Yes, I found the diary, and Charlie's wallet in the box you gave me. She was sad after her first baby was born, her second child died, stillborn, and she experienced another episode of depression. Have you read it?"

"No, but I'd read a letter from an aunt a few years ago. I don't want her good name dragged in the mud because she was sad."

I looked at my mother.

Mom jumped in. "Aunt Catharine, women have had the baby blues for thousands of years, but we didn't know how to deal with it until more recently. Did you know our daughter-in-law, Kathy, suffered from postpartum depression after the birth of her twins? It is nothing to be ashamed of. It's a medical condition."

She looked at my father, who spoke up. "As a man, I know nothing about that form of depression. But I've grieved when my great-grandmother and grandparents died, and when my big brother died, and people will not think less of her, I promise you."

Aunt Catharine sighed. "Matthew, I appreciate everything you did for my grandson, Lance, and I don't know if I've thanked you properly. I'm sorry to drag you over here in the middle of the day. I'm an old woman, and I spend too much time alone, brooding, in this big house."

"You're welcome, Aunt Catharine. I was glad to do it. He's a good young man. Lance has been a great helper with the pioneer cemetery update. We don't want you to worry so much. I know my father is concerned about you."

He continued, "This is a lovely home, but it's large for one person. Have you ever thought of getting an apartment where your sister and Gracie's Aunt Violet live? They have lots of activities, meals, and a nurse on call. It's a great place."

Aunt Catharine hesitated. "Yes, I've been jealous of Violet and Trina. But it would take a lot of work to clear out this place, and what would happen to it?"

Mom spoke up, "You have family, remember? We'd help you move. After all, we're getting good at it, after helping Mark and Kathy move into Violet's old farmhouse. Then moving Gracie and David into Vera's old farmhouse. We could ask around the families and see if someone would want to make an offer."

Aunt Catharine looked thoughtful. "Victoria might even be interested. It's big enough to rent out some rooms to college students, and she has talked about doing that for years."

We visited a little while longer. Mom excused herself to use the restroom down the hallway, which I knew was her excuse to snoop around. We left a half hour later with Aunt Catharine in a better mood and promising to call the Prairie View senior living place to get on their list.

We made a quick call to Vikki to give her a heads-up. "We've been talking to her for three years about doing just that. Thank you! I will check in on her and call them myself."

Mom called in an early lunch order, and I ran in to get it at Aunt Shirley's.

When I got back in the car, Mom reported on her inspection of her aunt's house. "I think she's tired of climbing the steps to her upstairs bedroom. It looked like she was sleeping on the daybed in the first-floor bedroom. There were just a few dishes in the sink, and I peeked in the fridge and not a lot of stuff was there. Canned soup and cereal. I think we need a family conference call. I'm worried."

"I agree. I'll call my father and set it up." Dad looked resolved.

Once we got to the newspaper office, I ate a quick sandwich and packed up for the museum.

"It's funny how we think we're so advanced, isn't it?" I asked. "Mental illness is still taboo. People are still uncomfortable talking about it or acknowledging people in their family who struggled with depression. It's a hundred years later, and Aunt Catharine is still afraid people will judge her grandmother for being depressed."

Mom looked at me. "You're right. If we break a leg, we go to get help. But if we're sad or angry or brokenhearted, we suffer alone." Her eyes filled with tears, and I knew she was thinking of Kathy.

Dad came over and put his arms around her, and said, "Kathy's going to be fine."

I thought about the haunted look in Kathy's eyes. What was going on in her head? Was she getting all the help she needed?

Forty-five

The War Ends, November 11, 1918
Mary

"Yesterday I visited the battlefield of last year. The place was scarcely recognizable. Instead of a wilderness of ground torn up by shell, the ground was a garden of wildflowers and tall grasses. Most remarkable of all was the appearance of many thousands of white butterflies which fluttered around. It was as if the souls of the dead soldiers had come to haunt the spot where so many fell. It was eerie to see them. And the silence! It was so still that I could almost hear the beat of the butterflies' wings."
~Unnamed British officer, 1919

As the fall of 1918 continued, with the flu ravaging the country, one bright moment came on November 11, when the guns fell silent in France. According to articles in *The Jubilee Times*, The Great War lasted for four years, killed 8.5 million soldiers, and wounded another 21.2 million. In the end, the German Kaiser gave up his throne and fled to the Netherlands, a neutral country. The American soldiers had helped to win the war, but at a bloody cost. Those of us who'd lost a loved one wondered what the war accomplished, other than destruction, death, and despair?

Life returned to normal. Anna, Mama, and I resumed sewing with Grandma, who survived the bout of flu but seemed to tire more easily.

The weeks passed, and 1918 gave way to 1919. It would take many months for Bruce and our other boys from Jubilee Junction to return home onboard the large ships from overseas and then home by train. Papa said we must work hard and be patient.

In April, we got word our boys would be home in the next few months. Then, in June, a telegram arrived saying we should expect Bruce home on the train in three days. We cleaned the house, aired things out, and washed the bedding in Bruce's room.

Family members gathered at the Jubilee Depot. Papa left the clerk and Grandpa in charge of the store and walked with us to meet the noon train. Grandma was eager to see her grandson and joined us.

A dozen soldiers got off the train, and families greeted their boys. We saw the O'Connor family waiting just a few feet away, and Mrs. O'Connor smiled and waved at me.

I went over and embraced her, just as Charlie's older brother, Liam, stepped down from the train with his duffle bag. He was thinner but looked so much like my Charlie, my first impulse was to hug him. I didn't, of course.

He caught my eye, walked over, put his duffle bag down, and took both my hands in his. "How are you, Mary? I'm so sorry about Charlie. He loved you so much." His voice was husky with emotion.

I fought tears and told him I was sorry to hear about Jane as well. "I was looking forward to meeting her. She sounded like a lovely girl."

"She was. . ."

We stood there for a moment, staring at one another, still holding hands. Then I dropped his hands and stepped away. "Look at us. Your family is waiting." I nodded an apology to Mrs. O'Connor and walked away, just as Bruce got off the train, shouldering his duffle bag.

The tears came then, and I didn't turn around. Liam's parents greeted him, thankful he was home, safe and sound.

We greeted Bruce, and he hugged everyone, even Papa. He hugged me a moment longer and whispered, "Mary, how are you? I'm sorry about Charlie. We were in different sections of the trench, but I heard the shouting. He was a brave man."

I sniffled in response. Anna squealed, and he turned to her, with Aidan clamoring for attention.

My papa scolded, "Now settle down. Bruce just got home, and everyone wants to talk to him. You'll all get a chance." But his eyes were tender, and he fumbled with a hankie, wiping his eyes. "We're thankful you're home." He shook Bruce's hand, man to man.

My mother put her arms around me, and I sobbed against her shoulder, then got out my hankie and we left, the two mothers smiling at each other and the fathers nodding.

Bruce was thinner, so Mama and Grandma made it their mission to fatten him up. They made all his favorite dishes, and he was happy to indulge them.

"I missed your good cooking, " he told them as he ate whatever they put in front of him. "I dreamed about your cooking…" he faltered.

Grandma wiped her eyes on her apron as she stirred something on the stove.

Mother brought over a plate of fragrant brownies and set it down next to Bruce.

"We prayed for you every day. We sent as many boxes as they'd allow. I worried about what you were eating in that terrible place." Mother touched his shoulder.

Bruce reached for a brownie and thanked her. Our eyes met, and he turned away. I understood it was still too painful to talk about.

I climbed the stairs to our bedroom, got out my box of letters and photos, and sat there until Anna came looking for me.

"Mary, we're starting supper. Are you coming downstairs?" She took one look and crossed the room to embrace me because I'd started weeping again. Finding my hanky, I tried to dry my eyes, but the tears kept coming. *Am I a horrible person?* I was happy Liam and Bruce were home, but ached for Charlie's embrace. *He promised me, didn't he? We would be together now if he'd just stayed in the trenches.*

Forty-six

Liam and Mary Share a Bond
Mary

"Every man and woman who volunteered to serve this country should be treated with the same degree of respect, gratitude, and dignity."

~Mitt Romney

"The cries of the wounded had much diminished now, and as we staggered down the road, the reason was only too apparent, for the water was right over the tops of the shell-holes."
~Captain Edwin Vaughan, 1917

The following week, the church hosted a big social event to welcome our soldiers home and remember those boys who did not make it back. I was reluctant to attend, but Bruce looked at me, and I changed my mind.

The town held the picnic at the newly named Jubilee Memorial Park on the outskirts of town, and everyone brought food and blankets. Men pushed six large picnic tables together, and we put our food there. Platters of fried chicken, bowls of baked beans with molasses, as well as containers of potato salad, pickles, rolls, cakes, and pies.

The pastor opened with prayer and thanked us all for coming. He turned it over to the mayor.

The mayor told us the town was raising money for a sign listing all those young men who had served during the war, with an asterisk beside the names of those who died. There was a collection box upfront, across from the food. For now, someone had painted the names on a large piece of wood, but the official sign would be metal.

My family spread out our blanket next to the O'Connor family's blanket. Bruce and Liam both looked uncomfortable about being honored. There were a dozen boys present, and another six who had not come home, including Charlie and his best friend, Frank.

Mama and Grandma put their casserole dishes on the tables and lingered to talk to the other women. Anna and I opened the picnic basket to get out the plates, cups, and silverware. Aidan soon wandered off with his friends, clutching his plate and silverware. Papa and Grandpa stood nearby, chatting with some men.

Only Bruce, Anna, and I still sat on the blanket.

Anna saw her girlfriends. She was taller now, almost seventeen, a beautiful young woman, and still my baby sister. She asked, "Will you be alright if I go over and talk to Nora and Frances?"

"You don't have to babysit me. I'll be fine." I gestured for her to go.

Bruce looked at me. "I'm glad to be home. But my name—all our names—going on some sign for a memorial park...that's for old men, isn't it?"

"I think they mean to honor everyone who fought for our country. We are all so proud of you, and…" I faltered, "…all our boys." I couldn't bear to say Charlie's name in public for fear I'd break down and cry.

One of his friends came over then to shake hands, and they talked. Bruce looked at me, and I gestured for him to go. I hated the idea my family thought I was so fragile when it'd been over a year since Charlie's death. My internal clock reminded me it'd been one year, two and a half months.

I'd brought a shoulder bag along and dug out a book to read. I could be self-sufficient, after all. After a few pages, someone put a hand on my shoulder. I looked up, and it was Liam.

"May I join you?" He asked.

"Sure." I laid down the book. We stared at each other.

He crouched down to talk to me. "I'm not ready to talk to them. They mean well, but I can't make small talk or answer their questions, and I don't want their sympathy."

"Please, sit down. I understand completely. I wish I'd thought of bringing another book."

He sat down, and we chatted, ignoring those around us.

"I'm not sure which is worse. The well-meaning comments about being young or the scripture verses," I told him.

He sighed. "Exactly. The wound is still fresh, so let it heal."

We traded examples of the worst things to say to someone who has lost a loved one.

"How about any scripture verse in any translation that means it's beyond human understanding?" I offered.

"It was her/his time."

"You're young." I was getting into it. "There are other fish in the sea."

"The good Lord needed another angel," he countered.

By the time we were done, we were both smiling.

A few minutes later, everyone lined up, chatting, to get their food. Liam and I sat, waiting until the tables were almost deserted.

Liam helped me up, and we walked over to the tables together as naturally as if we'd always done it. When we turned around, plates full, we ignored the stares and walked back to my family's blanket, next to his family. We settled down in the middle and ate.

Our families made small talk around us.

I relaxed a little, and Liam ventured a small smile. "Thanks, Mary."

"You're welcome, Liam."

All the soldiers were called up front for a special prayer at the end.

Bruce and Liam walked up together. Mrs. O'Connor leaned over and thanked me. "Liam didn't want to come today, but we told him Bruce would be here—and you would be here. You would understand his grief. Thank you for being his friend."

"You're welcome, but his presence comforted me. I didn't want to talk to people and answer questions either," I told her.

Anna, Aiden, and Bruce came back, and we packed up our leftover food, piled the dirty plates and utensils into a canvas bag, shook out the blanket, and Papa picked up the picnic basket. Mama carried the blanket. Liam came over before we left to thank me, and stood before me, holding my hand.

I said, "Don't let people's stares or clumsy comments get to you. They mean well. However, a year ago, I imagined I was on an island, and only a few people could reach me. I was in a fortress of grief on an island, the moat filled with alligators, and the drawbridge up."

He stared at me, "And now?"

"My island is more like a peninsula, connected to the mainland. I got rid of the alligators because they don't make very good pets. I venture out of the fortress, and the drawbridge is down for a few special people."

"You understand. The drawbridge comes down for only a few souls in my fortress. My mother and father, Bruce—and you—so far," Liam confessed.

We stared at my hand, and I withdrew it.

"Well, it was just lovely to see you today," I told Liam with an artificial lilt to my voice.

Our families looked at us and glanced away, the mothers looking at each other with a smile.

We walked home, Anna and Aidan talking about their friends and plans for the summer. Bruce took the canvas bag from me and walked alongside. I thought about my conversation with Liam and realized I'd been comfortable in his presence. Was it just because he made me think of Charlie?

No, I thought. *He and Bruce had gone away boys and come back men. What they'd experienced—what they'd lost—might not be fully understood. If ever there was a war to end all wars, this should be it.*

A few days later, Liam stopped to see Bruce, and they walked out to the garden to chat. Liam was upset. He didn't say hello when they walked past Anna and me, reading in the parlor. Once outside, he walked back and forth, gesturing.

Bruce nodded several times and stood up and put a hand on his friend's shoulder. Liam's shoulders seemed to relax. They stood, whispering now.

Curious, I slipped closer to the window, but stayed out of sight.

"I have nightmares about the trenches—about Frank, about Charlie. Do you?" Liam asked.

Bruce didn't hesitate. "Yes, of course. How could anyone forget the rats, the stink of the water in the trench's bottom, wet socks and wet feet, the awful rations, and the constant fear of being overrun by the Germans? The screaming of men who got shot. The collapse of the trench on poor Frank, that medic, and the soldier they were trying to help. I think they're getting less frequent. But when we first got home, Aidan came into my room and told me to stop shouting." Then he asked, "What's wrong?"

Liam's voice dropped. "That's why I'm here. Frank's father took it especially hard when his only son died. His wife found him out in the shed this morning. He shot himself. She called the Sheriff."

Bruce shook his head. "Oh, Liam, I'm sorry."

Liam shook his head. "The war is over, and it's still killing people. My parents visited the family and took his wife and children home. Then they let the pastor know. That leaves Frank's mother with three children to support."

Bruce stepped closer. "What can we do to help? How old are the children?"

Liam thought, "The oldest girl must be about twelve, and the little ones are eight and six. All in school. Frank's father was the ticket agent for the railroad. As soon as the news came about Frank, his father was notified immediately. He stayed strong for his girls at first, but then he started spending more time alone, drinking. My mom took the girls and their mother home with her so the sheriff could do his work. My father contacted other family members out of town."

Bruce said, "Let's talk to my parents. They may already know. I'll ask Dad if he can hire Frank's mother at the store."

Liam relaxed. "I knew you'd understand."

They turned, and I stepped back, flushing because of what I'd overheard. Lost in the depths of my despair, I hadn't suspected they both had nightmares from combat. Both men were so self-contained that I'd not had an inkling that they were also grieving. I hadn't stopped to consider how losing Frank, Charlie, and other soldiers had affected my brother and his best friend.

I returned to the parlor and sat by Anna and told her what I'd overheard.

Her eyes welled up in tears of sympathy, and she put her hand on my arm. "I'm sorry for all our soldiers have had to endure. The war has changed them. I see a look on Bruce's face I don't remember seeing before. Have you? He comes down the stairs and switches on a smile to let us know he's alright."

I knew the look she meant, but I hadn't recognized it. "He's trying to protect us, isn't he? He doesn't want us to worry about him."

The back door opened and shut, and Bruce and Liam came into the house, with Liam looking more like himself. He said hello.

"Have you seen Papa?" Bruce asked. "We have some news—and it's upsetting." He turned to Liam.

Liam sighed. "I'm sorry, Anna and Mary. I can't think of a good way to tell you this, but Frank's father killed himself last night."

Before we could react, Papa walked into the parlor, the newspaper tucked under his arm. He shook hands with Liam, put a hand on Bruce's shoulder, and exhaled. "I talked to your father at noon, Liam. The café was full of gossip about Frank's father. Your mother and my wife are coordinating food."

He continued, "We will find work for Martha. Don't worry. And we're pressuring the railroad to honor his life insurance policy. It isn't much money, but it'd pay off the mortgage on their house."

Bruce and Liam thanked him, and then the three of them talked in low voices.

Papa said, "The pastor is taking up a collection to pay for a casket and any funeral expenses. I wish I'd taken time to talk to Frank's father more." He exhaled. "I thought he was holding up fairly well."

Liam nodded. "I stopped by several times since we got back. He seemed quieter."

Mama came in and said she was on the phone planning meals with Liam's mother once Martha and the children could go back to the house.

I went upstairs, saddened by the events. What had Liam said— the war is still killing people? He was right.

Forty-seven

Bruce has Surprising News
Mary

*"It does good to no woman to be flattered [by a man] who does
not intend to marry her; and it is madness in all women to let
a secret love kindle within them, which, if unreturned and
unknown, must devour the life that feeds it; and, if discovered
and responded to, must lead, ignis-fatuus-like, into miry wilds
whence there is no extrication."*

~Charlotte Brontë, Jane Eyre

After that, Liam and I sought each other
out at social functions and church during the summer. We were
comfortable with each other. I understood he was still living on
his island, in his fortress. He had let the drawbridge down for me.
We could sit in silence or talk about anything at all.

Sometimes Liam came into the store for something, or I saw him
at the library, or he was with Bruce at our house. He acknowledged
me with a smile, but I knew where he was living, and he wasn't
ready to leave the fortress yet.

Then, one day in early August, Bruce popped into my bedroom
and told me he and Liam were returning to college in the fall. Liam
was studying law in Prairie Falls when he got drafted. Bruce was
going back to study business. They were going to be roommates.
Prairie Falls was about a half hour away by train. They hoped to
come home some weekends.

"Well, I'm happy for you two." I didn't mean to sound so bitter,
but it seemed my course was set. I'd be the sweet old spinster who

worked at the store and kept counting the days since Charlie died. Maybe I'd get a couple of cats and live alone in a rented room.

Bruce looked at me with a strange expression on his face. I thought—not for the first time—*he went away a boy and came back a man*. He came into the room and sat on Anna's bed.

I sat on my bed, trying to process his news. *Liam was going away again. I would sit alone this fall at all those gatherings.*

"Mary, can I tell you a secret?" he asked.

Thinking it was about France, I prepared myself. "Yes, certainly."

"Do you remember how Liam spent so much time here when we were in high school?"

I couldn't imagine where he was going. "Yes, you've been friends since you were young boys."

"There was another reason. We were, and are, best friends, sure. But Liam liked you."

I was incredulous. "Liam liked me. Are you sure? You and Liam are almost two years older, and lots of girls his age liked him."

"Yes, I'm sure. When he saw you and Charlie getting together, he backed off. He wanted you both to be happy."

"Why are you telling me this now?" I was bewildered. "It's too late. He's in love with Jane, and she died. I loved Charlie, and he died." My voice was trembling, and I was glad that I was sitting down, because I felt shaky suddenly—as if the ground underneath me had shifted.

"Liam still has feelings for you, and he's a wonderful man. You deserve someone like Liam. He's been my friend since we were little boys, and he's smart, funny, kind, and a hard worker. He's hurting, and you're one of the few people he talks to, besides me."

Bruce sat down beside me. "I didn't mean to upset you, but I thought you deserved to know."

"I don't know what to think about any of this. You and he are going away. Liam will meet a nice girl at college." I sat up straighter, ignoring the tears streaming down my face. *I've missed my chance for love. Charlie's dead. Liam's my friend. Bruce is wrong.*

Bruce looked at me. "Why did he ask me to tell you we're coming home many of the weekends?"

I flushed. *Liam is my friend, and Charlie's big brother. What is going on?* My heart was beating faster, and I was lightheaded.

Bruce sighed again and stood up, putting a gentle hand on my shoulder. "I didn't mean to upset you, Mary. I'm sorry. Just be open to love, okay? You're my kid sister, but you're also a sweet, smart young woman. You deserve to be happy."

He left the room, and I tried to shove his suggestion aside. *It's ridiculous. Liam lost the love of his life. He doesn't love me. We're just friends.*

Anna walked into the room, carrying some letters, and stopped and looked at me.

"What's going on? Have you been crying again? Your face is pale, and you look rather strange."

I told her what Bruce had said about Liam. She sat down on her bed, laid the letters down, and listened. Anna asked, "Liam enjoys your company, don't you agree?"

"Yes, we're both grieving. We're comfortable with each other."

She interrupted me. "Please, let's not talk about islands and fortresses again. You've worn black for a solid year. I miss my big sister, who loved colors, flowers, and laughing."

Anna stood up, opened my closet, and took out a floral dress in blues, pinks, and purple. "Don't you think it's time to stop wearing all black?"

"Anna, I would never wear such a pretty dress to the store. I suppose I could wear a white shirtwaist with my black skirts." I stared at her, and at the dress. *Yes, it had been a favorite when I was dating Charlie.* I considered her words.

Was I stuck in the past mourning Charlie? Would he want me to wear black until I died? What was I to do about Liam? Was Bruce correct—did Liam have feelings for me?

I sat down, the lovely dress in my arms, and burst into tears. This was all too confusing for me to understand.

Anna came over and took the dress from me and hung it up in the closet. My baby sister comforted me. "Mary, it's alright." She handed me a handkerchief.

After a few minutes, I calmed down and hugged her. "Let's go downstairs and see if we can help Frank's family."

Forty-eight

Digging Deeper
Gracie

"After we lost our second baby, a little girl, I went back to the walled-up fortress on the island of grief, with enormous waves that threatened to destroy me. Liam was so patient with me. He held me gently and let me cry. He cried too. Slowly, we healed together. Then I knew our love was strong enough to come back to land, leaving the fortress and the island behind."
~Grandma Mary's diary

After finding Grandma Mary's diary, I read it through in several sessions. It began with sewing in the parlor with her Grandma Carlson, mother, and sister. Mary described her romantic relationship with Charlie even as The Great War raged in Europe. She described the President declaring war and getting engaged. She wrote about her mother packing for Bruce to leave for the Army's training and taking a last walk with Charlie. Then she described working at the store with her father while Charlie deployed to France. He lost his best friend Frank, and then became a hero, saving two men's lives while sacrificing his own. Charlie had promised to come home to her, and breaking that promise broke her heart, but her mother and grandmother reminded her he died a hero, saving two men.

I cried when she wrote about Charlie's death and celebrated her healing, as her friendship turned to love with Liam. Then I went back and looked at Charlie's letters, and they were the sweet notes of a first love, a young man clinging to the hope he would return to his girl, Mary.

As I read her diary, I got emotional. This was the incredible woman who'd fallen in love with one brother, who died a hero, only to marry his older brother, who'd also lost his first love, Jane. I was confident by the time I finished reading her diary, it would tell me almost everything I needed to know. Then I could answer all of Angela's questions—and everyone else's.

Now I understood why the hope chest had a hidden compartment. Mary's father wanted to encourage her to move forward, while keeping her memories of Charlie. In addition, I knew Liam liked Mary before his younger brother Charlie pursued her, and then Liam backed off out of respect for his younger brother and Mary. However, he confessed his feelings to her older brother and his parents. When Liam returned, he and Mary shared a bond of grief, because his girlfriend also died in France. Their friendship turned to love.

Mary married Liam after he graduated from college. I hadn't understood why she became so sad after they got married. Yes, she'd lost her first love. But then she suffered postpartum depression after little Emma was born.

I couldn't fathom the sacrifices of those young men and the families left behind. How many young women had lost their husbands, boyfriends, brothers, and fathers in France? And then they lost family members and friends to the virus—and more soldiers died from the virus overseas and at home alike. It was heartache piled on heartache.

I showed the diary to David and summarized what I'd learned.

"World War I is often called The Great War, and it cost about 10 million soldiers their lives, along with seven million civilians. The destruction and horror of that war changed the world and left a deep impression on the lives of those who lost a loved one."

"I can't imagine it. Then they had the horrible Spanish Flu, and it killed young men before they reached the battlefield, and it spread here at home. Her diary makes the 1918 Flu Pandemic come to life," I told him.

David embraced me. "Good job, Gracie. Great-Aunt Catharine came through with her boxes."

An hour later, David climbed the steps back to my attic study, a book in his hands, looking pensive.

I sat at my desk, still pondering the diary and the war, my laptop open to an internet search.

He asked, "Have you heard of an Irish poet named William Butler Yeats? He wrote something in 1919 that captured the collective horror of that war. It's a long narrative poem called "The Second Coming." I wanted to show it to you." He laid the book open to the poem on the desk, stood behind me, and read it aloud.

"Turning and turning in the widening gyre
The falcon cannot hear the falconer;
Things fall apart; the center cannot hold;
Mere anarchy is loosed upon the world,
The blood-dimmed tide is loosed, and everywhere
The ceremony of innocence is drowned;
The best lack all conviction, while the worst
Are full of passionate intensity."

I listened to David's voice, thinking about all the religious, literary, and historical references.

David spoke up. "Of course, Yeats seems to suggest that such violence can only bring the anti-Christ. It's dark, but then the world had just experienced a terrible thing, a war given the name The Great War because it had drawn in all the world powers."

"Thank you. This is powerful. May I borrow the book?" I asked.

"Sure," he said. He kissed me.

I took Mary's diary to the museum the next day and used our special scanner to do OCR scanning and cleaned up the text. Then I shared the scans with David, Carl, and Charlotte.

Mary's vivid description of her life, and WWI on the home-front, impressed Charlotte. Her grief at losing Charlie, the ordeal of the 1918 Flu Pandemic, and her friendship turned to courtship with Liam were all recorded there. Carl and David looked for information about which branches local boys had served in, as well as where they were sent.

Charlotte said, "Mary had an eye for detail. I liked the idea of selling those patriotic records by playing them in the store."

Carl looked up from his photocopy of her diary. "Over a hundred thousand Iowans served during WWI and over thirty-five hundred died. Let me find those exact numbers." He looked at his iPad. "Yes, 114,242 served during WWI. Of those, 3,576 died in France."

We gathered the information we'd found from various sources. Charlotte and I went back to Ancestry.com and the family trees. I did some more research with her help. We looked at databases for births, deaths, and marriages.

Charlotte found a record for a baby of Liam and Mary that died: they got married in 1922, had a child—Emma—and then lost a baby. They had three more children, all healthy, living to old age. I wondered, *Did Mary suffer a depressive episode after losing the second baby?* It would be a normal response.

I went back to Great-Aunt Catharine's boxes and emptied them out. At the bottom of the second box, I found a smaller box marked Mary, and inside I found more letters from Anna and a second diary. From one of those letters, I found out Mary collected baby clothes in the hope chest.

Anna remained close to her sister, and they wrote to each other faithfully. One of Anna's letters asked about how little Emma was doing? Anna mentioned she was sending a darling little outfit and tiny sweater to add to the collection for the new little one. Another letter expressed concern and condolences for the death of the baby girl and asked how Mary was doing. She was coming home on the train to help.

Certainly, it would be normal to be depressed. I saw what Mark and Kathy had gone through with their miscarriage and could not imagine how difficult it would be to lose a child after giving birth.

Charlotte talked to her big sister, a nurse in Prairie Falls who worked with young mothers with postpartum depression. Her sister told Charlotte there was still a major stigma on mental health issues like depression, and Mary may have been ashamed. Doctors didn't have many tools to use in the early 1900s. They didn't understand postpartum depression any more than they understood PTSD.

We learned from other letters that Anna moved to Chicago and stayed with Aunt Eva for some time. After graduating from a secretarial school, she got hired at a large company, and moved up to management. Many years later, Anna worked to improve the lot of women and children. She went to California during WWII to help set up daycare centers for women working in defense factories. It was another reminder of the contrast between WWI and WWII.

During WWI, it was primarily the young, single women who worked. During WWII, the country needed more workers to keep factories, shops, shipyards, and other workplaces functioning. So, during WWII, they recruited single women, widows, and mothers to help fill the jobs left open, and daycare was a necessary incentive. Anna helped organize those daycare centers. Charlotte discovered a helpful article on the National Park Service website about women workers during WWII.

Approximately 12 million women worked in defense industries and support services across the nation, including shipyards, steel mills, foundries, warehouses, offices, hospitals, and daycare centers.

Women drove cabs and delivered mail, they refurbished railroad cars to carry troops and charted the positions of enemy aircraft. They worked on war bond drives and manned civil defense programs. They promoted community health programs through the Red Cross and entertained troops at canteens. Hollywood stars like Lena Horne sang for Richmond shipyard workers and the Andrews Sisters entertained soldiers recovering at Oak Knoll Hospital. Female staff at the Berkeley Public Library collected and mailed 11,000 books to servicemen as part of the 1941 national "Victory Book Campaign."

I talked to Shelly and Tiara about it, too. Tiara was back at work, recovered from surgery, and looking like a woman in love.

Shelly reflected, "Every family has a story about a young mother with the baby blues. I cried a lot after my son was born for a day or two, but then I was fine. But I have a cousin who suffered a severe case of postpartum depression. Her mother-in-law was a nurse and got her help, but my cousin told me she thought she was losing her mind."

Tiara agreed. "I was lucky. I didn't have it with the twins, but I remember a friend who was hospitalized for a few weeks. Her mother moved in to help with the baby."

As we talked, I thought about the famous short story "Yellow Wallpaper" by Charlotte Perkins Gilman. Published in 1892, the story describes a woman going mad. She's being treated for post-partum depression by the rest cure, in a room with yellow wallpaper. Her husband, a doctor, separated her from her baby, which seems cruel to us now. She locks herself in the room, and in her delusion, sees a woman coming out of the wallpaper. By the end of the story, the woman has gone insane. She sees herself as the woman who has escaped from the wallpaper. It was a compelling story, and part of my fiction unit.

The following week we discussed "The Yellow Wallpaper" in my literature class. As we talked about the story in small groups, I noticed one of my students looking upset. After class, I asked her if she needed to rush to another class, and she shook her head, saying she was on her way to the library. I asked if she would walk with me to my office.

Once there, we found a place to sit. I asked if she was all right. She confided, "I've had depression for several years, since my second child was born. The latest antidepressant is helping me to function better. But I could relate to the woman in the story. It seems so ironic that a smart doctor could be so stupid, doesn't it?"

I agreed with her. We chatted for a few more minutes, and she relaxed. I encouraged her to continue talking with her counselor and consider whether she wanted to talk about it with her small group.

She ducked her head. "I wanted to speak up but lost my nerve."

She thanked me for noticing and left.

I thought about postpartum depression—what we used to call the baby blues. Now we know that the hormonal changes taking place in a woman's body after giving birth are responsible for the depression. But a hundred years ago, doctors didn't understand any of this.

I needed to read Mary's second diary once I finished the letters. That night, I reached for the three-ring notebook and found my sticky note. I'd read the first nine letters. Charlie was on his way to Europe on board a large cruise ship.

Letter Ten

July
My darling Mary,
The days pass aboard this ship, and they try to keep us busy with drills and classes, but there are times to go on deck and walk around for exercise. Frank and I walk together and take comfort in seeing other ships not far away, but there's too much ocean!
Bruce and I talked the other day. He admitted he has not been good at writing letters home. Please tell your parents he's doing well. He and Liam spend time together with a few of the other older boys. But he and I also chat, and we've taken a couple of walks together on deck.
Our sergeant says we'll have more training overseas with real guns. He's only 25, but compared to the rest of us, he's the old man. He watches over us and notices if someone isn't eating or has been seasick a lot. Sergeant Smith comes from Omaha, Nebraska, and his father and grandfather raise cattle. He says so far, his experience as a non-commissioned officer in the Army makes him think herding cattle was good preparation for going to war.
Love, Charlie

Letter Eleven

My darling Mary,
We hope to dock tomorrow and are excited to get off the ship and onto solid ground. It'll be wonderful to sleep on a mattress again, even if only for a couple of weeks of training. I'll be happy to sail home to you, but don't want to spend any more time onboard these enormous ships. There are too many stairs to climb for me to smell fresh air.
Mary, I'm happy to hear that you are doing so well at the store. I can imagine you standing behind the counter, filling orders and

helping people. I'm sure your father appreciates your help. You sound excited to be learning so much about the business.

Jubilee Junction seems very far away right now, and I miss it, and you. If I didn't have Frank, Liam, and Bruce, I would feel very sorry for myself. We've made some friends and learned about life in other states.

I'll write more when we're off the ship and settled.

Love, Charlie

I chuckled at the idea of herding cattle being a good preparation for leadership in the Army. I'd never taken a cruise but tried to imagine what it was like to cross the ocean in 1917 and discover there's *too much ocean*, as Charlie wrote. Then I imagined the excitement those troops would feel to get on solid ground again after so many days at sea. His letters had fired my imagination. I tried to put myself in Mary's place and wondered what it would be like to have your fiancé deployed to war.

Forty-nine

Friendship to Courtship
Mary

*"Doubt thou the stars do are fire; Doubt thou the sun doth
move; Doubt truth to be a liar; But never doubt I love."*
~William Shakespeare

"Whatever our souls are made of, his and mine are the same."
~Emily Brontë

Fall 1919

few days later, Liam came into the store
with a list for his mother, and I gathered groceries while he waited
at the counter. I took Anna's advice and wore a white shirtwaist
today with a black skirt. After gathering the items, I brought the
basket back to the counter, began adding them up, and saw him
smiling at me. I touched my hair, wondering if it was alright.

Liam smiled. "You look beautiful today, Mary. I'm so glad to see
you wearing some white again. Charlie wouldn't want you to be
in mourning forever."

Then he asked, "Are you going to the library tomorrow afternoon,
after work? Perhaps I could meet you there and then take you to
supper. I'd like to talk."

I accepted, wondering if Bruce had told me the truth.

After work, I walked home alone because Papa had things to
do before he left the store. As I walked, I noticed the flowers in
people's yards, and I saw our neighbor's house was painted a light

yellow. A group of children were playing baseball in the vacant lot, and they waved, so I waved back.

I entered our house and smiled at Mama, who was cooking something on the stove. She put down her spoon and walked over and embraced me. She said nothing.

Then she stepped back to stir something and spoke, "We'll eat when your Papa comes home."

I set the table, and Anna came downstairs and helped. She called up to Aidan, who came down and filled the water glasses.

Bruce walked in before Papa, having come from the library. He smiled at me, and I felt a little self-conscious. *What did he know? Was he right about Liam?*

The next day, I dressed with care in a gold shirtwaist with gray accents, and a gray skirt I'd been saving for—never mind.

I asked Anna for help with putting my hair up, which she was happy to do.

I told Mama I would have supper with Liam. She began to say something and stopped. "You look very nice, Mary."

Papa and I walked to the store together, as was our habit, and he told me I looked pretty.

All day I worked, trying not to look at the clock. At six, I took off my apron and called "goodbye" to Papa, Grandpa, and our new hire, Martha, Frank's mother. I picked up my purse and walked to the Jubilee Library, wondering what Liam wanted to discuss.

Liam was sitting at the reference table looking at an enormous book. I walked over, sat down, and asked him what he was reading. He told me it was a legal reference book.

"When I first became interested in the law, my grandfather teased me that I'd have to memorize this book. I kept coming in and staring at the first couple of pages and later chapters. Then, I asked him if he could recite it for me, and he just laughed." Liam smiled, remembering.

"Oh Liam, my boy, it's indexed alphabetically. If you look up a topic half a dozen times, you'll remember some of the content there."

"How old were you?" I asked.

"Nine or ten. Back then, I couldn't even lift the book, much less memorize it. But Grandpa gave me an important study skill. Knowing how to find information is important. Understanding that you will get a better grasp of the content every time you go back to the book is also important."

We chatted about his interest in the law. Then he asked, "I suppose Bruce told you we're going back to college in Prairie Falls?"

I didn't know what to say.

"We plan to leave in two weeks. The semester starts soon, and we need to buy our books and move into the dorms before classes start."

"Yes, my mother is packing for Bruce."

Liam nodded, "Mine too. Shall we go?" We stood up, and he returned the enormous book to the bookcase and nodded at the librarian.

"See that? I can lift it now." He smiled and opened the front door.

He and I walked down Main Street, talking as we approached the Jubilee Café where we found a table and sat down. I put my purse on my lap.

We looked at the menu, and a server came over carrying glasses of water and took our orders.

We sipped on our water and looked around us at friends and acquaintances. Several smiled and said hello.

Our food came—hamburgers and two Coca-Colas.

"I thought about this café in France—proper food like burgers and meat loaf and beef stew," he said.

I nodded. "Sometimes, I felt guilty for eating Mama's good food and wondered what you and—Bruce—were eating." It was still difficult for me to mention Charlie's name in casual conversation.

His eyes were kind.

We ate our meals and lingered over slices of cherry pie with a scoop of vanilla ice cream.

Liam looked at me and smiled. "I mentioned I wanted to talk to you." He hesitated, and my heartbeat sped up a little.

He leaned forward, speaking. "Would you be willing to visit my mother from time to time? She's so fond of you. I think it's going to be more difficult for her to have me away at college, with Charlie gone and my sister married and living in Prairie Falls."

"Certainly." I looked down at my purse, wanting to hide my facial expression, feeling my cheeks flush. *Was that it? He wanted me to check on his mother while he was away at college. What did I expect? Why am I disappointed? We're just friends, after all.*

I realized Liam was speaking, and I wasn't listening. "Mary?"

I looked up, "Excuse me?"

"Mary? Are you alright?"

I stood, clutching my purse. "Actually, I should go home."

I turned, and he caught my hand. "Mary, please wait for me. I'm going to pay the bill and walk you home."

I exhaled, and he gestured to the server, who brought the bill and took his money.

We left the restaurant and walked in silence for half a block until we reached a park bench.

Liam stopped. "Sit down, please, Mary. That's not all I wanted to talk to you about."

I sat down, trying to calm myself, thinking *"all the men I love just keep going away,"* and then caught myself. *What?*

Liam took my purse and laid it on the bench beside us. Somehow, he was holding one of my hands and reached out with his other hand to turn my face towards him.

I was astonished and on the verge of tears.

Liam asked gently, "Mary, do you think you will ever be able to put your feelings aside for Charlie and care about another man?"

I flushed and hoped he couldn't hear my heart beating extra hard.

I recovered my wits. "A part of me will always love your brother. But we were so young—was it puppy love? I don't know. It's been two years since you left. For the first year after Charlie died, my heart had shattered, and I thought I could never care for another man. I was on the island of grief, locked up in the fortress. But in the past few months, I've thought of him less and realized I could care for someone else."

Liam looked into my eyes. "Is the drawbridge down?"

He was holding both of my hands.

I could hardly breathe. "Yes."

"Good. I grieved for Jane in France but kept thinking of you. I would never have come between my brother and his happiness. Please understand. But I've loved you for a long time. And I've enjoyed getting to know you this summer as a friend."

"Me, too. I couldn't have endured all those town picnics and church socials without you."

"Mary, do you think you could care for me as more than a friend?"

I didn't trust my voice.

He continued, "If yes, I'd like to court you when I come home several weekends a month. I'm not asking for a final decision tonight—"

I interrupted him. "Yes, Liam. Yes."

He kissed me then, several times. We were in our own world. We walked to my house, holding hands, both of us smiling.

The sun had gone down, and people were sitting on their porches talking with neighbors. Others had already gone inside. Several waved at us.

When we reached the front porch, I saw my sister peeking out of the upstairs bedroom window.

I turned to Liam. "You'd better come inside because otherwise, when they see me smiling, they're going to think I took opium or something."

We were walking up the porch steps when the front door opened, and Papa spotted us, trying to look innocent, with Mama right behind him.

"Well, look who's here. Come in, come in, Mary and Liam," Papa opened the door.

We entered, and Bruce was sitting with Liam's parents, drinking lemonade and eating cookies at our dining room table. He turned to grin and wave, holding up his glass.

Anna and Aidan appeared on the landing upstairs, smiling.

I turned to Liam. "Do we act surprised? Or just run?"

"I think we blame it on Bruce and go in for some lemonade."

So, we did.

Fifty

Seeing the Boys off to College
Mary

"Love is not affectionate feeling, but a steady wish for the loved person's ultimate good as far as it can be obtained."

~*C.S Lewis*

*T*wo weeks later, our families saw Liam and Bruce off at the Jubilee Junction depot. There were heartfelt hugs and handshakes, reminders to write, and jokes. Mama tucked a package of brownies in Bruce's hands, and Liam's mother had oatmeal raisin cookies in a package for Liam.

Bruce joked, "We won't starve on the train."

Liam held me close as he whispered, "I love you, Mary. I'll see you in two weeks." Then he kissed me, kissed his mother, and boarded the train. We stood there, one large family, with both fathers looking proud, and both mothers a little weepy. Anna, now eighteen, and Aidan, fifteen, stood on either side of me, as my protective guardians. How they'd grown! Aidan was almost six feet tall.

Unfortunately, love always seems to be tested. A few days passed, and I felt guilty. How do I dare love Liam when my Charlie lies in a faraway grave? Can Liam really want me? Is he going to leave me, too? And then I wonder if everyone will see me as Liam's second choice?

Or him as mine?

Liam writes to me faithfully, and I confess all my fears that, like an anchor tied to my heart, seem certain to drag me under, back to the island, back to the fortress.

Liam doesn't make light of my concerns, but addresses them each in his sweetly logical, analytical way. He reminds me I would have been his first choice if Charlie hadn't pursued me. Liam was waiting because he thought it unseemly to court a younger woman when she was still in high school. He tells me Charlie wouldn't want me to mourn forever, any more than Jane would want that for him. He's going to love me every day for the rest of his life, and no one can promise more.

His mother comes to see me, and we have tea. She tells me she grieves for Charlie but feels thankful I will be part of her family and loves me like a daughter. Liam told her about his feelings for me before he left for the military. She and her husband were unsure about what to do with the information. They prayed it'd all work out, but never envisioned Charlie would die in France. She said she didn't want me to feel guilty for being happy, and she and I would always share a bond of grief that Charlie had died so young.

Ruby and I rejoiced when Congress ratified the 19th Amendment, August 26, 1920. I bought extra copies of the *Des Moines Register,* and she and I hugged.

Aunt Eva called and invited me and Ruby to come back to Chicago for a victory party that weekend. We packed our bags and got on the train. Along the way, a dozen other women joined us for the trip to Chicago.

Once we arrived, Aunt Eva told us how a young man named Harry Burns listened to his mother and voted yes on ratifying the 19th Amendment, making Tennessee the 36th state to do so. Countless women and men, black and white, had worked for this landmark legislation for seven decades.

We were ecstatic until we heard the rest of the news. Sadly, the 19th Amendment would benefit only white women. Ruby couldn't join the newly formed League of Women Voters with me. I didn't understand why.

Aunt Eva couldn't hide her anger and disappointment. "My friend told me they didn't want to offend the southern suffragists. But it's a mockery, a cup half full, and it's wrong. The Black suffragists worked hard alongside us, and they deserved more."

Ruby and I agreed, and we were heartbroken.

Fifty-one

A Cup Half Full
Gracie

*"Every great dream begins with a dreamer. Always remember,
you have within you the strength, the patience, and the passion
to reach for the stars to change the world."*

~Harriet Tubman

I looked closer. There seemed to be teardrops on the page. The cursive writing was a little harder to read. I realized the tears were from my eyes. I closed Mary's diary and went to see Grandma Molly for answers.

"I don't understand, Grandma. I thought the 19th Amendment was a big deal for women because they won the vote. And the League of Women Voters helped prepare them to vote. But Mary's friend, Ruby, wanted to join the League of Women Voters from the very beginning, and they didn't let her join because she was black?"

Grandma Molly listened. "Yes, I understand your frustration. It made me angry and sad, too, when I first read about it. Sadly, the 19th Amendment only helped white women. It took forty-five years—until August 6, 1965—when President Lyndon Johnson signed the Voting Rights Act for Black women to get the vote. The Voting Rights Act is called a landmark piece of federal legislation because it prohibits racial discrimination in voting."

Grandma Molly continued. "Carrie Chapman Catt tried to keep the Southern suffragettes happy. When you called about Grandma Mary and the 19th Amendment, I checked a few sources." She consulted a document, laying on top of several books, reading out loud. "The Fifteenth Amendment, passed in 1870, granted all U. S. citizens the right to vote regardless of race, but it wasn't until the Snyder Act of 1924 that Alaska Natives and Native Americans—men and women alike—were granted citizenship. Other western states, such as Arizona, New Mexico, and Utah, didn't let Native Americans vote until the 1940s and 1950s. In Puerto Rico, women who could read and write won the right to vote in 1929, but Asian American women couldn't vote until 1952 when the Immigration and Nationality Act allowed them to become citizens."

I shook my head in frustration. "How can we talk about democracy and freedom if we don't guarantee those things for everyone? Freedom isn't freedom if it's only granted to a small group of people."

"Gracie, I know you're upset. I am too. The League of Women Voters is a wonderful organization and has accomplished great things, but it's not perfect. We must acknowledge our failure to make sure that women of color, Native American women—all women—have the same opportunity that white women have."

She exhaled. "We've come a long way since then, Gracie. I'm proud to be a member of the League. I found an article that may make you feel a little better." She picked up one article and read:

"In 1998, Dr. Carolyn Jefferson-Jenkins, of Colorado Springs, Colorado, became the first Black President of the League of Women Voters. Jefferson-Jenkins was a public-school teacher and administrator and had been in the league since 1982. She urged the organization to focus on local elections and work on registering more voters. Jefferson-Jenkins led the 1996 Get Out the Vote campaign, registering over 50,000 voters. She also helped us transition to using the internet with her 1998 project, Wired for Democracy."

Grandma Molly gave me a big hug. "Keep reading and gathering information, Gracie. I think you'll find your answers."

Fifty-two

Mary Finds her Purpose
Mary

"The purpose of life is not to be happy. It is to be useful, to be honorable, to be compassionate, to have it make some difference that you have lived and lived well."

~Ralph Waldo Emerson

A few days after Liam and Bruce left for college, Grandma took me aside and talked to me about the meaning of the word *promises*. It had brought me to tears for the past two years, feeling betrayed by Charlie's broken promise to come home to me.

"Remember, Mary, each new day brings a chance for happiness, and a second chance at love. Think about the promise of a newborn baby, a rose that has just bloomed, or a sunrise. You've been given a rare opportunity to love again. I know Liam will make you happy if you just open your heart and set aside your fear."

"Your grandfather and I have seen our share of sorrow and loss. We struggled with our farm when we were young and just starting out. Thank goodness for our family and neighbors who helped us out of kindness. Kindness is important, and we need to reward it by being kind to others. We cannot control what happens in this world, only how we respond," she concluded.

As I listened to Grandma, I knew she was right about kindness. I'd just finished reading something Liam and I planned to discuss in the next letter, a wonderful quote by Ralph Waldo Emerson that captured his imagination, and now mine.

"The purpose of life is not to be happy. It is to be useful, to be honorable, to be compassionate, to have it make some difference that you have lived and lived well."

I knew then what I must do—I needed to show kindness to someone else and stop being so self-absorbed. I wrote to Liam about my conversation with Grandma.

He was enthusiastic and asked me to report back on my ideas.

The next time I saw Ruby at the library for our weekly chat, I asked if we could sit down and visit. I had a notebook and pen with me.

"What do the poor Black and white children in Jubilee Junction need?" I asked her.

Without hesitation, she replied, "I'd say breakfast and a safe place to be before school and after school. Many of their mothers are working, leaving children to fend for themselves in the morning and after school."

I talked to the women in my extended family, as well as Papa and my grandfather, and then Liam's family. They were all supportive. We found a large empty building close to the school, which used to be a shop. I solicited money from my family and the O'Connor's to rent it, then got to work refurbishing it. I hired a handful of women to help me paint, clean, and haul away the trash. I worked half days for several weeks while we prepared the building.

Liam's parents came up with an idea, and Liam's grandfather drew up papers to create a foundation in Charlie's name to provide funding for our project. As word got out, with articles in *The Jubilee Times*, the foundation gained more financial support. Liam's family purchased the building and presented me with the deed as the Chair of the Foundation's Board.

We turned the building into a center for children before and after school. We provided a safe place for them, with a hot breakfast, and we sent a brown paper lunch for children who would not have lunch otherwise.

My friend Ruby Collins became the Director of the Jubilee Junction Children's Center, and we hired ten mothers to help at the Center. Two mothers welcomed the children each day and helped them with their coats and bags and made sure they were ready for school. Four prepared breakfast and lunches, and four provided some activities for before and after school. The Charles O'Connor Foundation paid for all of it.

We found volunteers to tutor the children and make sure they did their homework in the afternoons. Several women from our big families took turns going over in the morning to help the staff get the children ready for school. They were looking out for those children who lacked boots, winter coats, decent shoes, or other things. We then supplied these things, and the families appreciated it.

Later we expanded, taking on babies and toddlers and caring for them during the day while their mothers worked. We asked for donations of diapers, baby clothes, blankets, and cribs. We hired more women, young and old, to help take care of the babies. Some of them were young women widowed by The Great War and needing work.

Papa hired Frank's mother at the store, and she was taking over the duties I had once done, and her children were coming to the Children's Center.

I worked part time with Papa in the mornings and showed up at the Children's Center in the afternoons to read stories, help with homework, talk with Ruby about the day, and troubleshoot any problems.

Every letter to Liam included a report on what we had done the previous week, and he responded with encouragement.

The whole town wanted to help us: for example, the Jubilee Café offered to send over day-old cookies and pastries—and they did, every day. The Jubilee Clinic offered free checkups. One of my uncles owned the local dairy, and they sent over milk and butter, while Papa's grocery store delivered boxes of oatmeal, eggs, cheese, fruit, and bread. Thankfully, our family foundation supplied several iceboxes.

Ruby and I were thankful for community support and realized we were also helping women. We decided we'd expand programming and rename it the Jubilee Junction Women's and Children's Center.

We planned workshops about voting, to help women register to vote, and show them what ballots looked like to prepare them for voting.

A woman from Iowa named Carrie Chapman Catt had come up with the winning strategy for getting the 19th Amendment passed. Now she was organizing what she called The League of Women Voters, and I wanted to learn more. Unfortunately, her League would only be open to white women for now, because of the compromises made to gain support from the southern women. And the 19th Amendment would only give white women the guarantee of the vote.

I was angry and disappointed that Ruby couldn't join the League with me. Having met Aunt Eva's friends in Chicago, I wondered why anyone would question the need to include my African American friends.

Ruby was philosophical. "I'm not surprised. Did I tell you I'm now a member of the Alpha Club? Yes, I'd still like to vote someday and hope that happens in my lifetime."

I didn't know the future, but hoped Liam and I would marry and have a big family. Until then, I decided these children would become my children. These women would become my sisters.

As I talked with Liam, he supported me, as always. Of course, he had a strong mother and grandmother, and his family's newspaper covered all the news about the 19th Amendment. But it disappointed both of us that the League couldn't be more like the Alpha club in Chicago that believed all women of any race should be able to vote.

I told Ruby we still had work to do, and I wasn't giving up until every man and woman who were citizens could vote.

Fifty-three

The Big Truck Returns
Gracie

"Peace cannot be kept by force; it can only be achieved by understanding. Darkness cannot drive out darkness; only light can do that. Hate cannot drive out hate; only love can do that."
~Martin Luther King Jr

All summer we'd speculated about who was driving the big Ford truck with Confederate battle flags painted on its doors. Its driver seemed to make a point of driving by the newspaper, college, and museum every few weeks. One of the rare times that someone saw its license plate, it was splattered with mud, but Lt. Carlson didn't think it was an Iowa plate.

One night, the driver planted a small Confederate flag next to the town's welcome sign. Then he—or she—did the same at the pioneer cemetery, newspaper, museum, and college. The following week, he lit small crosses at all those places. Lt. Ben Carlson took the remains of the crosses down, but not before taking pictures and documenting the scenes.

After the problems we had with the white supremacy gang earlier this year, David's father, Harry, had supplied us with cameras. We could monitor traffic on the road that ran in front of Mark and Kathy's farmhouse and ours. Harry brought along a laptop and some other equipment to look at the traffic, and if needed, record it.

The men put all the equipment into David's man cave, and it became something every male in the county seemed to be curious about. Mark, David, Dad, and Ken gathered to look at the footage at least once a week. Most of the time, the footage didn't make for great TV, with deer, cats, dogs, people walking, and known cars and trucks. Occasionally, the cameras caught sight of the truck, and the driver—a big man at an estimated 300 pounds and six feet, according to Mark. But the pictures were never up close, and no one recognized him. And his license plate continued to evade identification. Either way, the server made a copy and sent it to Ben once a week.

My cousin Lance and his friends set up several motion sensing trail cams to monitor the back roads to the family farms. Since we lived a short drive from the pioneer cemetery, where the big truck's driver had left a threatening message, Ben was worried about our safety, and so were our parents. And then we didn't get any sightings for a couple of weeks.

As summer turned to fall, Ben got reports about the truck more frequently thanks to what Mom called *the cousins network*. Every business they owned with surveillance cameras checked their video feeds for signs of the truck and alerted Ben.

One Saturday in early November, I drove over to see Mark and Kathy and the babies while David worked on a project in his office after supper. It was only a mile away, so I rationalized I'd be safe. Kathy and I were planning our presentation to the family about Grandma Mary and what we'd discovered.

She and I reviewed what we wanted to cover using a simple outline and made a few changes. Then I sat down and played with the twins for a few minutes, planning to leave soon. It was almost their bedtime, anyway. Kathy and I chatted about the twins' new ability to grasp toys and raise their head and chest during tummy time.

Mark and Ken walked into the house, a little out of breath. The dogs followed at their heels. Mark had his phone in his hand. "Thanks for calling, David. Call Ben." He took the steps downstairs to the basement double time.

"Katie, Gracie, and Kathy, take the babies upstairs to the nursery." Ken ordered.

His voice was strained, and the three of us women picked up

babies, bags, toys, and snacks, and I grabbed my purse and messenger bag.

"What's going on?" Katie asked.

"No time," Ken said. "Get upstairs, now. David spotted the big white truck headed this way. C'mon, everyone!"

I thought, *Oh, no, he's found out where we live.* I reached the top of the stairs and glanced down.

Mark emerged from the basement wearing tactical gear. He handed a vest to Ken. "Put this on and get ready. Everyone, stay away from the windows."

He then held out a pistol and had one tucked into his belt.

Ken donned the vest and took a pistol and clips of ammo from Mark.

Katie handed me Sean and ran into her bedroom to grab several pillows and quilts. Hearts beating faster, we hurried into the nursery and huddled on the floor as far from the windows as possible. We cradled the fretful babies with pillows and quilts.

Katie adjusted the quilts around us. "It's going to be fine."

Then, we heard it—a large truck engine barreling down the access road to their driveway, going much faster than was safe.

What was he doing? Was he drunk? Was he going to crash into the house?

The dogs barked an urgent warning outside.

Then we heard a crash and felt the impact on the front part of the house directly below. I jumped as the house seemed to absorb the impact.

We heard yelling and cursing.

"What have you done?"

"This should have been our farm."

A short time later, we smelled fire.

What was going on? Did they just ram the front porch? Was the house on fire?

I handed Sean to Katie and crawled over to the window and peeked out.

The big white truck had indeed crashed into the front porch, climbing the front half-dozen steps and taking out the front door. I could hear the engine running, but the truck wasn't going anywhere. Then someone turned off the engine. The truck's doors were open, and one man stood watching while the bigger man planted a small wooden cross in the ground just a few feet away and lit it on fire. The man standing by the truck rubbed his head.

"The big guy's down there and he just lit a wooden cross on fire out front," I told Kathy and Katie. "There's another man with him."

The bigger man ran back towards the truck, carrying a weapon that he'd removed from his jacket's inner pocket. Suddenly, Mark and Ken were there, staring them down, carrying the pistols. Chewie and Han Solo growled a warning.

"Our guys are there!" I could hardly breathe, and my throat felt parched as I croaked, "Looks like a standoff." I opened the window to hear what was going on.

Then we heard more screaming and cursing—and sirens.

Mark yelled, "Don't take another step! The police are on their way."

"My great-great-great-grandma was your mama's great-great-great-grandma's sister. They had a farm right here in Jubilee County, somewhere near this farm. Her daddy moved us to his relatives in Kentucky. He didn't want to fight to free slaves. Now I'm back because my grandson Billy's in jail because of your family." The older man's voice was full of hate.

Mark stared at him. "Billy? He's right where he belongs."

Ken wasn't as patient. "You have the nerve to drive around in that big ridiculous truck with the flag of the loser. Iowa supported the Union. There are two babies and three women in the house, and you thought it was necessary to show how tough you were by gunning your engine and taking out our porch?"

The big man stared, panting, while his companion was passive, looking down, rubbing his head where he must have bumped it in the crash. Then Lt. Carlson arrived, and so did David.

After a scuffle with the bigger man, officers got the handcuffs on them. The younger one remained quiet and didn't resist arrest. Lt. Carlson read them their rights. The dogs crouched nearby, growling low and looking alert.

Dad walked up with Uncle Rich and Uncle Vern.

"What was your great-great-great-grandmother's name?" Uncle Vern asked.

The man told him, quieter, "Loretta May Nelson."

Uncle Vern shook his head. "I heard about your side of the family. Snuck out in the middle of the night, abandoned the farm, and didn't pay their debts. Someone else in the family took ownership of the farm and paid the debts. But my great-grandma said her great-grandmother grieved for her sister until the day she died."

"Yeah, and my granny felt robbed of the inheritance from this farm," the big man said. "Far as I'm concerned, this was my granny's place."

"Well, she wasn't here. Her family left. So there would be no inheritance, would there? We pass farms to the next generation who work them with us," Uncle Vern stated matter-of-factly. "My name is Vernon Nelson. This is part of my farm. What's your name?"

"James Joseph Flett, but everyone calls me Jimmy Joe," he replied.

My father stepped forward. "I'm Matthew O'Connor, editor of the town newspaper. Jimmy Joe, why didn't you just park the truck and come into the newspaper office to talk to us? You got our attention weeks ago, and you've been terrorizing people all summer. Most people in Jubilee Junction get upset when they see the Confederate flag. Our cemeteries are full of Union soldiers, including my family's plot in the pioneer cemetery. This is my son Mark, an Iraq war veteran. This is his farmhouse and part of the Nelson farm. His father-in-law, Ken, isn't too happy with you either."

Jimmy Joe's companion looked down, but Jimmy Joe looked belligerent.

Mark asked, "I want to make sure that I understand the situation. You're here because your grandson Billy got involved with the Proud White Boys and got arrested for threatening my father at the newspaper office and my sister at the museum? He staged a phony protest at the jail, but those were real pipe bombs in those backpacks. His gang tried to kidnap my sister at her house, and Billy wrote some terrible things in those notes. He broke the law six ways. I'm sure Judge Carlson is going to enjoy meeting you."

The big man shrugged. "I'm not ashamed of our beliefs. The White Race is superior. Why, it says so in the good book, doesn't it?"

Uncle Vern looked at him with a mixture of pity and weariness. "And just where does it say that? "

"I don't rightly know the chapter and verse," Jimmy Joe admitted. "But I've heard it preached all my life."

Uncle Vern responded, "Well, Jimmy Joe, you look at Galatians 3:28. 'There is neither Jew nor Greek, there is neither slave nor free, there is no male and female, for you are all one in Christ Jesus.' Those of us who fought in WWII heard Hitler's nonsense about the White race and how the Jews were inferior. It was wrong then, and it's an insult to our service. We're all God's children."

His companion looked down while Jimmy Joe stared blankly.

Uncle Vern looked at the younger man and asked, "Who are you, son, and how did you get mixed up with Jimmy Joe?" His tone was compassionate.

The younger man sighed. "I married his daughter, Roselyn. My name is Roger Jenkins, and I'm here because his daughters are worried about Jimmy Joe. And please accept my apologies for the damage done to your property. I tried to grab the steering wheel, but the old man was stronger."

Mark asked, "What happened to the air bags? Why didn't they go off?"

Roger shook his head. "I'm not sure. I know he had an accident a few months back."

Another officer escorted them to the squad car and drove them to the police station. Ben stayed to take photos of the big truck and smashed-in front door and porch.

My father looked at Uncle Vern. "Thank you for coming, Vern."

Uncle Vern said, "I'll defend my family as long as the Good Lord gives me strength."

Ken, David, and Mark came into the house to check on us then. We'd been watching at the upstairs window and holding the babies.

We came downstairs in time to see them remove their tactical vests. Mark handed his vest and pistol to Ken, who took them downstairs.

"Are you alright?" Mark asked us.

We looked at each other. Kathy held Sean, and I cradled Sophie, whose little chest was close to mine. She was whimpering softly. Mark held out his arms and scooped her up.

David put his arms around me and said nothing for a minute.

I took a breath. "David, I didn't mean to worry you. I thought I'd be home before you missed me."

He stepped back. "You're not the one at fault, Gracie. I can't believe what that man did, ramming into the house."

Mark led the way out the deck door and around to the front, where the truck had rammed into the front door and porch, wedged up into the door and steps. He walked over to see the damage and held Sophie tighter to his chest.

Ben took pictures of the door, porch, and steps, as well as the front of the truck. "Mark, could you help me? I think we can move the truck now if you have a tow chain. We can use the tractor. I'll have it towed away later."

Mark nodded and handed Sophie to Katie. He and David went to get the tractor and tow chains. When they returned, they connected the tow chains to the big truck. Mark climbed inside the tractor and carefully pulled the big truck back down the stairs. Pieces of the door frame broke off and the door itself fell into several large pieces all over the steps.

Ben took more pictures as we stared at the damage. I thought, *Thank God we weren't sitting out here. Thank God Aunt Violet doesn't live here anymore.*

When Mark got out, he turned to Ben and asked, "Did you see the gun rack in the truck?"

Ben nodded.

We went back inside the house through the door on the deck to see the damage from the inside. The closed-in porch had been a favorite place of Aunt Violet. With a ceiling fan, two rockers, and a small side table, it was a pleasant place to sit and read or visit. Now, it looked like a disaster zone, with debris from the broken front door, which would need to be replaced and reframed. Several windows were cracked, there was glass on the floor, and the side table lay on its side. The rockers were shoved several feet from where they were normally placed.

We walked into the living room and around the corner and into the front bedroom, where Kathy spent the last weeks of her pregnancy. I remembered visiting Kathy here and what a pleasant room it'd been. Now it was a mess. When the truck rammed the front of the farmhouse, it sent a shockwave of energy into the bedroom, and picture frames went flying from the walls and dresser. A dozen 8 x 10 pictures lay on the floor, frames twisted, and glass covered the floor. The window facing the front of the house was damaged, with more glass on the floor.

Katie put her arm around Kathy. "We can fix this, dear."

Kathy nodded, holding Sophie closer as she surveyed the damage. Ben took photos.

We'd been in the family room, on the other side of that wall, when I'd arrived. Kathy and I had gone out to the porch to talk about the presentation, while Katie watched the twins.

Mark looked grim, and his shoulders tightened. He and Ben exchanged glances. "We're all upset," Mark admitted, "but it could have been much worse. Jimmy Joe had high-powered weapons in his gun rack in that pickup truck. I'm still not sure what that old man's problem was, but he had it out for us."

Ben nodded and finished taking photos. "I think I'm done here. Let me echo what Mark just said. We're looking at property damage, among other things, but I didn't have to call for an ambulance because Jimmy Joe shot someone."

David nodded and exhaled. He put an arm around me.

Mark walked Ben to the door. He came back with my parents.

Mom hugged Katie and then Kathy and me. Dad talked to Mark and David quietly.

Ken entered the bedroom, looking disgusted at the messy room. His dogs weren't far behind, but when he saw all the glass, he told them to stay.

We returned to the family room where Kathy and Katie laid the twins in the crib. They were worn out from the excitement and half asleep.

The damage here was minimal, with some pictures off the walls, a chair out of place, and the portable crib moved.

Mom asked, "How are you all?" She hugged each one of us. The four of us women sat down, shaken. David, Dad, Ken, and Mark talked in low voices.

There was a knock on the deck door, and Mark came back with Uncle Vern and Aunt Maggie. She carried a large rectangular Tupperware container, which she put on the kitchen island and then opened. Her oatmeal chocolate chip cookies were legendary. She passed them around with napkins, and I accepted one with gratitude.

"Nothing like some chocolate to get you through a tough evening," she said cheerfully.

Uncle Vern looked around the room. "That man has brainwashed himself," he announced before getting a cookie and pulling up a chair for Maggie.

Dad was talking with Mark and David in low tones when Ken came upstairs from securing the weapons and gear downstairs. He and Uncle Vern joined the men.

Ken made a pot of decaf coffee, and Katie made tea and poured a big glass of milk for Kathy.

I munched on a cookie, which smelled amazing and tasted just as good. I closed my eyes.

Dad took his own photos of the damaged front door, steps, and porch, as well as the mess in the guest room. "We have insurance and can make a claim," he said to Uncle Vern, who nodded.

Mark left to check everything outside, and Ken and David followed.

I had essays to grade at home but was still processing what happened. *Jimmy Joe rammed into the front porch of Mark and Kathy's home and burned a cross. None of it makes any sense.*

Katie and my mom went back to the guest room and tried to salvage as many photographs as they could. Then they got brooms and dustpans and cleaned up the mess. Meanwhile, Aunt Maggie washed the coffee cups, and I dried, still thinking about what Jimmy Joe thought he was doing when he rammed into the porch.

Dad called his insurance agent, who promised to come out. When he arrived a few minutes later, the agent walked around with a notepad and made an inventory of what needed to be fixed.

Uncle Vern put his hand on Dad's shoulder before they left, and Aunt Maggie gave both the moms a hug. We finished the cookies and headed home.

Judge Carlson held court on Monday morning, and Jimmy Joe seemed more subdued. His partner cracked in jail and turned state's witness against his father-in-law. We were all there in the courtroom.

Roger confessed they'd been coming to town since late May, once a week. At first, his father-in-law wanted to visit Billy in the County Jail. After the FBI moved Billy out of Jubilee County, Jimmy Joe felt compelled to finish what Billy had started here. However, it wasn't clear what Billy wanted to accomplish beyond getting the attention of the Proud White Boys. But Jimmy Joe had raised his grandson since the boy's mother had died and his father had gone to jail. He felt responsible for the boy.

Jimmy Joe had overheard something in the Jubilee Café that fired him up about our family. He overheard some people gossiping about how those O'Connor children—Mark and Gracie—had moved into their own farmhouses off Highway 21. Not only that, but Gracie just got married, and her Uncle Rich gave her an RV as a wedding present. Jimmy Joe felt cheated and convinced that his whole family had been cheated, too.

Judge Carlson listened, hearing Roger out. "Did this person have any evidence?"

"No, sir, he didn't offer any. I didn't believe it, but Jimmy Joe latched onto it as the gospel truth, and we couldn't talk him out of it," the man admitted. "His daughters were worried about him, and I came along to keep an eye on him, but I couldn't convince him that the O'Connor family were good people and Billy needed to pay for his crimes."

"You were correct. Mark and Kathy are paying rent, and so are David and Gracie. Mark is working on the farm with his uncle and some cousins. Gracie's Uncle Rich loaned her the RV for three weeks for a wedding present. The allegations verge on slander and have no substance. I officiated at David and Gracie's wedding and know both couples well."

The judge looked at Roger. " Do you have any other information that might help me understand your father-in-law's motivation?"

Roger's face changed expression as his father-in-law glared at him from the defendant's table. "Jimmy Joe's wife, Shirley, died last Easter. His behavior became more erratic after that. He'd just retired, and they wanted to buy a big motorhome and travel. Shirley could get through to Jimmy Joe. It's no excuse, but he's not an evil man, despite all the terrible things he's done. My apologies for my part. My wife and I don't share his beliefs, and neither does her sister. I thought I could have more influence on him."

In the end, Roger got off with a warning, since it was Jimmy Joe who was driving and rammed the front porch door and steps. Judge Carlson charged Jimmy Joe with property damage, vandalism, vehicular assault, and harassment. He ordered Jimmy Joe to be held in jail, and assigned Jimmy Joe to a public defender who had his work cut out for him. Uncle Vern surprised us all and reached out to Roger for contact information for the two daughters and promised he would check in on Jimmy Joe on a regular basis.

Uncle Vern said, "Jesus told us to love our enemies in Luke. Jimmy Joe is not our enemy. He's a distant cousin. But he's been brought up to be racist, and he's the reason Billy's in jail. He believed gossip and felt jealous of our family's land. He needs our love."

Mark, Ken, Dad, and David got to work replacing the damaged doors and windows, repairing the damage to the front porch, and spackling and painting walls. Kathy and Katie rearranged the furniture in the family room, moving the portable crib away from the porch. It would take time for us to feel comfortable on the porch, in the guest bedroom, and in the family room and forget how vulnerable we were to someone intent on doing us harm.

Fifty-four

Cousin Lila's Memories of Mary
Gracie

"Maybe every once in a while we can take a break from doing everything faster and quicker to reflect on who we are and where we are going."

~Joe Plumeri, Author
The Power of Being Yourself

"Having somewhere to go is home. Having someone to love is family. And having both is a blessing."

~Unknown

A few mornings later, I was working at *The Jubilee Times* when I got a phone call from Aunt Violet. Her friend, Lila Carlson, wanted to visit with us. Lila was in her late 90s, and she was the cousin, and friend, of Anna and Mary. She wanted to tell us what she knew.

Aunt Violet asked when we could get together. I'd called her several weeks earlier to talk about my frustration. She promised to help. However, I'd neglected her since getting married and apologized. She said, "Don't be silly, Gracie. You're busy. You've done such a good job this year juggling a million things. Your Mom and I talk almost every day, and she keeps me updated on your doings with that handsome husband."

We set a time, and I agreed to bring along David, Carl, and Charlotte. I thought about it more and asked if Lila would be comfortable with Charlotte and Carl recording our conversation.

I also asked if Aunt Catharine could join us, and she agreed. I told my parents, and Mom phoned Aunt Catharine, who was receptive to the idea and agreed to come along.

The following Tuesday afternoon, we visited Lila at the Prairie Fields Senior Living Complex. We took treats and a carafe of coffee and another one of tea. She was pleased to see us. One of her daughters was there, as well as Aunt Violet. Lila used a walker, but her eyes were bright, she was dressed nicely, and very alert for a woman in her late 90s.

We made introductions and sat down around her table to chat. We sampled the pastries from Aunt Shirley's Café while we sipped tea or coffee. Carl and Charlotte set up their cameras and recording equipment.

Lila greeted Aunt Catharine with a hug, commenting they hadn't seen each other in almost a decade. I brought along a small album with photos of the hope chest. She smiled. "I remember that pretty chest. Their papa made one for Anna too."

Lila told us she knew Mary and Anna while she was growing up. She was only ten years old when Mary and Liam got married. Mary's mother was Lila's maternal aunt, so Lila was their cousin. Anna and Mary had babysat her. Lila remembered going to the O'Connor store with her mother and seeing Mary working there.

"Mary was a beautiful young girl, with lovely, big blue-gray eyes and dark blonde hair. She and Charlie were quite a striking pair." She looked at Catharine. "Catharine, you look like your grandmother."

Catharine smiled, but I saw some tears in her eyes.

Lila remembered her mother talking with Mary's parents, who were heartbroken when Charlie was killed. She told us, "They couldn't get Mary to eat, and she didn't want to see anyone. She was so grief stricken she stayed in her room for several weeks and seemed sad for months. Then, there was a letter, from the young medic whom Charlie saved, which seemed to help her. They corresponded during his rehab. He was kind to her and helped her see beyond the sorrow."

"Later, when Liam returned and courted Mary, my mother said

they were well-matched because they'd both suffered a loss. Mary told her Liam made her laugh again—and love again. They were friends before they fell in love."

She continued, "Anna and Mary were very close, friends and sisters. Liam became a lawyer. Mary became a suffragist like her Aunt Eva. She advocated for workers' rights, childcare, and equal treatment for women in the workplace. She was kind to me and encouraged me to go to college. And I did. I became a nurse, and when our nation entered the war in 1941, they deployed me overseas, and I worked in a field hospital."

Lila took a sip of her tea. "I remember how handsome Liam looked on their wedding day, and how beautiful Mary was in the simple, elegant dress." She opened her old photo album and showed us the photographs her father took.

Catharine cried, then, looking at her beautiful grandma and handsome grandpa.

I asked if I could return with a laptop and scanner for the album, and Lila agreed. Lila continued her recollections, "After Liam and Mary got married, they were blessed with a beautiful baby girl, Emma. Then they went through a dark period after losing their second baby. Sadly, it was premature and stillborn. Mary was so depressed again she didn't get out of bed for several weeks, couldn't see people, cried, and went back to the dark place."

"Emma asked her mother if the hope chest was haunted or cursed. Mary asked, 'why would you ask such a question? Children have such imaginations.' Emma replied, 'Once, when I was little, I came downstairs, and I heard you tell Papa, 'The baby died because the hope chest was cursed.'"

Catharine looked up, startled, at her mother's question. One of Emma's earliest memories was hearing her mama cry for the lost baby? We looked at each other. I spoke up, "But Emma was just a toddler."

Lila thought about it. "I think people remember early trauma like that."

"But, once her second bout with postpartum depression was over, Mary got better?" I asked.

"Oh yes, she and Liam were very happy with their family. Mary was a tireless worker at that center for women and children. She had the nicest smile. I can still remember seeing her with Ruby, holding a baby or talking to a mama," Lila said, smiling.

We thanked her for her willingness to talk with us, and her eyes sparkled. "I'm happy to help."

She and Catharine then embraced, laughed, cried, and talked some more.

Her granddaughter took pictures of Lila with Catharine. Carl took pictures of all of us.

Charlotte jotted down notes about things to check on the genealogy research we'd done.

A half hour later, we packed up the coffee and thanked Lila for seeing us.

Catharine promised to come back.

Carl and Charlotte discussed which one had a more portable setup to bring to scan in Lila's photos, and Lila mused she might have more photos of Mary and Liam.

We left with a better understanding of Liam and Mary's relationship. However, I still had questions about her bouts of depression.

David and I took Great-Aunt Catharine home. She was quiet in the car, so we made light chatter. When we reached her house, she thanked us for taking her along.

"Are you alright?" I asked her.

"Yes, it's amazing to hear the stories and see those pictures of my grandparents as young people. Thank you both for making the arrangements." David opened her car door, and I got out to give her a quick hug. She unlocked her house and turned back and waved.

The next day in my literature class, after reading and discussing a poem about WWII, I asked my class what they knew about WWI. Students looked at each other, waiting for the usual suspects to speak up.

"Okay, that was the war when soldiers were in the trenches, right?" one girl asked.

"We spent more time on WWII at my school," one boy confessed.

"That's when they flew those flimsy old airplanes," another boy ventured.

I told them about reading my great-grandmother's diary. I described Frank being trapped in a trench collapse, and Charlie's courageous rescue of two injured men in no-man's-land.

"Why should we care about a war that happened a hundred years ago?" I asked, looking around at the students.

They stared at me and each other.

"The war may seem like ancient history, but a number of young Iowans, not any older than you guys, died in that war. Pay attention the next time you visit a cemetery with your family, and you'll notice them. America entered the war late, in 1917, and helped win the war, but it was *a bloody slog*, as my Uncle Vernon would say," I told them.

"He's close to 90, and he was just a teenager when he entered WWII. So, imagine, just three generations separate me from WWII. Five generations separate me from WWI. Now, think of your family tree. You, your parents, your grandparents, their parents, their grandparents.

"Here is something for twenty bonus points. Look up the Wikipedia article for WWI. What was it called and how many people died? Then talk to your grandparents about WWI and ask if any of your relatives died in it. Write a paragraph or two about what you learned and post it in the bonus points discussion board on our blackboard site."

Almost two-thirds of the class took me up on my bonus points offer. My students' stories from their grandparents about WWI were both inspiring and heartbreaking. My students heard stories about feats of courage and acts of sacrifice. I added it to my syllabus for the next semester and tied it to reading poetry from the era of WWI.

At home, I kept reading love letters from Charlie.

Letter Twelve

My darling Mary,
We're in France. We paraded through the streets of a beautiful port city when we arrived, and people cheered for us. But I noticed the children seemed thin, and that everyone looked tired after three years of war. The name of the city is Saint-Nazaire, and they called us Doughboys.
When we arrived, we had mail waiting for us—several letters from you and my mother this week, and a small box with treats. My favorite oatmeal cookies, more socks, crackers, writing paper and pens, and a bottle of aspirin.
We have three more weeks of training with our new weapons before being assigned to the front. I'm so happy to be off that ship that I'd drill with wooden rifles again. It feels good to be on land, to walk on land, and to sleep in bunks that are not swaying back and forth. They're calling for us to drill or I'd write more.
Bruce and Liam send their love. We're all together, and that is a comfort. Frank is with me as well.
Love,
Charlie

Letter Thirteen,

My darling Mary,
We're at the front. It is far worse than I imagined.
The trenches are miserable, dirt walls reinforced with sandbags, barbed wire, and pieces of wood.
Rats run around in the dirt and there's dirty water in the bottom of the trenches.
Then, of course, people are shooting over our heads.
I think it's a miracle that everyone here is still alive.
At first, we didn't understand how close the German trench was to us.

*Our soldiers talked too loudly, and that riled up the Germans
who sent out a patrol across no-man's-land.
They were almost on top of our location when two English
soldiers shot them.
So, we had some action early on and learned a lesson.
Please pray for us.
Love, Charlie*

Letter Fourteen

*Dearest Mary,
Thank you for the package.
I enjoyed the cookies and reading your letters.
I'm sharing the clean socks with Frank.
He and I watch out for each other.
I'm sorry this letter is so short, but it's hard to write in here,
without much light.
Please pray for all of us.
Love, Charlie*

Letter Fifteen

*Dear Mary,
I find such comfort in reading your letters.
We need comfort.
Frank died yesterday trying to save some poor soldier trapped
in a section of trench that had partly collapsed. He saw a medic
struggling to reach the man and rushed to help.
I had gone to our forward trench for bread and mail.
When I was making my way back, I heard a loud noise—
We tried to dig them out, but it was too late.
I held him in my arms and wept like a child.
We'd been friends since we were five or six years old.
I loved him like a brother.
My sergeant came then and kneeled beside us. He put his arm
on mine and said,*

'Tough break, Charlie. Say a prayer for Frank. He died a hero.
Then we'll take care of him.'
They'll bury him here in France.
When they do, they will bury a piece of me, too.
Your heartbroken Charlie

Letter Sixteen

My dearest Mary—It's another miserable day here.
I miss Frank. I still can't believe he's gone, but he died a hero.
Whatever happens, be happy.
I'm closing my eyes and trying to get back to your parents' front
porch.
It seems a million miles away, so I got out my wallet and looked
at your face.
There is a commotion

I stared in confusion. The letter just broke off, and then I realized why. The young soldier had run out into no-man's-land and was about to be shot. Then the medic would run out to rescue him, only to be shot himself. Charlie was about to become a hero. Someone—maybe Liam or Bruce—found the letter and included it with his few possessions to send home to the family.I tried to imagine the scene, and my eyes filled with tears. Charlie ran out, put the wounded soldier over his shoulder, and grabbed the medic. He almost reached the top of the trench, with arms reaching up to help transport the two wounded men when Charlie was shot, and the medic, Gregory, talked to him once they'd pulled him to relative safety on the other side. Charlie died a hero, just the way his best friend Frank had died. Perhaps they buried them side by side in France. That thought comforted me, somehow.

Fifty-five

Mary Marries Liam
Mary

'i carry your heart with me (i carry it in my heart)'
~e. e. cummings

1922, Jubilee Junction

*L*iam graduated from college in the spring of 1922, and we planned a small wedding for early June. Both of our families drove over for the commencement ceremony. He was going to take the bar exam later that month, so we would have a short honeymoon.

We wrote to each other while he was away for those two years, and he came up with a clever idea. We read some of the same books, newspaper articles, and magazine articles and discussed them in our letters and when he came home for the weekend. Like a teacher, he wanted me to identify the big ideas, the supporting evidence, and the argument. He was, after all, training to become a lawyer. We shared common values, interests, and enjoyed discussing things. I felt I got to know him at a different level.

I also gained confidence and the ability to articulate an argument, write a paper, and speak about it. Liam encouraged me to go to college, too, because I had done so well. I decided I would think about it, but for now, I was busy between the store and the community center.

Anna and I shopped for my wedding dress. I couldn't bear the idea of wearing the pretty dress I'd found for marrying Charlie.

I gave it to a cousin who loved it. And then we found it, in the display window of a new dress shop in town—the perfect wedding dress, a simple, silky sheath with a lace overlay and dropped waist. Once I tried it on, I loved it.

I thought it went well with my wavy, dark blonde bobbed hair. Mama had been a little shocked, but it was all the style.

Anna said, "It's beautiful on you, Mary!"

The shop was owned by one of Ruby's aunts. She created a simple, elegant short headdress and veil, suggested my shoes and jewelry, and then found a dress for Anna. She was a talented woman, and my mother spread the word that Pearl could dress any bride.

Anna was my maid of honor. Bruce stood up with Liam. We planned a more somber reception—so many people had lost loved ones in the war, or to the virus. I now realized that I'd been a young girl infatuated with Charlie. Charlie was a wonderful young man and part of me would always remember him with great affection. However, Liam taught me a great deal about mature love and patience. He waited for me, and I waited for him. We grew closer through our separation.

We spent our honeymoon weekend at a fancy hotel in Prairie Falls. I was nervous about the physical act but amazed at how much I enjoyed it with Liam. He was gentle, patient, and very passionate.

He gave me a letter on our wedding day.

Dearest Mary,

If you ever doubt my love, remember this. We were friends before we fell in love, and it was friendship that drew me to you. However, I have loved you since I saw you one day at your family's home when visiting Bruce. You were only sixteen, but I was attracted to you by watching you reading poetry to Anna when Bruce and I walked by. It was some love poem, and your voice sent chills down my spine.

I thought, "I'm going to marry my best friend's little sister."

Maybe I was not your first love, but I promise to make you happy for the rest of our lives.

Love, Liam

We were immensely happy. A year after marrying, I became pregnant. We collected baby clothing and stored it in the old hope chest.

Our baby girl, Emma, seemed perfect. She was a delightful baby, and Liam was a wonderful father. Our mothers came and helped that first week. At first, I struggled with breastfeeding, but then things seemed to be just fine. I was tired for the first few days, and appreciative of the help. I told Liam I was eager to take Emma to the Community Center so Ruby and our friends there could see her.

Suddenly, a cloud descended, and I woke up one morning, feeling fearful and anxious. I worried I might drop the baby and that I might not be a good mother. Once our mothers left, I wouldn't know how to take care of her. I began having strange thoughts creeping into my head, and they frightened me.

Then I saw the fortress in my mind, getting closer. I couldn't sleep because I didn't want to wake up in the fortress. I was afraid to eat because I remembered the taste of the sand. I lay in bed, cried, looked at the baby crib, and felt inadequate. Again, I was drinking lots of tea but not eating much, so the baby cried when trying to nurse, and our mothers got formula and bottles and moved the crib out of our bedroom.

Liam and Anna saw I was troubled and encouraged me to get out of bed, eat, and get into the sunshine. They told me I was going to be fine, but I saw worry in their eyes. Our mothers focused on Emma and assured me she was a perfect baby.

Aunt Eva arrived a few days later. She came in with her mix of brisk efficiency and soothing assuredness. She sat on the bed and took my vitals. "Mary, please listen to me. It's hard work to have a baby—and to grow a baby. Your body has been through a great deal of changes, and you will recover. I've seen this in many other women in my nursing career."

She leaned forward. "Mary, you have a very handsome husband and a darling little baby girl. Let's bring her over to say hello to her mama."

My mother brought Emma over and laid her in my arms. She was three weeks old and seemed tiny, but she waved her little arms.

Aunt Eva talked to me soothingly as I held the baby, pointing out all the things I was doing right, holding the baby, and supporting her little head. Next, Aunt Eva praised me for breastfeeding, if even for only a couple of weeks. She pointed out how healthy and happy little Emma was, and how much she enjoyed cuddling with her mother.

Aunt Eva stayed several weeks, sleeping in my old bedroom across town.

By six weeks, I was feeling more like myself. The island was nowhere to be found. I was playing with Emma, taking her for strolls, showing her off to Ruby and the children at the Community Center. She cooed and waved her little hands at Ruby and the other women.

Liam and I enjoyed being parents. He held his tiny daughter in his arms so tenderly and told me how he felt blessed. We gave her baths together, and she loved splashing her little hands in the water as she grew.

A year later, I was pregnant again, and feeling more secure. Emma was toddling around, and we were excited about giving her a younger brother or sister. Unfortunately, the baby girl was born two months early and died. I couldn't get out of bed for days. It felt like after Charlie had died. I was back on the island, floating out to sea, and terrified.

My mother came and took care of me and little Emma. Liam's mother helped with meals and did laundry.

In my madness, I wondered if the hope chest was cursed. Could any hope be left?

Liam was patient, kind, and unfailing. He held me at night when I cried. One night he whispered, "I love you. I promise you we will have more children. See how Emma is growing up, healthy and happy? We will always grieve for our little one. Do you want to name her?"

"Yes, I like that idea. She existed. She was part of me for all those months. I don't know what I did wrong, Liam. What did I do to make our baby die?"

Liam held me. "You did nothing wrong. The doctor told me that this happens, and we don't understand all the reasons."

We named her Louise after an aunt.

I heard my mother whispering to Aunt Eva on the phone, who came down and spent several weeks with me.

She and I took walks, sipped tea, and talked about nothing at first. As we walked, I felt more myself. Aunt Eva taught me breathing exercises to help with the anxiety. Slowly, the drawbridge came down. I walked onto the land, and the island disappeared.

Our mothers took turns bringing little Emma to see me.

Emma clung to me, "Mama, Mama." She patted my tummy with her little hands. "Baby gone?" I nodded.

"Mama sad?" My eyes filled with tears.

"Hug." She stretched her little arms and reached up and we hugged.

I decided I must put my grief aside. But I stored blankets in the hope chest. My grief gave way to acceptance. But it would take more time to convince myself the island was gone for good.

We had three more children, two boys and another girl. Thank God, I only felt sad after one of them. I found a good man in Liam and held his words close to my heart. "I promise you I will love you every day of my life." And he has.

I no longer help Papa at the store. Aidan is a young man, taking business classes at the local college and working part time at the store. Bruce is the manager, and Papa keeps the books and helps with ordering.

Ruby and I work together at the Community Center, where we care for babies and children and educate women about voting. I continue to write letters to my state and federal legislators, advocating for expanding voting rights. Ruby and I have been back to Chicago several times to visit Aunt Eva and attend the Alpha Club. Each time, we come back re-energized. We have work to do!

1966

Ruby and I talked yesterday about the generations of women who worked for suffrage: white, Black, Hispanic, Asian, and Native American. Not only did we want the vote—but the opportunity to have a say about our lives, our community, and our nation. We remembered our excitement at the 19th Amendment being ratified, and then our disappointment that it was only for white women.

I would not have guessed that it would take forty-five years to rectify that injustice. Ruby never gave up hope, but I was angry and ashamed.

President Lyndon Johnson signed the Voting Rights Act into law on August 6, 1965. It guaranteed Blacks could vote and made it illegal for anyone to impose restrictions. The following year, Ruby and I voted together with our husbands at the community college. Then we celebrated with lunch at the Jubilee Café.

Ruby and I still work together at the Community Center, but we're getting younger people involved, too. I often wonder if our grandchildren will understand how momentous it was to walk into the polling station and vote with my friend.

I thought about the old red and green quilt my grandmother gave me years ago and the stories about Rebecca, a freed slave, who made it and then wrapped it around an injured soldier. There was a big yellow legal envelope attached. Grandma had never opened it, which made me reluctant to open it, but I knew what was inside— freedom papers for three slaves. She told me, "Remember, Mary, teach your children our family's stories and history. And remember how important kindness is—there isn't enough of it in the world. You're doing good work at that Center, and you and Ruby will see remarkable things in your lifetime." She embraced me. "Promise me you'll guard this quilt and keep it in the family."

One of those remarkable things I'd hoped for was for Ruby to vote. So, I finally got my wish. But I thought about Grandma Carlson's stories of the founding of Jubilee Junction. I wondered what my great-grandchildren would remember about us? I worried our stories might be lost from generation to generation. I wrote a note and wrapped it up in the old quilt. Like throwing a letter in a bottle into the ocean, it was an act of faith or foolishness. Time would tell. It might remind my descendants of what we valued and where we came from.

Fifty-six

Conversation with Kathy
Gracie

"My charge, then, in putting down my pen, and giving over this work to posterity, is this: Take the time. Take the time to preserve the stories, the photographs, the small mementos that mean so much. This is your legacy to future generations. Give it the attention it deserves. Your children and your grandchildren will thank you for it."

~Laurence Overmire

David and I visited Mark and Kathy one Saturday afternoon in mid-November. The babies were three months old and developing personalities. Mark left to do chores, and David offered to help, as did his father-in-law Ken, who'd taken to country life. Chewie and Han Solo padded after the men. They loved running around the yard and farm.

I sat with the babies, Kathy, and her mother Katie in the large living room. We'd laid down a blanket so the babies and I could get acquainted. I lay on the floor on my tummy and stared at them. They were on their tummies, drooling a little, and looking back at me, smiling.

"What do they weigh now?" I asked.

"About twelve to thirteen pounds each, the last checkup."

"They're so cute." I sat up and lifted Sophie into my lap. "Who's that lady over there? Is it Mama? Or is it the lunch lady?" She held her little head up, babbled something, and waved her arms.

Kathy laughed. "You're hilarious, Gracie. Even our genius kids can't say Mama at three months." She picked up Sean. He babbled back at her, and I sensed this little glow of something inside. I loved these babies.

Her mother got up to go change the loads of laundry.

Kathy sighed. "You wouldn't believe how much laundry we do now with these two."

"You look good, Kathy," I told her, as Felix walked by us and stopped to sniff each baby. The babies looked interested and waved their arms more. Felix backed off.

"Say hi to the kitty cat, Felix. We like Felix, right guys?" Sophie babbled and waved her arms. I petted Felix, who stayed out of Sophie's reach. The cat meowed and begged for more. The babies watched me, fascinated.

"Just watch. I told Mark that they would say 'Dada' before 'Mama' and they might say 'Felix' or 'cat' before they say 'Mama.' Of course, they also like Hans and Chewie."

She turned to me. "So, how is your research coming? Mark told me David was excited about an old diary."

"Yes, I have lots to tell you. But first, how are you? Are you still struggling with the baby blues?"

"I'm much better now, thanks. It took eight or nine weeks to feel normal. My lactation counselor was wonderful, and so were both of our moms. I hope you don't have this, though, because it's awful. When I miscarried two years ago, I was depressed, but I wasn't also nursing two babies and recovering from a C-section.

"I was weepy, tired, and sure that I could not produce enough breast milk to feed them, and they wouldn't flourish. So both our moms and my lactation nurse pumped me full of positivity—pardon the pun. They also kept repeating that it was temporary, that it was hormonal, and I would feel better soon. Fortunately, they were right, and I'm better. However, I'm glad I kept breastfeeding because I think it helped, too."

I told her then about Grandma Mary, and her struggles with postpartum depression, including her description of feeling she was on an island. Kathy's eyes got teary, and she began breathing faster. I held Sophie and talked to her, to give Kathy a chance to get her composure back. She held Sean, and he babbled. We made eye contact over the babies.

We were playing with the babies when Katie came in with a laundry basket. "I'm so glad we aren't missing any of this. They're growing so fast!"

"Kathy, would you be willing to share your experience with post-partum blues at our O'Connor family gathering? I'm going to share what I've learned about Dad's Great-Grandma Mary from her diaries and letters. Did I tell you we also found one of her cousins over at Aunt Violet's apartments? Lila will be ninety-eight in August, but she's alert and amazing."

Kathy didn't hesitate. "We have to talk about this, Gracie. Women have experienced this for generations and been afraid they were losing their minds. I was afraid. Fortunately, we had our moms, the nurse who came to visit us, and Charlene. And the problem is hormones."

She paused, thinking. "I talked to a friend whose baby was premature, two months early, and she was in a storm of emotions and hormones. The nurse told her that her body was sending two messages while she was in labor. *Dump the baby! Keep the baby!* No wonder she was a mess. We need to educate young women about postpartum depression before they have a baby, just in case. It varies from woman to woman, and too many suffer in silence, because they don't want to worry their family."

I looked down at Sophie. "Don't you have a smart mama?" Sophie made a strange squirty noise, and I smelled something horrible and handed her to her grandmother, Katie.

Katie carried Sophie over to the changing table, talking to her the whole time. Kathy teased me. "I dare you to go watch Mom change her. She has a technique."

I ventured six feet from the changing table next to the portable crib. "Yuck." I backed away, repelled by the appearance and smell.

Kathy's mom looked up and smiled. "I wasn't sure I could change dirty diapers either, but it's amazing what you can do for your family." Katie slid out the dirty diaper, rolled it up, and put it into the garbage can next to her. Then she wiped the little butt and cooed at the baby, who seemed enchanted, staring up at her grandmother.

"Who's my stinky sweetie?" Katie asked the baby several times. Sophie babbled back, and before you knew it, Grandma slid the new diaper on and secured it in no time flat.

I wished I'd timed her. "You could be on YouTube."

Kathy and her mother laughed, and maybe the babies thought it was funny, too, because they babbled.

Katie used a baby wipe for her own hands and sprayed some air freshener. Once she was all cleaned up, Sophie came back to my arms. Her hand reached out to touch my cheek, and I gave in to her sweetness. Maybe I could find the YouTube videos on changing diapers that Mark had shown me.

Could I ever master such a feat? I must remember that line—you're my stinky sweetie!

Fifty-seven

The O'Connor Thanksgiving
Gracie

"In our family histories, the frontier between fact and fiction is vague, especially in the record of events that took place before we were born, or when we were too young to record them accurately; there are few maps to these remote regions, and only the occasional sign to guide the explorer."

~Adam Sisman

We made plans to have an O'Connor Thanksgiving get together at Mark and Kathy's house, rather than Grandma Molly's, on Friday. It would be easier to come to them than ask them to pack up the twins and come to Grandma's house. We'd all bring side dishes, and 'the moms,' as we were calling them, would handle the ham and turkey, while the great-grandma and aunts would play with the twins. We'd also order pies from Aunt Shirley's.

An apartment was available in the Prairie Fields Senior Living Complex, so we were moving Aunt Catharine there the following week. Her daughter Vikki was moving into the big Victorian with her husband and turning it into a residence for college students. Angela and Judd were coming to town, showing off their new RV, and staying around for two weeks to help her mother pack and move. I'd return the hope chest and share what we'd discovered.

The O'Connor family gathered, including Grandpa Patrick and Grandma Molly, his three sisters, Catharine, Trina (Katrina), and Dorrie (Dorothy), along with Catharine's two daughters, Angela,

Judd, Vikki, and her husband Aaron. Aunt Violet came along as well to support Aunt Lila.

We'd set up two long tables in the dining room and used the dining room table for our buffet with the kitchen island for our desserts.

We made a few introductions and loaded our plates, feasting on too much food. The twins made cheerful noises from their big playpen in the corner. They'd already enjoyed their supper.

Then we cleared the table and put the food away, except for dessert. We settled in the large living room. David and Mark carried the hope chest into the room and draped the lovely wedding ring quilt over it. I explained my two tasks from Angela: first, find out why someone hid Mary's beautiful quilt and linens in the false bottom of the hope chest. Second, find out why Grandma Mary's hope chest was associated with sadness.

We'd asked Lila and her daughter to be our special guests. Lila shared the story of her cousin Mary, who experienced two episodes of major depression. The first was after Charlie's death in The Great War, and the second was after her second baby passed away.

She told us about her memories of Mary and Liam, who helped each other grieve the deaths of Charlie and Jane. Lila described the way their relationship blossomed into something more. She remembered how beautiful Mary was at their wedding wearing that lovely dress. Lila talked about the good work Mary did with Ruby at the Community Center, and how she and Liam were blessed with three more children.

Then I got up and talked about my research, finding the two diaries, the letters, and learning why the hope chest included a false bottom. Her father added the false bottom, hoping she could preserve her memories of Charlie, but look to the future. I held up the lovely old red and white wedding ring quilt made in anticipation of getting married.

"Mary recovered from the first bout of grief and depression, in part because of her wonderful family's support, including Aunt Eva. But it was the visit from Gregory, the young medic who brought her Charlie's wallet, and showed her the kindness that helped her heal. It also inspired her to do work with her friend Ruby at the Jubilee Community Center for the low-income women and children of Jubilee Junction."

Next, Kathy shared her story about being anxious and depressed after the birth of the twins. She pointed out that one in seven women will have postpartum depression. "But there's a stigma on mental illness and depression. It was even worse a hundred years ago, when Matthew's Great-Grandma Mary got depressed when Charlie died, and later, after the death of her baby with Liam. They didn't understand the hormonal changes going on in a woman's body after birth," Kathy pointed out.

I looked around the room. Everyone was listening, and every woman was nodding in agreement.

But before Kathy could continue, Trina looked at Aunt Catharine and said, "Yes, dear, we understand. After all, our sister Catharine got depressed after her first baby was born. We were all so worried about her."

What? Aunt Catharine broke down crying, while Angela and Vikki sat and listened, stunned. They'd never heard this story either.

Kathy and I looked at each other, and she sat down.

Aunt Catharine blew her nose and straightened, looking around. "Yes, that's right, Trina. Several days after giving birth, I woke up frightened, sad, and anxious. I was afraid I might hurt the baby—Angela—because she was so tiny. What if I dropped her? What if I didn't have enough breast milk? I got so worked up that I was in tears for days and thought I was going crazy. I'd just given birth to this beautiful baby girl, so why was I so sad? My mother came to help me with the baby, and my sisters helped, too, making meals, doing laundry, and taking care of Angela. She went home from the hospital, but I had to stay. They started her on formula while they tried to get me ready to go home.

"But I couldn't get out of bed at the hospital. I just lay there, sobbing, unable to stop. Of course, I wasn't sleeping well, either. I wondered if I'd forgotten to feed my baby, or if I'd left her some place. Doctors didn't understand what was behind the baby blues.

They wanted to make sure that I would not harm myself or my baby before they sent me home."

Aunt Catharine looked around the room. "I was young and scared, and the doctors talked about treatments that frightened me and my husband—electric shock, for example. Fortunately, with time, I got better. It took two months or more before I felt like myself again. Someone was with me every day. My husband was wonderful and very concerned. Mother came and helped with the baby, and she told me it would be alright. When I got pregnant with Victoria, I didn't think about the pain of childbirth. Instead, I worried I would go crazy again, but my mother and sisters told me they would be there, and they were."

Trina and Dorrie were emotional as well.

My mother recovered and found a box of tissues and passed it around, while Kathy and I stared at each other. We thought we'd uncovered the complete story and gotten all the answers. As always, it was messier and more complicated than we'd realized. The trauma of postpartum depression and the grief of losing a child echoed in the family through several generations.

"Years later, as the oldest daughter, my mother gave me the hope chest from Grandma Mary. I didn't know why, but I didn't want it in my house. I put it down in my basement," Catharine admitted.

Dorrie spoke up. "One of our cousins told me that the dead baby haunted the hope chest, and that Grandma Emma hated it because it reminded her of how sad her mama was. Emma was a toddler when Grandma Mary lost that baby. Someone must have told her stories, because Emma hated the hope chest and told us it was cursed. After all, Grandma Mary made a quilt to marry Charlie and stored it in the chest, and he died. Then she collected baby clothes, and stored them in the chest, and the baby died."

Aunt Catharine's daughters, Angela and Vikki, got up and went over and wrapped their arms around their mother, who was sobbing. Suddenly, this woman who had always intimidated us with her stern demeanor was just a frail older woman with secrets. Her sisters stood nearby, ready to comfort her.

I saw people's reactions to Aunt Catharine's story–surprise, sympathy, and recognition that we were talking about another family secret. Maybe it was Grandma Emma who felt sad remembering the loss of the baby girl, not Grandma Mary. We'd uncovered more of a story than we knew.

Lila looked upset by Catharine's distress, and Lila's daughter talked to her.

My mother stood up. "Oh, my. We appreciate all of you sharing those very personal memories. Let's take a break for some pie."

She wiped away her tears, thanked Lila, and assured her she'd been helpful. Grandma Molly wiped her tears and then chatted with Lila, drawing her and her daughter towards the kitchen.

We went to the kitchen to slice up the pies. The men all looked a little shell-shocked: my grandfather, Dad, Mark, David, Ken, Judd, and Aaron gathered in a group and tried to make conversation.

We ate pie and sipped coffee or tea.

Kathy and Mark, David and I sat together. Mark put an arm around Kathy with a tender expression that made me blink some tears away.

David whispered to me. "What's next?"

I exhaled. "Aunt Catharine's confession sort of eclipsed my research report. But Kathy did a great job of making it real."

David smiled at me. "You'll do fine with your wrap up."

One twin woke and cried. Kathy and her mother walked over to the portable crib, and each picked up a baby. They changed diapers and then brought the babies over to our group, handing them to David and Mark. Both women left to wash their hands.

David did a great job holding Sean and talking to him. Mark held Sophie, and she giggled as he talked to her. I looked at them both and felt a deep wave of emotion. *My brother and husband are both compassionate, gentle, and wonderful with the twins. David will be a loving father someday. Mark is doing an exceptional job.*

I knew what I would say to my family after we calmed down and finished our pie and coffee.

The three sisters were sitting and smiling, with Trina on one side and Dorrie on the other, holding Aunt Catharine's hands. She looked happy to have told her secrets, while her daughters looked relieved but still surprised as they stepped away to chat with their husbands.

Lila and her daughter were back in the room with Grandma Molly beside Lila, and so were Kathy and Katie.

I made eye contact with my mother, and she spoke up. "Let's hear from Gracie now."

I stood. "Thanks, Mom. I was sitting here, watching Mark and David hold the twins. The differences between parenting in my father's great-grandfather Liam's generation and ours seem immense. Men didn't do childcare or housework back in their day. Men weren't allowed to be there for the birth of their children when my grandparents were young. Now look at my father and Ken, Mark and David, and the twins: all these men change diapers, do laundry, help with meals, and soothe fussy babies. Kathy and Katie just handed the babies to Mark and David and look at what a great job they're doing holding them."

"There's a word that keeps coming to me after doing all this research—promise. Charlie promised Mary he'd return to her, but he died in France a hero. She became severely depressed. Later, Liam promised Mary he would love her for the rest of his life, and he did.

"The hope chest was something that Mary's father built for her, and he built a matching one for her little sister, Anna. It represented the love of her parents and their hope for their daughters to have a happy future."

I walked over to the chest and rubbed my hands over the roses and vines. "When I look at this hope chest, I see promise—the promise of love, of family caring for one another, and for making a better future for each new generation. The promise of sisters, mothers, and grandmothers being there to help new mothers. And the promise of modern medicine someday understanding something as distressing as postpartum depression.

"The lovely old aprons, pillowcases, kitchen towels, and the beautiful red and white wedding ring quilt are faded. Mary made them for her marriage to Charlie. The false bottom her father built was ingenious. He wanted her to look to the future, even if all seemed hopeless; to cherish her memories of Charlie, but move forward.

"There's another word that we must talk about—kindness. Kindness lifted Mary out of her depression when she received the letter from Gregory, the medic who was with Charlie when he died. He held Charlie's hand and told him he was loved. Gregory came to see her and brought her the wallet she gave Charlie when he left for The Great War. In doing so, he showed extraordinary kindness to her, as he had to Charlie, and that helped her heal. My Grandma Grace always said, 'There's not enough kindness in the world.' Mary's Grandma Carlson told her, 'Kindness is so important, and we need to reward it by being kind to others. We cannot control what happens in this world, only how we respond.' That statement made a big impression on Mary.

"While he was at college, Mary and Liam read and discussed the same books in their letters. Ralph Waldo Emerson's quote about the purpose of life spoke to her. She wanted to make a difference in Jubilee Junction. So Mary and her friend Ruby established a community center to care for the poor children, Black and white, in Jubilee Junction before and after school. They used money from the O'Connor family, who created a foundation in Charlie's name. That center is now part of the community college outreach program, going strong. There's a daycare center, available for little cost to low-income college students and community members alike. There's a literacy program, a GED program, and more. She and Ruby made a difference together, and yes, Ruby joined the League of Women Voters and was able to vote—but not until LBJ signed the Voting Rights Act of 1965. She was 65 years old and never missed an election until her death."

"Earlier this year, Grandma Molly asked me to investigate the red and green quilt she found in Grandma Mary's closet. The rustic rose quilt dated back to the Civil War era. We don't know why Mary didn't open the big yellow envelope safety-pinned to the quilt. If she had, she would have seen that Rebecca Stevens, a freed slave, made the quilt in Virginia and wrapped it around Daniel O'Connor on their trip to freedom."

"Instead, Grandma Mary wrote a note wrapped up in that quilt, asking that we find out who made it and reward them for their kindness. Regardless of whether Mary knew it, Rebecca's kindness resulted in her freedom and a second chance at life. She built a life here with Thomas, the love of her life. Her descendants still live here in Jubilee Junction.

Of course, it's also possible Grandma Mary wanted us to look at our history and discover that a freed slave became one of our ancestors—Samuel, a little light-skinned boy whose mother Rebecca was a slave. Sarah McDonald adopted him, and she married Michael O'Connor, and they are my great-great-grandparents."

I looked at Angela, "Thank you for the opportunity to learn about our amazing Great-Grandmother Mary. And to find out that each generation has faced some of the same challenges, and gotten through them, with the love and support of family."

I sat down. It was quiet for a moment and then people were clapping, and a few were grabbing for more tissues. David leaned over. "Great job, Gracie." Sean burbled at me and grabbed at my curls, but I ducked away. I'd already experienced having them grabbed by a cherubic little hand.

Angela came up to me and hugged me. "Gracie, you did it! I can't believe everything you learned about my mother and her grandma. Thank you!"

Vikki chimed in, "Thank you, Gracie. We appreciate everything you've done. Now, we can't wait to move mother into her apartment. Angela and I have been worried about her for several years."

Kathy hugged me. She whispered, "Now we know why Aunt Catharine was so upset with the hope chest, and World War One era quilt. Just when you think you've gathered all the information, there's more."

I agreed, so happy to have my cool, smart sister-in-law back.

Fifty-eight

Tracing Family Trees
Gracie

"We are the accumulation of the dreams of generations."
~Stephen Roberts Kuta

Charlotte called me a few days after our family meeting. I'd told her and Carl all about it. Charlotte said, "Gracie, can you stop by? I have something to show you."

I was there within the hour.

We sat down at her large reference desk, and she picked up a piece of paper and handed it to me. It was a family tree that we worked on earlier in the year.

"What is it?" I squinted.

Charlotte smiled. "I'm a little thunderstruck. I was straightening up some papers and saw this family tree. We'd set it aside. We traced Lucy to the modern day and Tiara. But we didn't finish tracing Rebecca's line."

I looked at the tree again and got excited. "Ruby Collins?" I asked. "Mary's friend, Ruby, was descended from Rebecca and Thomas Settler?"

Charlotte looked emotional. "Yes. I double checked. And Tiara's Aunt Phoebe? She's the daughter of Roberta Johnson. She's also on the tree, and Jerome Johnson is her grandson. Remember him? He's the deputy who helped us with the Civil War photos, acting as Thomas?"

I couldn't wait to tell my friend. "Great work, Charlotte. This is exciting. I wonder if Aunt Phoebe knows?"

I called Tiara and put it on speakerphone. "Got a minute, Tiara? Charlotte just told me something, and I think you should hear it from her."

When Charlotte relayed the news, there was stunned silence, and then a shriek.

"I want to see this family tree. I've never heard about this before. This is incredible," Tiara said. "I'll be there soon."

Charlotte's eyes sparkled as she made another copy of the family tree. When Tiara arrived, she brought Aunt Phoebe along, who was smiling. We sat down, gave them their copies of the family tree and chatted.

Aunt Phoebe said, "I wondered when my grandson Jerome said he might be related to that slave Thomas, who came back with Daniel O'Connor. Grandma always told us that one of our ancestors came from Virginia on a big wagon and then took the train to Jubilee Junction. But we weren't writing names down back then. We were trying to survive, mind you. Thank you, Miss Charlotte, for figuring it out, and you, too, Miss Gracie."

Tiara was quiet, unusual for her. She'd turned her face away from us. When she turned back, she was smiling and crying. "I wish my grandma was still here. She would be tickled to know that she and Aunt Phoebe were both related to the freed slaves who came to Jubilee Junction to get a fresh start on life."

Charlotte sniffled, but it was probably because of her allergies. She cleared her throat and looked at me. "Don't forget. Sarah was Gracie's great-great-grandmother. So, three of your ancestors made a treacherous journey with two children, a freed slave named Thomas, and four Union soldiers determined to get them to the train in Baltimore."

Alright, now I was crying and digging in my bag for a tissue. Charlotte grabbed a box and passed it around. We sat together, smiling through our tears.

The next day, I headed to *The Jubilee Times*. I sat down at my desk and turned on my computer before I noticed that Ken Daniels was in my father's office, and they were talking and laughing together.

Mom came over and sat down beside me.

"We have news. Ken owns a marketing publication company and couldn't decide if he wanted to retire or not. He produced the content and laid it all out. Then, a contractor took care of the printing. He and your father are discussing a way to merge our companies. We would print his publication, a magazine."

"He has several employees in Prairie Falls who could commute here or move. They gather the ads and write content. Ken would write some articles for the newspaper, and we would upgrade some equipment with the cash he brings. He wants to stay in town and enjoy his grandchildren. Ken said he was too busy when his own children were young, and he doesn't want to make that mistake again."

I looked at them. "I think they could be excellent partners. Ken's a hard worker and seems to like Jubilee Junction."

Mom agreed. "Katie and I've become friends. Ken took a six-month leave of absence, but she could tell he wasn't looking forward to going back to work. I hope they can work it out." She paused. "Isn't it amazing how much our lives have changed in the past year? All of our hard work moving Kathy and Mark into the big farmhouse has paid off, with those twins and Katie and Ken joining our family."

Then she smiled at me, and I stopped her. "Okay, Mom, I know you'd like another grandchild, but we're still newlyweds. Besides, I need to learn how to change diapers before I have a baby."

"I'm sure you can get a lesson or two without resorting to YouTube. Just spend the afternoon with Kathy and Katie and the babies." She gave me her famous *mom* look.

I couldn't think of a snappy comeback, so I turned back to my computer. I was working on a column about postpartum depression and society's ongoing silence towards mental illness of any kind. We needed more education for pregnant women and their families alike. Kathy had given me some good quotes, and I'd borrowed the book by Brooke Shields about her experience. Soon, I was absorbed in my work, but a small part of my brain was thinking about *stinky sweeties* and Kathy and Mark changing six thousand diapers in the twins' first year.

Fifty-nine

Moving Aunt Catharine
Gracie

"...what the next generation will value most is not what we owned, but the evidence of who we were and the tales of how we lived. In the end, it's the family stories that are worth the storage."

~Ellen Goodman

*O*ur family worked together to move Aunt Catharine into her new apartment at the Prairie View Senior Living Community. She liked her two-bedroom apartment looking out on the community garden. In a few weeks, it was hard to find her home because she was socializing, walking to her sister's apartment, or going to visit friends.

There was a lot to sort in her Victorian, and we let her daughters, Grandma Molly, and her sisters, Dorrie and Trina, handle that. Once they sorted things, the men would haul them off to donate, auction, or whatever. There were a few keepsakes, of course, and my mother suggested they make a list, talk to their mother, and take lots of pictures.

Then Angela called me and asked me to stop over at her mother's house after classes.

When I walked in, Grandma Molly, Catharine, Trina, and Dorrie were sorting things in the kitchen and dining room. My mother was sitting in the dining room chatting with Vikki and Angela, and the red and white wedding ring quilt was folded up on a table nearby in one of those protective zipper cases.

There was a row of Rubbermaid tubs against the wall and a lot of cardboard boxes already filled and labeled. They had been hard at work.

Angela greeted me. "Thanks for coming, Gracie."

Vikki said, "We've been talking. We appreciate everything you and David have done to help us get answers. Angela and I don't have daughters, so we'd like you to take Grandma Mary's Red and White Wedding Ring quilt. Then it stays in the family."

She walked over to the table, picked up the quilt, and handed it to me.

I found myself in tears. "Thank you! It's a beautiful quilt."

"And too beautiful to hide in the hope chest again," Angela said.

Vikki gestured to her mother, who was sorting a pile of kitchen linens and laughing and talking to her sisters. "My mother has mellowed—telling her secrets has made a big difference. We told her we wanted to give you Grandma Mary's quilt, and she said, 'What a good idea.' If you want to use it on a larger bed, Trina has ideas for adding a border. And if you want to use it in an exhibit, it's up to you. You don't have to worry about Mother any longer."

Angela hugged me. "I'm sure you have ideas of your own. You could display it on a quilt ladder, for example, the way you do at the museum."

"Yes, I like that idea. Thank you!"

David and I squeezed in coffee with Tiara and her handsome surgeon, Dr. Davis, at Aunt Shirley's late one afternoon. They sat down, and I noticed how much they were smiling.

We introduced ourselves. His first name is Terrence, but he said, "Away from the hospital, please call me Terry. "

He and David chatted while Tiara and I made a run to look over the pastry case and whisper. Maybe it was the giggling that gave us away because we glanced over and, of course, the men were looking at us and smiling.

Tiara said, "Things are going well. He's a good man, and he's worked hard on his career. He's supportive, funny, and has magic hands." She giggled.

I said, straight-faced, "I suppose you're talking about his surgical skills." Then I smiled. "I'm happy for you. You both look happy."

We picked out our pastries and headed back to the table.

David was telling Terry about his newfound love of tools and the cat tree, showing him pictures on his iPhone. I looked at my man with admiration. David had grown a short beard and looked very handsome in his new flannel shirt and sweater.

Terry said, "I'd like to see it. I have a very hyper cat."

Tiara told us the big news. "My daughter is getting married to that junior resident, and they're about to make me a grandma." She was excited.

David asked Terry, "So, you're dating a grandma-to-be? How's that feel?" He was grinning.

Terry said, "I can handle it. Besides, Tiara's a beautiful *young* grandmother, don't you think?" He took Tiara's hand and kissed it.

David nodded.

Tiara looked besotted and beamed.

"So how soon is she getting married? When's the due date?" I asked.

"We're going down this weekend for a simple ceremony in the chapel. The baby is due in six weeks, but you know first babies. They have a mind of their own. I want my daughter married before that child makes its arrival."

We talked more, found out that the good doctor is also a gamer and set a date to have them over soon. His eyes lit up. "I had a friend in medical school who used to play board games, and he got me hooked on the *Century Spice Road* game. Then I went to one of my rotations and found a gaming group. I hadn't found any gamers in Jubilee Junction—until now!"

He and David did some manly fist bump thing.

We made a date to game soon and told him that Mark and Kathy played board games and so did our cousins. I knew Tiara wasn't that enthused about playing board games, but she was about to embrace gaming.

Sixty

The Sweetness of Home
Gracie

"Do I love you? My god, if your love were a grain of sand, mine would be a universe of beaches."
~William Goldman, The Princess Bride

On the drive home, David was quieter than usual. We drove up our driveway, parked in the garage, and walked holding hands to the front door. Once inside, Agatha greeted us. We sat on the couch, and he held my hand.

Agatha raced around and climbed her cat tree. She looked at us from her perch on top.

David once told me that he thought she was sizing him up for breakfast when she perched up there—if only he were much smaller, and she much bigger.

Now he turned and looked at me. "Gracie, do you see how much this marriage has done for me? I'm wearing flannel shirts, jeans, and boots—and liking it. I've grown a beard, have tools, and helped build that cat tree with these two hands. You haven't tried to change me the way Cynthia did. I decided to make a few changes myself. I love living out in the country here with you and our crazy cat. Mom says I look like a country boy version of myself.

"But it's not just that. I now have guy friends—Mark, Carl, R. J., James, Ben, and who knows, maybe Terry. I reconnected with my Chicago friends like Cornell and want to stay in touch. I've gotten to know your father, Uncle Vern, Uncle Rich, and Grandfather Patrick. They're good men. I love how your family works together so well.

"Mom says Dad is coming around about me getting tools. I think he wishes I'd shown more interest in the hardware store when I was a teenager. But I've always been a history geek. Driving that RV cross-country has given me some street cred with him and Alex—don't laugh. Your dad was right about the whole *macho man* thing. I enjoyed our RV honeymoon and dancing to Stevie Ray Vaughan and rescuing Miranda from that human trafficking ring. But I also loved doing research at the Library of Congress and visiting all those battlefields and museums. I'm still an academic, and I've made good progress writing my book. The draft is almost done, but it's been fun to explore this other side of me. And it's all because of you, Gracie." His voice was strong and earnest, and I loved him even more.

"David, I've been watching you and loving the way you fit in with my family. You're a hard worker, and you respect my family, and they adore you. We're going to have so much fun living here. We can plant a vegetable garden where Kathy had hers, and more flowers. They planted all those hostas, and we have the fire pit area to finish. I saw you looking at gazebo designs with Mark. I think that would be wonderful next summer."

David's brown eyes sparkled, the gold flecks standing out. "Yes, wouldn't it be cool to walk out to our garden and get some fresh green beans, cherry tomatoes, maybe some zucchini and use them for supper? I think we have plenty of room for a gazebo. I asked Mark if we needed permission to add it, and he said he was sure the elders would all say yes to whatever we wanted to do."

I could almost taste the sweetness of those cherry tomatoes. "Yes, I agree. But before then, we get to decorate the farmhouse for the holidays. The only thing I ever did at my rental house was to hang a wreath on the front door. I don't have any real decorations for a Christmas tree because I've never bought a tree. I wonder if we should visit your dad's hardware store and get some expert advice about decorations and outdoor illumination."

"Yep. Dad would love it. I'll call him and see if he can think about something simple. I don't think we should go too crazy. But we can get a Christmas tree if our crazy cat leaves it alone."

"If nothing else, we could get something for the mantle. What do cat people do?"

"I'll google it. *People with cats and Christmas trees.*"

I started sorting mail and looking at our grocery list and menus. I felt like a real grownup. Our marriage had brought out another side of me as well—a domestic side. Grandma Molly taught me how to make her brisket. Aunt Maggie and Aunt Violet came to visit, and we made scones. We're planning a big family baking day at Mark and Kathy's house, making Christmas cookies. David and I cook together and enjoy it.

David popped back into the room. "I have it—I found a website with advice. Did you know cats hate aluminum foil? You put it around the base of the tree stand. Then you add some orange peels because they don't like citrus. You can also spray apple cider vinegar because they don't like the smell, but go easy. It's a great article. I emailed it to both of us and to Mark and Kathy."

He grabbed me. "We're going to have our first Christmas as a married couple in our farmhouse, and it's going to be wonderful, Gracie."

"Yes," I said, a little breathless from the embrace.

He left the room, and I wrote aluminum foil on our shopping list, lots of aluminum foil, and a bag of oranges. Then I squinted, trying to remember what kind of vinegar I had because I needed apple cider.

Just as I was getting up to go to the kitchen and search for the vinegar, my cell phone beeped. It was a text from Kathy.

    Time to chat?

I responded:

        Sure

The Depression-Era Crazy Quilt
Gracie

"A good snapshot keeps a moment from running away."
~Eudora Welty

I called Kathy. She was excited.

"Gracie, you know how our moms are becoming such great friends? The dads watched the twins yesterday and told our moms to go do something fun. They drove over to your parents' house. As they walked in, Mom saw an old crazy quilt draped over an antique bench in the hallway, and it made her think of her grandmother's pictures of a crazy quilt. This is going to sound, well, *crazy*, but when she came home, she dug through a Rubbermaid tub down in the storeroom and found her mother's old photo album.

"Gracie, she has pictures of several crazy quilts made by some little church sewing circle during the depression. She has a picture of your grandma's quilt and bench. But mom grew up in Peoria. How is that possible?"

I pondered her question. "I know the crazy quilt you're talking about, Kathy. When I was a child, I used to kneel on the floor next to it and look at the patches. It was at my Great-Grandma Ginny's house, draped over the big bench that held a lot of other family quilts. I'd love to see the photo."

"Mom wonders if you and David could figure this out. I know it's the holidays, but maybe you could investigate afterward?"

David walked back into the kitchen with a printout in his hand.

"Let me talk with David. I'm pretty sure we'll take the case. A depression era crazy quilt sounds intriguing. Talk to you later, Kathy. Send me the photo, okay?"

David looked up from the printout. "Can't I leave you alone for five minutes without getting us involved with another quilt mystery? What is it this time?"

I told him about Kathy's phone call, and he responded, "What are the odds that two identical crazy quilts would be out there in the world? How could someone who isn't from Jubilee Junction have a picture of your Great-Grandma Ginny's crazy quilt?"

Turning around to the desk, I tore off a sheet of paper from the underside of the menu notepad and started a list. "I need to see Mom's quilt and compare it to this picture. Then do some research on depression era quilts, talk to Aunt Violet, and see what Charlotte can find out for me in her archives."

David grinned, picking up my mini-clipboard to look at my grocery list and noting the tin foil and oranges. "Here's the article about cats and Christmas trees. Life is always interesting with you around. I'm going to call Dad about those Christmas lights." He kissed me and walked away. "No more quilt mysteries while I'm gone. We have our hands full."

Agatha followed him. I wasn't jealous, but she spent a lot of time on the cat tree and wandering back and forth between our offices. She turned and meowed at me, and I laughed at myself. Sure, I was sharing David with my cat, but I was pretty sure I had the better part of the deal.

I picked up my new to-do list and headed upstairs for a little research about the Great Depression, crazy quilts, and quilting circles. This was going to be fun.

The Recollection
A Christmas Novella

*J*oin Gracie and David as they untangle the mystery of two crazy quilts made during the Great Depression.

Gracie's mother, Becky O'Connor, and Kathy's mother, Katie Daniels, become friends when Katie and Ken come to stay with Kathy and Mark who are expecting twins. Katie visits Becky's house and sees an old crazy quilt draped over an antique bench, and it sparks a memory. So, Katie goes back to the farmhouse, finds her grandma's old photo album and shows Becky a photo of an identical crazy quilt on an antique bench. How that is possible since Katie grew up in Peoria, Illinois before moving to Iowa?

The other narrator in this novella is a young farm wife named Marie. She and her husband, Frank, have farmed with his father and mother for the past eight years. But the bank foreclosed on the farm, so she's packing everything she can fit into barrels and boxes.

It is March 1933, and the country is in depths of The Great Depression. Her father-in-law, Samuel, and Frank plan to head west to California to find work. They've built a truck house on Samuel's big farm truck with room for the two couples and her two little girls.

At least we won't be homeless, Marie thinks.

Acknowledgements

No one writes a novel—much less a series—without help and encouragement. I'm blessed with much love and support.

Thank you to Michael, my husband, for believing in me. He reads drafts, fact checks, and is my resident historian and IT staff rolled into one. He's also taken over much of the cooking.

Thanks to my adult children (Jon & Anna, Michelle & Sean) and grandchildren (Corbin, Mason, and Nora) for their encouragement. Mason has the makings of a social media manager. He's in fifth grade and reported that one of his friends checked out my book from the Waverly library and liked it! I thought, *I'm writing for ten-year-old boys?*

Then he asked, "Why don't we have any girl presidents?" Good question.

Thank you to Beth, my lifelong best friend and other sister, who tells me every book is better. She read the original drafts during COVID and gave me feedback.

Thank you to Hope, who spent an afternoon looking at my old quilts and helped me identify the patterns. She encouraged me to take the oldest one to the Grout Museum and have it verified—my 1860 Rustic Rose quilt. Her passion for quilts inspired me to write about them.

Thank you to my writing mentors Barbara, Gail, and Joy. They've provided feedback, encouragement, and support through the writing process for each book.

Thank you to Patricia, my talented illustrator, who creates a map for each book. She's translated my scribbles into Jubilee Junction in three time periods now. She's also created bookmarks with QR codes and "branded me" with a computer and a quilt square. Patricia then uploads the map designs to Spoonflower, which is a website for people who love fabric and quilts, and the map gets printed onto fabric.

Each time, I buy two yards of the fabric, and my friend Judy sews them into pillowcases and wall hangings. I sell them at my book events to raise money for House of Hope, Cedar Valley, my designated charity with WordCrafts Press. House of Hope provides housing for young women who've aged out of the foster care system and young moms facing homelessness. A shout out to Dusky Steele, their Development Director, and my contact there.

Check them out on Facebook at:

https://www.facebook.com/HoHCedaRValley

Thank you to Liz, who took me shopping for RVs for this book so I could describe the Greyhawk. She's my friend, former sister-in-law, and an expert quilter. She presented me with an incredible gift: a beautiful purple, black, and white quilt. She added signage at the bottom in a lovely block, congratulating me on my *Grandmother's Treasures* series.

Thank you to all the women in my family who quilted and handed down those quilts, especially Grandma Nellie and Great-Grandma Eva. They inspired me with their stories.

A special word of thanks to my mother, Charlotte (the inspiration for Grandma Grace) and father, Harry, who did research 'old school style,' driving around the state to visit courthouses and collect birth and death certificates.

Thank you to my beta readers: Mike, Lavonne, Judith, Barbara, Beth, Ambri, Mikki, Patti, Sheri, and Joy.

A special thank you to Lee Carver, my wonderful editor. You helped me fine tune the manuscript.

Thank you to my wonderful publisher, Mike Parker.

The Story Behind The Promise

$\mathcal{I}$ wish now that I had talked to my Grandma Nellie and Great-Grandma Eva about WWI. They lived through both world wars. Eva and Nellie were mother-in-law and daughter-in-law but acted more like mother and daughter. To me, they were just my two grandmas.

As my mother, aunts, and grandmothers decorated family graves in two different country cemeteries each Memorial Day, they may have pointed out the graves of WWI soldiers, but I don't remember it. However, visiting those cemeteries decades later, I'm amazed at how many soldiers are buried there from that war. Many of the quilts in my big antique bench would go back to this era.

It is also the era of Ruth Suckow, the novelist/beekeeper who captured my attention close to twenty-five years ago. My then boyfriend Michael took me to the annual meeting of the Ruth Suckow Memorial Association in Earlville, Iowa, and I was hooked. I loved her writing, and I loved the group. I began using one of her stories in my literature class and my students *got* her. She wrote about Iowa's farms and small towns during the 1920s through the 1950s. She captured the world that my mother, grandmother, and great-grandmother knew and came of age in, including two world wars and The Great Depression.

Researching The Great War made me realize how little I remembered from school.

I came across a fascinating article: "World War I Changed America and Transformed Its Role in International Relations: So Why Don't We Pay More Attention To It?"

Meredith Hindley. HUMANITIES, Summer 2017, Volume 38, Number 3

Historian and writer A. Scott Berg writes, "I hope audiences will appreciate the presence of World War One in our lives today—whether it is our economy, race relations, women's rights, xenophobia, free speech, or the foundation of American foreign policy for the last one hundred years: They all have their roots in World War I."

"I think World War I is the most under-recognized significant event of the last several centuries. The stories from this global drama—and its larger-than-life characters—are truly the stuff of Greek tragedy and are of Biblical proportion; and modern America's very identity was forged during this war."

You can find the article online at:

https://www.neh.gov/humanities/2017/summer/feature/world-war-i-changed-america-and-transformed-its-role-in-international-relations

Thank you for reading!

Follow me online at:

www.facebook.com/CherieDarganAuthor
https://cheriedargan.substack.com
https://www.cheriedargan.com

Author's Note

The horror that happened in the trenches inspired a poem that Irish poet William Butler Yeats wrote after World War One, named "The Second Coming." I've included it on the next page for your consideration.

The Second Coming

Turning and turning in the widening gyre
    The falcon cannot hear the falconer;
Things fall apart; the centre cannot hold;
    Mere anarchy is loosed upon the world,
The blood-dimmed tide is loosed, and everywhere
    The ceremony of innocence is drowned;
The best lack all conviction, while the worst
Are full of passionate intensity.

Surely some revelation is at hand;
    Surely the Second Coming is at hand.
The Second Coming! Hardly are those words out
    When a vast image out of Spiritus Mundi
Troubles my sight: somewhere in sands of the desert
    A shape with lion body and the head of a man,
A gaze blank and pitiless as the sun,
    Is moving its slow thighs, while all about it
Reel shadows of the indignant desert birds.
    The darkness drops again; but now I know
That twenty centuries of stony sleep
    Were vexed to nightmare by a rocking cradle,
And what rough beast, its hour come round at last,
    Slouches towards Bethlehem to be born?

Cherie Dargan

After nearly 30 years in education and 20 years teaching writing, literature, and educational technology courses at Hawkeye Community College, Cherie took early retirement in 2016. She joined the Cedar Falls Authors Festival planning committee, celebrating the five best-selling writers with ties to Cedar Falls—Bess Streeter Aldrich, Ruth Suckow, James Hearst, Robert Waller, and Nancy Price.

Cherie contributed two chapters for collections of academic essays: one about Iowa writer Ruth Suckow and the other about the literary history of Cedar Falls, Iowa. She is the author of the *Grandmother's Treasures* series, including *Book 1 The Gift*, *Book 2 The Legacy*, and *Book 3 The Promise* with two more volumes in the works.

She serves as President of the League of Women Voters of Black Hawk-Bremer Counties advocating for voting rights for all. She is Mom to four children and Grandma to three grandchildren. Cherie is married to retired librarian Mike Dargan, who serves as her tech support, fact checker, and head cheerleader.

Follow her online at:

Substack, https://cheriedargan.substack.com/
Facebook, https://www.facebook.com/CherieDarganAuthor/
www.cheriedargan.com